ROCK ~N~ SOUL

SOUL SEEKERS
~1~

LAUREN SATTERSBY

RIPTIDE PUBLISHING

Riptide Publishing
PO Box 6652
Hillsborough, NJ 08844
www.riptidepublishing.com

Rock N Soul
Copyright © 2015 by Lauren Sattersby

Cover art: L.C. Chase, lcchase.com/design.htm
Editor: Carole-ann Galloway
Layout: L.C. Chase, lcchase.com/design.htm

ISBN: 978-1-62649-311-7

First edition
January, 2016

Also available in ebook:
ISBN: 978-1-62649-310-0

ROCK ~N~ SOUL

SOUL SEEKERS ~1~

LAUREN SATTERSBY

RIPTIDE PUBLISHING

For those who read this story and gave me encouragement, all of whom are—shockingly—still speaking to me after months of listening to me complain my way through writing it.

For Sarah, because no one else can put up with my brand of crazy as well as she can and I'm eternally grateful for her.

And for the nameless bellboy I watched for a grand total of ten seconds one day, years ago, who I looked at and said, "Yes. This man is clearly having a love affair with a sarcastic ghost. I should write that." This one's for you.

TABLE OF
CONTENTS

Prologue 1
Chapter 1 7
Chapter 2 15
Chapter 3 23
Chapter 4 33
Chapter 5 39
Chapter 6 47
Chapter 7 53
Chapter 8 57
Chapter 9 61
Chapter 10 69
Chapter 11 77
Chapter 12 87
Chapter 13 97
Chapter 14 103
Chapter 15 115
Chapter 16 125
Chapter 17 133
Chapter 18 145
Chapter 19 151
Chapter 20 155
Chapter 21 163
Chapter 22 173
Chapter 23 181
Chapter 24 189

Chapter 25 197

Chapter 26 205

Chapter 27 215

Chapter 28 223

Chapter 29 233

Chapter 30 241

Chapter 31 249

Chapter 32 259

Chapter 33 273

Chapter 34 281

Chapter 35 287

Chapter 36 297

Chapter 37 305

Chapter 38 317

Chapter 39 327

Chapter 40 335

PROLOGUE

I didn't actually hear a chorus of angels singing when I saw the bag of grapes sitting on the refrigerated shelf of a tiny Asian food store at two in the morning, but I definitely heard it in the back of my mind. Here, sitting before me, was a miracle. Red grapes. In a store that was still open. The words on the bag were Korean so I had no idea if the grapes were seedless or not, but Chris Raiden had been waiting for his room service for over an hour now. Which meant we were quickly approaching the point where a famous rock star's wrath over late food might trump his wrath over seeds in said food, so they'd have to do either way.

Still, it's always best to know exactly why I'd be getting fired, so I reached into the bag and pulled out a grape, then popped it into my mouth.

And the angels sang again because there wasn't a seed. This beautiful, perfect plastic bag in this beautiful, perfect Asian food mart contained red. Seedless. Grapes.

"Hey," a voice called from the direction of the cash register. "You can't eat those. You have to pay."

"I know, I know." I snatched the bag from the cooler and trotted up to the register, giving the cashier a big lopsided smile. "Man, you don't even know how glad I am that you guys are open right now."

The guy shrugged as he rang up my purchase but didn't answer. Not that I blamed him. People who have grape-related emergencies at 2 a.m. aren't generally the type of people you want to be having a conversation with during said emergency. So I just closed my mouth and handed over the corporate card my boss had given me to make the purchase.

Cashier Guy could have been nicer, though. It wasn't like I'd *asked* to be out running around Beacon Hill in the middle of the fucking night looking for overly specific types of fruit to keep a drugged-out bass player from complaining to my boss, so I felt like I should get a pass on this one. Still, though, there wasn't time to explain, and I'm not usually that big on small talk with strangers anyway.

After paying for the grapes, I muttered a "Thanks," scooped up the bag, and started jogging back toward the hotel. I slipped my phone out of my pocket and hit Call on Richard's number.

"Tell me you got them," he answered.

"I got them," I practically crowed.

Richard let out a heavy, relieved sigh. "Thank God. How long will it take you to get back here?"

"I don't know. Fifteen minutes?"

"*Fifteen—*"

"I'm in Beacon Hill, Richard. It's gonna take me a bit." I stopped and scanned the street for cabs. And, in a burst of luck, one rounded the corner just as I was looking. I lifted the hand with the grape bag in it and started flagging like a lunatic. "Hold on. There's a cab. I'll be back as soon as I can." I paused for a moment, fumbling with the phone while I added my other hand to the flagging. "Is he bitching about it?"

"No, he hasn't called again. But it's only a matter of time. You know celebrities."

"I can imagine." The cab turned toward me and pulled up to the curb so I could get in. I slid in the backseat and gave the driver the hotel address, then went back to the phone. "I'm on my way."

The steak was done when I got there, but it took the kitchen staff a few minutes to wash and plate the grapes, and Richard's hovering and hand-wringing made it seem like the longest few minutes of all our lives. To make matters worse, by the time I finally got the room service cart wheeled out of the kitchen and down to the service elevator, my phone was buzzing like an angry hornet for the tenth time since I'd made it back to the hotel, and I knew who was calling. I considered just ignoring it, but I had a few seconds while I waited for the elevator and then while it took me up to the top floor of the hotel, so I decided I might as well answer.

Besides, Carmen and I had been together for almost a year, and even though she could be incredibly high maintenance and a class-A jerk when she was mad at me—which seemed like always, these days—I wanted to keep her happy. After all, if I was nice to her now *and* showed up with a Chris Raiden autograph when I got home tonight, the sky was the limit as far as the sex-having went. So I pulled my phone out of my pocket and answered.

"Hey, babe," I said, pushing the Up button on the elevator and tapping my foot while I waited for the doors to open.

"Have you seen him?" she asked in the sweetest voice ever.

I bit back a sigh. "Not yet."

"It's been over an hour since he called for room service," she pointed out, as if I didn't know that. As if Richard's increasingly frantic texts during my grape adventure hadn't been keeping me up-to-date on the subject. As if I don't know how to read a fucking clock.

"Thanks. I'm aware of that." I leaned against the wall by the elevator and pinched the bridge of my nose.

She *hmmph*ed loud enough for me to hear through the phone. "And you expect me to believe you haven't seen him yet?"

"I wasn't in the lobby when he came in," I told her, pinching harder like that would make the conversation end faster. "Mark took his bags up. And you know I've been out grape-hunting for the last hour. So no. I haven't seen him."

"Tyler—"

"I told you I'd call after I saw him, okay?" I was being sort of bitchy by interrupting, but there were only two floors to go and I needed to hurry this thing along "I'm working. Let me work."

The sweetness disappeared and there it was, the hard-edged bitchy voice that I'd gotten used to hearing lately. "I *am* letting you work, Tyler. You told me not to come down there, and I didn't. So *excuse me* for wanting to know how it was going."

The elevator doors picked that moment to open, so I pushed the cart inside and hit the button for the penthouse while I willed myself to be nice instead of snapping at her. "I found the grapes," I said, trying to make it into a peace offering. "Had to go all the way to fucking Beacon Hill to find some, but I got the stupid grapes."

"Good," she said, still bitchy but a little brighter. *Good work, Tyler.* "Are you sure they're seedless?"

"I'm sure. I'm not getting fired because I served a seed to Chris fucking Raiden." Rolling my eyes, I muttered "douche bag" under my breath, then tucked the phone against my shoulder while I heaved the cart out of the elevator and into the hallway in front of the penthouse suite. "I gotta go. I'm about to knock on the door."

"Put me in your pocket?" she begged, back to sweetness and light, and I sighed.

"Fine." I started to slip the phone into my pocket, then put it back up to my ear. "But you have to shut up so he doesn't hear you, got it?"

"Promise," she purred, and I rolled my eyes again and dropped the phone into my suit pocket without ending the call.

I took a second to straighten my suit, and then knocked on the door. "Room service," I called through the heavy wood, then stepped back to wait. And wait. And wait. I tapped my foot on the carpet and knocked again, yelling a little louder this time.

Still nothing. Typical. Rich fucks always thought they were so much more *important* than a working-class bellboy, which seemed to mean that they got their rocks off on making me wait in the hallway while they finished filing their nails or whatever. And rock stars were even worse, always wanting weird shit like red seedless California grapes even when they weren't in season and making me run around Boston in the middle of the fucking night trying to find a twenty-four-hour fruit store.

I mean, I assumed so. This was the first rock star I'd done room service for. But the fact that this guy actually *had* demanded weird shit seemed like good evidence for the generalization.

"Mr. Raiden?" I yelled through the door, in case he was having hearing problems from the concert he'd just come from. "*Room service.*"

After a couple of minutes had passed, I sighed and pulled out my master key card. "I'm coming in, sir," I called, wrinkling my nose at the *sir* but not wanting to offend a celebrity and lose my job. When there was still no response, I swiped my key card and let myself in.

Chris Raiden was passed out on the floor beside the bed, a pool of vomit in front of his face. I wrinkled my nose at the sight—leave it to a rock star to order a fucking rare steak and grapes and then waste my hard work by puking all over himself before passing out—and went over to him, then toed him with the tip of my shoe. "Mr. Raiden."

He didn't so much as twitch, so I sighed super hard and knelt beside him, calling his name again. No response.

He was so still, lying there on the carpet. His legs were twisted, like he'd fallen to the floor. His skin was pale and washed out, his eyeliner smudged everywhere. There was a trickle of blood smeared all down his arm, most likely from where he'd stuck himself with a needle. But most importantly, he wasn't breathing.

"Oh, *shit*." I pressed my fingers against his neck, feeling for a pulse, and didn't find one. "*Shit*," I said, louder this time, and scrambled to my feet.

Carmen was shrieking from my pocket, and I pulled the phone out and pressed it to my ear. "Shit, Carmen, I think he's dead. I think he's *dead*. What the fuck do I do?"

"Call an ambulance, you dumbass!" she yelled through the tinny speaker, and I stumbled my way over to the room phone and picked it up, dialing the front desk.

"Reception, Anthony speaking."

"Anthony," I said, a little bit of a whimper to my voice. "It's Tyler. I'm in Chris Raiden's room and I think he's dead and I need you to call an ambulance. *Now*."

"Shit," Anthony said. "Okay, okay, I'm calling." He hung up with a loud, resounding *click* and I raised my own phone back to my ear with a shaking hand.

"Carmen." I eyed the corpse on the floor a few feet from me. "Holy fuck. He's dead."

There was a long pause on the other end of the line. Then she took a deep breath and said, "You know this is all your fault."

I blinked a few times. "What?"

"You killed him," she said, her voice rising in pitch and volume. "If you hadn't taken so long to find the fucking grapes, he'd be alive."

"What?" I asked again, straining to hear her through ears that seemed to be filling with cotton. The edges of my vision constricted in on me as I stared at Chris's body. "What're you talking about?"

But she just kept *yelling*, and after a few seconds I let the phone fall to the floor as I looked down at the corpse of rock star Christopher Raiden and tried to figure out what I was supposed to do from here.

CHAPTER ONE

"No," I said. It seemed like a good response given the circumstances.

Richard crossed his arms and did a twitching-jaw thing at me. "You don't get to say no, Tyler. It's your job."

I eyed him, trying to figure out how much of a bitch-face I could give him before I crossed a line and got fired.

So far today he'd been mostly smiling and friendly despite his current hostile stance, but just to be safe I only dialed up my bitch-face to about seventy-five percent of its capacity. "Damn it, Jim, I'm a doctor, not a physicist," I said. Richard's mouth opened slightly, and he stared blankly at me. "I'm a bellboy," I explained, "not a maid."

"Mr. Kingston wants his room cleaned," Richard said, tightening his crossed arms and twitching his jaw even harder.

"Yeah, I know," I said. "That's housekeeping's job."

Richard let his arms fall to his sides, then shrugged. "He doesn't trust foreigners with his stuff."

"Okay, first off, that makes Mr. Kingston a douche. But second off, that pretty much just rules out Malika. Make the others do it."

Richard hesitated. "He says they're all foreigners."

I blinked. "Natalie was born in, like, Iowa."

"I know. Still. He says she's foreign."

"You can't *get* more corn-fed American than Iowa. And she doesn't even *look* foreign." Which was true. Natalie was gorgeous, a platinum blonde with bright-blue eyes who stood about five eight, with five feet of that being pure leg. I'd tried to hit on her once. It hadn't gone well.

"He thinks she's Scandinavian, and Scandinavians are raging thieves." He rolled his eyes. "According to him, anyway."

I stared at him for several seconds. "You're kidding me."

"I promise you I'm not." Richard looked *almost* sympathetic to my plight. "But he's a good tipper, so just go swab out his toilet and throw some new sheets on the bed and stop your complaining."

"I want security to give me a full, televised pat down after I get done." I crossed *my* arms. "I'm not going to jail because Mr. Kingston thinks I stole his gold-spun butt floss."

"Just go clean the room, Tyler." And then he turned around and walked into his office and shut the door.

I stood there eying the closed door for a moment while I regrouped, then headed to the lobby to see if any guests needed help before I had to go up to the stupid penthouse. I could do this. It wasn't like I hadn't been back up to the room since Chris died in it—it's the biggest room in the hotel and the people who stay there are usually VIPs, so excellent bellboy service is something they expect—but this was going to be the first time I'd been farther inside than just past the doorway. And even then, I'd made a point not to look deeper into the room, and especially not at the spot on the floor where I found him.

I'm not ashamed to say I'd had nightmares about it, at first. I'd woken up in cold sweats in the middle of the night and grabbed at Carmen for comfort, only to realize that she wasn't there anymore. And honestly, even if she had been, she would have just rolled away from me and said, "Fuck, Tyler, I'm trying to sleep." She'd never been much of a cuddler except on special occasions, and even less so there at the end of the relationship.

But anyway, the nightmares were weird, because he never got up and came at me like a killer zombie or anything. Most of the time in the dreams I just stood still and stared at his corpse, with its shallow glassy eyes pointed at the floor beside it, until my skin started to crawl, and no matter how much I tried, I couldn't move for anything in the world. The sight of him had been burned into my mind when

I found his body, and now my stupid subconscious kept making sure that I couldn't forget a single gory little detail.

But I am a grown man and I am not a coward, so I decided to stop being a baby about it and go clean the stupid room. Chris's body wasn't going to be there. It had been hauled off in a body bag and buried somewhere in New York state, which seemed weird since I'd read the band biography and as far as I could remember, Chris had never lived there. Maybe he had family in the area or something. Who knows.

Time was passing, though, and I definitely wanted to be done and out of the room long before Mr. Kingston came back from wherever he had gone and decided that my blond hair meant that I was Scandinavian too. So I left the empty lobby and walked very briskly to housekeeping and took a cart into the service elevator.

I had to remind myself to breathe a few times on the way up to the room. It helped to know that I, of all people, was sure that he was dead. Really dead. So his body wasn't going to be there when I opened the door. The nightmares weren't real, and I had to face them one of these days. It might as well be today.

I wasn't a huge fan of Incite the Masses. I mean, they were fine, I guess. Basic rock music, harder and edgier than the inoffensive bore-fest music that pumps out of the speakers at the hotel bar, but not thrashing death metal either. Alt-rock, maybe. What I'm saying is that if they came on the radio I wouldn't change the channel but I also wouldn't crank up the volume. They were okay.

I had a T-shirt, though. And all their albums. And I'd been to the concerts. I'd even gone to a fan convention once. But that was *not* because I was a huge fan—it was because Carmen Anders had great tits and tended to put out after listening to rock music, and she was a big fan of Incite the Masses. I mean, massive. Like when we started dating, she'd included a clause in our verbal contract that if she ever had the chance to sleep with any (or all at once if possible) of the band members, she was totally going to do it and I just had to be fine with it.

She hadn't felt the same way about me putting Zoe Saldana on my free-pass list. Or even of me *having* a free-pass list. But that's another story.

So anyway, playing the part of an Incite the Masses fan was sort of a requirement for getting to see Carmen Anders naked, and I didn't hate their music or anything, so I'd bought a T-shirt, learned a few of their songs and (*bam!*) got laid. And then I'd skipped out on paying my internet bill so that I could buy her mosh pit tickets, and then I had to pay Vic Mitchell fifty bucks to cover my shift so I could take her to it, and *then* I got punched in the jaw by a very burly, sweaty biker type for elbowing my way past him to get her right next to the stage, but it had been worth it because after the concert, she kept me up all night long. And I do mean that literally. All. Night. Long. And it was *awesome*.

Which was mostly because she swore up and down that Eric Painter had made eye contact with her in the middle of "Strike a Match" and it was apparently the hottest thing that ever happened to her. And I'm about ninety-nine percent sure that she'd been closing her eyes and imagining that I was Eric with his deep raspy singing voice and his spiky gelled hair while I was boning her, but you know what? Still counted.

And after that, wonder of wonders, she'd stuck around. For a while, at least. Over a year. Then Incite the Masses came back to Boston on this year's tour, and I'd been bare-ass broke and not in the mood to take a fist to the jaw again; plus, I'd been starting to get pretty tired of putting up with her shit, so when she'd not-so-subtly hinted that I needed to repeat last year and get her up to the stage again, I'd just told her I had to work. And she'd bitched and moaned and threatened to dump me, but I'd stood firm, man. I'd stood firm.

She hadn't dumped me, though, mostly because while we were having a big screaming match about it, Richard called me freaking out over how Christopher Raiden had booked a room at our hotel for after the show and how he was probably going to want a rhesus monkey skeleton and where the fuck was he going to get a rhesus monkey skeleton on short notice and on and on and on about the damn rhesus monkey skeleton until I couldn't even take it anymore and had to hang up. Not hang up *on* him, of course, because I need my job, but the "oops, I left the casserole in the oven gotta go" type of hanging up.

Carmen stared at me as I put my phone back in my pants pocket. "What the fuck, Tyler?"

"What? What did I do wrong *now*?" I picked up my jacket from where I'd thrown it on the floor earlier and fished around in my pocket for my keys.

"You took a phone call in the middle of an argument," she said, her voice rising slowly in pitch like the argument was about to start up again.

Luckily, I knew how to shut that down. "Chris Raiden just booked a room at the hotel. Richard's freaking out and talking about rhesus monkey skeletons." I pulled my keys out and curled my fingers around them.

Carmen's mouth dropped open. "Chris Raiden is staying at *your hotel*?"

I exerted a monumental amount of willpower and just barely managed not to roll my eyes so hard my retinas detached. "Yeah, that's what I just said."

"Well . . ." she said, a slow, dangerous smile spreading over her face. "Then I guess you know how to keep me, then."

I had put on my jacket. "No idea what you mean." After all, if you want your boyfriend to pimp you out to a rock star, you have to say the words.

"You're going to let me in his room." She leaned forward with an upsetting gleam in her increasingly cold eyes.

"Um, no." I patted the sides of my jacket, more out of habit than anything else since I'd already found my keys. "I'm not doing that."

"He's on my free-pass list, Tyler!"

"Yeah, well, fuck your free-pass list." I raised an eyebrow at her in a clear challenge. "I never signed off on that bullshit, and you'd bust an ovary if I asked you to let me fuck some other chick, so no. Not doing it."

"This isn't *some other chick*, Tyler. This is Chris *Raiden*. He's my *idol*."

"Oh, please," I scoffed. "He's not even your favorite band member."

"Well, no." She pursed her lips in her "trying to be alluringly sensual while deep in thought" expression. Which is duckface, of course. The crazy ones always think duckface looks sexy on them. They're also always wrong.

After several seconds of duckface thought, she nodded as if she'd decided something important and smiled at me. "Surely Eric will be there too?"

"Doubt it," I said, letting my words be clipped and harsh.

"But . . . they're best friends. And bandmates. Surely . . ."

"Pretty sure Richard would have said that *the band* has rented out our penthouse if that was the case. And he just said Chris."

"Oh, so you're on a fucking first name basis with him now? All buddy-buddy?" She put her hands on her hips and sneered at me. "You're some sort of bestie with Chris Raiden now and you won't even let me talk to him?"

I actually rolled my eyes at that. "Don't be ridiculous. I'm not sure if you can *stop* being ridiculous, but it would be fantastic if you could make an effort."

"Fuck you," she spat.

"That's pretty much the only reason I'm still with you," I snapped back.

"Let me in his fucking room, Tyler!"

"No. I'm not losing my job just so you can get a rock star to knock you up."

She narrowed her eyes. "Then get me an autograph. If you can't even do *that*, we're through."

"Yeah, whatever." I reached for the doorknob. And then, because I felt sentimental for some stupid reason, I didn't turn it. Instead, I sighed and looked back at her. "I mean, yeah. I can do that."

She raised her eyebrows. "You're not going to fight me on that, too?"

I shrugged. "Least I can do, I guess."

She came over and wrapped her arms around me, laying her cheek on my shoulder. "Thank you, baby."

I sighed and kissed the top of her head.

Apparently, the prospect of getting an autograph gets her off too, so I'd taken advantage of that newfound knowledge. Because only morons turn down chicks as hot as Carmen when they're pressed up against them.

I, Tyler Lindsey, am not a moron.

CHAPTER TWO

U p at the penthouse, I stood outside the room for longer than strictly necessary while I talked myself into going inside. Finally, in a wild burst of energy so I wouldn't have time to stop myself, I swiped my access card and wheeled the cart into the room. I closed the door behind me and eyed the carpet where he'd been lying, half expecting to see a body outline still there even though that was stupid.

But there wasn't a corpse on the floor this time, which was probably comforting for Mr. Douchey Kingston, being as the room was his now. I looked around at his boring businessy suits and his multiple spare briefcases—which were a huge difference from the guitars, eyeliner, and syringes I'd seen in here before, although I tried not to think about that—and then pulled the cleaning cart farther into the room and parked it where I usually park my luggage cart. I eyed the carpet where the body had been again.

You'd think that it wouldn't bug me. But it did.

It also shouldn't have bugged me that Carmen blamed me for Chris's death, since she's batshit crazy and there's no way any sane person could think it was my fault that the guy died. But when you get text after psychotic text about how if you'd just gotten off your lazy good-for-nothing ass and taken room service up five minutes earlier, you would have been able to save somebody's life, it starts to really fuck with your mind.

And apparently with my motor skills too, because when I tore myself away from staring at the boring hotel carpet and went into the bathroom to clean, I fumbled as I was reaching for the half-empty bottle of complimentary hotel shampoo sitting on the side of the tub. The bottle hit the ground and rolled under the claw-foot sink.

I groaned. I was going to have to reach down there, and God only knew when the maids last deep-cleaned under that thing. Whoever designed that sink was a complete idiot, because there was just barely enough room to get your hand through but not enough room to scrub, and you could forget about using any kind of cleaning tool, because it wasn't going to fit either. Mostly the housekeeping staff ignored the whole area unless somebody specifically complained about it, which hardly anyone ever did.

But I didn't want to lose out on tip money because Asshole Kingston decided to get on his hands and knees and shine a flashlight everywhere to catch me leaving something dirty, so I crouched on the floor and reached down to fish around for the bottle.

My fingers hit something small and cold. I frowned and raked whatever it was out from under the sink. It was a ring, white gold with Celtic symbols on it. Chris Raiden's ring, one that he'd gone on and on about in interviews until anyone even vaguely familiar with the band would have recognized it.

I peered at it for another few seconds, then put the ring on my hand. I mean, that sounds weird, but it's a basic human instinct. You find a ring, you put it on. That's totally normal.

What *wasn't* totally normal was that when I looked up, Chris Raiden was staring at me from the doorway of the bathroom. And he was . . . slightly transparent.

I blinked at the cart for a few seconds while my brain tried to process everything. Then, without planning to, I screamed.

"Shut up, dude!" the ghost of Chris Raiden said, holding his hands up. "I'm not going to hurt you."

"Like hell you're not," I shouted, and was pleasantly surprised that my voice had returned to its usual pitch. "I've seen *plenty* of horror movies."

Chris tilted his head a little and stared at me. "What?"

"You're going to drown me in the tub. Oh God." I covered my face with my hands and began . . . well, I won't say "whimpering" because that's totally not something a guy like me does, but . . . well, okay, whimpering. But come on, there was a ghost and the bathtub was *right there* and that was how someone always ended up dying in the first five minutes of a horror movie to show the audience how gory the whole thing was going to be. I'm not an idiot. I know how movies work.

When he didn't respond immediately, I peeked out through my fingers, and Chris frowned down at me. "What are you doing wearing my ring? And why the hell are you in my room when I'm still here? If you're trying to steal my shit, I'll have you fired so fast you'll leave your shoes behind."

A version of the truth was probably the best place to start. "Um . . ." I scooted backward toward the tub, even though that would just make it easier for him to drown me in it if he decided to. "I was just cleaning under the sink and I guess the ring rolled under there?"

"Why are you wearing it?" He scowled at me.

"I'm not *wearing* it," I said, even though that was clearly not true. I mean, come on. The thing was right there on my finger. "I just, you know, tried it on." I reached for the ring to take it off, but Chris took a step toward me and I cringed back against the tub, flinging my arm up to cover my face like that was going to help me not die.

"Dude, calm down. I'm not going to drown you in the fucking tub. What am I, a psychopath?" I peered up at him over the top of my arm, catching him mid-eye-roll.

Carefully, I lowered my arm the rest of the way and took a second to look him over. He was wearing the same clothes I'd found his body in, although the dried blood and vomit were gone, and his face and hands had lost their unsettling purple tint, thankfully. His eyeliner was back to stage-ready perfect, and his hair was freshly styled. In other words, he looked just like he would have if he hadn't been out of his mind on heroin and/or dead due to the heroin. Really, the only thing that made him seem ghostlike at all was the fact that I could sort of see the outline of the cleaning cart behind him through his stomach.

Carmen would have immediately commenced trying to fuck him. Ghost or no ghost.

"So . . ." I said, slowly getting to my feet. "What do you remember? You weren't in the room a second ago when I came in to clean."

"Are you kidding me?" He rolled his eyes. "I was lying on the floor. I mean, right there. You couldn't have missed me."

I raised an eyebrow at him. "Yeeeeah. I think maybe you're confused."

"I'm not confused. Now give me my ring and get out of my room." He held out his palm.

I pointed at his finger, where a see-through version of the ring in question was gleaming transparently. "You mean that ring?"

He inspected his hand. "Huh," he said after a moment. "You have a replica, then?"

". . . I think they sell them, yeah." I cleared my throat. "But dude. I might need to tell you something."

"What?"

"You're . . . well, you're dead, dude."

He narrowed his eyes and glared my own death at me. "Is that a threat?"

"No, it's an observation." I ran my hand through my hair for something to do. "You died like two months ago. In this room."

"I'm calling security. I don't care if you work here." He stalked back into the suite. I tagged along behind him.

"Security sounds like an awesome idea, man. If you're not dead, you have a lot of people who are going to want an explanation." *If* he's not dead. What a joke. I could see through the guy's abs.

He shot me a black glare and reached for the phone, then frowned. He tried again. We both watched as his hand went straight through the handset and into the nightstand below it.

"Huh," he said, then tried one more time. Silence fell as his eyes flicked comically back and forth between the phone and his hand. "Um . . . I guess that's pretty good evidence for your 'I'm dead' theory."

"Yeah, no joke," I said. "So . . ." I tried for a minute to think of a way to finish that sentence, but there didn't seem to be a good ending. "So."

He looked around the room, then lowered his eyes to the floor. "Right there?"

"Yeah," I said. "I was actually the one who found you. I was bringing you room service."

"What . . . happened?" His face was pale in addition to being transparent, and he sat down heavily on the bed like he couldn't keep his legs under him. The bed didn't move at all when he flopped down on it, which was way more unsettling than you'd think it would be.

But anyway, that was a dumb question, so I raised my eyebrow at him again. "You're seriously asking me what happened to you?"

"I don't remember much," he said, his voice soft in that way that makes men want to run for the hills before the crying starts.

"Um . . ." I swallowed hard. I mean, normally I'd just leave, push the awkward potential crying situation off on someone else, but I had no idea what the protocol was about leaving an emotionally compromised ghost to work things out for himself. Maybe that's where vengeful spirits come from: some guy bailed on them instead of giving them a ghost hug or whatever and so they start killing people in their sleep. I couldn't have that on my conscience. But I also couldn't think of anything to say, really. Who wants to be the one to tell a person how they died? Nobody, that's who.

But still. He needed to know. I cleared my throat. "I think they said it was a combination of anxiety medicine and, um, you know . . ."

He cleared his throat too. "The heroin."

"Yeah."

"Eric always said I was going to kill myself with that shit," he said, still alarmingly softly. "Maybe I should have listened to him."

"Yeah, you probably should have." I crossed my arms and watched as he stood up from the bed, then knelt to run his hand over the carpet where his body had been. After a second, curiosity got the better of me. "Can you feel that? The carpet?"

"Sort of," he said. "It's like . . . when you put your hand on the surface of water. You can feel the resistance, but it wouldn't take much to push your hand through." He dipped his hand into the floor and then pulled it back out. "How long has it been? You said two months?"

"Yeah. It happened in September. It's the end of November now." I pushed the toe of my shoe against the carpet, ruffling it up one way and then smoothing it back down. "Um . . . for whatever it's worth, I'm sorry, man."

He sighed. "My own fault."

"Yeah, but still. Sucks to die young." It was a dumb thing to say, but really, no amount of life experience prepares you for this shit.

He let out a huff of laughter that didn't sound terribly humor-filled. "Thanks, I guess." His eyes got wider. "Fuck, I'm *dead*."

"You're dead," I confirmed.

"No, you don't understand." His voice had an edge of hysteria to it that somehow made me less nervous than the thought of him crying. "I'm *dead*. I *died*."

I stared at him for a second, not intending to respond. But he just stared back like he was waiting for an answer, so I shrugged and said, "You're dead, yeah."

"I wasn't supposed to die," he said, a little louder. "It wasn't supposed to be like this."

"Calm down, dude." I spread my hands out in front of me in a helpless gesture. "There's not a lot you can do about it at this point."

"I'm not ready." He scrambled back to his feet. "Jesus, I should have called him. I should have apologized."

"Who?"

"Eric," he said, biting his lip and gazing at the carpet. "I told him I hated him, and I shouldn't have said that. Because I didn't, not really."

"Um . . ." I looked around the room like that was going to give me answers. "I guess I could send him a letter for you or something."

"No, he'd just rip it up." He closed his eyes and left them shut for a while, squeezing his eyelids together. When he opened them again, they were a little less wild.

"I'm sure he knew you didn't mean it."

Chris didn't answer that—he just poked the toe of his own shoe at the carpet like I'd done a few minutes ago. His foot disappeared through the floor. "I wonder how I'm even standing and not just falling into the room below?" he murmured.

"I don't know, dude. It's probably a matter of perspective. Mind over matter, you know. You think you can walk on the floor and so you can."

"I'm sure you're right." He met my eyes with a businesslike expression. "So . . . are you some sort of angel or something?"

I laughed out loud at that. "Oh God, no. What, do I *look* like an angel?"

"No," he admitted. "But I thought maybe you were somebody who took souls up to heaven or whatever."

I could have pointed out that borderline suicidal heroin junkies who sleep with dubiously legal groupies and go out in a blaze of stupid futile glory in their twenties probably don't make it to heaven, but that seemed unnecessarily cruel. And plus, I don't make the call. I guess if God's an Incite the Masses fan that might have some sway in the afterlife cabin assignments. So instead I just shrugged. "Not an angel. Just a bellboy. I work here."

"Oh." He pushed his foot through the floor again before straightening up and squaring his shoulders. "Well, I guess that's it, then. I'm dead."

"Yeah." I shifted uncomfortably. "So I guess you'll be wanting to . . . move on? Or whatever?"

"I don't know how," he said. "That's why I thought there would be an angel or a guide or something." His gaze slid around the room. "I don't see a light to go towards."

"Do you see a flame?" I asked, then wished I hadn't.

To my surprise, he laughed. "No, not one of those either. Although I guess that would be more likely for a guy like me."

I smiled, and he smiled back.

It was at that moment it hit me: I was talking to a ghost.

The screaming started again.

CHAPTER THREE

I only screamed for a few seconds, but by the time Malika rushed into the room I was crouched in the corner of the suite, hugging my knees to my chest and rocking back and forth. It was actually a little pathetic, and I was glad it was Malika who found me, because Vic or Natalie would have given me so much shit about it that I would have been forced to leave the country. Anyway, Malika saw me and ran over, falling to her knees beside me dramatically.

"Tyler! What's wrong?" She reached for my arm, and I yanked it out of her reach. Frowning deeply, she tried again. "Do I need to call an ambulance?"

"No," I whimpered, hoping she could hear me through my knees. "It's him."

"It's who?" Malika's eyes flitted around the room. "Mr. Kingston? Did he hurt you?"

"No!" I summoned all of my strength and lifted my head. Chris was standing behind Malika, his brow knitted and his arms crossed tightly against his chest. I pointed at him. "*Him.*"

Malika turned and scanned the room behind her, then looked back at me with a ridiculously calm expression. "There's nobody there, Tyler."

"He's there." I pointed harder at Chris. "Can't you see him?"

She glanced around again, checking for longer this time before slowly turning back to me. "Maybe you should lie down. I'll help you to an empty room, okay?"

I stared at Chris. "Let her see you."

"I don't know if I can." He frowned for a minute, then shrugged. "Doesn't seem to work."

Malika pursed her lips a bit. "Tyler. Who are you talking to?"

"Chris Raiden," I said. "He's here."

"Oh yeah," Chris said, rolling his eyes. "If she can't see me, she's totally going to believe you."

Malika got to her feet. "I think maybe I should call that ambulance."

"No!" I glared at my legs and tried to will them to straighten out and agree to support my weight. "I'm okay. I'm just . . . maybe you're right. I should lie down. I'm just . . ." I glanced at Chris again and then tried to act like I *wasn't* seeing an apparition in the room. After all, I'm too pretty to go to a psych ward. I swallowed hard and turned to Malika. "It's been a long day. I'm just tired."

She narrowed her eyes.

Chris poked her experimentally. His hand went through her neck.

"I'm going to lie down," I said. Even though this was our largest, most luxurious room, it suddenly seemed claustrophobic. "Is 612 empty?"

"Yeah. Are you sure you're okay?"

"I'm good," I said, finally managing to scramble to my feet. "Can you just throw some sheets on this bed for me?" She nodded, and I gave her a bright smile. Really, it was probably a few shades *too* bright, but it was the best I could do under the circumstances. "Okay, then. I'll be fine in a bit. I just need a little nap."

"Okay," she said. "I'll come check on you in an hour if you're not up by then."

"Thanks." I forced my feet to move. After a few steps had proved to me that I could walk on my own without face-planting, I sped up and went to room 612 at a trot, then passed the management key through the room card reader and went inside.

I went directly to the bed and sat down. I put my head in my hands and took a moment to gather my thoughts.

"So that was awkward," Chris said.

I looked up at him. "I'm crazy," I said after a moment. "I've lost my mind."

"I don't know what you are, man. Maybe *I'm* crazy. I've never had a trip like this, though, so it seems weird." He crossed over to the bed and put his hand on it, then slowly lowered himself to sit down. "Huh. I guess I can sit."

I thought about mentioning that he'd already found out he could sit in the other room, but I didn't really have the stability to string together a long sentence yet. I put my elbows on my knees and focused on breathing normally. Chris reached over and touched my knuckles.

"Can you feel that?" he asked.

I moved my hand so that his fingers dipped into it. "No. Not really. Not at all, actually."

"The movies say ghosts are cold. It's not cold or anything?"

"No." I pulled my hand away. "But it's weird, so stop it."

"All right," he said, pulling his own hand back.

"Could *you* feel it?"

He shrugged. "Same as the floor and the bed. I can tell when I'm touching something, but it doesn't feel like *really* touching it. Just like there's a barrier there. A little token resistance." He dipped his hand into the mattress. "But it's easy to break through."

I nodded, then sat up a little straighter. It was time to get back to business. "You appeared when I put on your ring, so . . ."

He jumped to his feet and jabbed his finger at me. "Aha! So it's not a replica! You *did* steal my ring!"

I rolled my eyes. "Dude, I told you. I found it on the floor and tried it on. That's not the same thing as stealing."

"Give it back," he demanded, holding out his hand. "It's mine. My dad's wedding ring, man. It's important to me, and I need it."

I laughed. "And where are you going to put it? In your ghost pockets? It would just fall right through you."

"Take it off. It's not yours to keep." He scowled and shook the hand he was still holding out like he was reminding me it was there.

"Okay, okay." I reached for the ring, then paused. "You appeared when I put it on. So if I take it off, you might disappear."

He considered this. "I'm not afraid."

"You're not? That must be nice. Because I'm fucking terrified, let me tell you."

He gave me a Look. "You're not the one who's dead."

"Maybe not, but I *am* the one who's sitting in an empty hotel room talking to a ghost while my coworker is probably on the phone with the guys in white coats, so I think of the two of us, I'm worse off right now."

"How is that worse than being dead?" He started pacing back and forth.

I watched him for a few seconds before answering. "Well, it's not like you're getting any *more* dead. But I could potentially be getting crazier and crazier by the second."

"I think it must vacillate back and forth between more and less crazy," he said, and for some reason the fancy GRE word sounded natural in his voice.

I raised an eyebrow. "How do you figure that?"

"Well, you were screaming," he pointed out. "And then you were pretty chill with the whole thing for a little while. And then you started screaming again. And now you're back to chill. So you've gone from crazy to not crazy and back to crazy and now you're back to not crazy."

I thought about this for a moment. "Well, maybe. But I think maybe the screaming was the not-crazy part and the chillaxing is the crazy coming back out."

"That could be true," he conceded. "So . . . good-bye, I guess."

I blinked. "What? Good-bye? Are you, um, moving on?"

He stopped pacing and turned to face me. "Not that I know of. But if you take the ring off and it launches me into whatever afterlife I'm headed for . . . good-bye."

"Yeah," I said, drawing out the word. I put my fingers on the ring again, but still didn't pull it off.

Poor guy. He'd just learned he was dead and now he might be getting even deader, despite what I'd said earlier. That must suck. I've always thought it might be better to die suddenly, without any warning, because although it would be shitty to die without saying your good-byes, at least you didn't have to lie there dreading the last moment. I raised my eyes to meet his and felt like maybe I should, I don't know, say a few words.

"You were a good musician, you know." It was really all I could say, since I didn't know the guy personally. But maybe it would be enough. "Your music and your life meant something to a lot of people."

He swallowed, even though that must be pretty useless for a ghost. "You're a fan?"

"Not really," I admitted, then felt bad, both because maybe it would be better for him to be talking to a fan right now and because it's not *strictly* true that I'm not one. "Well . . . I'm not a hardcore-psycho-screaming-in-the-mosh-pit kind of fan. But I like Incite the Masses, yeah. And my girlfriend was a *huge* fan."

He tilted his head. "Was?"

"Yeah, was." I paused, then realized what he meant. "Well, she still is a fan. She's just not my girlfriend anymore. Hence the past tense."

"Oh," he said. "Well, I guess it's good. That people appreciated me."

"They did," I assured him. "And you know, the fans went crazy when you died. There was weeping and gnashing of teeth. Some kids ran out and got tattoos in memory of you. There are fan sites and oh my God, you should have seen the crowd outside the cemetery where they buried you."

He blinked. "I'm buried?"

"Yeah," I said. "Why? Does that surprise you?"

"A little, yeah," he admitted, hugging his arms to his stomach. "I mean, it shouldn't. I'm dead." He blinked hard, then sighed. "How many people get to stand there saying 'I'm dead' and mean it literally?"

"No idea, man," I said, shrugging. "I really don't know how widespread ghostism is."

"So you're not Haley Joel?" He laughed awkwardly. "I mean . . . you don't see dead people all the time? Walking around like regular people? Who don't know they're dead?"

"Not all the time, no," I answered. "You're my first. But who knows? Maybe finding your purple corpse awoke some latent psychic powers in me or something."

"Maybe— Wait. Purple corpse?"

I rolled my eyes. "Yeah. What, you thought after you shot yourself up with that much smack you'd look pretty?"

"I kind of hoped I wouldn't look *dead*," he snapped. "Or even *be* dead, for that matter."

"Well, when you die of a heroin overdose you're purple. The more you know." I shot him a pointed glare. "But you looked okay otherwise, I guess. Well, and the fact that you'd puked yourself. So that wasn't very attractive either. And your makeup was everywhere."

He grimaced. "I really didn't think I took enough to die of it."

"The entire medical community disagrees with you," I said. "And you know what they say about heroin, dude. Not even once."

"You mean you've never tried it? Not even once?"

"Um, no," I said, letting the contempt creep into my voice. I mean, sure, I'll be nice to the guy to help ease his transition from life to afterlife so he doesn't become a vengeful ghost and rethink the whole not-drowning-me-in-the-tub thing. But I wasn't going to sit there and defend hard-drug use to him like it was a good idea that went tragically wrong.

"I find that hard to believe." He crossed his arms and leaned back against the wall, slowly and carefully like it was an experiment.

I raised my eyebrow again. "Dude, not that many people actually do heroin. I mean, pot, okay. Meth. Even crack. But heroin is a pretty small subset, as far as I know."

"Just about everybody I know has at least tried it."

"Well, you're a rock star. You have a skewed sample," I pointed out. "I bet everybody you know has boned Zoe Saldana, too."

He laughed. "Not her specifically. But I guess I see what you mean."

I offered him a smile, then let it slip back into a less amused expression. "But seriously, dude. Why'd you do it?"

He closed his eyes and took a deep breath. "I don't know. I really don't. I tried it because I wanted to try new things. Experiment, you know. And then I just didn't stop." He opened his eyes again and gazed past me, unfocused and distant. "Eric told me to stop. But all I could think was, you know, fuck Eric. So I did what I wanted and now I'm dead."

"I thought you and Eric were best friends." And I really did. They acted like besties in all their interviews, elbowed each other and smiled and giggled and told stories about shenanigans and hijinks they'd gotten into. I'm pretty sure there's a subset of fans who are convinced that they had been doing it too.

Chris pondered that for a few seconds. Finally, he sighed. "We were. But that was over a while ago. We've been barely civil to each other for a long time now."

"So the interviews where you said you were like brothers . . . that was all for show?"

"No, we're still like brothers," he said, chuckling bitterly. "Just brothers who don't like each other and only hang out when we're obligated to."

I nodded slowly. "Hence the separate hotels."

"Yeah." He tried to push away from the wall and almost fell backward through it.

I shouldn't have laughed, but I did. He just looked so ridiculous, flailing for balance as his limbs disappeared into the wall and out of it, and then the dark glance he shot me set me off more.

"It's not funny." He wrinkled his nose and crossed his arms. "I nearly busted my ass."

"Your ghosty ass!" I said, laughing even harder.

"Shut up," he demanded, but his mouth twitched.

"Okay, okay." I took several deep breaths and managed to compose myself. Barely. "So anyway, should we try the ring thing? See if that sends you on into the hereafter?"

"I guess so," he said, his voice getting a little soft and vulnerable again. "Thanks, man."

"For what?" I asked, my fingers pausing on the ring.

He worked his jaw for a moment. "For . . . I don't know. I guess for explaining what happened. Could you, you know, pass on a message for me?"

I raised an eyebrow at him. "A message. To who?"

"To Eric. And to my sister."

"That you love them? That you're sorry?" I guessed.

"Yeah, tell Allison that." He grimaced. "And tell Eric . . . I don't know. To go fuck himself. Or that he was right. Or that if he gets Nathan Vale to replace me, I'll find a way to come haunt the shit out of him."

I raised both eyebrows. "Um. Well, this is awkward."

Chris's mouth dropped open. "He did *not*."

"They said it was only for the rest of the tour," I pointed out helpfully.

"He did *not*," he said again, louder this time. "That fucker!"

"Don't drown the messenger in the tub." I spread my hands in the universal "please don't kill me Mr. Ghost" gesture.

"I'm going to find that asswipe and *haunt* him. I'm going to make his life miserable. He'll regret doing this."

"Hey, now, don't go all vengeful spirit on me." I gave him an exaggerated wide-eyed look. "I don't want to have to shoot you with a salt gun."

"With a what?" He stopped grinding his ghosty teeth and frowned at me.

"A salt gun," I said. "Because you're a ghost and, you know, salt . . ." He still looked completely in the dark. I rolled my eyes. "And then I'd have to burn your bones."

"What in the hell are you talking about?" he demanded.

Jeez. Richard didn't get the Star Trek references and Chris Raiden had never watched *Supernatural*. I was surrounded by cultural cripples, all the time. "Never mind. If you didn't watch any decent shows when you were alive, it's too late to start now."

"What show is that from?"

"*Supernatural*. It's pretty good. They hunt ghosts and monsters and shit."

He tilted his head again in what I was already starting to recognize as his thinking stance. "They hunt ghosts? Let's watch it."

I blinked at him. "Are you serious?"

"Yeah, as a heart attack," he said, then went to the bed and sat down facing the TV.

"Or as a lethal dose of junk," I muttered, then picked up the remote. "It's probably not even on, anyway. And the hotel TVs don't have internet access."

"Just find it on pay-per-view." He flipped his hand like he was saying "any time you're ready. Slowly McTakesforever."

"Um, no," I said. "Richard will kill me if I use pay-per-view in a guest room."

"Then charge it to me." He smiled like this was the greatest plan ever. "You still have my credit card information on file, don't you?"

"Yeah," I said. "But. You're. Dead. I'm pretty sure they cancel your credit cards when you're dead."

"Oh." He paused and looked lost for a second.

And there was no way I was going to deal with a crying ghost if I could possibly help it, so I smiled super brightly and patted his ghost hand as best I could without being able to feel it. "Well, let's just try the ring thing. Maybe you'll go to heaven and then God can get you Netflix access or something."

"Or I'll go to hell," he grumbled.

"Then you can watch *Rock of Love*," I said. "Surely they play that one in hell on repeat."

He laughed. "I like you, Tyler."

I rolled my eyes. "Just because you're stuck with me right now."

"Well, yeah," he admitted. "But you seem all right."

"'All right'? I can live with that." I gave him a half smile. "So . . . are you ready?"

"Yeah." He stood up. "If I disappear, can you put the ring back on before you just get rid of it? See if I come back when it's on your hand again?"

"Sure. But if you don't . . . well, it was good to meet you."

"Same here." He took another deep breath.

I watched him for a few seconds, then slipped the ring off of my finger.

CHAPTER FOUR

C hris Raiden was a tall guy. Not freakishly tall, but easily six feet. A little taller than me. He had dark hair, almost black, and dark-brown eyes. He was slender with decently muscular arms, and he liked to wear tight T-shirts on stage to show off his biceps. He was the sort of guy who was attractive enough on his own, but fame suited him well. However, the most unusual thing about Chris Raiden was that he was still there.

I looked at the ring in my hand, then put it down on the bed beside me so that I wasn't touching it at all. He stood there in front of me with his eyes squeezed shut.

"Any day now," he said after a moment.

"I already did it," I told him. "And you're still here."

He opened one eye and peered at me. "I didn't disappear?"

"Nope. Not even a flicker." I pointed at the ring on the bed.

"Well," he said, opening his other eye. "That explains a lot."

I raised an eyebrow. "What exactly does it explain?"

"I have no idea," he admitted. "But if we knew what the hell was going on here, I have a feeling it *would* explain a lot."

"That's extremely helpful," I said sarcastically. "But it doesn't help the situation."

"What's the situation exactly?" He started pacing again.

"That apparently you're just, you know, *here*. And you're not seeming to go anywhere." I leaned back onto the bed and held myself up by my elbows. "Still no light to go toward?"

His eyes slid out of focus, and he gazed off into the corner of the room for a few seconds. "Nothing. I get the feeling that I *can't* leave. Or at least that if I tried, something bad would happen."

"Something bad like what? An explosion? Tearing open the fabric of space and time?"

"No, more like . . ." He paused and tilted his head. "More like I won't like where I go if I leave now."

"Oh." There was a little bit of awkward silence while every hellfire and brimstone sermon I'd ever heard ran through my head. None of that seemed helpful, though, so I just sat there and let my head fall back to stare at the ceiling.

After a few seconds, he cleared his throat. "So . . . if it's not the ring . . . why you? Why you and not that girl?"

"I have no idea, man. None." I considered making up a story about séances or another arcane ritual, but I'm not really that good a bullshitter. "Maybe because I was the first one to touch the ring? Or because I was the one to find your body so there's some sort of connection to your soul?"

"I wonder if it really is just you," he said, sounding a little lost in thought. "Maybe I could show myself to other people if I tried harder."

I shrugged. "You can try. But I've got to finish my shift. Richard will fire my ass for sure if I don't. And even if he doesn't, Malika will probably have me committed for my own safety unless I get out there and start acting normal again."

He gave me an extremely dubious look. "You're going to go back to work after all this?"

"Yeah," I said. "Bills don't pay themselves, man. And also, you owe me a tip."

"I owe you a tip? For what?"

"For bringing you room service and stiffing me on the gratuity," I clarified.

". . . when did I stiff you on a gratuity? I'd never met you before tonight." He blinked at me, his forehead wrinkled up. It was almost endearing, his confused face. Made him seem more like a real human being instead of an untouchable rock star.

"About two months ago," I said. "You ordered a steak, medium rare with a bleu-cheese crust, and a side of grapes. *Grapes*. And not just any grapes, but red seedless grapes. We had to run out and find some grocery store that was open in the middle of the night and sold red seedless grapes because we didn't have any in stock. It was so weird, dude. I didn't know heroin gave people weird pregnancy cravings, but whatever."

He stared at me, and I decided that it must not be possible to hear the gears turning in someone's mind because if it *was*, I'd be hearing them now. But I saw the exact moment when he figured out what I meant.

"I didn't stiff you," he said, his voice rising in volume with each word. "I was *dead*."

"Yeah, well, tell that to my cable bill." I raised an eyebrow. "That was a hundred-dollar steak, man. Twenty percent of a hundred dollars is *twenty bucks* that I was counting on taking home."

"You're so bad off that twenty bucks is the difference between paying your bills and not paying them?"

"Zoe Saldana, man," I said.

"What? Oh." He looked a little sheepish, to his credit. "Skewed sample again, I guess."

"Yeah. Welcome to the world of the working class." I pushed myself up and off the bed. "Speaking of the working class, I have to get back to it."

He looked around. "What am I supposed to do?"

"I don't know." I smoothed out the wrinkles in my bellboy jacket. "Didn't you say you wanted to go haunt some people? Maybe you could do that. That would be fun for you."

"I guess I could," he said. "All right, then. I suppose this is good-bye."

"Yeah." I picked up the ring and put it in my pocket. "I'll mail this to your manager and he can get it to whoever."

"Probably my sister," Chris said. "Thanks again."

"Yeah, no problem." I gave him a weird little salute and headed out of the room and down the hallway. Before I got to the elevator, though, I heard Chris speak from right behind me.

"So . . . this is kind of unsettling."

I stopped and turned around to glare at him. "Why are you following me? Don't you have people to haunt?"

"Yeah, about that . . ." He shifted. "I'm not sure I can be away from you."

I raised both eyebrows this time. "What do you mean?"

"You got about twenty feet down the hall and then I had to follow you."

"Well, that's sweet and all, but I don't think I'm your type," I snapped. "Go away. Go find your sister or Nathan Vale or some groupie with a nice rack. I've got work to do."

"No, I mean . . . I really had to follow you. As in, when you walked away, I *had* to follow you. It wasn't optional." I scoffed, and he continued, "I'll show you. Walk away."

"That's what I'm trying to do," I said. I turned my back and walked another fifty feet or so toward the elevator again. When I looked over my shoulder, Chris was about twenty feet behind me.

"I didn't move on purpose. You dragged me with you."

"I dragged you with me," I repeated. "What the fuck does *that* mean?"

He glared. "Walk backwards and watch me."

I rolled my eyes but did as I was told. For every step I took, Chris stumbled forward a little, reluctantly, as if someone was pushing him along. He could have been faking it, I guess, but it was pretty convincing.

"Huh," I said, super eloquently.

"Yeah," he said. "So there's that."

"So not only am I the only one who can see you, and not only do you not disappear when I take off your ring . . . but I'm stuck with, like, a restraining order. Except instead of you needing to be *more* than twenty feet from me at all times, you have to follow me everywhere."

"Yeah, that seems about right." He motioned at my pocket. "Or it's the ring I have to follow."

"Guess we should test that, huh?" I turned away from him and pulled it out of my pocket. "Here goes." I squatted and rolled the ring along the floor away from him, then twisted around to look at him. He was standing in the same place.

I stood and took a big step backward, and Chris stumbled forward again. "Guess that answers that," I said.

He scowled and walked toward me so that we were at a normal speaking distance again. "No offense, man, but this sort of blows."

I laughed. "You have no idea."

"Well . . ." He ran his hands through his hair again, and I watched it slowly fade back into its unmussed state, like he was resetting to always look the same. "What are we going to do?"

"I'm going to finish my shift, and you're going to stay back and be quiet. And then when I get off work, we're going to figure out what to do." I walked over to where the ring had stopped rolling, then picked it up and put it on.

"So I just . . . follow you around and watch you do your job?"

"Pretty much, yeah. Maybe it will be educational for you. To see how the common masses live when you're not Inciting them."

"I guess I could do that," he said. "After all . . ." He paused dramatically. "It won't kill me."

I groaned. "Okay, you're going to have to stop with the ghost jokes."

"That's the only one I've told," he argued, looking ridiculously put out by the whole thing. "Come on, man, I just found out I'm dead. Worms are currently eating my liver. The least you can do is give me a couple of free passes on ghost humor."

He had a point. I sniffed so he knew how generous I was being, then shrugged one shoulder. "Fine. You can have a *couple* of ghost jokes."

"Really?" He gave me a lopsided smile that would have sent Carmen into spasms of pleasure. "Thanks, man. That means a lot."

"Don't think you can just smile at me and get anything you want, though," I warned, even going so far as to waggle my finger at him. "That only works on girls."

He opened his mouth to say something, then closed it. I gave him a moment to decide whether or not he was going to try again with the speaking thing, but he didn't, so the seconds stretched on until they got sort of weird.

"Anyway," I said to break the awkward silence. "I have to get downstairs. Just be quiet and, I don't know, try and figure out if you can float."

"All right," he agreed. "Lead on."

CHAPTER
FIVE

When I made it back up to the front counter and found Richard, his eyes immediately fixed on me with an unnerving intensity. I raised my eyebrows at him like I didn't know what he meant by that, but he didn't seem fooled by it. He motioned me into his office and closed the door behind us.

"Sorry," I said, trying to placate him before the yelling started. "I just had a little bit of a flashback and it freaked me out. Malika finished up Mr. Kingston's room."

"She said you were curled up in the fetal position screaming your head off," Richard said. "We got complaints from other guests too. About the screaming."

Chris walked over and sat on Richard's desk. I watched him for a second before I realized that it probably wasn't a good idea to watch ghosts walk around the room when people could track my eye movement. I wrenched my eyes back up to meet Richard's. "Yeah. Like I said, I'm sorry. It was just . . . weird."

Richard narrowed his eyes, but with concern instead of anger. "Because of Christopher Raiden?"

Chris glanced up at the mention of his name from his perusal of whatever paperwork Richard had spread out on his desk. I flicked my eyes over to him for the briefest instant before I remembered again that I wasn't supposed to look at him.

"Yeah," I said after a beat of silence. "I just hadn't been back in that room since then."

Richard's frown softened a little. "I understand. If you need to go home, take the rest of the night off . . . well, I'm sure Vic would be happy to have the extra shift."

"Nah," I said, waving my hand dismissively. "I'm fine. I promise."

"Listen, Tyler . . ." Richard tugged at his collar. "If you need to talk to somebody about the whole Christopher Raiden incident . . ."

"Don't worry about it, Richard," I said quickly. The last thing I wanted was to have to talk to my boss about my fears. About the nightmares. About anything related to my life, really.

"I didn't mean *me*," Richard said, his eyes widening. "I'm not exactly qualified to talk about, you know, posttraumatic stress and issues like that."

"Oh." I paused for a moment. "I don't have posttraumatic stress."

"Well . . ." Richard pulled at his collar again. "What I'm saying is that this happened to you on the job, so the hotel would be happy to pay for a few sessions for you. If you think you needed some help working through everything."

"Um . . ." I considered the offer. On the one hand, I didn't think I needed counseling.

And telling a therapist that I was seeing ghosts would probably get me thrown in a mental institution or doped up on antipsychotic meds, and I'd seen how well that worked for my cousin Chad, who'd ended up with pancreatitis and the total inability to sit still. So no thanks on the clozapine. I'd just take my healthy pancreas and put up with my rock star ghost for a while.

Still, though, if it would be on the hotel's dime, I might as well at least leave the option open.

And then I realized that I hadn't actually answered Richard, so I shrugged. "Thanks. I'll give it some thought."

He peered at me for several seconds before speaking. "Okay. Well, let me know if you need anything."

"I will," I promised. "Should I go back to my post now?"

Richard nodded, and I got up and walked out of his office. Chris followed along behind me.

"You really hadn't been back up to the room?" he asked.

"No," I muttered. "Be quiet."

"Why not?"

I didn't want to explain everything to him, so I went for nonchalant. "No reason. I just hadn't."

"Were you, like, messed up by it?" He walked a few paces in front of me and then turned around and started walking backward so he could keep watching me.

"By finding a dead guy in his hotel room? Yeah, that was sort of a bummer." I wrinkled my nose at the memory.

A woman who was waiting in the lobby gave me a very strange look, and I suddenly remembered how odd I must look walking along and talking to myself. I clamped my mouth shut and kept walking.

Chris wasn't interested in being ignored, though. He kept walking backward, his gaze locked on me. "Seriously, did it mess you up?"

I did my best to stare straight through him instead of letting my eyes focus on someone nobody else could see. The semitransparency helped a little. When we got close to the door leading to the foyer of the hotel, I reached through his stomach to grab the door handle and pull the door open.

"Wow," he said. "That was weird." I walked past him, and he continued tagging along after me.

The foyer, where I usually stood chatting with Mark the doorman until guests arrived, was empty at the moment, so I frowned and let my eyes focus on Chris. "If you don't want people sticking their hands through you, don't stand in front of them," I snapped. "And you're really going to have to stop talking to me while I'm working. It's hard to concentrate on just, you know, working and smiling and *not looking at you* when you're walking in front of me and chattering away."

He furrowed his brow. "I'm not really used to sitting back and being quiet."

"Well, do your best. Think of it as a personal challenge." A taxi pulled up to the curb in front of the hotel, and Mark whisked in from the lobby to get the door for them. I lowered my voice so he wouldn't hear and muttered to Chris, "Please, just be quiet. Just while I take their shit from them, okay?"

"If I do, will you take me up in the service elevator?" He seemed ridiculously excited by the prospect, so I nodded and then grabbed one of our shiny gold luggage carts and wheeled it out to the taxi. Mark was busy juggling the purses and backpacks of a woman and her two teenage daughters while her husband eyed him suspiciously.

Even though it was really Mark's job, I went ahead and opened the trunk of the taxi to get the luggage while he handled the ladies' things. Chris stood back close to the hotel doors, clearly trying hard to be quiet and still. Apparently, though, the prospect of riding in the service elevator only appeased him for about seventeen seconds. Then he trotted over and leaned in beside me as I pulled a large pink polka-dotted suitcase out of the taxi's trunk.

"Do you ever rifle through their stuff while you're taking it up?"

"No," I whispered. "I need this job, dude. That would get me fired so fast that Einstein would have to rethink relativity." I put the suitcase on the luggage rack. "Now shut up before they hear you."

"They can't hear me," Chris pointed out, smirking so obnoxiously that I would have been tempted to punch him in the teeth if he'd had corporeal teeth to punch.

"Yeah, well, you can't hear *me* unless I talk to you out loud, so it doesn't do you any good to talk because I can't answer you while they're in earshot." I smiled and waved at the family belonging to the pink suitcase and hefted the other luggage onto the cart while Chris, shockingly, wandered away from the taxi.

Then I had a thought. *So . . . can you hear me?* I mentally projected at Chris.

He continued stalking an unsuspecting pigeon that was strutting its way down the sidewalk. That answered that question, then.

I pushed the cart back toward the door and then stopped and smiled at the family again. "I'll have your belongings up in your room in just a few minutes," I said, offering my best "I'm a nice guy who isn't going to steal your shit" impression.

"You sound so earnest!" Chris called from behind me, where I assumed he must be ghost-petting the oblivious pigeon.

I didn't dignify him with a response. Which was probably a good thing, since the man of the family already seemed very distrustful and likely wouldn't have appreciated me talking to invisible people right in front of his kids. After a moment of awkward silence, though, the man just nodded and shepherded his family inside and up to the reception desk.

Mark had his face set in an expression I knew too well. It was the "fuckers didn't tip me" look. Which could only mean . . .

"Booked online?" I asked him.

"Yep," Mark said. "And not only that, but some *discount* site."

I groaned in sympathy. "So I shouldn't expect anything, then, huh?"

"Who knows? They might surprise you. But I wouldn't get my hopes up." He touched his hand to his earpiece. "They're in 419."

"All right. I'm off, then." I saluted and pushed the cart toward the service elevator. Chris caught up with me.

"What's wrong with booking hotels online?" he asked. "I thought that was the way of the future. Everybody books online."

"Yeah," I said. "But people who book fancy hotels online are usually getting some kind of special deal pricing, so they're getting hotels that they normally couldn't afford."

"Which is terrible. How dare they." He rolled his eyes.

"Well, it's great for them," I admitted. "But people who don't stay in luxury hotels very often don't realize that they're supposed to tip. So they don't. Or they tip badly."

"You're really hung up on this tip thing."

I pushed the button to open the service elevator and then shrugged. "It's my living, man. They don't pay me worth shit here because they assume I'm getting tipped."

Chris just stared at me blankly. I sighed. "You wouldn't understand. You have money and you don't have to wonder how you're going to pay the bills."

He narrowed his eyes. "I can still understand it."

"Yeah, right," I scoffed. "You probably have all your bills on auto-pay."

He stared at me blankly again.

I laughed. "Dude, you don't even understand what a luxury auto-pay is. You can only be on auto-pay if you're sure the money will be there when the day rolls around."

"How much do you make?" he asked, peering at me.

I made a face. "That's none of your business."

"It's my business," Chris said. "Everything about you is my business."

My eyebrows shot up so far they almost got lost under my bellboy cap. "*How* is everything about me *your* business?"

"Well, you're my ride. So until we figure out how I can move on, I'm at your mercy and so I need to know what I'm dealing with."

"I have a hole-in-the-wall apartment and a beat-up TV that has a weird green spot in the top-right corner," I said. "So clearly I'm not rolling in the dough."

"You have a nice suit, though."

"Company-provided," I told him. The elevator stopped on the fourth floor, and I wheeled the cart out and down the hall to room 419. I paused in front of the door and eyed Chris. "Please be quiet. I'm begging you."

"I was quiet," he said. "I was playing with a pigeon and I was very well-behaved."

"True," I admitted. "But still. Quiet."

"Fine, fine." He crossed his arms and poked out his bottom lip.

I knocked on the door and was immediately greeted by the father of the family, who gave me a very sour look.

"About time," he grumbled. "Mary was about to call down to the desk."

"I'm sorry, sir," I said. "The service elevator can be a little slow. I have your luggage. Where would you like me to unload it?"

The man scowled at me. "Just inside the door. We'll put it where it goes."

"Yes, sir." I unloaded the heavy suitcases just inside the door and stepped back outside, but before I could even turn around, the door slammed unceremoniously shut behind me.

Chris raised an eyebrow. "Wow, he was a dick."

"At least he didn't collapse and get blood all over the carpet," I pointed out. "So he's better than *some* people I could mention."

"Blood?" he asked. "There was blood?"

"Yeah." I turned the empty cart around and headed for the service elevator. "Well, I mean, not a ton of it. It wasn't a murder scene or anything. But I don't think you were terribly careful with the needle jabs there at the end, is what I'm saying."

"There at the end," he repeated, his voice going scary soft again.

"Don't do that," I said, pinching the bridge of my nose. "I've had a rough day and I really can't deal with you getting weepy over your entirely preventable death."

He glared at me. "Thanks for being so supportive and reassuring."

"You do the smack, you pay the price," I said. But then I felt sort of bad, because it's not like addiction means you *deserve* to die, so I sighed again and continued, "But like I said, lots of people miss you. So I guess there's that."

"Yeah," he said. "That's good. You'll have to show me the fan sites."

"Oh, I'll show you the fan sites." A grin spreading across my face as I remembered coming across extremely interesting fan art of him and Eric. "I will *definitely* show you the fan sites."

"What does that creepy little voice mean?" he asked, folding his arms across his chest.

"It means I'm going to show you some very special fan sites," I said. "Just wait. It'll be worth it, I promise."

CHAPTER SIX

When my shift was over, I got my coat from the employee closet and put it on, then wrapped a scarf around my neck and pulled on gloves and a knit cap. Chris watched me intently.

"Why are you bundling up like that?" he asked.

"It's November now." I headed for the front door, and Chris followed. After pushing open the heavy doors and stepping outside, I immediately shivered and pulled my hat down to cover my ears. Chris stared at me like he was having an epiphany, and I sighed and started walking toward my apartment.

"I'm never going to feel cold again," he said after following me for a few seconds. "I'm never going to feel hot again, either. I'm never going to sweat. I'm never going to . . ." He stopped walking. "I'm never going to have *sex* again," he said, clearly just noticing this problem.

I stopped too and turned to face him, trying to look like I was admiring the buildings instead of staring at nothing on the sidewalk. "You don't know that," I said. "You might end up finding a nice ghost lady and settling down to have ghost babies."

He grimaced. "That sounds even worse than celibacy."

"What?" I smirked at him. "Not the family man type?"

"Oh, God no," he said, wrinkling his nose. "I would be a terrible dad, anyway."

"Yeah, with the drugs."

He narrowed his eyes at me. "You know, I'm more than the drugs, dude. I'm a person."

"I know you're a person," I said, looking down at a candy bar wrapper on the sidewalk at my feet.

"Really? Because so far, you've mostly just ragged on me about overdosing and told me that people like my music."

He had a point. I could have been nicer to him. But truth be told, he wasn't being terribly awesome himself, and I felt the need to mention that to him. "Well, all you've done is distract me at work and tell me I'm an idiot for expecting tips."

He considered my words then nodded. "All right. Let's just agree to be nicer to each other while we figure out what to do about this."

"I wouldn't go that far," I said. "I'm not nice to anybody, really. I'm kind of an ass. That's just me."

He laughed. "I get that, man."

I turned around and started walking again. Chris kept pace with me, and we continued in awkward silence for a few minutes, then I cleared my throat. "So, um, where are you from?"

"You don't know? I thought all the fans knew."

I did know, honestly, because apparently every sentence of the stupid band biography was burned into my memory banks, but I didn't really want him to know that I knew even *more* about him. "I probably knew at some point. I've forgotten. Enlighten me."

He stuffed his hands in his pockets. "I tell everybody that I'm from Cincinnati."

Which was a huge opening, so huge that I almost refused to take it on principle. But I was curious, and I'd just promised to try to stop being an ass. "But you're not?"

"Yeah, I am," he said. "Or I'm from there as much as anywhere else."

More awkward silence. *This* hadn't been in the biography. Really there wasn't much about Chris's early life in there—most of the stories started at the time when he and Eric met. Which I hadn't realized was weird until now. "So . . . military?"

"Missionary," he said. He stared off down the street and let his eyes focus somewhere far away. "I don't talk about that much. It made reporters ask a lot of questions about religion and shit I didn't feel like answering. So I started just saying Cincinnati and moving on with the interview."

I wondered why he was suddenly being so open, with me of all people. About things that he didn't advertise. "So . . . can I ask about it?"

He looked at me out of the corners of his eyes. "I guess so, if you care. You're the exception to the rule right now."

I couldn't help but ask. "Why's that?"

"Because without you I don't have anybody to talk to." He shrugged, still staring off down the street. "And I figure I should try to keep you interested in talking back."

"Okay, fair enough." I turned down another, less trendy street and kept walking. "So. Missionary. Like in the Congo and shit?"

"No, more boring than that," he said. "At least then I would have had awesome stories to tell. Nope. We were church planters."

I raised an eyebrow. "Church planters."

"Yeah," he said, rubbing his neck and staring at the ground as we walked. "We went to places in the United States that didn't have enough churches, started one, and stayed just long enough to get it established before moving on to somewhere else."

I chuckled. "I didn't know there were any places in the United States that didn't have enough churches."

"Well, 'enough' is relative," Chris pointed out. "Dad thought that any town with fewer than one church per hundred residents was woefully lacking in religion."

"Okay," I said. "So why did you pick Cincinnati, then?"

"It's where I was born. That much is true. And it's where we ended up when Dad died. Mom had family there. We buried him there."

"What happened to your dad?" I paused and thought about what I'd said. "I mean, if you don't mind me asking."

"Heart attack," he said, his voice kind of short and clipped. "He was hanging up some pictures of Jesus in the new church, and then that was it."

I didn't say anything at first to give him the chance to keep talking if he wanted to. Then I turned to look over at him. "That's terrible. How old were you?"

"Fourteen." He bit his bottom lip, then shrugged. "And I wasn't . . . sad. I was just relieved that we could stop moving around and I could have friends and girlfriends and not have every moment of my life dominated by talk about church and God and Jesus."

I kept silent. This didn't seem like a topic I could contribute anything meaningful to.

After a moment, he continued. "I didn't feel sad for a long time. And then I started feeling like a monster for *not* feeling sad." He shrugged. "So I was angry instead. Furious. At everything. And I picked up a guitar and started trying to make sense of my life through music."

There was a long pause again, and after a bit I felt the need to fill the silence. "Did that work?"

"Sort of. I mean . . . I was never a very good songwriter. I wrote a few that were pretty decent, but I wasn't ever ready to play them for anybody. Especially since they were so, you know, personal. About my dad and about my life and about grief and not-grief and feeling like there's something evil inside you that keeps you from feeling things you should feel." He pulled his hands out of his pockets, fluttered them around for a few seconds like he didn't know what to do with them, then put them back in his pockets. "Besides, it would have killed my mom. To hear what I thought of it all."

"Is that when you joined up with the band?" It seemed like a safe question.

"When I was fourteen, I went to this place where local musicians played," he said, almost like he hadn't heard my question. "Just a coffeehouse, really low-key. And there was this guy on stage with a guitar and a microphone and he was amazing. He said he wrote all the songs he was singing and everything he did had so much soul and emotion to it, and I just stood there with my mouth open."

"That was who? Eric?" I turned down yet another street and sped up. It was getting even colder, so I wanted to get home.

He smiled. "Yeah. And after the show I went and talked to him. He asked me if I could play the bass and I lied and said I could even though I'd never played bass before. I figured if I could handle six strings, I could handle four."

"How'd that work out?" I asked, my lips quirking up into a tiny little smile of their own accord.

"Pretty well, I guess," he said. "I've been playing bass ever since."

"Do you ever play a six-string anymore?"

"Sometimes." He frowned. "Although I guess those days are over."

I frowned too. "Sorry, man."

He shoved his hands in his pockets as we walked. "I think that's even worse than not having sex again."

We'd made it to my apartment building, but I paused in front of the outer door and looked at him. "For real?"

He gave it some more thought. "Yeah. Definitely."

"Wow." I tried to think of something else to add but came up empty, so I turned around and put my key in the door and shuffled inside with Chris at my heels. "Why's that?"

"Music literally saved my life," he answered. "I mean, that's cliché and cheesy as hell, but it's true. I was lost and I didn't know what to do. The guitar and the band gave me a purpose and a voice that I didn't have before."

"I guess I get that." I headed up the stairs toward my apartment door. "It must be nice to have a purpose."

"It is," he said, then grunted softly. "Well, it was. Before I blew it."

"Because you died?" I unlocked my door, but I wasn't quite ready to go inside, so I paused with my hand on the doorknob and waited for his answer.

"Because I let some dumb shit come between me and Eric," he said. "Well, me and the rest of the band, too. But especially between me and Eric."

"And so . . . you stopped being friends?" I ran my hand over the doorknob absently.

"We were going to break up," he muttered, staring at the floor.

I blinked. "You and Eric were . . ." What did the gays like to call it these days? Boyfriends? Partners? I wasn't sure.

He looked at me, his forehead wrinkled, and then his eyes went wide. "Oh. No, me and the *band*. The band was breaking up."

"Oh," I said, trying to keep my embarrassed cringing internal-only. "Well. Okay. Carmen would have hated to hear that."

"The girlfriend?" he asked, then kept talking before I could answer. "Well, she doesn't have to worry anymore. Not now that Nathan Vale is rocking the arenas better than I ever could."

I shrugged. "He's not better than you. At least not from what I've heard."

Chris raised an eyebrow at me. "Thanks for the compliment," he said, in a voice that clearly indicated that he did *not* think it was a compliment.

"No, I was being serious," I insisted. "I was reading articles about it after you died, and they all said that he was, you know, decent. Passable. But people said he didn't have your, you know, passion. You know." Ugh, could I have thrown a few more "you knows" in there? I kicked myself thoroughly.

"Well, thanks," he said, a little more sincerely this time. "But still. I'm pissed about it."

"Yeah," I said, then cleared my throat. "I guess we should go inside."

His forehead wrinkled again, and he looked around the hallway like he hadn't even noticed we were in the building. "Oh. This is it."

"Yeah," I said, then I gave him a stern look. "And before we go in, I don't want to hear any lip about how cluttered it is and how you've been in bathtubs bigger than the whole apartment. I live by myself and rent is a bitch in this city and this is all I can afford." I deepened my frown.

"Okay, okay." He rolled his eyes. "May we enter?"

I sighed and opened the door. Chris breezed through the doorway in front of me and then burst out laughing.

It was at that point I remembered I had a giant poster of him hanging over my couch.

CHAPTER
SEVEN

Well, not him specifically. It was a concert poster of Incite the Masses, and it was really more focused on Eric than Chris, but still.

Chris was laughing so hard he started to wheeze, although I'm not sure why a ghost needs to breathe at all so the wheezing was probably just to be obnoxious. I crossed my arms. "Laugh it up, Casper. Go ahead and be a dick."

"You have . . ." He tried to compose himself but clearly failed. "You have a poster of me on your wall."

"Yes. Thank you for the observation. Good to know you're not blind as well as dead." I tightened my crossed arms and scowled. "Besides, it's not my poster. It was Carmen's. I just never took it down after she left."

"Yeah, I'm sure of that," he said, finally stopping with the laughing. "Did 'Carmen' also leave behind her copy of that magazine where I was shirtless? And if so, do the pages still open right or are they all stuck together?"

"You're a douche," I grumbled. "I told you not to rag on me."

"No, you told me not to mention how small the apartment was, and I didn't." He looked around again. "Dude, though, is that your bed?"

"Shut up," I snapped.

"It's in the *living room*," he said, his eyes sparkling.

"It's called a *studio apartment*. Meaning there isn't a bedroom. And I'm lucky I can afford it."

"Come on, man." Chris turned and raised his eyebrow at me. "Surely you can get something better than *this*."

"I can't, you asshole." I hoped he couldn't see how red my cheeks were getting. "It's hard to pay for this as it is. So maybe you should have thought about that before you went around stiffing people like me on the tips. I can't even keep the heat on in the winter because it's too fucking expensive. I have to save the heat for nights when I'd freeze to death without it, and every other night I just pile on like six blankets and hope for the best. So you can take your rich dick privilege and shove it, you got me?"

He huffed and then clamped his mouth shut, and I couldn't bring myself to give even a single shit about it. After a moment of awkward silence, he asked, "Couldn't you just get a roommate?"

"Yeah, I had one," I muttered. "And then she left because I killed you."

He blinked a few times, rapidly. "Because you killed me," he repeated in a monotone.

"Yeah." I pulled one glove off my hand, a little more viciously than necessary, then yanked off the other glove too. "It's not that uncommon a theory among the people who think there was foul play."

"There are people who think I was murdered?" he asked, raising his eyebrows almost all the way to the ceiling.

"You're a famous rock star who died suddenly and young," I said. "I mean, come on. Cobain blew his brains out after writing an actual suicide note and people still think he was murdered. Of course there are crazies who think you were too."

"But why *you*? We didn't even know each other. You had no motive." He started drifting around my apartment, running his fingers lightly over things even though he couldn't feel them.

I shrugged, more for myself than for him since he wasn't watching me. "I found your body. So I'm a suspect."

He did turn to me at that. "You were a suspect?"

"No," I said, rolling my eyes. "Not to anybody who wasn't two brain cells away from comatose. But to the crazier conspiracy theorists, sure." I took off my hat and tossed it onto a table by the door along with my gloves. "And to Carmen, yeah. She kept saying I'd killed you, or at least that it was my fault you died because if I'd gotten to your room sooner I could have saved you. But whatever. She was a bitch anyway and I'm better off without her." I grabbed some warm clothes out of my chest of drawers and gave Chris a look. "I'm going to go change out of my work clothes. Try not to die any more than you already have."

He pursed his lips, clearly affronted, but I just turned around and disappeared into the tiny bathroom before he could say anything. I stripped out of my formal work clothes and draped them over a towel rod, then quickly bundled myself in a sweater and a pair of sweatpants. I sat down on the closed toilet lid and put on two pairs of socks, then just stayed there, my elbows on my knees, and tried to process everything.

To be honest, I wasn't absolutely sure that I wasn't losing my mind.

I mean, I was handling it pretty well, I guessed, all things considered. Either there was a ghost standing in my living room putting his ghosty hands all over my shit, or I had gone off the deep end and needed psychiatric help. Really, neither option would bode well for me. Haunted or crazy. Talking to a ghost or talking to myself. Normal people don't have to wonder about this sort of thing.

I sighed and stood up, putting my hands on the edge of my bathroom sink and leaning forward to gaze into the mirror.

"Tyler," I said to myself, "you crazy." I nodded knowingly at my reflection. But I didn't really look like an insane person. Most crazy people have wild beards and eyes that are way too white around the edges, and I was just a clean-shaven bellboy with dirty-blond hair and greenish eyes that were the appropriate level of white around the edges.

I pushed away from the sink and opened the door back into the living room. Chris was looking through my movie collection. Probably judging me, the fucker. But it wasn't like I'd had time to run home and hide all the embarrassing shit before he decided to be less dead than I'd expected and follow me to my apartment. He was just lucky there weren't days-old bags of fast-food scraps all over the floor and several nights' worth of used tissues in a pile beside the bed.

I leaned against the bathroom doorframe and crossed my arms. "Find anything interesting?"

He glanced up at me and shrugged. "You don't have terrible taste. You definitely are a nerd, though."

"Yeah," I said, walking over to the couch. "Did you want to watch *Supernatural* or what?"

"I do." He straightened up from the stooping position he'd taken to see the bottom row of movies. "Put it on."

I found the remote, then settled down on the couch and tucked a blanket around me. Chris walked over and perched on the other end, watching me curiously.

I navigated through the menus of the streaming service and then couldn't stand the staring anymore. "What?" I asked, letting the exasperation creep into my voice.

"So..." He shifted a little on the couch. "You weren't lying. About the not being able to afford heat."

I frowned and pushed play on the first episode.

CHAPTER EIGHT

"So he's spent his whole life tracking and killing monsters and demons and shit, and he's afraid of *airplanes*?"

"Yeah," I said, yawning. "They said that like two minutes into the episode. It took you the whole time to figure it out?"

"I thought there would be a twist or something." He rolled his shoulders and clapped his hands together. "But oh well. That was pretty good. What's the next episode?"

"Are you serious?" I groaned and pulled the blanket over my head. "We've got to stop for the night, dude."

"Why?"

I lowered the blanket enough to be able to see him. "Because we've watched four episodes in a row after I did a full shift at work, and I'm *tired*."

"Oh." He looked around the room. "I'm not."

"You're a ghost. I doubt you'll ever get tired again. But I'm human and I need to go to sleep."

He stood and wandered through the room. "What should I do while you're sleeping?"

"I don't know." I reached up and rubbed my eyes with my fists. "And honestly I don't really care, as long as you don't stand there watching me sleep all night long."

"I have nothing to do." His mouth did something pouty that was almost cute. Almost.

"Well, entertain yourself. Find a book or something."

"I can't turn the pages." He frowned even more deeply.

"Fine, then watch TV," I suggested. "I'll put in some earplugs, and it'll be fine."

"Can you just push Play and let me keep watching?"

I rolled my eyes and yawned again. "Sure. But when it times out on you, don't expect me to get up and push Play again."

"I won't," he said. "I promise."

I didn't really believe him. He hadn't proved especially trustworthy so far. But still, I gave him the benefit of the doubt. I pulled up the next episode, then pressed Play. "Okay. I'm going to bed."

He sat back down on the couch and nodded. "Okay, sure. Thanks."

"Yeah, yeah. Good night." I walked over to my bed, put my earplugs in to block out the sound of the TV, and lay down. Normally I would have rubbed one out and gone to sleep with my hand down my sweatpants, but I was sure Chris would have noticed what I was doing and that was just weird to think about. So instead I just burrowed under the covers and let out an involuntary half moan of pleasure as I stretched my limbs at the end of a long day, then fell asleep almost immediately.

It felt like only a few seconds later when I opened my eyes and saw sunlight filtering in through the small window in the living room. I sat up and rubbed my face, then had a brief moment of panic that I'd gone deaf before I realized that I still had the earplugs in. I gingerly pulled them out.

"Good. You're awake. I need you to push Play."

I blinked at Chris slowly. "You're still here."

"Of course I'm still here," he snapped. "And I am bored out of my mind, dude. It timed me out like five hours ago and went back to whatever channel you had it on before. Which was an infomercial channel, if you're curious. So I've pretty much just been sitting here not-watching-you-sleep for forever."

I snuggled back under the covers. "Whatever," I said. "I'm going back to sleep."

"Oh no you're not." Chris jumped up and crossed the room to sit on the bed beside me. "You've got to entertain me, man."

"Go away." I put the pillow on top of my face to block out the sight and sound of him. "It's my day off, and I can sleep in if I want to sleep in." I thought about getting my earplugs and putting them in again, but that would require me to put my hands back into the icy world, so it didn't seem like a priority at the moment.

"No," Chris said, loudly enough for me to hear him through the pillow. "Get up and push Play at least."

"Fuck off," I muttered.

"No, *you* fuck off," he snapped. "Come on, man, I'm going crazy."

I pulled the pillow off of my face and glared at him. "You've been alone with your thoughts for five hours and you're already losing it. That's kind of pathetic."

"I've been alone with my thoughts while a big freaking poster of a nondead me stares down at me," he said, then eyed the poster and grimaced. "And let me tell you that Eric is not exactly someone I want staring down at me either."

"Ugh," I said. "Fine. I'll put the damn show back on if you promise to leave me alone for another four hours."

"You're the most boring person I've ever met."

I frowned at him. "You know, for somebody who can't use a remote, you're being an awfully big bitch to the one who *can*."

He tilted his head, then nodded. "You're right. Please could you play the next episode for me?"

"I have a better idea," I said. "Now that you've made it totally impossible for me to go back to sleep, I'm going to get up and then we're going to go find a psychic."

"A . . . psychic." He wrinkled his brow. "What good is a psychic?"

"Well, I figure maybe they can tell us what we need to do," I said. "To help you, you know, move on."

"Maybe I don't want to move on," he muttered.

I'd heard him just fine, but I scowled at him anyway. "What was that?"

"Nothing," he said, louder this time. "Never mind. A psychic. Sure."

"I don't even know where to find one," I said. "But I have some hippie friends who might know."

Chris stood and nodded, frowning slightly. "Fine. I guess it couldn't hurt."

"Yeah," I said. "Worst-case scenario, it's a waste of time. But we have to figure out *something* before I get really super freaked out by you watching me sleep."

"I *wasn't* watching you sleep," he said. "I told you that. And anyway, you were all tucked down under your covers and so even if I wanted to watch you, I wouldn't have been able to see anything interesting."

"By 'anything interesting' you of course mean my cock," I said, swinging my legs out from under the covers and testing whether I could feel the cold wooden floors through my double layer of socks.

"Yeah," he said, rolling his eyes. "I mean, big famous rock star like me totally feels the need to ogle a bellboy's micropenis."

"It's probably for the best." I stood up and went to my chest of drawers to get clothes for the day. "I wouldn't want you to be jealous because yours is nonexistent."

"Whatever, dude," he said, waving his hand dismissively. "Lots of people know better than that. Who knows, maybe even Carmen. I lost track of all the groupies I've fucked a long time ago."

"You didn't do Carmen, trust me," I said. "She never said anything and you can bet that if she'd done you, she would have literally never stopped talking about it."

"I make everybody sign a confidentiality agreement," he said, grinning.

"Yeah, I really don't think that would have mattered to Carmen." I wadded my clothes into a ball and carried them over to the TV. "I'll change the episode for you and then I'm going to go take a shower." I pulled up the next episode and pushed Play. "And I swear to God, Chris, if you come bother me in the shower, I'll go out and buy a Justin Bieber album and put it on repeat all day long, and there will be nothing you can do to stop it."

He grimaced. "Noted. Go ahead."

I stood there for a second, watching him settling down on my couch to watch yet another episode, and then turned around and went to take a shower.

CHAPTER NINE

Madame Destiny was an older lady dressed in stereotypical psychic-gypsy attire, complete with the mystic do-rag on her head. She even had an honest-to-God crystal ball sitting on her table. The dark room was hung with tons of tapestries embroidered with dragons and Celtic symbols and pentagrams and all sorts of pagan-type illustrations while she bustled around, muttering something about auras and life force and shit. I tried to speak a few times, but she shushed me and said that the spirits needed a moment to acclimate themselves to my presence.

"I'm pretty acclimated, dude," Chris said, peering into the crystal ball. "Did you know you make little grunting noises in your sleep? It started out being endearing and then it just got really fucking irritating as the hours dragged on."

I shot him a dirty look but didn't answer because Madame Destiny would have scolded me for talking. Not to mention she probably would have thought I was crazy. Better to explain the situation first.

Finally, after another awkward few minutes, in which Chris continued to bitch about my sleep grunting, Madame Destiny fluttered back over to her chair, across the table from me. She did a weird waving gesture with her hands and took a deep breath, then exhaled slowly.

"So, young man," she said, folding her hands in front of her. "What brings you to Madame Destiny today?"

I wanted to do the belligerent disbeliever thing and tell her that a psychic would already know why I was here, but I figured she got that a lot, and I hate being predictable. So instead I just smiled at her and said, "I'm being haunted by a spirit."

"I see!" she said, leaning forward with a big, toothy grin. "And you'd like to know who the spirit is and what he or she wants from you?"

I paused. "Something like that."

"Ah," she said, running a hand lightly over her crystal ball. "I sense . . ." She closed her eyes. "I sense that this spirit is . . . male?"

"Yeah. Listen, I know who it is."

"Please be quiet and only answer my questions with a yes or no," she said, somehow managing to use a stern schoolteacher voice while her face remained relaxed. "I sense that this is a man who meant a lot to you. Perhaps a father figure?"

Chris snorted. "A father figure? Is she even *trying*?"

I *did* shoot him a dirty look this time since Madame Destiny still had her eyes closed. "No, I don't think so," I told her. "Listen . . ."

"Silence, please," she snapped. "Yes, I see it now. Not a father figure. Someone *you* felt fatherly feelings for. Someone you felt you needed to protect?"

"No," I said. "Listen, Madame . . ."

"Ooh," Chris chirped, "I just wrote a new song. It's called 'This Lady is Mentally Unbalanced and/or a Charlatan' and it goes like this . . ."

"Chris, if you don't shut up I'm going to punch you," I growled.

"Chris!" Madame Destiny echoed triumphantly, like she'd figured it out on her own. "Was Chris your brother?"

"Yeah, you know what? I'm just going to go." I stood up. "Thanks anyway."

She opened her eyes. "Don't walk away from this. Time is short, but all is not lost. He still has a chance to tell you that he loves you. To show you."

I rolled my eyes. "I'm pretty sure I know *exactly* how he feels about me." I grabbed my scarf and wound it around my neck. "And he's not my brother."

She glared at me. "My fee is nonrefundable."

"Keep your lousy ten bucks, then." I turned around and stalked out of her shop, stepping back out onto the street and heading for the next address on my psychics-for-hire list.

"Can you afford to just leave ten bucks with her, or will that cut into your ramen budget for the month?" Chris smirked, matching my pace and walking close beside me.

"Stop being a dick." I frowned. "I'm trying to help you and you're just giving me shit."

"Fine, fine. Where next?"

"Lady Hazel," I said, pulling out the list to confirm that I was walking in the right direction. "A few blocks from here."

"Is she perhaps . . . a witch?" Chris asked, then gave me that look you give people when you've just told a joke and are waiting on everyone to laugh.

After a couple of seconds, I decided that I must have missed the punch line. "What?"

"Like . . . witch hazel. Get it? Because her name is Hazel and she's into, you know, new age stuff and shit."

I rolled my eyes. "You were a pretty good bass player, but it's a good thing you never tried to branch out into stand-up."

"What are you talking about? I'm awesome at comedy," he said, smiling.

I eyed him suspiciously. "What's got you all chipper?"

"Nothing," he said. "Well . . . actually, it's being out in the sun."

I stared up at the sky. It was frigid, especially in the wind, but there wasn't a single cloud anywhere and the sun was pretty nice. He had a point there. "I guess the sun is okay."

"It's weird," he went on. "I guess you don't realize how much of a night owl you are until you get up early to go find psychics with a bellboy."

"I'm pretty much a night owl too, you know," I told him. "I have late shifts most of the time and I'm almost never up this early."

"Well, I guess this is unusual for both of us, then." He walked through a cast iron streetlight pole and puffed out his chest, smiling over at me.

"It's not really impressive that you can walk through stuff," I pointed out. "You *are* a ghost, after all."

He gave me the stink eye. "I can't have sex or play my guitar or eat ice cream ever again. Let me have my small pleasures."

"Touché," I said. "So . . . I think this is it." I stopped in front of the store, which was almost identical to Madame Destiny's except more . . . orange.

"I don't know about this plan," he said, raising one eyebrow while lowering the other. "I think these people are probably all con artists."

"You're probably right," I said, "but I don't have any better ideas."

He looked up and down the street. I shivered and then crossed my arms to conserve body heat. After a second, he nodded toward a coffeehouse nearby. "You're cold. Let's run down there and get you some coffee or something to warm you up."

I felt a rush of gratitude, but his motives were suspicious. "What's in it for you?"

"You just look cold, okay?" He seemed genuinely offended, so I decided to let it go.

I unfolded my arms and started walking toward the coffeehouse. "Okay. Thanks. I'll even let you smell my coffee if you want."

"Oh my God, that would be wonderful," he practically moaned. "I'm going to miss coffee. And ice cream. And sushi. And bananas. And—"

"Jesus, shut up. You're making me hungry and it's not time for lunch yet." I pushed open the door to the coffeehouse and let myself enjoy the warmth and the heavy scent of coffee and pastries.

Chris walked over to the pastry case, ghosting straight through a hipster couple to survey the selection. "Can you buy one of these blueberry scones?"

I maneuvered my way around the hipsters so I could be closer to Chris. I looked less crazy when I could speak softly. "Why?"

"So I can watch you eat it," he said, his voice weirdly earnest.

"Because that's not creepy. Not at all."

"Ghostly pleasures, man," he reminded me.

"Fine," I muttered. "I'll get you a scone and I'll eat it for you."

"Will you . . . Will you tell me how it tastes?" His eyes were big and pleading.

I swore under my breath. "Oh my God. You're going to drive me insane."

"Probably," he said, cheerfully. "So . . . scone? Oh, and a caramel macchiato."

I glared at Chris, then noticed the barista giving me a funny look. "Caramel macchiato," I told him. "And a blueberry scone."

Chris legitimately cheered, pumping his fist in the air and then doing the devil-horns rock-and-roll hand gesture with both hands.

"You're a dork," I whispered to him. "You think you're this big sexy rock star, but you're actually a huge dweeb."

He just grinned at me and did the devil-horns thing again, this time sticking his tongue out. I rolled my eyes at him.

The barista called out my order, and I picked it up and retreated to a tiny table by the window. Chris followed me, making sure to leap straight through the body of every customer he encountered and grinning to himself. I settled down to eat my scone, and he sat on the chair across from me and focused his eyes on the scone with an intensity bordering on creepy.

"You're going to watch me eat this," I deadpanned.

"Yeah," he said, not taking his eyes off the pastry. "I told you I was."

"I thought you were joking." I took a sip of my coffee and moaned happily as the warm liquid started raising my body temperature. Chris just kept staring at the pastry.

"Are you going to eat it?" he asked after a few seconds.

"Yes," I told him, "but you're going to have to stop staring at it like that. It's weird."

"I can't," he said. "I'm starving."

I raised both eyebrows. "You're hungry? But you're a ghost."

"I'm not . . . physically hungry. I think my body still thinks it's alive because I'm feeling . . ." He paused for a second, tilting his head. "It's hard to describe. It's like when you're bored-hungry, you know? You don't *need* food but it's all you can think about and you can't get the idea of eating something out of your head."

I lifted the scone. "I guess I can understand that."

Chris's eyes snapped back to the pastry. He licked his lips.

I put the scone up to my mouth and took a bite of it. Chris let out a borderline-sexual sigh and swallowed hard.

"Dude," I said, putting the scone back on my plate. "Did you just go from six to midnight?"

"Shut your face," he snapped. "I fucking love scones."

"Wow. With the rare steak and the scones and the very specific grape needs. Who knew you were such a foodie?" I thought about asking if it was a junkie thing instead, but that seemed mean, so I just picked the scone up again and took another bite.

He waited until I was done chewing and then answered: "I don't think that liking seedless grapes makes me a foodie."

"It makes you picky as hell, though." I grinned at him and took another bite, trying not to notice the way he watched my lips and throat while I chewed and swallowed.

That went on until I'd finished the scone, and he made me pick up even the smallest crumbs and eat those too. I'd polished off my coffee and had gotten up to leave when I saw a girl sitting at a table in the corner by herself, holding a deck of what appeared to be tarot cards. She drew several, then scowled at them as if they'd personally offended her.

I took a step closer.

"Dude," Chris said. "Are you going to go hit on that chick?"

"Shut up," I muttered, then walked over to her. "Hi. I'm Tyler."

She looked up at me and did not seem impressed. "Can I help you?"

I glanced at the deck in front of her. The illustrations on them were beautiful, patterned like stained glass with gold foil leafing for highlights. The one I could see best was a picture of a woman holding on to the mane of a lion. It was labeled *Strength*.

"They're tarot cards," she said like she got this question a lot, even though I hadn't actually asked it out loud.

"For telling the future, right?"

She rolled her eyes. "Yeah. For telling the future. I'm busy. Can you maybe leave me alone?"

I leaned over to inspect the cards again. "What's that one mean?" I pointed to a picture of a crumbling castle turret.

She followed my gesture and frowned deeply when she saw what card I was pointing to. "That's the Tower."

"Cool. What does it mean?"

"It means I'm fucked." She gathered up the cards and put them back in the deck.

"Well, at least you know about it," I said. "Whatever it is. So if you know it's going to happen, you can change it, right?"

She shook her head. "That wasn't the future. It was the present."

"Oh." I shifted on my feet. "That sucks, then."

She shrugged. "Yeah, well, not much I can do about it at the moment. What do you want?"

"Can you tell my future?" I smiled at her.

"Oh my God," Chris said. "You're not as smooth as you think you are."

I ignored him and kept smiling.

The girl gave me a once-over and then sighed. "Fine. But it's not as much about your future as it is about helping you understand what's going on now and what attitude you should have." She shuffled the cards and fanned them out for me. "Pick one."

I thought for a moment, moving my hand over the cards, and then pulled one out. I turned it over and peered at it. "The Knight of Cups."

She nodded. "So there's someone in your life who's kind of an emo-narcissist?"

Chris laughed out loud. "I'm not sure there's a more apt description of me than that. Although really I'd argue I'm more goth or moody than emo."

I resisted the urge to shoot him a dirty look. Or just to shoot him. "Yeah, you could say that. He won't leave me alone."

She raised an eyebrow. "Boyfriend?"

"No," I barked out. "God, no. I'd hang myself if he was my boyfriend."

"Thanks," Chris said dryly.

"You're welcome," I answered without thinking.

Her other eyebrow shot up to join the already-raised one. "Who are you talking to?"

I tried to appear super innocent. "Nobody. Sorry. I thought I heard my name."

She kept eyeing me suspiciously, but she didn't press me for more information. "Well," she said after a moment of awkward silence, "that's your major issue right now, then. Whoever he is must be making your life difficult. You need to focus on fixing that part of your life."

Chris scoffed. "I don't like the implication that I need to be fixed."

"How can I fix it?" I asked her, pointedly ignoring him.

She shrugged. "The cards don't tell you everything. Some stuff you have to figure out on your own."

"Well, can you maybe do a more in-depth reading?" I prompted. "I really want to know what's going on with everything."

She glanced around the coffeehouse. "Not in here. I'm already getting stared at enough as it is."

"Where, then?"

"In your bed," Chris said. "That's what you're hoping for, isn't it? You want to do a tarot reading off of her boobs."

"I don't know," she answered, then paused for a second. "There's a new age bookstore nearby. They have some tables for customers, and I wouldn't get stared at in there."

"Let's go, then." I stood and smiled. "I'm Tyler," I said again.

She gave me an appraising look, then visibly relented, standing and half smiling. "Gemma."

CHAPTER TEN

"All right," she said, spreading the cards out facedown in a wide arc. "So think about your friend and pick two cards. To symbolize what you think the problem is."

I eyed the cards. "Just . . . pick two cards?"

"Yeah," she answered. "Hover your hand over them and wait until one feels right."

"Okay. Sounds easy enough." I did as she told me and held my hand over the cards.

Chris squatted down beside the table. "This girl already seems more legit than Madame Destiny."

I pulled one card out and then hovered my hand again for a few seconds before picking another. "These two."

"All right, then turn them over." Gemma pushed her hair behind her ear.

I flipped the first card so that it was faceup. "The Devil," I said, reading the title off the card.

Chris snorted. "I can see how you'd think that about me."

My eyes darted over to him before I caught myself. Gemma must have noticed because she narrowed her own eyes slightly. I flipped the other card before she could say anything. "And the Moon."

She studied the two cards for a moment. "So he's an alcoholic? Or is it drugs?"

Chris stood up. "You're shitting me. That's got to be a coincidence."

"Probably both," I told her. "But definitely with the drugs. Hard ones."

"So are you worried about him?" she asked.

I thought about that. "Not really. He's already dead."

Her eyes widened. "And he's still your big problem?"

I decided to go for it. "He's haunting me. He's a ghost."

Gemma snatched up the two cards, shoved them back in her deck, and stood. "I have to go."

"No, I'm serious," I pleaded. "I'm being haunted, and I need to figure out how to—"

"You don't have to be an asshole and make fun of me."

"I'm not," I assured her. "I just thought . . . you were doing tarot and I've spent all morning going to fake-ass psychics and I thought maybe you could help."

She crossed her arms, clutching the cards in one hand. "Uh-huh."

"I can prove it," I said. "I can talk to him. Hold up a card where I can't see it, and he'll tell me what card it is."

"I'm not your fucking lapdog," Chris snapped. "And I keep telling you I'm more than just my addictions."

"Shut up, Chris," I said, then looked at her again. "He doesn't like me ordering him around. But he'll do it."

Gemma frowned but nodded curtly. "I want you to know that I don't really believe you," she said, then drew a card and held it where I couldn't see it. "What's the card?"

Chris scowled at me. "I don't feel like it."

I figured it couldn't make her think I was any more crazy than she already did, so I turned my head and glared at him. "Just do it, you dick-weed."

"Fine," he said. "But only because I want to get away from you." He stalked around behind her and leaned in to peer at the card.

"It says 'The High Priestess.' That's pretty on the nose, don't you think?" He pursed his lips and looked generally pouty.

"It's the High Priestess," I told Gemma.

She blinked at the card and her jaw tightened. "Again," she said, picking a different card.

"The Three of Cups," Chris muttered.

"The Three of Cups," I repeated.

She drew another card.

"This is getting hella old," Chris said. "But it's the Five of Swords. And it's upside-down."

"Five of Swords," I told her. "Upside-down."

"Reversed," she mumbled. "One more."

Chris rolled his eyes. "That's not even a card. It just has some contact info for where to order more decks from."

"He says it's a contact information card and not a real tarot card."

Gemma turned around and looked behind her, then back at me, eyes wide and a little dazed.

"No mirrors or anything," I said. "Just a ghost standing beside you telling me what he sees."

She scanned the room behind her again, then moved slowly back to her chair and sat down. "For the record, I'm still not convinced there's a ghost," she said, giving me a stern glare. "But I'm intrigued enough to listen."

I smiled at her only for Chris to scowl at me, which made me throw my hands up in exasperation. "What is your problem, dude?"

He crossed his arms and stared off into the distance. "Nothing. I just thought that maybe I'd get a few days before I had to witness your grotesque mating rituals."

"Shut up," I told him, then turned my eyes back to Gemma. "He's very . . . self-centered. He doesn't like it when I talk to anybody besides him."

"I don't give a fuck who you talk to," Chris said, raising his voice. "I just don't know why this chick is suddenly your best friend."

"Shut *up*," I said, louder this time. I gave Gemma an apologetic smile. "I think he's jealous."

"I am *not* fucking jealous," he yelled. "I just think we should be focusing on getting me to heaven or wherever. Then once I'm gone you can get all the girls you want."

Gemma raised her eyebrows in a clear question, and I shrugged. "He thinks we need to focus on figuring out how to help him move on. I guess he has a point."

"Okay," she said, drawing the word out. "So . . . if you can talk to him, why do you need a psychic? Isn't that usually for when you can't communicate with a spirit?"

I shrugged again. "I can talk to him fine. But he doesn't know why he's still here, so he doesn't know where to start."

"I guess I can get that," she said. "But seriously, I'm not an expert on the spirit realm or anything."

Chris let out a disgusted snort, then walked through the wall and went outside. I frowned at the place where he'd disappeared, then turned back to her. "But you know how to read the cards."

"Well, yeah. I'm decent at it. But I'm just saying that if you expect me to go all mystic seer on you and tell you what he needs to do to clear up his unfinished business, then you're going to be pretty disappointed."

"I just figure it can't hurt. To get some ideas."

"I can do another reading," she said, "just don't expect to get all sorts of answers from it."

"I won't," I assured her. She picked up her cards and started shuffling them again while I leaned back in my chair a little. "So how does this work?"

"Tarot?" she asked, still shuffling. "Well, it works on the principle that the collective unconscious—you know, the universal spiritual connection we all have with each other and with the world—guides you to draw or choose the cards that will give some clarity to your situation."

"So the Force."

She paused. "The Force?"

"Yeah, from Star Wars."

"I know what the Force is," she snapped. "But you're comparing the collective unconscious to hokey religions and ancient weapons."

I laughed. "Will you marry me?"

Gemma rolled her eyes, and Chris stuck his head through the wall and glared daggers at me. "Oh my God, that's so fucking lame."

"Well, come back in here and listen," I told him. "And stop being a jerk, because she's going to try to help us."

Gemma followed my gaze to the wall where Chris's head was. "He's over there?"

"Yeah," I said. "And he's a jerk. But that's what you'd expect from a rock star."

She gave me a "bitch, please" face. "A rock star."

"Yeah. Christopher Raiden." I practiced my completely earnest expression.

"You're being haunted by the ghost of Chris Raiden," she deadpanned. "Just so I have this straight."

"It's not as glamorous as you'd think," I said. "Mostly he just watches me while I eat scones and bitches about how small my apartment is."

She pursed her lips. "I want it on the record again that I'm not convinced."

"But you'll still help us?"

"I'll do readings," she said. "But like I told you, I don't know how helpful that's going to be. Tarot isn't super great at telling the future, really. It's more about getting insight into the present and the past and what your attitudes should be about things. All of the future stuff turns out pretty vague and only tends to make sense when you think back on it later."

"We'll take what we can get," I said.

Gemma finished shuffling the cards and spread them out in an arc on the table again. "Well, why don't you ask him to choose a card that represents what you are to him?"

Chris scoffed, and I raised an eyebrow. "What I am to him?"

"Well, like he's the Knight of Cups for you. That's how you see him. So how does he see you?" She gestured at the cards.

Chris pouted. "I don't want to pick one. This is bullshit, and it's a waste of our time. Let's go find Witch Hazel and see if she has any pointers."

"Just pick a card, Chris," I said. "Please."

He narrowed his eyes at me, then leaned forward and tapped a card with his finger hard enough that his hand went through the table. "That one. I hope it's called the Grand Vizier of Douchebaggery, because that's what you are to me."

I rolled my eyes and pointed at the card he'd picked. "That one, he says. And just so you know, he's being very hostile about this whole thing."

Her eyes widened. "Is he going to start killing people? Is he that kind of ghost?"

"No," I said. "He's just a bitch, is all. But I think he was probably like this when he was alive, too."

"I'll take your word for it." She pulled the card out of the arc and flipped it over. "The Hierophant. Interesting."

I peered down at the card. The man it depicted, sitting between two columns and frowning, didn't strike me as very pleasant. "This is what he thinks of me?"

"Yes," she said. "The Hierophant is all about . . . traditional values. Doing what's right from a religious or moral sense."

I looked over at Chris. "So he sees me as, like, a moral compass?"

"A moral compass that doesn't point north," he muttered.

"Was that a *Pirates of the Caribbean* reference?" I asked him.

"You're not the only one who knows some pop culture," he snapped. "Don't sound so fucking surprised."

I sighed and turned back to Gemma. "I don't think he agrees with your interpretation."

Gemma shrugged. "Well, the card's about traditional values. But it's not necessarily totally good. Given that the cards you picked about him were all about his narcissism and drug use, this could mean that he thinks you're being too high and mighty. Judging him too much and not trying to see his point of view."

Chris smirked. "That's exactly right. Maybe I like this chick after all."

I sat back in my chair and let out a huff of breath. "I guess I could be nicer to him."

"Damn right you could," Chris said. "And you can start right now."

"If I'm going to start being nicer to you, then you have to stop bitching about how worried about my tips I am," I countered.

Chris rolled his eyes. "You need to let go of your materialistic concerns and live life without spending all your time thinking about money."

"*I'm* materialistic?" I crossed my arms and glared at him. "You're the one who wears designer underwear and drinks champagne that costs more than my rent."

"I don't really drink that much champagne."

"Yeah, because you're too busy guzzling Jack," I snapped.

"Only if he asks nicely," he shot back.

"Well—Wait. What?"

He widened his eyes at me super innocently. "What?"

"Are you talking about giving guys BJs?"

Gemma waved her hands in the air in a no gesture. "Okay, okay, listening to one side of this conversation is weird enough without the sex talk coming out."

"The sex talk isn't the only thing coming out, apparently," I muttered.

"It was a joke, you douche bag," Chris said. "Perhaps you've heard one or two of them before. I recommend knock-knock jokes if you're a beginner."

"Shut up," I said.

Gemma sighed. "Look, I'm not a couples' counselor. I'm just a finance major with a deck of tarot cards."

"Finance, huh?" I said. "I guess I get it. Wanting to make money."

Chris groaned. "Always with the money and never with the not-money."

I pinched the bridge of my nose. "You know, the only people who have the luxury to *not* talk about money are people who have lots of it."

"Enough!" Gemma almost yelled. "I'm only hearing half of this and it's still exasperating. *You*," she pointed at me, "stop making everything about how he doesn't understand the poor life. And *you*," she pointed vaguely in Chris's direction, "I don't even know what you're saying, but it sounds like you're intentionally antagonizing him and you need to quit."

Chris and I both smirked at each other, then frowned almost in unison.

"Anyway," Gemma continued. "Tell him to pick two cards that show what he thinks *your* issues are. Even though I think it's really frickin' obvious."

Chris touched a card, then thought for a moment before choosing another card. I pointed at them and Gemma pulled them out of the deck. She flipped over the first card.

"The Five of Pentacles," she announced. "Of course. The poverty card. The card of financial strain and hard times and things like that."

"That's pretty on the nose, don't you think?" I asked, mimicking Chris's voice from earlier.

She shrugged. "You picked textbook addiction cards for him. It makes sense that he'd pick a classic financial struggle card for you."

"She's right," Chris said. "You subconsciously pick bitchy cards for me, I subconsciously pick bitchy cards for you right back."

I rolled my eyes again. "Go on," I told Gemma.

She flipped over the second card. "The Wheel of Fortune, reversed."

"The Wheel of Fortune?" Chris scoffed. "Seriously? Is there a Vanna White card too?"

"He just made a Vanna White reference," I told her. "I feel like you should know that."

She sighed. "I get that all the time. But no. The Wheel of Fortune has to do with change and growth and finding new paths in life that fulfill you."

"Ha!" I said, pointing at Chris. "So you think I'm on the right path."

Chris opened his mouth, probably to argue, but Gemma spoke first. "Actually . . . that's what the upright Wheel of Fortune means. Reversed, it means stagnation. Refusal to change. Staying in a bad situation because you don't want to put forth the effort to move from where you are."

"Which is true," Chris said. "I mean, you're a bellboy."

"And you're a bastard," I retorted.

"Listen, guys, I really do have to go," Gemma said. "But here . . . let me give you my number. We'll meet up again in a few days and do some more readings if you want."

I pulled out my phone and let her type her number into it. Then she gave me the phone back, smiled, and left the store.

"Good riddance," Chris said.

I punched him. It didn't do any good.

CHAPTER
ELEVEN

"You can't ignore me forever," Chris said, waving his hands through the frying pan I was trying to make an omelet in.

I didn't answer. I'd been getting pretty good at not focusing my eyes on him and not responding to what he said. It had been four hours since I'd stormed out of the new age bookstore and started willfully ignoring him, and it was clearly starting to bug the guy. "I think you're being really childish," he said, stepping into the stove so that his torso was sticking out of the burner.

I set my jaw but didn't say anything. If he was going to be a bastard and make everything about how I'm too obsessed with money, he could just spend some time stewing about how nobody can talk to him if I'm not there.

"And it's just bitchy not to let me watch any more TV," he went on. "I'm dying here. Well, I'm already dead. But you get the point."

I'd thought about putting in one of Carmen's concert DVDs and making him feel awkward by forcing him to watch himself on stage, but knowing Chris he'd just find the whole thing fascinating. I wondered if he fantasized about himself while he jacked off.

"I have all these things I could tell you if you would talk to me and be nice to me," he said, letting his voice melt into a cajoling tone.

I flipped the omelet and got the bottle of apple juice out of the fridge. I considered pouring it into a glass, then thought about how much I hated washing dishes, so I just picked up the jug and put it on the end table beside my spot on the couch.

"Like about who I've seen naked," he said. "Beautiful women. You'd recognize some of the names. Maybe even a *lot* of the names."

I went back to the stove and finished cooking the omelet, then put it on a plate and went to the couch. I picked up the remote and tried to think of the most boring thing I could possibly make him watch, then decided on C-SPAN. It seemed like something that a narcissistic rock star wouldn't like one bit.

Chris came over and sat on the couch beside me. "You wouldn't believe the freaky shit some of those actresses are into, man. And don't even get me started on the hip-hop ladies and the professional tennis players."

I took a bite of my omelet and tried to look engrossed in whatever the hell the old white guys on C-SPAN were talking about.

"Like . . . who is it you have a thing for? Zoe Saldana? Totally fucked her."

And really, that was too much. I snapped my eyes over to him and scowled. "You're lying."

"Well, yeah," he said, smirking obnoxiously now that he'd busted through my concentration. "Of course I'm lying. She wouldn't give me the time of day. But! I'm not lying about having a lot of really impressive conquests."

"I'm sure," I said, determinedly turning my eyes back to C-SPAN.

But now that I'd broken my silent treatment, he just talked *more*. "I do have lots of conquests. Seriously. And I can prove it. I've got video."

"You have *video* of yourself boning famous chicks," I repeated in a monotone.

"Yes," he said, beaming. "All totally legit too. I got permission and everything."

"Yeah, well, pics or it didn't happen," I said. "And since you can't provide me with the pics, it didn't happen."

"I saved them online." You could practically see the canary feathers plastered to his face.

I stared at him. "You've gotta be shitting me, man."

"Why?" He grinned. "You don't believe me?"

"How the hell do you have video saved to the cloud of yourself banging famous chicks and that's never gotten out on TMZ?"

He shrugged. "TMZ doesn't know everything."

"Oh yes they do," I said. "And they haven't hacked your password to your secret porn stash?"

"I don't really advertise it," he said. "I just like to have it for the memories."

"The memories," I deadpanned. "Of you doing the horizontal tango with Scarlett Johansson."

He rolled his eyes. "If you keep throwing out names, you'll probably hit on somebody I *have* done the horizontal tango with. But not Scarlett Johansson. Sadly enough."

"So tell me somebody you've boned. Somebody I'd know."

"Victoria Sinclair."

I waved my hand dismissively. "Doesn't count."

"Why not? She's hot."

"Because number one, she's not that famous," I started.

"Yes, she is." He crossed his arms. "Everybody in the music industry knows who she is."

I gave him a look. "Everybody in the music industry knows who *her brother* is. She's just that chick who acts like his manager and who occasionally took a roll in the hay with you."

"Fine," he said. "I still respectfully disagree, but whatever."

"And number two . . ."

"There was a number two?"

"Yes, you idiot," I said, exasperated by the interruption. "If there's a number one, there's got to be a number two. It's the rule."

"Fine. Number two?"

"Number two is that she was your girlfriend, so she doesn't count as a conquest," I told him, folding my arms and smiling.

"Um, that's ridiculous," he said. "To even get to girlfriend status means I conquested her."

"Conquested? Seriously?"

"Shut up," he snapped. "And anyway. You don't get to exclude people from my 'famous people I've slept with' list because I actually dated them instead of just having a wild night of passion with them."

"Fair enough," I said, using my best magnanimously condescending voice. "But still. You can do better than that, right? Because if not, then I call shenanigans on your whole 'I've fucked a lot of famous people' story."

"Well, now I don't want to show you my stash anymore," he said, pouting. "Because I'm sure that no matter who I say, you'll assume I'm lying or you'll argue that they don't count, so forget it."

I sighed. He did seem pretty offended. "Sorry. I'm just an asshole."

"Well, me too," he said, and his face relaxed a little back into his baseline douchey expression. "But anyway. How did Tori handle it? Me dying?"

My first instinct was to lie and say she'd been devastated, but word on the street before Chris's death had been that they weren't getting along and that it was just a matter of time before they broke up. And from what Carmen had said, Chris hadn't seemed too heartbroken about his impending singlehood. I could probably tell him the truth.

"Very well, actually. She cried some pretty tears and then drove away from the funeral with that punk-ass drummer from Cold and Furious."

He narrowed his eyes. "I hate that guy. Almost as much as I hate Nathan Vale."

"Well, they're happy together," I told him. "If by 'happy together' you mean 'already on the brink of a fiery breakup.'"

He rolled his eyes. "She's a crazy bitch, man. I'm lucky I got away from her when I did."

"You mean you're lucky you *died*?"

"No," he said quickly, then paused before shrugging. "I guess there are fates worse than death, and ending up shackled to Tori Sinclair is one of them."

"Even if that would have meant having a connection to Gabriel Sinclair?"

He scoffed. "If you think that buffoon has anything on me, you're dead wrong. He's a pompous prick."

"A pompous prick who managed not to join the 27 Club, though," I pointed out.

"Only because he's too busy being a Goody Two-shoes," he argued. "I mean, I like him. We're friends. But that doesn't mean he's not an asshole. Anyway. Enough about him. Let's talk more about me."

"There's the narcissist I know and love," I said, letting the sarcasm drip from my voice like processed nacho cheese.

He laughed. "Well, anyway, I'm not particularly destroyed by Tori deciding to move on. Good for her."

I sighed. "I wish I could do that."

"What?" he asked, tilting his head at me. "Move on? Are you still pining over Carmen and her breasts?"

"Mostly just the breasts," I admitted. "We weren't really good together, but regular sex was nice. I miss that part."

"Was it good sex? Or just regular?"

I shrugged. "It was fine. She liked to close her eyes or be blindfolded so she could pretend I was one of you guys. She even called me Eric in bed. More than once."

Chris raised his eyebrows. "On purpose?"

"Yeah," I said. "And she got in a snit when I told her to cut it out."

"Just Eric? Or all of us?"

"Mostly just Eric. Although she wouldn't have kicked the rest of you out of bed. But I think she's legitimately in love with Eric."

Chris laughed. "Who isn't?"

I gave him a strange look. "Me. As one example."

"Well, good for you," he said, rolling his eyes. "I guess you must be president of that club by default since you're probably the only fan who's not a member of it."

"I'm not a fan."

He glanced around the room, resting his eyes pointedly on the posters and concert DVDs and framed autographed CD.

"I'm a casual fan," I corrected myself. "Who unfortunately had a ridiculously obsessed girlfriend and who is too lazy to redecorate now that she's moved out. Besides, all this got me some pretty awesome sex with a hot chick once, so who's to say that won't happen again?"

"Uh-huh."

"Anyway." I put my omelet plate on the end table beside me and twisted around to face him. "We need a game plan."

"A game plan for what?"

"For figuring out how to get you to heaven," I said. "Or into whatever afterlife you've gained yourself entry to."

"Oh." He raked his teeth over his bottom lip. "I imagine it must be heaven, right? Otherwise why am I even here? It seems really mean to give me a chance to make things right and then send me to hell anyway."

I shrugged. "I'm not a philosopher, man."

"Well, I figure maybe I have unfinished business," he continued. "I mean . . . isn't that why ghosts usually stay behind?"

"In the movies, sure," I allowed. "But up until you showed up, I wasn't convinced that this sort of thing was even possible, so what do I know about it?"

"Well . . ." He looked around the room again. "It's somewhere to start, at least. Can't hurt."

"True. So what business do you have left?"

"There are three people I want to see," he said. "You'll have to help me talk to them, though. We can figure out a way to convince them I'm really talking to them through you."

"Sounds like a bucket of laughs," I said sarcastically. "Who are the three?"

He counted them off on his fingers. "Jerri Walker, my sister, and Eric."

Sister I could understand, and it was obvious who Eric was, so I ignored those. "Jerri Walker? Who's he?"

"You'll see," he said. "And she's a girl, actually. Jerrica's her name, but she goes by Jerri." He paused. "She'll probably be the easiest one. We should do her first. Get it over with."

"So . . . your chick on the side, then." It seemed like a likely prospect.

He laughed briefly. "No, nothing like that. Totally platonic."

"Why is that funny?"

He shrugged. "You'll see. She's . . . Well, she's not what you'd expect."

"So . . . lesbian." Which *also* seemed like a likely prospect, given the laughter.

"Nope," he said. "Not as far as I know."

"Who is she, then?"

He shook his head. "Just a friend. A good friend."

"All right, be mysterious," I said. "Tell me where to find her."

"Los Angeles," Chris answered. "She lives on—"

"Los *Angeles*?"

He raised an eyebrow. "Yeah. That's where I spent most of my time."

"I am not flying out to Los Angeles, man. There's no way I can afford that."

"Then drive," he suggested. "Take a few days off and—"

"And *drive* from *Boston* to *Los Angeles*?" I took a mental inventory of my eyeballs to make sure they were both still attached to my brain instead of just bugging all the way out. "Are you insane? I mean, seriously, Chris, are you legitimately insane?"

He crossed his arms and frowned. "I need to see her," he said. "And Eric, who's probably there too if the tour is over."

"Well, I'm sorry about that, because I can't do it." I crossed my arms back at him. "I really truly am sorry. But I don't have a shiny black credit card I can just wave at the gate agents and get sent right through to LAX."

He waved his hand. "I'll pay for it."

I laughed at that. "Using what?"

Chris wrinkled his forehead in thought. "Using my bank account."

"Dude, I can guarantee you that your bank account is closed. You've been dead for two months and they don't just leave your cash lying around in a bank vault in case you get resurrected." I leaned back against the couch and gave him a challenging look.

He opened his mouth to speak, then closed it again. Finally, he said, "Touché."

"And anyway, man, even if your account was still open, I'm really not going to prison for fraudulent use of a dead celebrity's bank account. I'm too pretty to go to prison."

He scoffed. "You're too scrawny to be *really* pretty."

"Hey!" I bristled. "Chicks dig skinny guys."

"Skinny guys, sure. *Scrawny* guys, not so much." He grinned.

I tightened my arms across my chest and pouted.

"I'm joking, man. You're attractive enough. Don't worry." He let the grin morph into more of a genuine smile, which made me a little nervous. "So show me a picture of this Carmen chick. I want to know what league you're in."

I rolled my eyes, but pulled out my phone and found a picture of her. I held it out so he could see. "This was right after your concert last year. She swore up and down that Eric made eye contact with her, and then that night I got some spectacular action, so it was win-win."

"Did she ever make you role-play about us?" he asked, leaning in to see her. "Wow, she's a looker, man."

"I know. But she's crazy. And I don't say that in the 'I'm a man who got dumped and so I'm going to call all women crazy' sense. I mean that in the 'I actually think she should be on serious medication' sense." I clicked the button to turn the screen off and put the phone back in my pocket. "And yeah. Mostly it was Eric. I got called Eric a lot."

"Duly noted," he said, smiling. "So . . . did you love her?"

"Who?" I asked, then felt stupid because it wasn't like we'd been talking about a whole slew of women. "Carmen?"

"Yeah. Just curious if you're, you know, heartbroken about the dumping." He turned so that he was facing me, too.

I put my elbow on the back of the couch and propped my head on my hand. "I guess I must have loved her a little. I don't really know. There were times when it felt real." I glanced up at the Incite the Masses concert poster and then back down at Chris. "What about you?"

"I was in love a long time ago, and it didn't work out very well for me," he said. "Tori was just a warm body. And she knew that, and that's pretty much what I was for her too."

"So we're both recently out of relationships with girls who are borderline psychotic and who we don't miss other than for sex," I said.

"Thank you for summarizing that for me," Chris said. "I don't know how I would have been able to figure out the bottom line without your assistance."

I gave him a bitch-face. "There you go, being a jerk again."

He shrugged and turned his body so he was facing the TV instead of me. "It was starting to feel like we were ten seconds away from giving each other pedicures and talking about boys. I thought I should nip that shit in the bud."

I twisted back around too. "Probably for the best. No good ever comes of guys sharing their feelings."

"None at all."

There was a slightly weird, slightly companionable silence for a few seconds, then I cleared my throat. "But I'll try to save up for a plane ticket to LA. I've always wanted to go there anyway."

He glanced at me out of the corner of his eye, which I saw out of the corner of mine. "You'd do that for me?"

"Ugh," I said. "Not when you say it like *that*."

"Sorry." He smiled softly. "I mean . . . that's cool of you, bro."

"No homo?" I said, grinning.

He pretended to think, tapping his fingers on his chin and gazing up at the ceiling pointedly. "Well, less than five percent homo. I did just tell you a few minutes ago that you were attractive enough to get a prison boyfriend, so I think that bumps it up to four point five at least. But then I only said that because I thought you were about to burst into tears, so that lets me deduct about three percent, so . . . I'd say it was only one point five percent homo. Tops."

I grabbed a pencil off of my end table and threw it at him. It went through his nose and he laughed.

"When you're not harping on my drug problem, you're pretty chill, man," he said. "We could have been friends."

"Not with my girlfriend wanting to bone you. That would have made things awkward between us," I pointed out.

"Eiffel Tower, bro. And anyway, I'd be boning *her*. Not her boning me."

"How very literal of you," I replied. "But honestly, if you were down for it, I don't think she would have been too picky about positions."

He shrugged. "I'm adventurous. I'll try anything once."

I paused. "I want it on the record that you just gave me a perfect opening to continue talking about your drug abuse and I didn't do it."

"And *I* want it on the record that I haven't called you poor or mocked your proletariat lifestyle in like ten whole minutes." He smiled. "So we're both making progress."

"Go us," I said. "Hooray." I went back to watching C-SPAN.

After a few seconds, Chris let out an exasperated sigh. "Can we watch something less dull than this? Have you made your point yet?"

"Fine," I said, reaching for the remote and holding back a sigh of relief. "But I'm picking what we watch this time."

CHAPTER
TWELVE

"How much did he give you?" Chris craned his neck as if that would let him see into my pocket.

"You know, it's really rude to keep asking me how much I'm making in tips," I said. "But it was a five."

"That brings us up to . . ." He tilted his head while he calculated. "Twenty-three dollars for tonight."

"The night is young," I told him. "People get more generous as it gets later."

"Because they're drunk?"

"Not usually," I said. "Well, some of them are. But most of them are just tired and so they're at that stage where they'll shove whatever bills they have at you just to get to their room faster."

"And you take advantage of people when they're tired?"

"Yes. And I feel zero shame for that."

"Well, you need to make like a hundred more dollars tonight so you don't have to dumpster-dive for food in LA," he told me. "So hop to it."

"Um, your math is faulty, man," I said. "Because sure, the food will be about that much, but I have to make that much *on top* of what I need for my rent and my bills before I can go to Los Angeles on a whim."

"It's not a whim," he insisted. "It's a necessary trip."

"So you can tell Eric Painter to go fuck himself and then go see Jerri What's-Her-Name for your mysterious reasons that you won't tell me about?"

"Yes. And we're going to see Jerri *before* Eric. Not after."

"Why does it matter?" I asked. "You need to see them both, don't you?"

"Yeah, but if I see Eric first he'll tell me not to go see Jerri." He paused, then wrinkled his nose. "Well, honestly, if I go see Jerri first she'll tell me not to go see Eric, too. But Jerri I can ignore."

I raised an eyebrow at him. "When do I get to find out who Jerri is and why you have unfinished business with her?"

"I'm planning for never. I was just going to have you stand twenty feet away and wear headphones while I talk to her."

"Yeah, that's not going to happen," I said, crossing my arms. "If I'm flying across the country for you, I at least get to hear the juicy gossip. And besides, you can't even talk to her without using me as a translator, so you'll just have to live with me hearing the conversation."

He grimaced. "Fine. But you'll disapprove."

"Yeah, man. I mean, probably. If you're not telling me who she is, that probably means I wouldn't like it."

"You don't like a lot of things," he said, but he gave a little half smile so I didn't take it as an insult.

"Well, what you see is what you get," I agreed. "Anyway, this is a lot of trouble, going all the way out there. Are you sure it's necessary to go in person? Can't I just call them and tell them what you want them to know?"

"I won't be able to convince them I'm real over the phone. And besides . . . I kind of want to see them. Even if they can't see me, I want to see them one more time."

I could understand that. I mean, if I was dead I'd want to see my grandma again before I left. And if we were going to do this whole unfinished-business thing, we might as well do it right. I really did want to see LA, and I wasn't likely to ever have a good enough excuse to justify the trip again, so it was worth it.

"We'll figure something out," I said. "But seriously, it's going to take me some time to get the money. So you'll just have to stay with me and try to entertain yourself while I work for a while."

Chris huffed out a sigh. "Well, I guess I can wait."

"So are any of the people you want to see nearby? So we can start with them, maybe?"

"My sister lives in upstate New York," he said, "but I don't want to see her yet."

"Why not? Save the best for last?"

He shook his head. "Save the worst for last. Save the most awkward for last. She hates me. We haven't spoken in years."

I don't have siblings, so I couldn't *really* understand, but that still seemed pretty shitty. "I'm sorry, man. So you just need to, what? Tell her you love her?"

"Something like that," he said. "Honestly, I have no idea what to say to her. She hates everything about me. The drugs and shit, yeah, I get those. But she also hates that I'm a musician. She thought I should have done what Dad did and kept planting churches."

"She wanted you to be a traveling preacher?" I asked, then paused for a moment to think. "That makes sense, actually."

He laughed. "You can see *me*, a drug-addicted screwup who films himself having sex, being a *preacher*?"

"Well, preachers and musicians have similar skill sets."

He didn't look terribly convinced. "Do explain."

I stepped into the service elevator and pressed the button for the lobby. "Well, both callings require you to be really charismatic and to connect with an audience from a stage. And they both gather followers and inspire people to convert to their way of seeing and doing things." I shrugged. "And I'd imagine they both get tons of chicks. Maybe pastors don't take the chicks up on their offers, but they probably have lots of women who want to bump uglies with them."

"My father would have had an apoplectic fit if he'd heard you say that," Chris said, smiling slightly.

I smiled back. "Well, I guess the end goals of the women are different. The pastors get women who want to marry them and have godly lives and raise little godly children with them."

"Whereas the bass player just wants to bone them," he finished for me.

I shrugged again. "I don't know what you want from your chicks, man. I assume it's boning, but maybe there's a romantic down in there somewhere."

He didn't say anything, and that was surprising enough that I looked over to make sure he hadn't spontaneously moved on, but he was just standing beside me watching the numbers on the elevator move slowly down to one.

When the elevator made its dinging sound letting us know we'd arrived at the lobby, he spoke up. "I can be a romantic. I just have to be with somebody who's worth the effort."

"Like your girlfriend Jerri?" I asked, smirking.

"Jerri isn't my girlfriend, you fucker."

I smiled again, and when the doors opened I walked back out into the lobby.

"She's *not* my girlfriend," he said, louder this time.

There were guests around, so I didn't answer him. I kept smiling, though, enough that Richard gave me a funny look. I headed for the front door to see if Mark had any new guests arriving who might need my help.

A woman was climbing out of her cab and shoving a largish suitcase to Mark, so I hurried over to grab it. She handed it to me and took a moment to brush a nonexistent crumb off of her ample bosom. I didn't take the bait and instead kept my eyes safely above the neck.

"I'll take your bags up to your room, ma'am," I said, warmly enough to give her the impression that I was a nice guy but not *so* warmly that she would expect me to show up at her room door later wearing a Speedo and carrying a bottle of wine.

The woman smiled back at me, but her smile was substantially less innocent than mine had been. "Well, aren't you just the helpful one," she purred.

Chris laughed out loud. "She's hitting on you."

I flicked my eyes to him while Mark was opening the door for the woman and directing her to the front desk for check in. "Yeah," I mumbled, trying to move my lips as little as possible in case somebody was watching. "It happens."

Mark told me the room number, and I started dragging the suitcase inside.

"Do you bone guests ever?" Chris asked.

"No," I said. "Shut up."

"She'd probably tip you better if you boned her."

"I'm sure she would," I muttered. "But I'm not going to do it. I'm not a whore."

"Which is good," he said. "I don't know if I'd want to watch you having sex."

I hauled the suitcase into the service elevator and headed up to the floor the lady would be staying on. "Well, you might have to get over that at some point," I told him. "Because if you're stuck with me forever, I'm not staying celibate just to avoid offending your delicate sensibilities."

"Ugh," he said, making a disgusted face. "I guess I can just sit out in the hallway of the apartment."

"I'll hang a sock on the door," I offered. "But you said I was pretty, so maybe you'd like to watch." I gave him an exaggerated 'come hither' eyebrow waggle for comedy's sake.

He rolled his eyes. "I've never been much of a voyeur. I've always wanted to be in on the action."

I shrugged. "Beggar ghosts can't be chooser ghosts."

"That's probably true," he admitted. "But I don't know if Gemma would be okay with it, seeing as she already knows I'm here."

"Dude, Gemma is totally not into me."

"She is," he argued. "But whatever. There's no accounting for poor taste."

I shot him a look and pulled the suitcase out into the hallway and carried it to the lady's room. She wasn't there yet, so I took the suitcase inside and put it down next to the dresser, then went back outside to wait for her.

"So you're just going to stand here?" he asked.

"Yeah," I said. "I mean, for a few minutes. To see if she needs anything else. And to give her a chance to be a decent human being and tip me."

"I think she's expecting *you* to tip *her*," he said, then leaned in closer. "With your cock."

"Yes, thank you for clearing up that completely subtle innuendo," I snapped. "I never would have figured it out otherwise."

"Always glad to help," he said, bracing his shoulder against the wall and smiling.

"For my own personal information," I said after a moment, "if I'd let Carmen in your room, would you have done her? Or would you have just called security and gotten me fired?"

"Probably both," he said. "Well, that's not true. I wasn't very picky there at the end. Tori was pissing me off and Eric was pissing me off and . . . well, everybody was pissing me off, is what I'm saying. I was spending my life with both middle fingers in the air because . . ." He closed his eyes and wrinkled his forehead, reaching up to pinch the bridge of his nose. "I don't know. Whatever. Let's talk about other stuff."

"Okay." I glanced away for a second to give him a tiny bit of privacy and then turned back. "Sorry."

"No problem." He opened his eyes again and relaxed his face. "I just . . . I shouldn't have died. You know?"

"Nobody should die as young as you."

"Yeah. And nobody should have to wait around afterwards. I mean, if ghosts were super common we'd have more evidence that they existed. So why don't we?"

"I don't know, man." I put my hands in my suit pockets and focused on the floor. "I guess it's just one of those things."

"You're not even curious about it?"

"I'm not *not* curious about it," I answered. "I just doubt there's any way to really know for sure and so I don't think about it too much."

"Is that your stance on religion too?"

I shrugged. It seemed like a nuanced enough answer for such a broad question.

"I guess I would agree with that." He opened his mouth like he was going to continue, but then he closed it again.

"What?" I prompted. The conversation was still weird from the Carmen question, and it felt like we were skirting up against some kind of edge and I couldn't stop myself from tiptoeing a little closer to it.

He sighed, then sniffed like it wasn't a big deal. "I was just going to say . . . that Allison would love me more if I was religious." He paused again. "Not that I'm *not* religious. I'm just not . . . actively religious. Whatever."

"I'm sure she loves you," I said. "She's your sister."

Chris snorted. "Yeah, talk to me about that again when you meet her." He looked past me down the hall. "Your girlfriend's coming. Act cool."

I followed his gaze to the main elevators. The flirty lady was walking toward me, swaying her hips a little too much and giving me eyes.

"Oh, my, you're still here," she breathed when she got close to me.

Chris laughed at that and then started whistling and making catcalls. I did an Oscar-worthy job of pretending I didn't hear him while I smiled at the woman. "I wanted to make sure you didn't need anything else, ma'am."

"Hmm," she said, giving me an up-and-down appraisal that was even less subtle than the one outside the cab had been. "Well, that depends on what services you provide."

Chris stage-whispered, "She wants to know if she can ride you like a bronco."

I crossed my arms behind my back so the guest couldn't see my hands, then flipped Chris off, which just made him laugh. Ignoring him, I smiled at the woman again, still pretty brightly although I turned down the warmth a bit, and did what I usually did in these situations. "Well, I can send room service up for you if you want. Or I can have the concierge make you reservations for dinner or a show. I can also have housekeeping bring up extra pillows or towels if you need them." *You'll notice how none of that involved me taking off my pants.*

She kept eyeing me for a moment, then opened her door and stepped inside. "I expect you want a tip, right? Come in and let me get my purse."

It took a massive effort for me not to stare pointedly at the purse hanging off her shoulder. "No, thank you, that's not necessary," I told her, even though it kind of was. But I didn't need her lousy dollar enough to risk a hospitalization to get her tongue surgically removed from my throat, so it was probably best to just let that one go. "Have a good night." I gave her one more smile and then walked away toward the stairwell.

"You're not going for the elevator?" Chris asked me as he trotted along behind me.

I hadn't heard the door to the room close, so I assumed that the woman was still standing there watching me. I spoke low so she couldn't hear. "I'd have to stand there in the hall and wait for it, and she'd be leering at me the whole time. This way I get out of here quickly."

"Fair enough. So how often does that happen?" He matched my speed, and our hands would have bumped if Chris were more solid, so I angled a little more away from him.

I opened the door to the stairwell and started trudging down the steps. "Not *that* often. I mean, maybe once every couple of months? It's always the businesswomen in their forties, too. I guess they're bored."

"No business*men*?" Chris said. He raised an eyebrow at me, and I rolled my eyes at him.

"Sometimes," I admitted. "I turn them down too."

"So you've never porked a guest. Not once."

"Nope," I said, then decided to be honest for whatever reason. "Well, not while they were guests. There was this one girl who was here for a bachelorette party who gave me her number. After she was safely not a guest anymore I called her up."

"You devil, you," Chris said, chuckling.

I smiled. "Well, it didn't amount to anything, anyway. And then I hooked up with Carmen. And that concludes my dating history for the past two years." I paused with my hand on the door to the lobby. "That sounded more pathetic than I meant it to."

"I applaud your moral standards," Chris said. "I won't rag you too much about it."

"Thanks," I said, rolling my eyes again. "But really it doesn't have as much to do with moral standards as it does with my deep fear of unemployment."

"So would you have porked Horny Lady back there if you knew you wouldn't get fired for it?"

"*Please* stop saying 'porked.'" I wrinkled my nose. "And my girlfriend dumped me the night you died and I've only had myself for company since then, so . . . I don't know. Maybe."

"Carmen dumped you the night I died?" he asked, and judging by the way his eyes widened, he must have been pretty surprised by that.

"Yeah," I told him. "It was sort of a shitty day for me all-around."

"Before or after?" he pressed.

"After." I opened the door and walked back into the lobby. Mark was outside watching the cars go by and nobody seemed to need help at the moment, so I headed into the lounge area and started straightening pillows on the couches so that Richard would think I was busy.

"She dumped you after you'd had to deal with finding a dead body in a hotel room?" Chris asked.

I almost ignored him, but he would probably keep harassing me until I answered. "I told you, she's not very nice. And besides, it was pretty much over anyway. She was just sticking around in case I did manage to get your autograph."

"I honestly don't know if I would have given you one." Chris flopped down on the couch and smirked at me. "I was kind of an asshole that night."

I laughed. "Dude, you're *still* an asshole." Then, because I didn't want to come off as a dick myself: "But I guess you're a cool asshole."

He gave a half smirk at that. "Thanks. You're a cool asshole yourself."

And there it was, that edge we'd been sneaking closer to. "Dude, are we . . . *friends*?"

He tilted his head and looked up at the ceiling. "I think we are, yeah."

"Wow," I said, and it did seem pretty amazing, especially since I hadn't made any friends since I dropped out of college. I still had some friends from a long time ago who I kept up with loosely on social media, but nobody I could call or go hang out with. Which was even more pathetic than my sexual dry spell, so I didn't mention it. "Shame nobody would believe me. I could get so many chicks if I claimed I was friends with the ITM bassist."

"Well, once we go out to LA you can tell them you know the ITM front man, and that will probably get you even *more* chicks, so you can thank me for that later."

He smiled, and I smiled, and it occurred to me that maybe friendship wasn't the edge we'd been approaching after all.

CHAPTER THIRTEEN

"N o," I said emphatically as I locked the door behind us. We'd just gotten back from having lunch with Gemma, and Chris had been bothering me about watching TV for the whole walk home. "I'm sorry, Chris, but in the past two weeks we have watched *four seasons* of *Supernatural* and I am frankly really, really fucking tired of it."

"Sucks to be you, then," he said. "Because season five is going to be *awesome*."

I rolled my eyes. "I'll watch to the end of season five, but if you think I'm watching past that, then you can go fuck yourself."

"Well, fine," he said. "You're such a spoilsport."

"And anyway . . . I needed to talk to you. So no TV right now." I sat down on the couch and turned to look at him.

He narrowed his eyes at me. "Is this the Relationship Talk?"

"No, you idiot," I said, then thought better of it. "Well, sort of. It's the 'I have to go home for Christmas and hang out with my stupid family and since your soul is weirdly attached to my aura, then that means you have to come too so please don't be an asshole about it' talk."

"Christmas, huh?" He rubbed his chin. "It's been a long time since I had a Christmas that didn't involve hookers and blow."

"Well, my family gets pretty crazy, so I wouldn't rule that out," I said, laughing.

"This sounds like my kind of event, then." He grinned at me.

I found myself grinning back, which irritated me. "Seriously, it's probably not going to be very exciting. We'll go, I'll eat, Aunt Greta will tell me I've gained weight even though I haven't, Crazy Cousin Chad will pace around the living room, we'll watch some football, and then I'll leave again and maybe we can find us a hooker." I paused. "Well, not really. I can't afford that shit. But we can come back to Boston and I'll eat a scone for you and we can watch a documentary about the real Saint Nicholas or something."

"I guess that sounds not completely terrible," he allowed. "It will be fun to meet your family without having to make small talk with them."

"That's the spirit," I said, then smirked. "Get it? Spirit? Because you're a ghost."

He tried to pick up a pillow and throw it at me before he remembered he couldn't. I laughed, and he joined in.

"So you'll come?" I asked him after the laughter faded.

He shrugged. "I'll come. I don't have much of a choice, though, do I?"

"Not really," I admitted. "But if you actually *agree* to go, then maybe you'll be nicer about it than if I just dragged you along without your consent."

"I'll go. It might be fun to meet your family. See why it is that you are—" he gestured up and down me "—the way that you are."

"I don't know how enlightening it will be for you," I warned him. "I have your run-of-the-mill family."

"No family is really run of the mill," he said. "Every family is weird and dysfunctional in its own special and unique way."

I thought for a moment. "Well, there *is* Crazy Cousin Chad."

"Oh yeah, Crazy Cousin Chad. You mentioned him a minute ago. What's his story?"

"He's crazy. And not just normal 'my family is soooo craaazy' crazy. Like literally mentally unbalanced. He's on antipsychotic meds."

Chris raised his eyebrows. "What brand of crazy? Like hearing-voices crazy or like homicidal-rage crazy?"

"Why? Are you afraid he'll kill you deader?" I let the corner of my mouth quirk up into a tiny half smile.

"I'm afraid he'll kill *you*," he retorted. "And then who knows what would happen to me? I'd rather keep you alive than take my chances."

"That's very heartwarming," I said, rolling my eyes again. "But I guess he's more hearing-voices crazy. I don't really know. We're not super close. I mean, he's around my age, so we played together at family events when we were younger, but we haven't been buddies as adults. But to the best of my knowledge he's never tried to murder anyone."

"It must be terrible for him to see and hear something that no one else can see and hear." He cocked an eyebrow at me.

"Yeah," I agreed. "It must make him feel like a major nutjob. I can certainly relate."

"I don't think you're crazy," Chris said, sounding oddly serious about it.

I smiled again, and it wasn't even a sarcastic smile. "That sounds like something that my psychotic hallucination would say if I *was* crazy."

He chuckled. "Very true."

The fucker had dimples. *Dimples.* What the hell was he doing with dimples like that? And why the hell was I noticing them at all, much less thinking about how they made him look like a genuinely nice guy? I doubted Eric had dimples, so I don't know why Carmen wouldn't have liked Chris more. But maybe she was into bad boys. I don't know. I don't care. That whole line of thought was stupid.

The silence had apparently stretched on a little too long, because Chris awkwardly cleared his throat and continued. "So tell me about your family. There's Crazy Cousin Chad and some aunt who's obsessed with your weight. Who else?"

I swallowed hard, pulling my eyes away from his stupid cheeks. "Well." I drew out the word to give myself some time to regroup. "There's my grandma. I call her Grandma. Because I'm creative like that."

"Cool. Grandmas are pretty nice, from what I hear."

"You don't have any?"

"No, my parents sprang forth from the foam of the sea," he deadpanned.

I threw a pillow back at him—or, more accurately, through him—and he ducked, grinning. I smirked at getting a reaction out of him. "Jerk. You know what I mean."

"I know what you mean. And no, I don't have any. They were still around when I was a kid, but they've been gone for a while. And before you apologize, it's cool. Made my peace with that a long time ago."

It was pretty hard not to apologize anyway. Basic human reaction. But since he'd told me not to, I suppressed the urge. "Well, I hope Grandma makes it for a few more decades. She's basically my mom. She was the one who raised me."

He opened his mouth to speak, then looked uncertain.

I took pity on him. "My mother didn't want kids. She was pretty young. Not *16 and Pregnant* young, but young enough that she didn't think she'd be a good mom. So when I was born, she foisted me off on Grandma and hit the road."

Chris frowned. "So you don't have contact with her?"

I shrugged. "I don't really know where she is at any given time. But she sends postcards every once in a while. And she sends me a birthday card when she remembers to, which has been about five times in my life. And sometimes—very rarely, but sometimes—she shows up to family functions."

"Will she be at Christmas?"

"I sincerely doubt it," I said. "The last time she came to a family holiday was the Thanksgiving when I was nine. She called Aunt Greta an insufferable, nosy know-it-all right there at the dinner table and Grandma threw her out of the house and it was *awesome*. But only in retrospect. At the time, Aunt Greta was crying and Crazy Cousin Chad was crying and Grandma was beet red and furious and Mom was waving a turkey leg in the air and telling Grandma she couldn't throw her out because she was *leaving of her own accord* and then she tripped over her chair and started cussing a blue streak and I was pretty sure that nobody was going to get dessert, which to a nine-year-old was the worst possible outcome."

Chris was laughing, a hearty genuine-sounding laugh. "Did you get dessert?"

"Yeah," I said, grinning. "And I think Grandma let us have extra because she felt bad that Mom had caused a scene. So it turned out okay in the end."

"I almost hope I get to see something like that."

"Well, don't get your hopes up," I warned him. "Seriously, every other holiday has been pretty low-key."

"Still," he said. "I'm actually looking forward to this."

"And if you're *really super nice*," I paused dramatically, "I'll even let you watch me eat a slice of Grandma's special-recipe strawberry-rhubarb pie. You can sit real close and watch me chew and everything."

He laughed again. "You'd do that for little old me?"

"Only if you're nice."

"Then I will *definitely* be nice," he promised.

CHAPTER FOURTEEN

C razy Cousin Chad was out on the porch pacing when Chris and I arrived in the taxi. He looked up at me and then immediately turned around and went in the house.

Chris watched as the door slammed shut behind him. "Well, that was certainly a warm welcome."

I headed up the walkway to the house. "He probably just hasn't taken his meds today. Sometimes he doesn't take them because he says they make him feel fuzzy, and Aunt Greta tries to crush the pills up and hide them in his food, despite the fact that that's never worked, not even once, because he can taste them. And also because he's a human and not a Golden Retriever."

"So that wasn't a reflection on your relationship with Crazy Cousin Chad?"

I shook my head. "Nope. Chad is like a box of chocolates. You never know what you're gonna get."

"That was lame. But I forgive you."

"How very magnanimous," I said. "Now stop talking to me before Aunt Greta spikes my cranberry sauce with clozapine."

He scoffed. "Technically I can talk all I want. It's just up to you not to answer me."

"Well, then just don't be an ass. I'm going inside now." I paused in front of the door, took a deep breath, and went into the house.

"Tyler!" Grandma's voice announced from the kitchen. "You're here! Wait just a second, I need to dry off my hands."

Chris raised an eyebrow. "Did Chad tell her you were here?"

"Fuck if I know," I murmured back. "But Grandma always seems to know the instant I walk in, so probably not."

Chris nodded and immediately started snooping through my grandmother's stuff, examining every knickknack on the shelves in the front room. After a few seconds, Grandma came bustling out of the back of the house, beaming and holding her arms out.

"Come give me a hug, you bad grandson you."

I hugged her tightly. "Why am I a bad grandson?"

"Because you have a girlfriend and you're trying to keep her a secret," she chided, pulling back and wagging her finger at me.

"Who?" I asked, genuinely surprised. "Carmen?"

"No, not Carmen," she said. "I know about *that* hussy and good riddance, is what I say to that. No, I mean this Gemma girl who keeps posting on your Facebook."

"Oh, Gemma," I said. "She's just a friend."

"That's not what it sounds like on the Facebook," Grandma insisted.

Chris looked up from Grandma's collection of porcelain thimbles. "She *does* post a lot on your wall. And we do have lunch with her sometimes while you try to pretend you're not staring at her tits."

I almost argued with him since I definitely had not been staring at Gemma's chest during our lunches, but I wouldn't give him the satisfaction of seeing me break my personal "no talking to invisible people in front of family" goal this soon into the day. So instead I just smiled at Grandma. "I wouldn't lie to you, Grandma. If I start dating someone, I'll tell you."

"Promise?" she asked, wagging her finger again.

"I promise."

"All right, then," she said. "Now go wash your hands and come help mash the potatoes."

"Okay, Grandma." I kissed her on the cheek and headed for the bathroom, where I didn't even have the door closed behind myself before Chris started chattering away.

"You're going to help her mash potatoes? Isn't that a woman's job?"

I faced him and crossed my arms. "Okay, first off, that's incredibly sexist of you. A man can mash potatoes just as well as a woman can and women are not objects who exist to fuck you and make you dinner. And second off, no, I'm not going to help her mash potatoes. Every single year she tells me to go wash my hands and come help her mash potatoes, and every year I tell her I'll do it and then I escape."

Chris smiled. "Family traditions, man. They're weird."

"I guess so," I said. "Now get out."

"Why?"

"Because this is a bathroom and you need to get out." I made a grand "go ahead" gesture at the door.

"I had no idea that washing your hands was such a personal matter."

"It's not," I snapped. "But I need to take a leak and I don't want you ogling my privates while I do it."

"I am *not* going to 'ogle your privates.' I mean, come on." He rolled his eyes.

"Then it shouldn't be a problem for you to kindly fuck off for forty-five seconds."

He pouted. "I'm bored."

"Yeah, well, I have to pee. Now get out." I gestured at the hallway again.

There was a quick tapping on the door, and I jumped.

"Tyler?" It was Chad's voice. "Are you all right?"

I cleared my throat. "Yeah, Chad, I'll be out in a minute."

There was a beat of silence, then Chad spoke again. "I heard you talking to somebody in there."

I glanced over at Chris. "Yeah, I'm on my phone. I'll be out in a second."

Another long pause, long enough that I was sure Chad had left. Then: "Do you have it on speakerphone?"

"What? No," I said. "Go away, man. You're giving me a shy bladder." I looked at Chris with an eyebrow raised, and he just shrugged.

After another pause, Chad said, "Okay," and I heard him shuffling down the hall.

"That was weird," Chris said. He sat down on the closed toilet lid.

"I will straight-up pee through your torso if you don't move," I warned him. "I swear I'll do it."

"Fine, fine," he grumbled. "Spoilsport."

"I fail to see what sport I'm spoiling for you, exactly," I said, "unless it's privates-ogling."

"Geez," he said, rolling his eyes again. "Okay, okay, I'll go out in the hall."

"Thank you," I said, then crossed my arms and pursed my lips while I waited on him to leave. Chris stood up and gave me a cheeky salute before walking through the door and out into the hallway.

I finished up in the bathroom, then poked my head into the kitchen to tell Grandma and Aunt Greta that I was going to check on something in the backyard, which was my very unsubtle way of saying that if the potatoes were going to be mashed, they weren't going to be mashed by me. Grandma just sighed and waved me off instead of waggling her finger and telling me to stop stalling and lend a hand. I headed out into the backyard and sat in the tire swing hanging from a big oak tree.

Surprisingly enough, there was no snow on the ground and it was fairly warm for December. Chris sat down on the grass and put his hands on the ground behind him, then leaned back and tilted his head up toward the sun, his eyes closed. I watched him for a few seconds, wondering how the sunlight could hit his dark-brown hair like that and turn it almost red in places when he didn't actually have corporeal hair for the sun to touch.

"Can you feel the sun?" I asked him after a bit.

"No," he said. "But I can remember feeling the sun and I can pretend." He left his eyes closed and tilted his face up farther. A soft breeze started, and it ruffled his hair even though that didn't make any sense either.

When I didn't say anything, he opened one eye and peered at me. "What?"

I shrugged. "I was just thinking about why, since you don't have a physical body, the sun and the wind and things affect you."

He opened his other eye. "Do they? How?"

"Well, your hair moves in the breeze," I told him. "And the sun kind of glints off it. Did you know that it's sort of bronzy red in the sun?"

He shook his head. "Nobody looks at me in the sun."

"I do," I said, then realized that my answer could be interpreted as more than five percent homo and so I continued. "Well, I mean, I'm looking at you right now. And I'd guess that stage lighting makes it reddish too."

"Probably," he said, sounding a little distant.

"Did you like it?" I asked after a moment. "Being a rock star?"

He pushed himself into a more upright sitting position. "It's like any job. There are things you like and things you hate. All in all it's a better job than most, though. And like I said, the music is important to me." He paused. "Well, the music *was* important to me. I guess now I can't make any more of it."

"You could compose," I suggested.

He just shook his head and didn't respond for a long time. "My birthday's coming up," he said finally.

A bell rang deep in the back of my mind. "January 7?"

"Yeah," he said, looking genuinely surprised. "How did you know that?"

"Honestly, I have no idea," I said. "Carmen must have mentioned it. Or maybe I just remember it from the book."

Chris raised both eyebrows so far that I was concerned they'd escaped and made a break for his hairline. "The *book*?"

"Yeah. The unauthorized biography of the band," I said. "Which let me tell you was not overly detailed or helpful or even interesting. I think it got a lot of things wrong."

"Oh really?" He smiled. "Like what?"

"It strongly implied that Brent and Paul were knocking boots."

"Totally untrue," he said. "Although I'm pretty sure they were both sleeping with the same girl without realizing it at one point. And if you believe the safe sex ads, that's basically the same thing as sleeping with each other."

I rolled my eyes. "Maybe from an STD standpoint. But I refuse to consider that I've essentially slept with Danny Carter from the liquor store, so I reject the idea on the basis of my sanity."

He laughed. "Such as it is."

I rolled my eyes again. "Yeah, I don't have much to prove my sanity these days. When even Crazy Cousin Chad starts asking me if I'm talking to myself, things have gotten pretty bad."

"Do you think . . ." He paused, looking strangely vulnerable in a way that did something odd to my extremities.

I prompted him. "Do I think what?"

"Do you think you really are hallucinating me?" he asked. "I mean . . . what if I'm not real? Or what if I'm only as real as you're making me?"

I thought about this for several seconds. "I don't know," I finally said. "I strongly doubt I'm just hallucinating you."

"How can you be sure?"

"I can't, I guess," I said. "I mean, how do I know that I'm seeing any of the things I think I'm seeing? How do I know this tire swing is really here and my grandma exists and rain smells like lemons and batteries? I don't *know* any of that. I could be living in a human farming pod the machines are raising for food like in *The Matrix*. I could be a fetus having a dream before I'm actually born. I could be God and I just don't realize it. And since I can't know anything for sure, my personal coping method is just to go with it."

He didn't say anything for a moment, then sighed. "I can't decide whether I should ask you why rain smells like lemon and batteries or if I should just jump right ahead into making fun of you for thinking you might be God. If I went with the first option, I could maybe get some interesting insight into how your weird little brain works. But if I went with the second option, I could call you a hypocrite and point at you and go 'Aha! Who's the narcissist now?' which would be pretty fun for me. So . . ."

I smiled. "Well, you could do both. Don't let me stop you from doing what you want to do."

"You can't cage me," he said, smiling back. "I am a free spirit."

We both laughed at that, and then Chris leaned back again and turned his face up to the sun. I watched him for a while before speaking.

"But I don't think I'm imagining you, man," I said, making my voice a little gentler than usual. "You know too much about Chris Raiden to just be my own personal idea of what Chris Raiden would be like."

"I could be lying to you. About everything." He didn't look at me. "You don't know. I could tell you all sorts of random shit and you wouldn't have any idea if it was really some kind of insight into what I'm really like or if it's just your inner craziness making shit up."

I shrugged and kicked the ground to make the tire swing sway. "Well, like I said. I cope with existential uncertainty by going along with what seems real to me."

"I guess that's the only way to live life," he said. "Or death. To live death."

"Do you believe in God?"

He closed his eyes, still facing toward the sky. "I believe in God," he said after a minute. "I just don't know how often I even cross his mind. Probably never. There are a lot of people in the world who deserve divine intervention more than I do."

I couldn't think of anything to say to that, so I just pushed myself on the swing with the toe of one foot for a while.

"Anyway," he said. "Let's talk about other things."

"Who's Jerri?" I asked, trying to come across as a little cheeky.

"Nope," he said, smiling and looking back at me finally. "You'll just have to wait and see."

I laughed, then quickly broke off as I saw Chad come out the back door and start shuffling across the yard toward me, doing a weird sort of walk that was fast and nervous while at the same time his feet dragged the ground like it was hard for him to lift them properly.

"Hey, Chad," I said, partly to be sociable and partly so that Chris would know we weren't alone anymore. Chris sat back up and peered at Cousin Chad, clearly excited to get to see what the guy looked like up close.

"Hey, Tyler." Chad rubbed the back of his neck, and when he spoke, it was the same as his walking gait—somehow both fast and slow at once, the words running together and slightly slurred. "Grandma says you need to come inside now. She's setting the table and it's almost time to eat."

"Cool." I ducked through the center of the tire swing and stood up. "Let's go in." We started walking, Chris trailing along behind us. "So how've you been, Chad?"

"My psychiatrist says I'm making progress," he said, then frowned. "But he's been saying that for years and I don't feel any different."

Ah, the awkward family gathering tradition of discussing one's health in depth after someone asks a filler question like *How are you?* I suppressed a sigh. "Well, I guess he'd know, right? Or maybe you need to switch meds?"

He shook his head quickly. "There aren't any other meds. You only get this one if nothing else works and after this, they just shake their heads at you and start talking about putting you in a padded cell and then you start telling them you're better so they won't commit you."

Which wasn't something I had a ready-to-go response for, so I laughed like it was a joke and changed the subject. "Do you know if Grandma made the cranberry sauce? Or is it just the canned kind?"

Chad shrugged. "I don't know. Probably homemade." He stopped and turned to face me. "How are *you*, Tyler?" he asked, weirdly earnest sounding.

Which was odd, implying that he didn't want the "I'm fine" answer from me either. I shifted onto one foot. "Um, I'm fine." It was worth a shot, anyway.

"Are you sure?" he asked, leaning forward. "You seem strange."

"I seem . . . strange," I repeated. *Don't look at Chris, don't look at Chris, don't look at Chris.* "What do you mean?"

"Like you're . . . distracted. Like you were sitting out here talking to someone."

I raised an eyebrow at him. "Phone, man."

"I didn't see a phone." He gave me a very suspicious gaze.

"I hung up when you came out the door."

He watched me for a few more seconds, his eyes narrowed and his lips pursed, then sighed. "We should go inside." He turned back around and fled into the house, leaving me standing just outside the door.

"That was weird," Chris commented.

"Yeah, well, that's Crazy Cousin Chad," I said. "At least maybe you can tell he's not a homicidal maniac. Just a normal maniac."

"Has he always been like this?"

I shrugged my shoulders. "When we were little, he was a normal kid. And then all the sudden he, you know, wasn't."

"Sad," Chris said. "I mean, I had my problems, but when I hallucinated I knew they were hallucinations. And I knew they were my own fault."

"Forgive me if I'm not too sympathetic to you on that front," I retorted. "I have to get inside."

"Yeah, that's fine. Let's go."

Once I got inside, I sat down at the table and took inventory of the family members who were present. Grandma and Aunt Greta and Chad, of course. Aunt Greta's husband, Uncle Tim, who always seemed uncomfortable around his son, like he was genuinely afraid that Chad was going to flip the homicide switch and bludgeon him to death with a chair leg. Grandma's sister Aunt Jane and her two sons and their wives and their four combined kids, ranging in age from two to about twelve. Uncle Tim's adult daughter from his first marriage and her husband. It wasn't the fullest Christmas we'd ever had, but it was crowded enough to have that Big Family Event feel to it. Chad sat in a chair across the table and diagonal from me.

Chris stood behind my chair, then leaned down and whispered, "Is your mom here?"

I shook my head very slightly.

"Is she coming?" he asked.

I tried to give a tiny shrug, but Uncle Tim saw it and gave me a strange look. I smiled at him. "Shoulders got stiff from sitting on the train."

Unlike Chad, Uncle Tim just let it go. Train-related aches and pains apparently weren't as suspicious as talking to unspecified people on invisible cell phones in bathrooms and backyards. I could understand.

Grandma called everyone to order and made us all bow our heads while she said grace over the meal. I opened one eye and turned my head so I could see Chris. He had his head bowed too, his eyes closed tightly, like he was actually listening to the words of the prayer. I closed my eye again—it seemed like I was intruding on his privacy and something in my conscience balked at that.

After the prayer, pandemonium broke out, with everybody half standing up from their seats to rake food onto their plates. I had scoped out the seat with the best access to Aunt Greta's famous corn casserole, so I immediately spooned up as much as I could without angering the rest of the family with my greediness. Then I passed my plate to one of Aunt Jane's sons so he could fill it up with turkey.

I glanced at Aunt Greta while I was waiting. She was surreptitiously sprinkling what had to be ground-up psych meds into Chad's mashed potatoes. Our eyes met briefly, and I gave her the "I see what you did there but I'm not saying anything about it" look before turning back to get my plate. A few more passes to other family members for farther-away foods, and then I sat back down to eat.

Chris crouched and watched me eat every single bite. By now, this sort of thing wasn't creepy. It had started to be a little unsettling how normal I found it, though, so maybe it would cycle back into creepy before too long. This time, though, I just let him watch and did my best not to let it distract me from my conversations with the nondead people at the table.

Aunt Greta motioned at my helping of corn casserole. "Is it as good as you always say it is, Ty-ty?"

Chris snorted. "She calls you *Ty-ty*?"

I didn't answer him. Instead I just gave Aunt Greta a winning smile and assured her that it was delicious. I was lying a little bit, though, which was upsetting. Aunt Greta's corn casserole was one of the things I looked forward to all year long, and this time it just tasted kind of off, like she'd gotten a bad batch of corn or something. Still, since she had noticed me eating it, I made a point to finish the helping I'd put on my plate.

By the time the feeding frenzy had slowed, I was deep in a debate with Uncle Tim about whether the Star Wars prequels were terrible or not (they were, obviously, but I was playing devil's advocate to keep the conversation interesting) when I yawned, midsentence.

"Tired?" Uncle Tim asked.

I raised both eyebrows at myself. "I don't know. I guess so. Sorry, the food's just lulling me to sleep or something."

Aunt Jane piped in then, talking about tryptophan and how turkey makes people sleepy, and I tried to listen but my eyelids were drooping a little. I made it through the meal, then muttered some excuses and went upstairs to my old bedroom.

When I closed the door behind myself, Chris stepped in front of me, concern in his dark-brown eyes. "Are you okay?"

"Yeah," I said, making a huge effort to keep my eyes open. "I'm just hella sleepy, man."

"You look drugged," he said, frowning.

"You would know," I snapped, then had the odd sensation that I should feel bad for saying that, except that I was too drowsy to care.

Chris frowned more deeply, but I walked straight through him toward my old bed. "I'm sorry, dude, I just need a nap and I'll feel better."

He said something back to me, but I didn't catch it before I fell asleep.

CHAPTER
FIFTEEN

The light outside was fading when I woke up. I sat up in bed and blinked, momentarily disoriented. Chris was sitting in an armchair beside the bed, staring at the floor. I yawned. "How long have I been asleep?"

"Four hours," he replied without looking up. "You..." He stopped, visibly clamping his mouth shut.

"What?" I glanced down at my feet. "I didn't even take off my shoes. Man, I was out like a freaking light."

"You fucking scared me, man," Chris said, his voice soft in volume but disturbingly hard in tone. "Don't fucking do that."

"Don't do what?" I asked, starting to get annoyed. "Don't have basic human needs like sleep? My bad, man, I'll try to be more ghostlike in the future."

"*That*," he gestured at the bed, "was not a basic human need. That was your Aunt Greta putting drugs in your food."

I blinked. "What?"

"Your Aunt Greta. She drugged you," he said, still staring at the floorboards like they had personally offended him. "And when people take drugs they die, so I'm a little sensitive about the matter these days."

"Did you ... Did you *see* her put something in my food? I mean, I saw her slipping Chad some clozapine, but she didn't even touch my plate."

"No, I didn't *see* it," he snapped. "But she's obviously not above drugging people if she does it to her own son and doesn't give a shit."

"It's for his own good," I said. "Because he won't take it himself."

"Yeah, whatever, I'm sure she thought *this* was for your own good too." He scowled.

I took pity on him since he did seem genuinely upset. "I don't think she drugged me," I said. "She has no reason to drug me. But I'll be careful from now on, okay?"

He looked up then, catching my eyes with his and not speaking for a moment before he sighed. "Okay."

"Dude." I kept my voice low so Chad wouldn't hear it and come ask what was going on. "I'm fine. And besides, even if Aunt Greta *did* drug me, she wouldn't have wanted to *hurt* me. So I'm fine. Promise."

Chris just nodded. The silence stretched for a few seconds, then he cleared his throat and asked, "Is this your room?"

I glanced around even though I knew exactly how it looked. Grandma had tidied it up after I moved out, of course, and changed the curtains and the bedspread. But the room was essentially the same as it had been when I was living here. Framed pictures of me and my high school friends were still on the wall. There was still a black fake leather beanbag chair and my telephone shaped like the starship *Enterprise*. It was still my room, just not a sacred untouched shrine to my former self. I liked that about it.

"Yeah," I said after I realized I hadn't answered him. "This is where I grew up."

"I'm guessing that's your phone and not your grandma's." His voice was a bit uncertain, but it was gaining back his usual note of bravado. Slowly.

"Hey, you don't know," I said. "Grandma was a huge fan of Shatner-era *Trek*."

"I'm sure she was," he said with what was clearly an involuntary smile.

I swung my legs off of the side of the bed. "I guess I should go back downstairs." I pushed myself to my feet and swayed just a little before finding my balance.

Chris stood and walked over to me. He touched his fingers to my forehead in a "let me see if you're feverish" gesture, which was weird because of the total lack of tactile sensation that came along with it.

"Can you tell if I'm feverish?" I asked.

"No," he said, frowning. "I'll have to take your word that you're not."

"I don't feel feverish," I said. "But I promise to tell you if I start feeling sick."

"Deal," he said, then seemed to notice how close he was standing. He backed up, looking down at the floor again.

I started to say something (maybe his name? Hell if I know), even getting so far as to open my mouth, then decided against it and closed my lips again.

There was a quiet knock at the door. "Tyler?" It was Chad's voice.

Chris snapped his eyes over to the door and glared at it.

"Yeah, come in," I called.

Chad slowly opened the door, hesitated for a second, then shuffled inside and closed the door behind himself. He looked furtively around the room as if to make sure no one else was there, then took a few steps closer to me. "Did it help?" he whispered.

Chris let out a sound that was almost a growl, and I nearly turned to look at him before I caught myself. I smiled at Chad. "Did what help? I just took a nap."

"No you didn't," Chad said. "The meds make you sleepy and unfocused and that's why I walk and talk like I do. But did it help?"

"The meds," I repeated. "Chad, did you put something in my food?"

He had the decency to appear ashamed of himself. "Yes," he said after a moment. "I saw you talking and you looked like I used to look before I learned to stop talking and I thought it would help. Did it help? It doesn't help me. But did it help you?"

"I don't know what you mean," I said, starting to get a little freaked out.

"*I* know what he means," Chris growled. "And I'm going to strangle him."

"Shut up," Chad said, pointing straight at Chris. "You're not real and you're just confusing him, so shut up before he gets like me."

My mouth dropped open, and it took me a few seconds to remember how to close it again.

Chris looked just as surprised as I felt. He crossed his arms. "You can see me?"

"Yes," Chad mumbled. "Not that it matters since you're not real."

I snapped my eyes back and forth between them. "This is . . ." There didn't really seem to be an appropriate ending to that sentence.

Chris came up with one, though. "Bullshit. This is bullshit."

"Um . . ." I let a nervous laugh bubble up. "I was going to say something more like 'weird' or 'unusual,' but okay."

"No, it's bullshit," Chris insisted. "If he can see me and he can hear me, then he *knows* you're not crazy, but he still spiked your green beans with antipsychotic medications that are prescription strength for a *reason*."

Chad shrugged. "I was trying to help."

"Well, stop trying," Chris shouted. "You could have killed him!"

"Whoa, whoa, let's take a step back, guys," I said. "No sense yelling and getting flustered and making me pull out the salt gun."

"That wouldn't work anyway," Chad said. "Tried it. I've tried everything. I even ordered some special powdered jungle root and tried rubbing it on the soles of my feet during a quarter crescent moon. Nothing works."

I frowned. "Not even the clozapine?"

He crossed his arms over his stomach as if to hold his insides in. "Especially not the clozapine. But Mom keeps giving it to me and like I said earlier, if I stop taking it, then they'll throw me in a psych ward. So I pretend to take it and then I pretend that it's helping. And I just . . . try not to talk to anyone unless I'm sure they're actually there."

"That stuff is serious, though, man," I said to him. "I mean, I only had one dose and it knocked me out faster than a heavyweight boxer."

"I know." He sighed. "Believe me, I know."

Chris pointed at him. "Look, I'm not sympathizing with you after you tried to kill my ride."

"I didn't try to kill him," Chad said. "Just to make him stop seeing you."

Chris glared. "Fine. But still. You stay the hell away from Tyler."

Chad ignored him and instead focused on me. "You think you can see him, I guess," he said, the tiniest sigh escaping his lips after the words. "But . . . can you see others?"

"Other than Chris?" I shook my head. "No, just him. Are there others?"

"Oh yes," Chad said. "Hundreds. Thousands. I mean . . ." He shifted. "They're not *that* common, really. They're not just *everywhere*. But they're common enough that I'm not surprised when I see one." He shrugged, averting his eyes. "I didn't really expect to see one at Christmas dinner, though."

"Well, let me introduce you," I said, then half turned toward Chris before Chad yelled, "No!"

I turned back to him with my eyebrows raised. "No?"

"No," he said, shaking his head emphatically. "If you talk to them, then they become more real in your head and then it gets harder to convince yourself that they're not there."

I peered at Chris. ". . . but he *is* here."

"He's not," Chad insisted. "He's just a product of your mind, okay? He's not real. He's not there. You're imagining him."

I glanced at Chad, then looked back at Chris, then at Chad again. ". . . but he's here."

"No!" Chad said, raising his voice again.

"Shhh, dude." I lifted a finger to my lips. "Do you want Uncle Tim to come running up here to check on us?"

Chad crossed his arms. "I'm just trying to keep you from becoming like me, okay?"

"I get that, Chad, I really do," I said. "And I appreciate the thought, but . . . if Chris wasn't actually here, then how would we both be seeing him? The same guy? And hearing him say the same things."

Chad slid his arms down to wrap around his own stomach again. "I don't know what that means. But I know he's not real."

I thought about Chad for a moment, trapped in a world where everyone said he was crazy. That could have been me, if Chris had happened earlier. When I was still learning reality from imagination as a kid. It made me have a little more sympathy for the guy. "Can I ask you a few questions, Chad?"

Chad didn't look particularly happy about it, but he nodded.

"Do you have someone like Chris?" I asked. "Someone attached to you?"

Chad's eyes darted around the room, and for a moment I wasn't sure he was going to answer.

"I did," he said after a long time. "She's gone now. And then there was another one but he's gone too."

"Who were they?" I asked.

"Nana. Dad's mom. She was with me for a long time and then she wasn't. When she left I started to see more of them. Then I found Lucas and he stayed with me for a while, but I never stopped seeing the rest of them. And then Lucas left. And now I'm alone. But it's easier this way because I just pretend like I don't see the others and they leave me alone and I can almost act normal sometimes."

Chris and I exchanged a glance, then Chris cleared his throat. "You said they left. How did they leave? Where did they go?"

"I don't know where they went," Chad said, staring down at the floor and catching his bottom lip in his teeth before continuing. "They just disappeared. Maybe my meds kicked in or something. Who knows."

"Okay," I said. "Well, let's pretend for a second that they were real. Where do you think they went?"

He shifted on his feet. "Heaven, I guess. I don't know. Lucas didn't think he was going to heaven since he was a suicide. But I don't know what happened after they left, only that they were gone." He met my eyes for a second and then looked away again. "Not that I'm saying that they're real. But if they were."

I nodded. "Okay. Fair enough. But how did they leave?"

He shrugged. "I guess they just didn't want to be here anymore. They finished what they wanted to do and then they left."

"So . . ." I waved my hand at Chris. "Unfinished business, then?"

"I guess," Chad said. "I have to go. I'm sorry. I need to go lie down."

I wanted to make him stay, to keep asking him questions, but he suddenly looked so bone-tired that I couldn't bring myself to stop him. "Okay, buddy. You go nap and we'll talk more later."

Chad nodded and stumbled out of the room, tripping over his own feet and moving like he was already at least sixty percent asleep.

Chris watched him leave, then faced me. "That shit's messed up."

"Yeah," I agreed, yawning. "But that makes a lot of sense, I guess. Poor guy."

"Poor guy?" Chris said, scoffing. "He drugged you."

I glared at him. "You have no sympathy for your fellow man."

"I have sympathy for people who don't drug other people," he grumbled.

"You know, for a guy who did so many drugs he died from it, you're awfully judgmental about this whole drugging thing."

He tensed up and glared daggers at me. "That is *totally* different."

And it was, of course. I knew it was. So I relented. "Yeah. I know. I'm sorry."

"Will I ever be more than just a walking syringe to you?" he asked, anger tinting his voice. "I mean, really? Will you ever let go of that?"

"Why didn't *you* let go of it?" I shot back. "All the people you loved told you that you should stop before you hurt yourself. They begged you to do it. And you didn't stop because *why*?"

He worked his jaw a little. "Because it's my life and they don't control me."

"Well, I guess you showed them," I said bitterly.

"It wasn't like that."

I shrugged. "Whatever. You just tell yourself that none of it was about you being a selfish prick."

"*Everything* was about me being a selfish prick." He turned away from me and started pacing, his hand tugging at his hair while he walked. "And by the way, my sister and Eric told me that all the time. If you think you're being original, you're not. And I did it because I could, okay? Because it was something I could do. Something I could choose for myself that didn't depend on anybody else giving me permission. Something that my sister could hate me for that made sense because *I* hated myself for it. And it was a way to show Eric he didn't control me."

I watched him for a few seconds. "It was still selfish."

"I know," he ground out. "That was the point."

Silence fell, and it wasn't the companionable silence we'd started enjoying recently. It stretched on for so long that I physically *had* to move, so I crossed and then uncrossed my arms.

"I'm sorry," I said at last. It wasn't enough, but I couldn't think of anything else to say.

After another long pause, Chris shrugged and looked away. "I just want to stop talking about it. I want to be myself again and since I don't *need* the heroin as a ghost, I can be. But I need you to stop harping on my drug use. I need to be more than just a junkie to you."

"Why to me?"

"Who else is there?" he said back. "I mean, no offense, but you're literally all I have in the world. It's in my best interest to be friends with you."

There was yet another moment of even more awkward silence. "It's just hard to get past it."

"Well, it's not like I'm *proud* of it," he grumbled.

I let out a long breath through my nose. "You sound proud. Talking about how it gave you control and talking about how you used it as a big fuck-you to Eric and to your family."

"I'm *not* proud of it," he said. "I was selfish and I was vindictive and I was just a giant douche to everyone who knew me, and I hated myself for how I was acting. I'm not making excuses or expecting you to understand it or to agree with my reasons. I'm just telling you . . . why."

". . . Okay."

He sighed. "And besides, this is why I need to go talk to Eric and to Allison before I can move on. I need to tell them why. To let them know why I did it and how bad I feel about it."

"What about your mom?" I asked. "Are you going to apologize to her, too?"

He shook his head. "She doesn't know."

"Really? Everybody knew. It was common knowledge."

"Yeah, well, not to my mom." He kicked at a nonexistent rock on the floor and watched his own foot move. "She has early-onset Alzheimer's. She—" He broke off, then continued a few seconds later. "She thinks I'm twelve. She thinks Dad is still alive. She doesn't know and even if I told her, even if I came totally clean about everything, she'd forget it the next day."

"Oh." I wrinkled my nose and squinted up at him. "I'm sorry."

"I'm not," he said, quickly. "She'd be so hurt if she knew. So it's better that she doesn't."

I nodded while I processed that. Dead father, amnesiac mother, sister who hates him. Maybe my messed-up family with the absent mother and the psychotic cousin was actually better in comparison. "I get that. But . . . you should still see her. Tell her good-bye."

"She won't remember it," he said again. "I thought about going to see her, but it won't matter. She won't remember."

"But you will," I pointed out. "And really, maybe moving on is about *you* saying good-bye rather than the living people saying it. We could go stand over your grave and get our closure, but this is your only chance."

"I guess that makes sense," he said, but he didn't continue the conversation and I didn't particularly want to keep talking about it myself, so I let it go.

"Okay, enough fighting," I said. "Let's just get through the rest of Christmas and then go home. I'll see if Richard will let me put in some extra shifts and maybe I'll be able to get a cheap red-eye flight or something before too long."

He offered me a small smile. "Thanks for doing all this for me."

"Yeah, yeah, you don't deserve it." But I smiled back, and he seemed comfortable with that.

CHAPTER SIXTEEN

The rest of Christmas passed uneventfully. My mother didn't show up, and Grandma gave me a new coat and an envelope that she made me promise not to open until I got home. Chris stayed grumpier than usual and kept Chad well in his sights at all times, but in general it was a nice holiday. Grandma begged me to stay over, so I did, and it was only slightly awkward to go to sleep knowing that a rock star was going to spend all night sifting through the weird shit that Teenage Tyler had been into back in high school.

Chris was his old self on the train ride back home the next morning, gleefully jumping through people and climbing under the bottom of the train to see the tracks rushing along underneath us. It was still reasonably warm for Boston in late December when we got back, so I stuffed my gloves in my coat pocket and walked home a little more slowly than usual, taking in the sunshine.

Chris seemed to enjoy it as well. I wondered if he'd get used to being out in the sunlight or if it would always seem strange to him after his rock star routine.

"So," he said as we walked along the red brick line in the pavement that marked the Freedom Trail. It wasn't strictly on our way home—actually, it wasn't on the way home at all, if you wanted to be honest about it—but there was some human interest in watching the tourists taking pictures and pretending to knock on Paul Revere's door. "Do you like it here? In Boston?"

I paused to let a group of tourists get farther ahead of us so that they wouldn't hear me. "Yeah. I love it here. It's my spirit city."

Chris looked over at me. "Your spirit city?"

"Yeah," I said. "You know, sometimes where you are is just a place where, you know, you are. Or a place you grew up. And you like it okay, or you hate it, or whatever. And then you go somewhere else and suddenly you have this rush of *home* from it, even if you've never been there before. You feel the rhythm of the place and it seems like . . ." I thought for a moment, but couldn't come up with another way to say it. I shrugged. "Well, it seems like home."

"I can understand that, I guess."

"Haven't you ever felt like that? You've traveled all over the world. Surely there was someplace that felt right to you."

He seemed lost in his own mind for a few seconds. "Denver."

I raised an eyebrow at him. "Denver?"

"Yeah," he said. "First time we did a show there. When we were leaving, I made Brent give me the window seat because I wanted to watch while we flew away from it. That was about the only time I really wished we had a few days between gigs."

"Seriously?" I asked. "Denver?"

He glared at me. "What's wrong with Denver?"

"Nothing," I assured him. "I just thought . . . you've traveled the entire world and instead of choosing, like, Paris or Moscow or Bora Bora, you pick Denver."

He shrugged. "You asked me if anywhere felt right. Denver felt right."

"Okay," I said. "Sounds legit."

He looked away. "But I never wanted to *move* there. It was just a really great city."

"I knew the minute I stepped out of the car here," I said. "Granted, I thought what I was feeling a connection to was Harvard. But turns out it was the city in general."

"You went to Harvard?" he asked, sounding surprised enough that it sort of annoyed me.

"No," I said, then decided to brag a little. "But I got accepted to it."

He stopped walking and stared at me. "You got accepted to Harvard and you didn't go?"

Which was a perfectly normal follow-up question to what I'd said, but somehow I hadn't expected it and it just annoyed me more. I shrugged my shoulders and avoided his gaze. "I got a full ride to Emerson. And Grandma said she'd figure out some way to pay for me to go to Harvard if I got in, but I couldn't ask her for that. They probably would have worked with me on the tuition and if I hadn't had a full scholarship somewhere else I could have figured it out, but . . ." I shrugged again. "It seemed selfish to make her struggle to help me pay when I could go somewhere else for free. And they had a pretty cool degree in political communication and social advocacy that I was really interested in, so I signed up."

"So . . . wait. You're not in school now?" He crossed his arms. "You haven't been skipping class to work, have you?"

"No," I said, frowning. "I'm not in school. I did four semesters and then I just . . . never registered for more classes."

"You gave up a full-ride scholarship."

"Yes."

"You had a full-ride scholarship and you gave it up."

"You already said that," I pointed out.

"*Why?*"

I wrapped my arms across my chest. "Grandma went to the doctor, and they said it was cancer. They did like a thousand tests on her and found out that the tumor was benign, so they just removed it and she was fine. But the time between when the doctor first said the *c*-word and when they said she was going to be okay was, you know, stressful. And I missed my registration date because I was pacing outside the surgery unit, and then when I went to register, this one class I really needed was full. The professor said he'd put me on the waiting list, but I didn't get in because nobody dropped. So I figured I'd sit out a semester and then go back in the spring. And then I didn't."

"Why not?"

"I don't know," I said. "Because just working was the path of least resistance, I guess."

"You bitch constantly about how poor you are," he said. "I mean, *constantly*. And you just walked out on college because you didn't feel like getting your ass to the registrar's office?"

"It wasn't like that," I snapped. "I always intended to go back. It wasn't a conscious decision. It just . . . never happened."

"I see," he said, then angled his body away and started walking again. I trailed along behind him for a while, feeling pretty ashamed of myself, before he slowed down his pace significantly to let me catch up with him.

"So anyway," he said, way too brightly, "do you want to see what Evie Tellerman looks like naked?"

I raised both eyebrows at him. "You have nude pics of Evie Tellerman?"

"Nude *video*," he corrected. "Of me boning her."

My mouth dropped open. "You're shitting me."

He grinned. "Not kidding. Of course, this was before she got her Oscar. She was less pretentious back then."

"You boned Evie Tellerman."

"*Hard*," he said, still smirking. "And I know, pics or it didn't happen, so I'll show you the pics."

I thought for a minute. "Isn't that, you know, unethical? Showing me video of her without her permission?"

He shrugged. "She knew I was videotaping it. And she told me not to sell it to the paparazzi or leak it online or give it to the media. She never said I couldn't show my friends."

"That seems . . ." I thought about it. "I don't know. Still seems skeevy."

"The way I see it, since it's only you, it's basically personal use," he argued. "And besides, I know you won't leak it."

"How do you know that?"

"Because you could have taken pictures of my corpse and gotten reasonably rich off of selling them," he pointed out, "and you didn't."

"That's true, I guess."

"So if you promise me you won't let the videos get out, I'll show you."

I probably should have said no, but curiosity apparently kills both cats and bellboys, so instead I just nodded. "I promise."

"All right." He waved in the direction of my apartment with a flourish. "Then let's get home."

I walked a lot more quickly after that. Chris was practically bouncing on his heels as we walked, and I was alternately turned on by the thought of seeing an A-list actress doing the horizontal tango and weirded out that it was *Chris* she was going to be doing it with.

When we got back to my apartment, I made Chris wait while I changed into lounging-around-the-house clothes and fixed myself a glass of water, mostly because I enjoyed listening to him whine about how slow I was going. Then I settled myself on the couch with my laptop in my lap and pulled up my internet browser.

He gave me the website, and I typed it into the address bar. It was one of those mass cloud storage sites where you could upload your files and access them from anywhere. I clicked on the username box and Chris told me what to type.

"I still can't believe you saved your porn stash on the internet," I told him as the page loaded.

He rolled his eyes. "It's not *just* porn. It started out as nonsexy pictures and things I was writing. I only put the porn in there later, when I got paranoid that people would steal my computer."

"So you uploaded it to the hackable internet," I said as I typed in the password.

"It seemed like a good idea at the time," he grumbled. "Anyway, it's good for you that I did. Because you wouldn't be able to see it if I hadn't." He motioned at the screen. "It's the Vids folder."

I opened the folder. There were a good many videos in the file, all titled with initials and dates. He pointed to one about halfway down the list. The file name was "CR_ET_091611." I opened it.

The video was of decent quality, but it was obviously a home video. It started out with the usual amateur porn Awkward Talking About How We're Going to Bone. I slid the time bar ahead, and Chris and Evie went from Awkward Talking to bed-shaking sex immediately.

"Wow," I said. "I mean . . . wow." I tilted my head at the screen.

"She was fantastic," he breathed. "I mean, really amazing."

"She's so . . ." I tilted my head even more as if that would let me get a better angle on the scene. "Flexible."

"Wait until you see the part where she sits on my dick and spins around," he said, smirking. "I thought my head was going to explode."

And sure enough, after a few more seconds, they switched positions and she started bouncing up and down on his cock, then did something with her legs that made her spin around on him. It seemed like a move that you shouldn't try at home, at least not without a spotter and some sort of pulley system, but she made it seem graceful. Well, as graceful as sex ever is.

"Get a load of those tits," Chris said, sighing softly. "They tasted like apples. She had some edible body butter or something on."

"Jesus, dude," I said. "I know you told me this was a sex tape of you and Evie Tellerman, but . . . this is a sex tape of you and Evie Tellerman."

"Sure is," he said, beaming and looking ridiculously proud of himself.

"Who else do you have?" I said, closing the screen and going back to the file list.

He scanned over the list and then pointed at "CR_VN_070111." I clicked on it.

"Oh my God," I said. "Is that Valerie Nobles?"

"Sure is," he crowed. "I didn't actually fuck her, but she spends like half an hour deep-throating me. It was mind-blowing. Here, skip forward a little." He pointed to a spot on the time slider, and I moved the video there.

Valerie was deeply involved in the cocksucking by that time. Video-Chris had his head thrown back and his hands tangled in her hair. The noises he was making were . . . well, very interesting. I glanced over at him without even meaning to.

"Don't watch *me*," he said, not making eye contact. "Watch the video."

I turned my eyes back to the screen. Valerie pulled her mouth off of Chris's cock to lick the tip of it, which made us both shiver and made Video-Chris moan loudly.

I cleared my throat. "I've jacked it to her before."

"Yeah, me too." Chris's voice was a little gravelly, but as per the Bro Code of watching porn with other dudes, I very tactfully didn't mention it. "And I have since, actually."

I laughed at that, the sound coming out almost as much a gasp as a chuckle. "I can definitely understand."

Chris—the one sitting on my couch—was hard by that point, which answered the question I'd never asked myself about whether or not ghosts could get erections. But the Bro Code covered that too, so I didn't say anything. After all, the only thing keeping my own interest from being totally obvious was the laptop pinning me down.

But still, I had to ask. "So . . . can you jack it now?"

He turned to me, eyebrows raised. "You want me to jerk off on your couch?"

"No," I said quickly. "I just mean . . . can you? As in, do you have the ability to, or are you just . . . stuck?"

He looked down at himself, and my own eyes flicked to his pants before I caught myself in total violation of the Code and snapped my eyes back to the screen.

"I don't know," he said after a moment. "I haven't tried it, surprisingly enough. I mean, I can feel it when I touch my arms or my hair or things. So I guess I can?" He chuckled, a little breathily. "Doesn't seem like the most prudent time to try it, though. I'll report back later."

"Deal," I said. "It doesn't really matter. I was just curious."

He laughed again at the same time as Video-Chris started vocally encouraging Valerie to go faster and take him in deeper. My dick twitched at that, and I told myself it was totally in response to Valerie.

I clicked away from the video quickly.

Chris gave a tiny whimper. "Why'd you click away? It was almost over."

"I don't really want to see a money shot from a guy who's sitting right beside me," I explained. "That shit's awkward, bro."

"Fair enough," he said, "but you might have to excuse me to the bathroom if you keep doing that."

I laughed nervously. "Yeah, we might have to do that anyway." He gave me a strange look, so I tried to clarify. "Seeing these A-list chicks naked would give a hard-on to a monk."

He rolled his eyes. "You must not watch much porn."

"As much as the next guy, I guess," I said. "But usually it doesn't star people like this." I scanned the list. "Who's G. S.?"

"Who?" He peered at the list, then rushed into a dismissal. "Oh, nobody. Just a groupie. Why don't you click on the M. R. one? That's somebody you'd know."

I hovered my mouse over the M. R. file, then glanced back up at the G. S. one. "If it's just a groupie, then why would you care if I clicked on it?"

He frowned. "It's boring. You'd hate it. I should have deleted that one before, actually."

"Uh-huh." I moved my mouse back up to CR_GS_080410.

"Don't you dare, Tyler," Chris said. His boner had totally gone away, not that I noticed.

"Well, now you've got me curious," I said, grinning.

"I mean it," he growled. "Just step away from the file."

"Yeah, dude, there's no way I'm not clicking on it now." I clicked on the file and immediately slid the timer about halfway into the video, then pressed Play.

CHAPTER
SEVENTEEN

"Oh," I said, tilting my head at the screen like that was going to help me process the video any better. "That's ... unexpected."

Chris stood up and punched the wall, which did nothing to either damage my apartment or his fist since his hand went right through.

I cleared my throat again since it suddenly felt extra tight. "That's ... a cock."

"Thank you, Sherlock," he snapped. "Close the fucking video."

I started to say *That cock is in your ass*, but that seemed excessively obvious. Instead I just peered at the man who was pounding Chris doggy-style. "Holy shit, is that Gabriel Sinclair?"

"Yes," he grumbled, then sat back down and ground his teeth. "Clearly."

"You boned Gabriel Sinclair," I said, just for clarification's sake. "Well, I mean, he boned you. I guess."

He gave me a hostile glare, crossing his arms tightly over his chest. "Are you going to be a fuck-wad about this?"

"Probably, yeah," I said. "But I mean, do what you gotta do, man. Or who you gotta do. Just know that I'll rag you about it."

"Shut up," he snapped. "You're just making this even more awkward."

I looked at the screen again. Gabriel had his nails dug into Chris's hips and was holding him in place while he fucked him, fairly slowly but apparently pretty hard. Video-Chris had his eyes closed and was moaning with each thrust, trying to rock his hips back to take Gabriel even deeper. "You . . ."

"I told you not to watch it," he said petulantly. "Now close it and we can pretend it never happened."

"You're, um, gay?" Video-Chris clenched his hands in the sheets and moaned louder. Gabriel was muttering meaningless sex things about tightness and God, and my own cock started pressing hard against the bottom of the laptop.

"No," he muttered. "And that's exactly why I never told anybody. You tell anybody that you like getting fucked in the ass and they assume that's *all* you like. And I do like girls. A lot."

"Okay." I moved my hips slightly to try to take the computer's weight off of my boner. "So bisexual, then?"

"Yeah," he answered. "I mean, clearly." He motioned vaguely at the screen but didn't look at it.

"There's no shame in that."

"I know there's not. But the entertainment industry disagrees with us."

"So . . . you fucked your girlfriend's brother," I said.

"Shut your mouth," he said. "Me and Tori . . . we were in an off-again phase at that point. And anyway, Gabe and I were just fooling around. It didn't mean anything."

Gabriel was speeding up his thrusts now, the steady rhythm he'd been following earlier starting to stutter and become irregular. He looked down at the place where their bodies joined and groaned, and I couldn't help but imagine what it would look like, what it would *feel* like.

Chris was watching the screen again, apparently encouraged by the fact that I hadn't tried to lynch him for being a homosexual yet. "He was, um, pretty good too," he said, softly.

I gave a breathy little chuckle. "I can tell."

Gabriel slammed into Chris and clenched his eyes shut, then came so hard you could see his whole body twitch. Video-Chris yelled out and shifted his weight onto one hand so he could reach down and jack himself with the other.

"You might want to click away," Chris said, his voice sort of raw. "If seeing me jizz would be weird for you."

"I can handle it," I said, my eyes glued to the screen. Somewhere far in the back of my mind, a warning bell went. I ignored that bell.

Gabriel started to pull out, but Video-Chris slammed his hips back. "Stay in," he moaned. "Just another second, I'm so fucking close . . ."

Gabriel whimpered and pushed his already softening cock back into Chris, who groaned loudly and then started coming onto the bedsheets. The arm that was holding him up gave out and his face hit the bed, which only muffled the moaning a little bit. Gabriel held himself inside until Chris went limp, then pulled out and flipped Chris over onto his back. He climbed up over him and kissed him deeply, pressing their bodies together.

I did click away then. "Um . . ."

Chris picked at a thread that had come loose on the couch. He didn't say anything.

My cock was straining against my pants, and even the slight friction of moving the laptop off of it sent a spike of energy through my body. "Um . . ." I said again, then put the computer onto the cushion beside me and stood. "Two minutes."

Chris glanced up at me, searching my face, then let his eyes slide down to my obvious tent, which was completely and unambiguously against the Bro Code, but we seemed pretty far past that at this point. I gave him an embarrassed smile, and he nodded.

I practically ran to the bathroom. It didn't take anywhere near two minutes.

When I came back out into the living room, Chris had regained some of his composure. "So," he said. "You're bi, too? I mean, I don't know your life or anything, but you did just jerk off to gay porn, so I figure you're at least bi-curious."

I shrugged and plopped down onto the couch. "I guess so."

"Have you ever, you know . . ." He waved his hand unhelpfully in the air.

"Fucked a dude?" I finished for him. "No, I haven't. I mean, I've made out with a couple of them. But we didn't get past second base."

He whistled. "I figured you for a straight guy."

"Yeah," I allowed. "I mean, I guess I'm mostly straight. Like eighty percent of the people I'm attracted to are women. But there's the occasional dude who gets me going."

"Like Gabriel Sinclair, apparently." He gave me a lopsided smile.

It wasn't Gabriel who had gotten my dick so hard, but I wasn't going to tell *Chris* that. Especially since I hadn't quite worked out if it was Chris himself I'd been turned on by or just, you know, sitting there watching porn. After all, when I was watching the videos of him with Evie and Valerie, I was mostly watching the boobs. So maybe it wasn't Chris. Maybe I was just horny.

But still, the sounds Chris had been making and the way my cock had responded when he came . . . it hadn't *not* turned me on. That much was absolutely certain.

I realized I hadn't answered him. "I guess he's attractive enough. I hadn't really ever thought about him like that before." Which was true. I wasn't a huge fan of the guy's band—they were too sentimental to be real *rock*—and so I really hadn't given him much thought at all, even in a nonsexual way.

"He's a pretty good fuck," Chris said. "I've done him too. I'm not just a bottom."

I shrugged. "Wouldn't really matter if you were. I don't judge."

Chris raised an eyebrow and gave me a "bitch, please" look.

I laughed. "Well, okay, I totally judge. But not because I'm not cool with you being whatever you want to be. Just because I like messing with you."

"Well," he said, "that's appreciated."

"You're welcome," I said. "See, we can be civil to each other."

He smiled, and I smiled back, and then neither of us said anything for a little while.

"This feels like awkward after-sex talk," he said. "I feel like I should be putting my pants back on and promising I'd call you."

I rolled my eyes. "You wouldn't call."

"I did sometimes," he said. "I mean, not for the groupies unless they were *really* amazing. But for the ones I knew outside of bed, I usually called."

"How very chivalrous of you," I said, then motioned vaguely at his crotch while making absolutely sure not to look where I was pointing. "Do you need a turn in the bathroom?"

"Nah," he said, looking a little sheepish. "Turns out ghosts can jerk off after all."

"Dude, you jerked off *on my couch*?"

"Don't worry," he said. "Apparently ghost spunk disappears after it leaves my body."

My eyes widened a little bit without my permission. "It does?"

"Well, it glowed blue on the couch for a few seconds, but yeah, it disappeared," he said. "And it's a good thing, too, because I wasn't sure how I was going to clean it up if it didn't."

"I am *not* cleaning ghost jizz off of my furniture," I said. "So yeah, you're very lucky it went away."

After seeing the video, I didn't have any trouble picturing what Chris would look like when he came. That thought was both incredibly weird and pretty exciting. I focused on the weird.

"So did you and Eric . . ." I trailed off intentionally, motioning at the computer.

"No," he said, after a very interesting beat of silence. "No, we never did."

"That doesn't sound especially convincing."

He frowned. "Well, we didn't. We didn't do anything. We didn't even kiss. Eric is hella straight, I guess. At least he never gave me any indication that he wasn't."

"Did he know about you?" I asked.

"Yeah," Chris said, then ran a hand through his hair. "I came out to him when I was sixteen, after I'd had my first gay experience. And once we'd made it big, I wasn't that discreet. It's a miracle none of the gossip channels ever got wind of it. There was one time that I'm pretty sure I fucked a roadie in my dressing room without even closing the door."

"Wow," I said, because that was the only response I could think of.

"That one's not on tape, though," he pointed out. "I don't have very many from when I was high. The camera seemed too complicated to fuck with then." He paused, tilted his head. "I was always careful, though. You know. With protection."

"I see." I sighed and leaned against the back of the couch, gazing up at the ceiling. I was tired of talking about his drug habit, so I wanted to change the subject, but things seemed a little . . . soft. Fuzzy around the edges in the way that only a good orgasm can cause. And he was right: it felt like the two of us had actually fucked. There's something not entirely platonic about two dudes coming at the same time after watching the same porn, even if they're in different rooms when it happens.

So instead of changing the subject, what I said was: "Would you want to fuck me if you could?"

Which was dumb. I knew that the minute I said it. But it was too late by then.

Instead of answering immediately, he looked up at the ceiling too and seemed to consider the question, which was even more awkward than the quick, embarrassed stammering I'd expected. "Yeah," he said. "I mean, probably. I'm kind of a slut."

I nodded slowly. "Cool," I said. "I was just curious."

"Do you bottom?" he asked. "Or would you want to top? I'm just trying to imagine it here."

I blushed and hoped he didn't notice it. "I told you I've never had sex with a guy."

"Well, yeah," he said. "But . . . you've thought about it, right?"

I nodded again. "I mean . . . I guess you never know what you'll like until you try it. But I'd be willing to give bottoming the old college try."

He stared at me for a long time before he spoke again. "I wonder if I could kiss you."

My cock gave an exhausted twitch at that, but something in my throat tightened and I shook my head. "Don't," I said. "It doesn't feel right. Not after . . ." I motioned at the computer. "Not after that. It would just complicate things. If it even worked."

He sat back in his seat, which made me realize that he'd been leaning forward since he'd asked if I would bottom for him. I could feel every centimeter of the distance between us, and it made me strangely unhappy.

Chris bit his bottom lip for a moment. "You're right. I only thought about it because it's been a while since I've had sex."

I let out an awkward chuckle. "Me too, man. I mean, it's not like I can really have sex with you in the room with me. I'm not into exhibitionism."

"You could, you know," he said. "I mean, I'd wait outside. I don't want to totally ruin your life. We can work out a sock system or something."

"Thanks," I said. "But I'm sort of shit at picking up chicks. It was a miracle I got Carmen."

"You've been doing pretty well with Gemma so far," he pointed out.

I thought of Gemma then, with her pretty wavy hair and her sarcastic smile. With a heaping dose of luck, I could probably talk her into bed with me if I really wanted to. But now there was Chris, who complicated things even when he wasn't watching my lips and possibly mapping how his might fit against them.

I shrugged. "I don't know. She's nice and she's hot and all, but I don't really want a relationship and I doubt she'd fuck me without one."

He nodded. "You're right. She did seem like the type who doesn't bone indiscriminately."

"Yeah," I said. "But still, thanks. I might take you up on your offer to wait outside sometime."

"No problem."

"So . . ." I said, "do you want to watch more *Supernatural*?"

He shot me a disbelieving look. "You said you'd rather have your earlobes eaten off by rats than watch that show ever again."

"I only said that after you'd forced me to binge-watch it for days," I told him. "And since I've had a little time off, I could be convinced to watch a few more episodes."

Chris sat there for a few seconds with an odd look on his face, like he was holding back. Then he smiled a huge smile. "Let's watch it."

I fished the remote out from between the couch cushions and started up the show, but I fell asleep on the couch in the middle of an episode. I think I woke up again partway through the next one, with Chris sitting very close to my side and his arm around my shoulders, which were tingling with the not-quite-weight and not-quite-warmth of his arm. At least I thought they were. Maybe all of that was a dream, though.

When I woke up the next morning, I was still sitting on the couch, but at some point during the night I had curled up against the armrest to use it as a pillow. Chris was watching some vapid-sounding show that seemed to follow the lives of several college-aged girls who lived on a ranch and had aspirations to become country singers.

"What the hell are you watching?" I asked, rubbing my eyes.

"It's called *The Meadow Larks*, and it's the dumbest thing I've ever watched in my life," he said, not taking his gaze off the screen.

"And yet you're watching it." I sat up and tried to stretch my cramped muscles.

"Well, your streaming service timed out and went back to TV when I ran out of *Supernatural* episodes, and I couldn't change the channel, so I was stuck with this. And it's a marathon too, so I've been watching for a while," he said. "Except now I'm *involved* in this ridiculous thing, so shut up so I can see if Martha chokes during her big moment."

I peered at the screen. "Are they at a rodeo?"

"Yeah," he said. "And Tina was supposed to sing the national anthem but she got kicked in the throat by an angry sheep and she's in the hospital recovering, so Martha has to sing it, except she's terrified of the high note, so everybody thinks she's going to bomb spectacularly. And Kelly just found out that there are talent scouts in the audience—"

"Wait," I interrupted. "There are music scouts in the audience of a rodeo?"

"Yes. And so Martha—"

"Why?"

He glared at me. "Why what?"

"Why are there music scouts in the audience at a rodeo?" I repeated. "I mean, what do they think they're going to do there?"

"Well, somebody has to sing the national anthem," Chris said. "It's a rule or something."

"So some big-time music scouts flew all the way out to Indiana to watch this one chick sing the national anthem even though she may or may not be able to hit the high note?"

He gave an exasperated sigh. "First off, it's not Indiana, it's Tennessee. Second off, yeah, I guess they did. I don't write the show,

I'm just telling you what happened. And third off, shut up. I'm only interested because I was forced against my will to watch this all night long."

"Whatever," I said. "You like it."

"Shut up," he said again. "And if you're just going to talk through it, you might as well go take a shower or whatever you have to do for your morning ritual, so that you can leave me alone to finish this episode."

"A shower sounds pretty awesome, actually." I stood and stretched again, making an involuntary whimper as my muscles popped back into place with that deliciously satisfying kind of pain.

"Then go," Chris said, fluttering his hand toward the bathroom in a "hurry up" gesture. "Go go go. And be quiet. Martha's about to sing."

I rolled my eyes at him but obeyed, grabbing some clean clothes out of my dresser before going into the bathroom and starting the shower. I let the hot water soak into my skin for a long time before I started washing.

"I'm sorry I said I wanted to kiss you."

I shrieked and nearly lost my footing. "Chris! What the hell!"

"Oh," he said. "I'm also sorry I nearly scared you to death just now."

I glanced around the shower to make sure he wasn't sticking his head through the curtain or anything equally intrusive. "Well, apology accepted, but Jesus, dude. Couldn't you have waited until I got done in the bathroom instead of just barging in like some crazy-ass poltergeist?"

"I could have," he said. "But I was bored."

"You had Martha," I pointed out.

"Yeah, well, she takes this big deep breath to start singing and it goes to credits," he said, sounding very put out about the whole thing. "And wouldn't you know it? That's the last episode available. So I'm going to need you to check on when the next one airs."

"Fine, fine. I'll look it up when I get done in the shower. So if you want to know, then go away so I can finish washing."

There was silence for long enough that I thought Chris might have gone back into the living room. It was hard to tell when he didn't have audible footsteps and didn't need to open and close doors.

Then he spoke up. "I really am sorry. About last night."

I forced myself to keep washing like it was normal to be having this type of conversation. "It's cool, man."

"I'm not some creepy pervert who wants to take advantage of you," he continued. "It was just idle curiosity. Whether I could maybe touch you or somebody else or if I'm going to be flying solo forever. I didn't mean . . . I didn't want you to think I was going to do anything you didn't want me to do."

"It's cool," I repeated. "It was a weird night. No offense taken, and we can, you know, move on."

"And never speak of it again?"

I shrugged even though he couldn't see it through the shower curtain. "Not unless it becomes relevant, I guess."

"Becomes relevant how?"

Like if we started actually lusting after each other, I thought. But it didn't seem like the time to bring up that possibility, not when I wasn't sure I wanted it to happen and not when he was already so upset about possibly offending me by suggesting that we try to make out. So instead I said, "I don't know, man. I just mean we don't have to keep talking about it unless there's a reason to."

"Yeah," he said. "That seems like a good idea."

"So don't worry about it. We're cool."

Another silence, although not such a long one this time. "And you're cool that I'm bisexual and that I've boned dudes before?"

"Totally cool." I finished rinsing off and then just stood there, shifting from foot to foot. "I was just surprised, you know? I assumed you were this big ladies' man."

"I was," he insisted. "Don't you be like that too. Just because I'm into guys doesn't mean I've been lying to all the women. I just, you know, like both."

I sighed, because being bisexual myself I understood that reaction, which made me feel like kind of a tool for causing it. "I get that. That wasn't what I meant to say."

"It's cool," he said, his voice a little stronger and more confident than before.

"So, you know, you can get out of my bathroom now," I said. "Especially when I'm in it."

"Okay," he said. "But hurry up. I'm bored."

I groaned and pulled back the shower curtain a little so I could glare at him, but he was already gone.

CHAPTER EIGHTEEN

"This is stupid," Chris said. His eyes were shut but his eyebrows were raised. "You have no secrets from me. Why do I need to close my eyes?"

It had been a few days since the porn incident, and we'd managed to get past the residual weirdness. Mostly, anyway. I'd at least managed to convince myself that it would be unethical to download his sex videos to my laptop in case the site ever crashed. And I'd even done better by convincing myself there wasn't one video in particular that I'd want rescued if it did. Small victories.

"Just shut up and humor me." I faked like I was going to hit him in the stomach—not that it would have worked—and then once I was satisfied that he wasn't cheating, I walked over and picked up the box Gemma had brought by that morning.

She'd been pretty awesome helping me get the supplies, which was great since it wouldn't be much of a surprise if Chris saw me buying streamers. I'd texted her a list of what I needed while he wasn't looking, and we did a furtive drug-deal-style exchange just outside the door when she brought the box over. I didn't have a hell of a lot of money to spend on the whole thing, but it wasn't like there was much I could buy for Chris that he'd be able to use even if I'd been loaded, so this was good enough.

"How long do I have to stand here like this?" He tapped his fingers on his upper thigh and raised his eyebrows even more.

"Well," I said, tearing into a pack of royal-blue streamers, "you have to stand there with your eyes closed until I tell you to open them. But there's no time limit on how long you have to stand there scowling like a douche, so you can stop *that* whenever you feel like it." It kind of worried me how sure I was that he'd be able to hear the smile in my voice.

He snorted. "I just don't know why I can't watch whatever you're doing."

"Shut up," I told him. "It won't kill you to stop being a voyeur for, like, five minutes." I dragged my beat-up plastic stepstool out and started taping streamers to the ceiling.

"I'm bored," he whined.

"If I had a quarter for every time you've said that since I met you, I wouldn't be living in this shitty apartment." There was a banner in the box too—one of the ones that had each letter cut out in metallic cardboard and strung together. I taped that up over the TV and attached streamers to the sides of it.

After I was done streamering, I looked around the room. It wasn't going to win any party-planning awards, but it was festive enough for a low-budget affair. I pulled a stupid green party hat out of the box and put it on. "Okay, you can open your eyes now."

Chris's eyes snapped open, and he gave me bitch-face for a second before the decorations registered. "What is this?"

"Happy birthday!" I chirped, and I reached back into the supply box. There was a packet of confetti inside, and I ripped it open and threw some in the air above Chris's head. It floated down through him, and he rolled his eyes. I grabbed a plastic kazoo from the supplies and blew it at him.

"You're throwing me a birthday party," he deadpanned. "I'm dead and you're throwing me a birthday party."

"Well, I could throw you a deathday party if you'd rather, but you'll have to wait a few months for that," I told him, giving him a challenging look. "And besides, that's pretty morbid."

"We'll see how I feel once the time rolls around," he said. "What else is in the box?"

I pulled out a bag of scones and a pack of candles. I took out a raspberry scone and held it up. "I'm going to stick a candle in this and then I guess I'll have to blow it out for you. And *then* I'm going to let you watch me eat it and I'm not even going to bitch about how creepy it is."

He stared at me for a second. "Why?"

I shrugged one shoulder and tried to look nonchalant. "Because it's your birthday, dude. And I wanted to do something nice for you." It had nothing to do with the way his hair shimmered in the sunlight. Nothing at all.

He just kept staring at me, and eventually it got weird.

"What?" I asked him. I blew into the kazoo again and then felt stupid for doing it.

"Nothing," he said, shaking his head like he was trying to clear it. "I just didn't really expect a birthday party."

"Hence the term 'surprise party,'" I told him. "And anyway, it's some streamers and a scone. It's not exactly the Grammys' after-party or anything."

He laughed a little at that, which broke some of the tension. Then he smiled an almost genuine sort of smile and said, "Thanks. Really. This is . . . nice." He paused like he was thinking, so I let him think and didn't do the kazoo thing again. "It's been a while since someone was nice to me."

"Well, don't get used to it," I warned. "I like snarking at you too much to be *nice* to you. But every man ought to get a birthday scone, you know?"

"It would be better if I could actually eat it," he said, the barest hint of a whimper in his voice, "but I'll take what I can get. Will you make 'oh my God, this is so delicious' noises while you eat it?"

I raised an eyebrow. "Probably not." That sounded like a terrible idea, to make orgasm noises in front of a guy who'd started appearing in my morning-shower fantasies with alarming regularity in the last few days.

"It's my birthday, though," he whined, and he gave me puppy-dog eyes that were just completely unfair.

I waggled my finger at him. "Don't push your luck. I might take back my offer to not call you a creeper while you watch me eat it."

"Okay, okay," he said, and he was grinning, and that made my toes feel warm, which was also alarming. "You're pretty cool, you know?"

"Yeah, I'm aware." It seemed like a good time to blow the kazoo again, so I did that. "Also, I got you presents."

His eyes widened, and I considered for a second if I should give eyeliner another try before I remembered that I was a skinny blond dude and eyeliner always looked dumb on me. It didn't on him, though. He was one of the rare guys who could rock eyeliner and still look like a total badass.

It wasn't until he spoke that I realized I'd been staring. "You got me *presents?*"

"Don't get too excited," I cautioned him, but I pulled two wrapped packages out of the box and showed them to him.

"I wonder what on Earth they could be," he said, and if sarcasm was a liquid he would have ruined my couch with it.

I tried to smack him with one of the packages. "Don't be a douche. Besides, okay, they're obviously movie-shaped, but you don't know *what* movies."

"True," he said, dimple-smiling at me with one side of his mouth. "Okay, unwrap them for me. I want to see what you think I'd like."

I put one of the packages down on the couch and started unwrapping the other one, but a weird tremor of nerves went through me before I'd torn the paper enough for him to see the title. I paused. "I didn't have a lot of cash so they're just used copies. But it's the thought that counts, right?"

He nodded and met my eyes, which was definitely not going to help matters in the shower the next morning. "It's cool. I'm sure I'll love it."

"Okay." I tore the rest of the paper off and held up the case for him to see. "Ta-da! You've probably seen it before, but every rock star needs a copy of *This Is Spinal Tap*."

"I *have* seen it, but it's been a long time," he said. "It'll be cool to see it again."

"And now you have your very own copy and all you have to do to watch it is harass me until I put the disc in for you." I put the case down on the couch between us and picked up the other package. "This one I'm already regretting getting for you." I tore off the paper quickly and held it up.

Chris let out a bark of laughter and flashed me a toothy grin. "Oh my God, you got me *The Meadow Larks*."

"The complete first season," I told him. "I figured you didn't get to see the first few episodes and I thought you might like to."

"I can't believe you're going to subject yourself to this crap," he said, but he was smiling from ear to ear and my toes curled in my socks at the sight of it.

"It gives me a breather from *Supernatural*." My throat was a little tight, and I didn't try to think about why that might be. "So I guess I'll survive."

"You're awesome, Tyler," he said, meeting my eyes again.

I really should have looked away a lot sooner than I did, but my eyeballs staged a mutiny and ignored my brain's commands for a full five seconds before I finally got them back under control and wrenched them back to the box of supplies. The only other thing in it was a lighter for the candles, so I pulled that out and busied myself with putting as many candles in one of the sconces as I could. "I hope raspberry is okay," I said when it got weird that neither of us had spoken.

"Raspberry is fine," Chris said. "Hey."

I looked over at him even though I wasn't entirely sure that was the greatest idea ever. "Yeah?"

"Thank you," he said again. "Really, I mean it."

"You're welcome." I tried to put my attention back on lighting the candles, which more or less worked. Then I held up the plate with the scone on it and grinned at him. "Make a wish and I'll blow out your candles."

He rolled his eyes, but there was no real annoyance in it. "Okay," he said after a second. "Wish made. Go ahead."

I blew out his candles, making sure to get them all with one breath because I didn't want to screw the poor guy out of his birthday wish. "Ta-da!" I announced. "I hope you made a good wish, because I totally rocked that candle-blowing for you."

He shrugged. "I always make the same wish anyway. It's never come true before, so it probably won't now."

"Well, maybe it hasn't come true before because you didn't have *me* on candle duty." I pulled the candles out of the scone and held it up. "Ready?"

"Yeah." He scooted a little closer to me on the couch and leaned forward to get a good view.

I put forth a massive effort and managed not to call him a creeper for watching my mouth so intently. I *had* promised, after all. I took a bite of it and chewed slowly while he kept his eyes locked on me, and I didn't even roll my eyes when I swallowed and he watched the movement of my throat all the way down. Then he slid his gaze back up and locked eyes with me again, which was really way too much eye contact for one evening, so I got up and put *This Is Spinal Tap* in my old crappy DVD player.

When I sat back down on the couch and pressed Play, I made sure there was more distance between us than there was before, just to be safe. That didn't stop me from watching him out of the corner of my eye for the entire movie, though, and wondering how in the hell my life had gotten this complicated. And whether I was cool with that or not.

CHAPTER NINETEEN

A few days of shitty tips passed, and I'd started to get frustrated with how long the whole "saving for a plane ticket" thing was taking me. Chris was being relatively cool about the delay, but he must have been keeping a meticulous count of my income and expenses in his head because he kept updating me on my progress all the damn time, and even though flights were getting a little less expensive as the holidays ended, we were still months away from affording a ticket. Which was less of a bummer than I'd thought it would be, since I'd decided Chris was pretty cool to hang around with.

But anyway, the porn incident and the birthday party had distracted me so much that I'd almost forgotten about the envelope Grandma had given me at Christmas. I was sorting through my mail and trying to decide whether I should open my utility bill or whether I should save that bad news for another day when I came across it.

Chris was draped over my couch with his legs up on one of the couch arms while he watched a Black Sabbath documentary on TV, and the mail was doing a decent job of distracting me from how much he looked like a fucking male model, lying there with his limbs stretched out and his stupid fucking eyeliner and the way his shirt fit around his biceps like he'd had it tailored to fit them.

It had been easier to ignore this kind of bullshit when I didn't know what he looked like naked and sexed-up. I sighed and tore open the envelope from Grandma.

"Holy shit," I said, and Chris looked over at me.

"What's up, buttercup?"

I shot him a Look. "Don't call me buttercup," I told him. "But again I say . . . holy shit."

He sat up. "What's up, Mr. Lindsey?" His tone would have made me roll my eyes again if they hadn't been locked on the contents of the envelope.

"Grandma gave me *five hundred dollars*." I held up the money so he could see it.

"Holy shit." Chris leaped up from the couch in one obnoxiously graceful movement and walked over to me.

I examined the card, which I'd mostly ignored when the cash started falling out of it. It just said *Merry Christmas, Tyler*. No explanation, nothing. Just five freaking hundred dollars with a generic holiday message. I whipped out my phone and called Grandma's number.

"Hello?" she said, using that questioning tone even though she had caller ID and must have known it was me.

"Grandma," I said. "I can't take this."

There was a chuckle on the other end of the phone. "I guess you finally opened your present?"

"Yeah, sorry, I forgot about it," I admitted. "But holy shit, Grandma, I can't take this."

"Language," she warned. "And yes, you can. And don't you dare use it all on bills, either. You need to have some fun. You looked very stressed at Christmas and I wanted you to have a little cash to do something nice for yourself. Buy a new computer or some sort of gadget. Take a trip. Just have fun with it."

"You don't have the money to just give me this, Grandma." My voice sounded weak, but I was honestly proud of myself for not letting my knees buckle.

"Oh, don't worry about me. I sold that old motorcycle Jane left in my garage. Turns out it was a classic or something. So this isn't coming out of my retirement fund or my Social Security. I promise."

"Oh my God," I breathed into the phone. "Thank you."

"I'm serious about the fun," she said, and I could just picture her Serious Face over the phone. "I'm not afraid to ask you for receipts to prove you spent it on something frivolous."

"Well," I said, "I'd been thinking about trying to save up and fly out to California for a few days. See somewhere new."

"Do that, then," she chirped. "Take lots of pictures and have as much fun as you can without getting arrested."

I laughed. "Thanks, Grandma. Really. Thank you."

"Anything for my boy," she said. "Don't tell your cousins, though. They'll all start dropping by to milk the cash cow."

I laughed again at that and took a second to appreciate having such a cool grandmother. "I won't tell a soul."

"Technically I'm nothing *but* a soul," Chris pointed out, "and I'm pretty sure you're going to tell *me*."

I rolled my eyes at him. "I love you, Grandma."

"I love you too, Tyler," she said. "I have to go now, though. My show's on."

"Okay," I told her. "Thank you again." We said good-bye, and I hung up the phone and stared at Chris. "So how do you feel about a trip to LA?"

He grinned at me. "Pretty good. Is that enough to pay for it?"

I did a little mental math and then shrugged. "I'll have to get a cheap hotel and eat off of dollar menus while I'm there, but with that and what I've saved up so far, I can probably swing it."

"Awesome," he said, pumping his fist in the air. "Let's do it, then."

I tucked the money into my wallet and picked up my laptop. I did a quick search and found a few flights that looked decent. "How do you feel about the beginning of February?"

"That long? We can't go now?"

I made a face at him. "The work schedule's already set for the next three weeks. I can't take a vacation without paying Vic to cover my shifts. But I can ask Richard to keep me off the next schedule for a few days and that would probably be okay."

Chris sat down beside me and looked at the computer. "That's fine, then."

"You'll just have to put up with me for a few more weeks." I ran another search on a different website, but the prices were about the same.

"I guess that's cool," he said. "I kind of like hanging out with you. I can do it for a while longer."

I glanced over at him. "You know," I said, drawing my words out a bit, "I kind of like hanging out with you too. We could wait a little longer if you wanted. Maybe go out there during the summer sometime."

A sudden, cold rush of fear prickled my skin. My heart sped up, pounding against my rib cage, and my throat constricted around breaths that had become shallow and quick. It wasn't *fear*, not exactly—more like dread: the feeling you get when there's a knock on the door at 3 a.m. and you can see the police parked outside. I swallowed hard, gripping the sides of my laptop with white knuckles, and squeezed my eyes shut as I willed myself to calm down. When I finally took in a deep breath and looked over at Chris again, he was staring at me with eyes that were probably only *slightly* bigger than my own.

"I'm guessing that felt awful to you too?" he asked. His voice was rough and unsteady at the same time, and I didn't blame him. "When you said we could wait . . ."

"Yeah." I gave my shoulders a hard shake and tried to get rid of my goose bumps by sheer force of will. "Something out there thinks that's a terrible idea."

"But that hasn't happened any of the other times we've talked about how I was going to have to be patient."

I took a steadying breath. "Maybe that was because until now, we *couldn't* go. And now that we can, we're not allowed to put it off any longer?"

He sighed and ran a hand through his hair. "I guess that's as good a theory as any. So beginning of February?"

We both paused, muscles tensed in case the feeling happened again, but it didn't. "I guess they—" I waved my hand at the ceiling "—are okay with that?"

"They seem to be," Chris said. "Okay, February it is."

CHAPTER
TWENTY

C hris lost patience as soon as we arrived at the airport. I started toward the line at the check-in kiosk and he kept walking toward the special carpet of the first-class priority line. It took him all the way to the twenty-foot barrier before he realized I wasn't following him.

He stomped back over to me. "I don't know why you couldn't have just sprung for a first-class ticket."

I touched the earbud of the cheap hands-free headset I'd bought to make it look like I wasn't just wandering around talking to myself. "Yeah, well, you saw my bank account. I can't afford first class. Not if I want to buy groceries and keep the lights on at my apartment."

"Eric will give you money," Chris insisted. "He'll reimburse you. I know he will."

"Okay, number one, you've done nothing but talk about how Eric doesn't *own* you and how he was angry with you and how he didn't want to ever see you again," I said. "And number two, you have to have the money up front for people reimbursing you to even be a thing that happens." I fished out my ticket receipt and started punching my information into the kiosk.

Chris grumbled. "I guess that's true. And yeah, Eric hated me there at the end, but it was a complicated kind of hate. He'll forgive me if I talk to him."

"You won't be able to," I said. "Unless you've figured out how to possess people." I got a couple of weird looks at that one, so I laughed like it was a joke.

"I've tried a few times. No luck yet." He sighed and ran a hand through his hair. "I just wish I could say my good-byes directly."

"I can get that, man." I picked up my backpack and took the printed boarding pass from the kiosk. "I wish there was a way you could, too."

An airport employee gave me a narrow-eyed look. "Sir, you'll need to turn off your headset when you go through security."

I smiled at her with my best "I am not a terrorist so please do not cavity search me" smile. "Yes, ma'am," I said. "Just finishing up my call now."

She gave me the stink eye, so I made a show of pushing the button on my earpiece.

Chris grinned at me. "So now I can just talk at you about all sorts of shit and you can't say anything back or else the security guards will block you from boarding."

I shifted my backpack on my shoulders and joined the line to go through security.

"Man, I'd forgotten how the common folk fly," Chris said, looking around at the crowded queue. "I guess being famous does have its perks. They give us private security screenings so we don't get mobbed by fans. And then we get to sit in the executive lounge and have cold beverages while we wait."

"I'm sure that's nice for you," I muttered under my breath.

"I'm sorry? I couldn't hear you over the sound of how much better it is to fly first class." He smirked at me, and I tried very hard to be mad at him. But Jesus, the dimples. I smiled back in spite of myself.

He continued chattering all the way through security, getting a huge kick out of yelling at the top of his lungs that he could see my double-ended dildo on the x-ray scan. I blushed even though I knew that a) I didn't have a double-ended dildo, in my carry-on luggage or anywhere else, and b) no one else could hear him. He looked triumphant at getting a reaction out of me, so I rolled my eyes in his direction as I was putting my shoes back on after the scan.

"You're an ass," I grumbled.

"I know," he said, grinning. "But you still like me."

"I have no idea why," I said, then stood up and went to the gate to wait on boarding.

Chris got bored with trying to talk to me on the plane. I couldn't answer him at all since I was sitting close to other people and they wouldn't have bought my "I'm on my phone" bit for very long, especially since I wasn't supposed to be using it during the flight. So when we started to taxi for takeoff, he went out to sit on the wing of the plane, and he stayed out there the whole flight except for one incident when he stuck his head through the side of the plane and told me about how he'd been buzzed by a goose.

We landed in Los Angeles late, at about eleven in the evening, so I put my headset back on and then told Chris I was just going to go to the hotel and then figure out how to find Jerri in the morning.

Chris scoffed. "It's 11 p.m. The city just woke up."

"The nightclubs just woke up," I corrected. "But it's 2 a.m. in Boston and besides, I'm not really that much of a clubber, so I'm just ready to go to bed, thanks."

"Are you sure?" he asked. "I kind of want to see you at a club."

"Why?" I shouldered my backpack and went out to find my airport shuttle.

"Because I think you'd be cute dancing," he said, winking outrageously at me.

I rolled my eyes. "You're ridiculous."

He shrugged, still grinning. "I'm just glad to be back in my homeland."

"Los Angeles isn't your homeland," I pointed out. "You never even lived here."

"I lived here while we were recording last time," he said. "But you're right. Not my homeland, exactly. But it does feel like I'm among my people here."

"The hedonistic megalomaniac people?" I asked, shooting him a little bit of a smile. "Sure, I guess I can see that."

He smiled back. "Well, anyway, I think you should go to a club. Maybe a gay bar. It might be interesting to see you grinding up against a dude."

"Um, no," I said. "That's not going to happen."

"Why not?" he whined. "You got to see me with a cock in my ass. The least you can do is let me see you dancing with a guy."

"Not going to happen," I assured him. "I'm bi, sure, but I'm not what you'd call 'out' about it."

"Who cares?" Chris said. "Nobody knows you here. And besides, you said you made out with a few guys. That's pretty out."

"I made out with a *couple* of guys I knew pretty well in the privacy of their homes," I pointed out. "Not with some random stranger on a dance floor in a town where if you're *not* photographed you're doing something wrong."

"But it would be really sexy," he argued.

"For you, maybe. For me it would probably be sweaty and beery and awkward."

"Killjoy."

"And proud to be one," I agreed. "But seriously, maybe someday. Just not tonight. I'm exhausted and I'm probably going to be comatose levels of unconscious before I even get my blankets situated."

"So no jerking it together tonight?"

I blushed and sputtered a little, then lowered my voice so that the other people waiting for the shuttle couldn't hear. "We do not make a habit of jerking it together, Chris."

"We did the other night."

"That was *one time*, like a month ago," I insisted. "And we didn't do it *together*, we just sort of did it at the same time."

"It was hot, though."

"It was hot because we'd just watched porn," I said, turning away from the gathered crowd slightly so I could waggle my finger at him like he was a little kid who needed to stay out of the cookie jar. "Not because of anything else."

Chris was silent for a second, which was weird enough that I looked over at him. He met my eyes for a moment before shrugging. "No, you're right. It was just the porn."

I opened my mouth to say more, but then the shuttle rounded the corner and pulled up next to us. Chris wandered off to jump in and out of the other passengers while I climbed into the stuffy, slightly sweat-damp van and settled down for the ride to the hotel.

Chris sat on the hood of the van for the whole ride, which was very disorienting for me. I knew the driver couldn't see him and so he wasn't blocking the guy's line of sight, but the driver had a heavy foot when he braked and every time I thought it was because he'd suddenly lost his view of the road. Chris, though, seemed to be having a good time. He was leaning back on the hood like he had been that day in Grandma's backyard, the wind from the drive making his hair whip around his head. I couldn't see his face, but I knew he had his eyes closed. You could just tell from his body language that this city, with all its glitz and glamour, was where he wanted to be.

Not back in Boston living in a tiny studio apartment with a bellboy. That sort of thing wasn't big enough to hold a guy like him. That much had been obvious from the beginning.

I plugged in my earphones to try to avoid conversation with the other passengers. I'd managed to score the seat by the window, so I watched the city speed by, bright and alive like Chris had said it would be.

I only had my backpack and my laptop bag, so I wouldn't have needed the hotel bellboy's services even if the place had *had* a bellboy, which of course it didn't. Chris followed along behind me as I walked into the lobby, commenting on how much nicer the hotel where I worked was from the one I was checking in to. I got my room key and went up to my room, which smelled faintly of cigarette smoke even though it was advertised as a nonsmoking room, and collapsed face-first onto the bed.

Chris sat down beside me. "You going to sleep?"

I left my face buried in the blanket when I spoke. "Yes, probably."

"You don't want to, like, order a pizza?"

I turned my head to the side, laying my cheek against the bed, and peered up at him. "So you can sit there and watch me eat it?"

"Yeah," he said, "and also because you have to be hungry."

"I'm okay." I knew he was right—I *should* be hungry. But the adrenaline of flying and landing and being all the way across the country from my happy place, combined with the total lack of energy remaining in my body for ordering and chewing and digesting food, made it hard to care that much. "I'll just eat a big breakfast in the morning."

"You should eat something," he said, frowning down at me. "All you've eaten today was a bagel right after check-in and your pack of airline peanuts somewhere over Utah."

"I'm okay," I repeated. "Seriously, it's cool. And besides, I ate some of my in-flight meal."

He gave me a look. "You ate one bite of the chicken, made the worst face I've ever seen anyone make, and then nibbled on one corner of that gingerbread cracker thing like an anorexic rodent until the stewardess took away your tray."

I wrinkled my nose. "They prefer 'flight attendant' now."

"Not the point." He reached out to touch my arm and looked almost surprised when his hand passed through me. "I don't want you to starve."

"Well, I don't want *you* to be dead," I said without thinking. Then, because he didn't respond immediately: "And yet here we are."

"If I wasn't dead, you wouldn't have met me," he said after a moment.

I rolled my eyes. "If you weren't dead, I would have met you, but you would have stiffed me on my tip."

He smiled at that (fucking *dimples*) and shrugged. "I would have given you like a dollar."

"Don't even lie," I said, smiling back. There was something about his smile that just invited reciprocation, and that was annoying. It was like I didn't have any choice in the matter. Chris smiles, I smile. Gross.

"Well, the new-and-improved Chris would have," he said. "The one who's slave to the whims of someone who lives on tips."

I toed off my shoes and let them fall onto the floor beside the bed. "Well, I'm incredibly glad I've had a positive effect on you."

"In spite of all my efforts to the contrary." He stood up. "If you're not going to eat something, you should get some sleep."

I eyed the space where he'd been sitting. "Did you just move out of my way?"

He looked back down at the bed. "Yeah, I guess I did."

I rolled onto my back and sat up. "I thought I might take a shower before I went to bed to get the airplane smell off of me, but fuck that."

"You get used to it," he said. "The airplane smell. The tour-bus smell. The smell of traveling to places you don't really want to go. It's all the same after a while."

I stared at him. "Dude, it's way too late to get so philosophical."

He glanced pointedly at the clock on the nightstand, the glowing "12:30" in blue digits. "It's actually way too *early* to get philosophical. Wait until you're up with me past 3 a.m. for the first time and then prepare to bust out the Sophocles."

I laughed, a little weakly. "Deal. I'll make sure to have a tape recorder on hand too."

"You should get to sleep. You're starting to weave."

I nodded and eyed the bathroom. Ever since Chris had showed up in my life, I'd gotten into the habit of only changing clothes in the bathroom, and since I slept so bundled up during the winter, it occurred to me that he hadn't even seen me with my shirt off. Which seemed weird since I'd seen him totally naked, at least in videos, but whatever. Anyway, the bathroom door seemed way too far away to fuck with, and it wasn't like I was going commando under my jeans, so I started taking them off.

Chris widened his eyes. "Dude, you're stripping in front of me."

I shimmied out of my jeans and left them on the floor with my shoes. "I'm wearing boxers, dude. Don't get too excited." And then, because I had apparently lost all my common sense, I took my shirt off too.

Chris sucked in a breath and glanced away.

I rolled my eyes. "What?"

"I just didn't know you were ripped, is all."

I peered down at my midsection, which was flat and slender enough, but wasn't anything approaching what you would call "defined," much less "ripped." Then I looked back up at him with an eyebrow raised. "Thanks, but you need to work on your vocabulary."

"What?" He blinked.

"Well, saying I'm ripped implies a six-pack. I don't have a six-pack. I don't even have a four-pack. I don't even have a *pack*." I pulled back the covers and snuggled down under them, letting out an involuntary sigh.

Chris walked over to the side of the bed. "You don't sleep like that at home," he said, looking like he was off his game.

Something in my stomach gave a strange twist when he said "home," but I ignored it. "What do you mean?"

He motioned at the lumpy expanse of person under the blanket. "Like that. You usually wear, like, flannel. Shirt and pants and everything."

"At home there's three inches of snow on the ground and it's ten degrees outside. Here it's maybe fifty, and you can smell the ocean."

He laughed. "I think that's smog, dude, not the ocean."

I flopped over onto my side and got comfortable. "If I want to believe it's the ocean, let me have my dreams."

"Okay," he said. "I guess I can do that."

I drifted off to sleep without noticing that he hadn't asked me to turn on the TV.

CHAPTER TWENTY-ONE

Another thing I didn't notice before falling asleep was that I'd forgotten to put in my earplugs.

"Tyler," Chris said loudly. "Tyler. Wake up. Tyler. Tyler. Tyler."

I opened my eyes and squinted up at him. "*What*, Chris?"

"It's ten in the morning," he said. "I let you sleep more than eight hours and now I'm *bored* and it's time to get up and go find people."

I blinked several times. "It can't be ten. It's still dark out."

"That's because you left the curtains closed, you dumbass. I would have whipped them open with a dramatic flourish but I'm noncorporeal at the moment, so you'll just have to imagine it." Chris grinned and flopped down on the bed beside me, which was weird because my body's muscle memory expected the bed to heave and the covers to pull in predictable ways, but of course nothing happened, not even a breeze. He continued. "I also considered brewing some of that disgusting-looking coffee in the room's coffeepot and yanking your covers off of you, but I can't do those either, so you'll have to imagine that as well."

"Making me coffee, huh? That's extremely domestic of you," I said, swinging my legs through him and off the side of the bed, then pulling the covers back. No morning wood today, and thank goodness for that, because he was awfully close to me and I wasn't sure how I'd keep him from noticing it when all I was wearing was boxers.

Chris carried on talking. "Once you're ready, I'll tell you Jerri's number and what you should text her to get her to meet you. And we need a game plan for how to convince her you're legit."

I grabbed my backpack, pulled out my hella-manly toiletry bag, and walked into the bathroom. Chris followed me in. I thought about shooing him away, but I figured he knew what he was getting into, following a guy into the bathroom, so I just turned my back to him and prepared to relieve myself.

Chris raised an eyebrow. "You're just going to piss with me standing here? After all the times you've yelled at me to leave and not ogle your privates, suddenly you're okay with it?"

He had a point, and I really wasn't up to figuring out exactly when I'd gotten this comfortable with him. "Think of it as a public restroom. Keep your eyes on your own urinal and you'll be fine," I told him. "And besides, you followed me in here. What did you think I was going to do?"

"Shower?"

I rolled my eyes at the peeling paint on the wall. "I don't see how that's substantially better. You'd still risk seeing my junk by accident." I tucked myself back in my boxers and then turned around to look at him. "Okay, showering. Get out."

"But I'm bored," he whined.

"You'd be bored even if you stayed in here, and so if you're going to be bored either way, then you might as well do it somewhere else. Like out there." I motioned toward the room.

He pouted at me. "You're no fun."

"I'll be plenty of fun once I'm out of the shower." I pulled my little soap bottle out of my bathroom bag. "A regular ball of sunshine. You just wait and see."

He scoffed and then smiled. "I wouldn't want you to be a ball of sunshine," he said. "Sunny people are boring."

I raised an eyebrow. "I'm not sure if that's a compliment or not."

"It is," he insisted. "You're a lot of things, but you're not boring."

I waited to see if he was going to snap his fingers and go "Psych!" at me, but he didn't, so I nodded. "No sunshine, then. Just regular me."

"Good." He hesitated for a second, his mouth slightly open like he'd barely stopped himself from talking.

"What?"

He wrinkled his nose. "I was going to ask if I could stay. Not look. But, you know, talk to you. Through the curtain."

It was my turn to hesitate then. On the one hand, no. Dudes do not let other dudes sit outside the shower and talk to them. But on the other hand . . . for some reason I didn't want to make him leave. "If you promise not to sneak a peek," I said finally, "then okay."

"Really?" he said, standing up a little straighter.

I shrugged and reached down to turn the shower on. "Sure, whatever. But you have to *swear*."

"Dude, you've seen *me* naked," he pointed out, "so I don't see how this is any different."

Shit. *There's* the morning wood. I shifted a bit so he couldn't see things perking up. "Not in person," I said, trying to fight back the mental images of Chris twisting the bedsheets in his hands and begging Gabriel to stay in just a little longer. "So that makes it *way* different."

It was starting to seem conclusive that my bathroom session after the video incident didn't have much to do with Valerie Nobles and Evie Tellerman, because it was never *them* in my head when I thought about the videos and felt the blood rushing away from my brain, despite how much I always tried to wrangle my thoughts back to the women. Fuck. This was very bad news for my sex life, given that the object of my lust didn't have an actual body anymore.

"Touché," he said, and his voice sounded closer, like he'd taken a step toward me.

I couldn't turn around to find out, though, because the boxer-tent was pretty well pitched at that point, so I just stuck my hand under the water to test the temperature. It was still a little cool, but I couldn't really risk staying on this side of the curtain for much longer, so I straightened up with my back still to him and said, "Close your eyes."

"They're closed," he said, and yeah, his voice was *definitely* closer.

I sighed. "Back off, Chris. You promised no peeking."

"Sorry." When he spoke again, he sounded farther away. "Go ahead. They're closed. For real."

I turned around to double-check—not that I didn't believe him, but just in case—and then dropped my boxers and practically leaped into the shower. I yanked the curtain closed and said, "Okay, I'm in."

"Cool," he said. "Thanks for keeping me entertained."

"Yeah, yeah." I turned away from the water and tilted my head back, letting the gradually warming water run through my hair and down over my shoulder blades. "So you wanted to talk. Let's talk."

There was a long pause. "I didn't really have a topic picked out."

"Okay." I reached up and ruffled my hair to get it fully wet. "Then tell me about little bitty Chris Raiden. What did he want to be when he grew up?"

He chuckled at that. "A veterinarian firefighter."

"Can you be both?"

"Itsy bitsy Chris thought so," he answered. "I was going to cuddle puppies by day and put out fires by night, I guess."

"That's aggressively adorable," I said with a laugh. "Cuddling puppies. Jesus."

"I can be adorable. When it suits me, anyway. What about you?"

I thought about his stupid dimples and then decided to stop thinking about them. "International spy." I poured some shampoo into my hand and started washing my hair.

"Really? Tyler Lindsey, the international spy?"

I smiled even though he couldn't see me, and the worst part was that I was pretty sure he was smiling too. "Yeah. They always got the girls. I didn't know what I would *do* with a girl at the time, but it seemed to be the goal as far as movies and shit were concerned, so I figured why not?"

"Makes sense to me," he said. "Okay, so when did you figure out what to do with a girl?"

I started rinsing my hair. "Do you mean when did I learn what sex was, or when did I do it for the first time?"

"First time."

Sighing deeply, I tilted my head into the water again and rinsed more soap out of it. "Senior prom," I said. "Her name was Katerina. Exchange student. I lasted like five whole minutes."

He laughed. "Good job, man."

"Hey, I was very proud of myself." I turned around and when the warm water hit my still-optimistic morning cock, I almost moaned. "And anyway, don't even lie. You know you didn't last long either your first time."

"True," he said. "Well, with a girl. The guy took longer. More logistics involved, you know."

"When was that?" I asked, even though I knew I shouldn't. "The guy, I mean."

"I was sixteen. It was at church camp," he said, and I busted out laughing.

"Seriously? You had gay sex for the first time at *church camp*?"

"Yeah. I was a rebellious teenager." It was really disturbing that I could tell just from his voice what facial expression he was wearing. That spoke to way too much time spent thinking about his expressions. But anyway, he was sort of half smiling. I'm sure of it.

"Sounds like it," I replied. "*Church camp*."

"His name was Adam, and—" He broke off.

"Oh, come on," I said. "You can't leave me hanging like that."

A couple more seconds went by, and then he spoke again: "He had a tattoo on his chest. A lion. I liked to dig my fingernails into it. I heard he got it removed after that summer."

"Can you blame him?" My hand brushed my cock, and it seemed to have gotten even harder since getting in the shower. I frowned down at it as if that would help. It didn't.

"Nah. Especially since he repented and married a woman and now he's a youth minister." He chuckled, which definitely didn't make the situation I had going on any better.

But I'm a dumbass who doesn't think things through, and so instead of steering the conversation away from sex-related topics, I asked him, "Who was the first girl?"

"Fuck, I don't remember her name. Claire or Clarissa or something like that," he said. "I was nineteen, and it was at a party. Eric introduced us. I didn't last very long."

I laughed, and it was a throatier laugh than I would have liked to give. "Even though you weren't a virgin?"

He shrugged at that. I couldn't even see him and I knew he was shrugging. Fuck. "Well, I'd never been the one doing the fucking before that, if you know what I mean."

My dick certainly knew what he meant. It gave a cheerful little twitch, and I frowned at it again. *Don't touch it, don't touch it, don't touch it.*

Hopefully it was just the combination of the time of day and the fact that before Chris showed up in my life, I'd been in the habit of jacking it at least once a day, sometimes more, and so I had a lot of built-up tension. It had nothing at all to do with the way Chris's laugh made my skin feel tight or that I was naked and five feet from a guy who'd made it into the top twenty of the Sexiest Rockers Alive list last year. Nothing at all.

But fuck, I had to do something about it. It wasn't going away and I couldn't shower forever. I wrapped my fingers around myself and started stroking even though I kind of hated myself for doing it. "So who was the best guy? Was it Gabriel?"

"Yeah, probably," he said. "Well, there was this one random groupie who was better. I never got his name. He could do some wicked things with his tongue, though."

"What did he look like?" My voice was a little breathless, but I decided that it wasn't enough to tip Chris off, so I sped up my strokes and ignored the part of my brain that was telling me not to think about Chris's o-face while I beat one out.

"Shortish," he answered. "Really dark hair, but I think it was dyed because I saw the drapes, if you know what I mean. Green eyes like yours." There was a pause. "Well, not exactly like yours. Yours are brighter. More spring-y."

I couldn't have him talking about my eyes while I had my hand on my cock, so I asked another question. "Who was the best girl?" A good question. Good job, Tyler. Get this thing back on the heterosexual track.

"I don't know," he said. "I mean, probably Evie, I guess. The spinning move was cool."

"And the body butter," I said, because thinking about tits was the sort of thing I was used to doing while I jerked off.

"Yeah. Tori wasn't any good. If you're curious."

I hadn't been, but that didn't matter. "Why not?" I got my other hand in on the action to try to speed things up, stroking with both hands and fighting to keep my breathing under control.

"She used me like a sex toy," he said. "She didn't want me to do anything, just lie there while she bounced up and down on my dick."

Fuck. Don't think about bouncing up and down on Chris's dick. I didn't even know what that would feel like, so it shouldn't have turned me on so much. But then Chris's money shot from the Gabriel video flashed across my mind and combined with a vivid fantasy of me riding Chris hard and slow, with my face tilted up toward the ceiling. That really didn't need to be the image I ended everything on, but my cock had other ideas, and I bit my lip hard to keep from moaning out loud while I shuddered a few times and fought to keep my legs underneath me.

"Shit," I mumbled under my breath, because I couldn't keep *totally* quiet, and now that the lust haze had cleared from my eyes, I was a little weirded out that Chris had taken over my sex fantasies so completely. I didn't want him like that in real life. Did I?

Goddamn it, I probably did. Fuck.

But whatever, jerking off had released a lot of tension and so I would count the shower session as a win. I let go of myself and concentrated on finishing up with washing as quickly as I could.

"You okay?" Chris asked.

"Yeah, fine, why?" My voice was almost back to normal, which was nice.

"I just expected you to have follow-up questions or something."

I shook my head hard like that would clear it. "No, I got a pretty good mental image of Tori using you like a dildo, thanks."

He chuckled again, which still did weird things to my skin even when I wasn't harder than a calculus final, and fuck if I knew what to do with that, so I rinsed the last of the soap off of my body and turned off the water.

I stuck my head around the curtain and looked over to where he was perched on the closed toilet lid. "Okay, I'm done. Out."

"Can't I just close my eyes again?" He gave me a look that I couldn't quite translate. Probably for the best.

"No, you can't. Come on, man, give me five minutes of privacy. Then you'll have me to bother for the rest of the day."

"Promise?"

I rolled my eyes. "Yeah, I promise."

"Deal." He stood up, then hesitated for a second before he shook his head and walked through the wall and back out into the hotel room.

I finished drying off and getting ready, then checked myself one last time in the mirror to make sure that he wouldn't be able to read "I just jizzed in the shower thinking about you fucking me" all over my face. None of the girls I'd dated had ever been able to read that sort of expression, but I got the feeling that Chris was going to be the exception to this rule too. The bastard was becoming way too much of an exception these days.

When I was finally satisfied that my poker face was firmly in place, I walked out of the bathroom. "Come on," I said. "I'll find us a coffee shop and I'll eat whatever you want to watch me eat."

"I want to see you eat something *you* like," he said. "That's what I miss. I mean, you eat scones for me and you drink the drinks I like and you make your spaghetti the way my mom used to make it just so I can watch you eat it, but that's not what I miss. I miss the *pleasure* of eating. I miss . . . having something on my tongue that makes my eyes roll back in my head." He slid his gaze over and locked it on me. "Is there anything that does that to you?"

I thought about it for a moment. "Caramel cake," I said, nodding decisively.

"Can I watch you eat caramel cake?" He licked his lips, and I hated that I traced the motion with my eyes.

"I don't know, dude," I said, my mouth dry all of the sudden. "That sounds really intimate."

"Yeah," he agreed, but didn't elaborate.

"If we find caramel cake in Los Angeles," I promised him, "I'll eat it for you."

He scoffed and waved his hand dismissively. "This is one of the biggest cities in the country. We can find you some caramel cake."

"Hey, I've only got a few days here," I pointed out. "And we need to find Jerri and Eric and let you talk to them. That's priority one. And then after *that*, we can look for caramel cake if we still have time."

He smiled. "Deal. Okay, so, Jerri first. Text her."

I pulled out my phone and typed in the number he told me. "What do I say?"

"Say 'Meet you at the store at one thirty.'"

I raised an eyebrow at him. "What store?"

"It's a florist's shop. Neutral meeting place," Chris said. "Jerri's very careful about who she meets up with."

"Uh-huh," I said, pouring all of my distrustfulness into the sounds. "Who's Jerri?"

"You'll see," he said. "And if you could just stand back and let me talk to her while you plug your ears, that would be great."

"You keep saying that," I told him, "but you keep forgetting that you *can't talk to her*. You need me to relay for you."

Chris paused with his mouth open like he'd already begun to rebut my argument. "Damn."

"Yeah," I said. "So just man up and tell me who she is."

"Not yet." He grinned at me and motioned at my laptop case. "Now pull up a map, and I'll show you where to go."

CHAPTER TWENTY-TWO

An hour later, I found myself standing in an abandoned florist shop staring into the barrel of a shiny silver handgun that managed to look both delicate and badass at the same time. For several seconds I just stood there staring blankly at the gun. My blood rushed in my ears and for a moment the whole thing seemed so fucking surreal that I almost laughed at it instead of reacting appropriately. To a gun. In my face.

"Dude, don't shoot." I'd never really expected to say that phrase for real. It was the kind of thing people said in the movies but not in real life.

Jerri glared at me, an unlit cigarette hanging out of her mouth. "Who the fuck are you?"

"I'm nobody. Don't shoot." I put my hands in the air. Surely she could already see that I wasn't armed, but it seemed like the sort of goodwill gesture that you should perform when on the wrong side of a gun. I swallowed hard and tried to exude *I'm not worth shooting* vibes by shrinking into myself and looking as small as possible.

"Your *name*, motherfucker."

"Tyler Lindsey," I said, quickly before she could get any angrier. I was, after all, pretty motivated to *not die*. "I'm nobody, I'm just . . . I just came here to talk."

"Honestly, I don't give a damn what you came here for. But I don't like being contacted without a reference, you understand?" She took a step closer to me, and I flinched backward. "I want to know who told you to send me that text."

"Um . . ." I looked at Chris, who was standing a couple of feet away. "Little help here, Chris?"

Jerri swung her gun around toward the door, then turned it back to me. "Who's Chris? Your backup?"

"No," I squeaked. "He's a friend. He's your friend too."

Jerri glared for a few more seconds, then slowly lowered her gun. "No sudden moves or I'll shoot you. I swear to God I will. But fine. Talk."

"Okay." I took a deep breath. It was amazing how much better it felt to not have a Glock in my face. But still, I probably ought to put out a disclaimer before I hopped right into the ghost thing. "Just, um, let me finish before you start shooting or whatever, okay?"

She narrowed her eyes. "No promises."

"Well, I'm here because Christopher Raiden wanted me to come talk to you. I was, um, the one who found his body." That much seemed . . . well, not *normal*, but not outside of the realm of possibility. Maybe I'd gotten some message from Chris before he died that he'd wanted me to pass on. That sounded reasonable.

Jerri didn't seem particularly convinced, but she nodded. "Fine. Okay. What did he want to say?"

"Look, this is going to sound really crazy." Yet another phrase I never thought I'd actually say. "But, um, I'm sort of a psychic or something and I'm being haunted by his ghost—" Her gun came back up to point at me, and I sped up "—and I know that sounds like I'm fucking with you but I can prove it."

"Ten seconds, motherfucker."

"Talk fast, Chris," I said, a little squeakily.

Chris, to his credit, looked incredibly freaked by this development. "Tell her that I told you that she's sexually obsessed with Abraham Lincoln and this one time she made out with this guy at a party because she totally thought he was Abe reincarnated."

I stared at Chris. "Are you fucking kidding me? *That's* what you want me to say?"

Jerri waved the gun a little, and I sighed. "He says you have a sexual thing for Abe Lincoln and once you fooled around with a dude at a party because you thought it was him?"

Jerri's eyes narrowed even more, and I wondered briefly if she could even see through them at this point. "I need more than that."

Chris ran a hand through his hair. "Tell her I never told anybody about the pot brownies she donated to that nursing home."

I closed my eyes. I was going to get shot for sure. "And you took pot brownies to a nursing home but he never told anybody."

Jerri just stood there.

"We're convincing her," Chris said. "Now tell her that her sister has a birthmark on her bikini line, and she's always felt weird knowing about it but she does."

"I am *not* telling her that," I snapped at him.

Jerri waved the gun again. "About what?"

I let out a huff of breath and tried to prepare for the afterlife as best I could in just a few seconds. "About the birthmark on your sister's bikini line."

Jerri lowered the gun. "I don't believe in ghosts," she said doubtfully.

A rush of dizzy relief washed over me, and I took a deep breath to settle my nerves. "Yeah. Neither did I, until this one got attached to me."

"So . . . why does the spirit of Chris Raiden want to talk to me?"

"Fuck if I know," I said. "He's being very secretive about the whole thing."

Chris made a face in my direction. "Tell her she's my friend."

"He says you're his friend," I repeated dutifully.

Jerri frowned again, but this time it was a saddish frown. "I told him a million times that we weren't friends."

"Really?" I said. "Well, he thinks you were. He made me come all the way here from Boston to talk to you."

"To talk to *me*?"

"Well . . . you and Eric Painter," I clarified. "But you first, yeah."

Chris stepped forward. "Tell her to shut up about us not being friends, because she knows that's bullshit. She's been like my sister and I want her to know that she meant a lot to me and that I'm glad I knew her."

I looked between them. "He says you mean a lot to him and you're like a sister to him and you should stop saying that you weren't friends."

"You can't be friends with your customers," Jerri said. "It's the rule."

"Yeah, well— Wait." I gave her an up-and-down appraisal. *Customers* implied one of two things here. She was slender and pretty enough, but Chris hadn't seemed to be lying when he said it was platonic and it wasn't like he was the sort of guy who would have needed to pay for sex anyway, so that ruled out prostitute. Which only left one possibility.

Chris groaned. "Here we go."

"Is Jerri your *dealer*?" I stared at him, incredulous.

Jerri twitched the gun. "Yeah, I'm going to need you to keep your voice down. Narcs are everywhere."

I dutifully lowered my voice, but kept my tone the same and kept staring at Chris. "You made me fly to Los Angeles to have a tearful good-bye scene with your *drug dealer*?"

Chris shifted on his feet. "Um, yeah. But she's really more of a friend? I mean, really, we've been buddies for years now."

"You are the biggest douche I've ever met," I said to Chris. "And *you*," I pointed at Jerri. "It's your fault he's dead."

Jerri frowned again. "No, it's not. If I wasn't selling, he would have found someone else. And besides, I'm very up front with my dosages, man. I tell 'em how much to take and if they do more than that, it's their own asses."

"She's right," Chris said. "She always told me to go easier on the stuff. And don't blame her for this, dude. Don't. You don't know anything about what was going on."

"Oh no," I said, shaking my head. "I am not going to let you defend your drug dealer to me from *beyond the grave*."

Chris frowned too. Frowns all around, then. "I just wanted to tell her good-bye, okay? Because there at the end she was the only person in the world who would take my phone calls."

I blinked and looked at Jerri again. "Is that true?"

She raised her eyebrows. "I'm only getting half the conversation here."

"Oh," I said. "You were the only one who would talk to him?"

"That's what he said." She shrugged. "I mean, he said Eric would talk to him about strictly business band-related stuff, and that Gabriel

Sinclair would text him. And I guess he and Tori fucked sometimes, but he didn't really look forward to that."

"That's incredibly sad," I said, turning my gaze to Chris. "One of the most popular men in the world and nobody would take your calls."

"Yeah, thanks, Tyler," he snapped. "I really wasn't able to figure out how shitty my life was without you summing it up for me."

I looked between them again. "Well." That was all I could think of to say.

Chris crossed his arms. "Will you let me finish saying good-bye now?"

"Yeah," I said, a little more softly. "Yeah, go ahead."

"Tell her that I appreciated her. And that it's not her fault."

I repeated that to Jerri. "Do *you* think it was your fault?" I asked afterward.

Jerri tucked her gun back into her jacket. "It was his own fault. Not mine."

"She's lying." Chris stepped a little closer to her, watching her carefully. "I know her too well for that."

"Well," I said to Jerri, "*he* thinks that you think it was your fault."

"He doesn't know my life," she said, then made a big show of rearranging her jacket and not looking at me.

"He knows about your Lincoln fetish and the birthmark thing," I pointed out. "So clearly you were pretty good friends."

Jerri gave a humorless chuckle. "We got along well, I guess."

"So is he right?"

She turned her eyes to the tile on the floor and then sighed. "I usually don't let it get to me. But when I heard about him . . . it sort of did."

"Tell her I don't blame her for it and that she needs to move on," Chris said.

"He says you should move on. He doesn't blame you," I repeated. "And you should find a job that's less likely to kill people. He didn't say that part, though. That part was me."

"You're very judgmental," Jerri said, cocking an eyebrow at me and crossing her arms. "Especially to people you don't even know."

I shrugged. "I've gotten kind of fond of Chris, despite my better judgment. And I wish he wasn't dead. But I guess he's right, and you're right. You didn't force the syringe into him that night. That was all him."

Jerri nodded. "I told him, man. I told him to stop."

I looked back at Chris. "Dude, when even your *dealer* tells you to quit, you should really consider quitting."

"Point taken," Chris said dryly. "I'll check myself back into rehab tomorrow."

"Is that all?" I asked him.

Chris looked at Jerri for a long time. "Ask her . . . if Eric said anything to her. Afterwards."

"He wants to know if Eric said anything to you after he died," I repeated.

Jerri's eyes darkened for a second. "Eric . . . Well, all he really said to me was a pretty impressive string of cuss words and a threat to go to the police."

"But he didn't?" It seemed like the kind of follow-up question Chris would have.

"No," Jerri said. "But I think that was mostly because he knew me and Chris were close. Friend-ish. And at the time, he was all about doing what Chris would have wanted."

Chris nodded slowly. "Good."

"He says that's good."

"And hey, Chris." Jerri paused. "Where is he? I want to pretend I'm making eye contact."

I motioned at Chris. "Over there. And here are his eyes." I poked at them with two fingers, and Chris flinched backward.

Jerri made almost eye contact with him. "You shouldn't go talk to him, man."

"Why not?" Chris said. I repeated after him as unobtrusively as I could.

"Because nothing good will come of it," Jerri said. "He'll just say the same shit he always says and you'll come out of it feeling worse than you did before. Like always."

Chris stayed silent, his eyes locked on Jerri's, and after a moment Jerri looked at me. "What did he say?"

I shrugged. "He didn't say anything."

Jerri returned her eyes to where I'd pointed. "You know it's true. Don't do it."

"I have to," Chris said. "I have to say good-bye." I relayed the words and Jerri frowned again, still sad instead of angry.

"Well, good luck, man," she said. "And you get Tyler here to come talk to me again if it goes badly and you need to vent."

Chris nodded. "I will. And if I finish moving on after I say my good-byes, just know that I'm glad I knew you."

I told Jerri what Chris said. She smiled and nodded. "Me too."

Chris looked at me. "Now hug her."

"What?" I gave him my most dubious double eyebrow raise. "I'm not hugging her."

"Hug her," Chris demanded. "It's part of my moving on. Vicarious good-bye hugging."

I looked at Jerri. "He wants me to hug you good-bye from him."

"Seriously?" Jerri said.

"Yeah, unfortunately." I held my arms out.

Jerri gave me a quick, hard hug and smiled. "Thanks for . . . whatever it is you're doing. And good luck with Eric."

I stepped back to a safe distance and returned her smile.

CHAPTER TWENTY-THREE

We left the florist's shop and went back to the hotel to regroup. Chris seemed to alternate between being happier now that some of his unfinished business was resolved and nervous now that he was closer to talking to Eric. I could understand that, I guess. But still, the pacing was getting a little annoying.

"Dude, sit down," I said after a while. "The back and forth and back and forth is about to put me into deep-stage hypnosis."

"I've got all this energy," Chris said. "And I can't do what I normally do to relieve it, so you're just going to have to learn to live with the pacing."

I had a flashback of Chris releasing energy with Gabriel Sinclair, which made every inch of my skin tingle. Then I realized he was probably talking about the drugs, and the pleasant mental image was replaced with a detailed memory of what Chris looked like lying dead on the floor of the hotel. That image made my skin tingle too, but instead of making me want to reach for him or ask him if he wanted to try to touch me, it made me want to think about absolutely anything else.

And strangle him for dying, too, but that was both impossible *and* counterproductive.

"Let's go out." I stood up and tried to smile at him. "You can show me the city. Maybe we'll see someone famous and you can tell me gossip about them. That will be fun for you."

He paused in his pacing. "We have to go see Eric."

I waved my hand in the air to dismiss his objections. "We have five more days here before we have to go back," I said. "Eric can wait. We'll take some time to digest the Jerri thing and you'll feel better afterwards." *And also you can take a few minutes to stop wigging out about seeing Eric.*

Chris was silent for a few seconds, but he was clearly thinking, so I just let him do his thing. After a bit, he nodded. "I guess that would be fun. I can show you the city."

"Then let's go."

We wandered around for a while. It turned out that Chris didn't have many stories from Los Angeles after all . . . he claimed he'd been too busy to get out much when he'd been here before. After a couple of hours of random walking, I decided it was time to take a break. The sun was getting low in the sky—I guess even in California the days were short at this time of year. Something about that was vaguely disappointing.

Chris had gotten quiet again, and he had that look in his eyes that I was mentally calling the "Oh Shit I've Gotta Talk to Eric" expression. It was really starting to bug me. Part of me wanted to stomp up into Eric's house right then and get the bullshit over with so Chris could go back to smiling. Because as gross as it was that I was apparently physically obligated to smile when I saw him smile, it was even worse that Chris being sad made *me* sad. There were implications of that sort of thing that I didn't really want to contemplate.

We walked past a little hole-in-the-wall bar with a couple of neon beer signs in the windows, and I stopped. There was guitar music leaking out from the doorway, but not the blaring music of a bar that's trying too hard to be cool, so it seemed like a good bet for a beverage. Chris kept walking for a few steps before he realized that I wasn't following. He turned around and quirked an eyebrow at me.

"I'm thirsty," I said, jerking my thumb toward the bar. "Mind if I go in?"

Chris shrugged. "No, go ahead. Maybe I'll people-watch for a while."

The moment we got in the door, Chris made a strangled noise in his throat, whispered, "Holy shit, is that a Strat?" and made a beeline for the girl sitting up on the tiny stage in the corner of the bar, her fingers flying over a black guitar while she sang a slowed-down version of some pop song I'd heard hundreds of times but never quite caught the name of.

I rolled my eyes at his back and went over to the bar, sliding onto a stool and waiting patiently for the bartender to notice me.

Two songs and half a beer later, a tall guy with sandy blond hair sat on the barstool next to me.

"You checking out the talent?" he said after a few minutes.

I tore my eyes away from the stage and turned to him. "What?"

He used his drink to motion at the singer. "You seem to be infatuated with the chick on the stage."

Which wasn't true, but it's not like he had any way of knowing that, so instead I shrugged and gave him a half smile. "I have a thing for guitarists, I guess," I said, feeling dumb as the words left my mouth.

"Who doesn't?" he replied, laughing even though what I'd said wasn't that funny.

I did the half-smile thing again, then turned back to the stage. Chris was sitting on an empty barstool next to the guitarist, watching her fingers move and nodding his head to the beat. The "Oh Shit Eric" look was gone for the moment, and instead he looked . . . content. It was a strange expression to see on his face.

The girl finished that song and then started up another one, a power ballad from one of those eighties hair bands. Chris's face dissolved into a big grin, and when she started singing, he joined in, harmonizing with her. His voice was a little too hard-rock for the song and the harmonies weren't perfect since he was obviously making it up as he went, but he had a decent singing voice that did weird things to my toes, and when he looked up and our eyes caught, for a second I forgot to give a shit about acting cool and unaffected.

His grin softened into a more genuine smile (fucking *dimples* again) and I smiled back, and fuck if it didn't feel like the world stopped spinning for just a moment before it remembered the laws of physics and carried on.

Which was pretty fucking terrifying. I looked back at my beer and took a deep breath to steady myself.

The guy beside me leaned over. "Are you going to ask her out?"

"Who?" I asked, then felt stupid again. "Oh. Guitar girl. Um, no. Probably not."

"Why not? You were staring at her like you wanted to undress her right there on stage."

I raised my eyebrow at him. "Actually, no. I just like the music."

"Do you come here a lot, then?"

I let out a short burst of laughter. "Are you serious?"

He frowned. "What?"

"You're seriously using that line on me," I said, reraising the same eyebrow. "Do I come here often."

His frown faded and almost reversed into a smile, but not quite. "Seemed like a good way to ease into flirting if you were into it."

I looked back at Chris. He wasn't watching me anymore. "I'm Tyler," I said to the guy on the barstool.

"Brandon," he said. "*Do* you come here a lot?"

"First time." I gave him a long look. He was pretty tall, taller than me and even a little taller than Chris, and he had light-blue eyes and a nice square jaw that gave his face character. Good muscles too, from what I could see.

Brandon smiled more brightly. "Then let me buy you a drink."

A few drinks later, I'd reached that stage of intoxication where I wasn't drunk, not exactly, but I was feeling extra cheerful and probably shouldn't attempt to operate any machinery. Brandon was smiling and laughing and telling jokes, and the combination of his attractiveness along with listening to Chris's stupid damn singing voice belting out some Madonna cover was making me smile and laugh and tell jokes back.

"So," Brandon said, leaning in a little closer. "Do you have a boyfriend?"

It was a pretty obvious pointed question, and if I hadn't been buzzed and distracted I would have seen it for what it was, but Chris chose that moment to get bored of singing and start fucking *sauntering* his way over to me, and I hesitated just a second too long before answering.

Brandon gave a low whistle. "Should I back off, then? He's not going to come in and beat the shit out of me for hitting on you, is he?"

Chris heard that and made a half-laugh-half-choke sound. "Oh my God, this guy's trying to pick you up. He must be into scrawny twinks."

Says the guy who called me ripped and would have tried to jump my bones just this morning if he wasn't see-through, I thought, but I wasn't drunk enough to start talking to invisible people in front of someone else, so instead I just shrugged at Brandon and said, "No. He can't do shit about it, actually."

"So I'm your boyfriend now?" Chris asked, smirking. "I thought I was an entitled asshole who you wouldn't touch even if you were in full hazmat gear."

I tried to shoot him a *shut-the-fuck-up* look without Brandon seeing. Not sure how successful I was, but it made me feel a little better. I mean, Chris *was* an entitled asshole, but that wasn't why I hadn't ever touched him, and I was pretty sure that we both knew it.

Also, just last night he'd been telling me he wanted to see me doing the dirty with another guy, and the beer had given me some courage. I let the smile I was aiming at Brandon get a little warmer and reach my eyes a little more as I turned my body even more toward him.

Brandon was talking again, and Chris had moved around behind me, so I met Brandon's gaze and tried to seem totally engrossed in our conversation just in time to hear him ask, "So should I keep flirting, or . . .?"

"He's hot," Chris said. The nape of my neck started to tingle like he was breathing on it, which wasn't possible but which pissed me off anyway because I just *knew* that the fucker was standing that close behind me, and he needed to step off before I did something stupid like forgetting he wasn't solid and trying to lean back against his chest.

Not that I would do that. Of course not. I smiled at Brandon. "I'm not saying no, am I?"

Chris must have stepped away from me, because my body's newfound ghost proximity detector stopped beeping at me. "Wait," he said. "For real?"

I put my glass of beer down on the counter and stood up. "I'll be right back, okay? Don't go anywhere." Brandon nodded, and I headed for the men's room with Chris trailing along at my heels.

It was a one-seater with a lock on the door, which was excellent news because I could avoid people seeing my conversation with the air. I locked the door behind me and turned around to look at Chris. "So . . ." I absently reached up and rubbed the back of my neck. Way to seem cool and nonawkward, Tyler. "At the airport, when you said you wanted to watch me grind up on some guy . . ."

Chris had what appeared to be a very carefully constructed blank expression on his face. "Yeah?"

"Were you serious?"

"You're thinking about fucking that guy?" He looked back out toward the bar even though he couldn't see it through the bathroom wall. Or at least I assumed he couldn't. But having x-ray vision seemed like the sort of thing he would have talked about, so I was betting on not.

I shrugged. "He really seems more like a top, which I guess is cool with me. Jumping in with both feet, you know."

"Wow," he said. "You come out to LA and you become way less of a prude practically overnight."

The whole not-being-able-to-punch-him-in-his-stupid-perfect-teeth thing was really starting to grate on me. "I wasn't a prude in Boston either," I said. "I just have a problem with having random gay sex with some dude I might run into again later in the line at CVS."

"So this guy is perfect for you, then," he said. "Well, you have my blessing. Bone away."

"Is he somebody you'd like to watch me getting boned by?" The redness in my face was *totally* just about the beer. I'm way too cool to be blushing about sex talk.

Now it was his turn to shrug. "I can give you guys privacy. Wait in the hall or something."

"That's very generous of you, but no thanks." Geez, he wasn't getting it. Maybe it was intentional. Or maybe he was being a dumbass. I decided to give him one more chance to figure it out before I explained it to him using small words.

"So . . ." He stared at me, the blank expression replaced by one of confusion that was completely not adorable, not at all, why would anyone assume I thought it was adorable? Ugh. This fucker. This. Fucker.

"So I kind of want you to watch," I said after a moment of incredibly awkward silence.

"You . . . do?" The confusion on his face deepened, and I gave an exasperated sigh.

"Yes, you moron, I do," I snapped. I mean, really, this wasn't that hard to understand. "You said it would be hot to watch me doing the nasty with a guy. You said Brandon was hot. We're both sexually frustrated and judging by how you ogled me shirtless last night I'm guessing you're horny as hell, so I'm saying I'll do this guy for *us* if you want me to." Then I realized how couple-y the emphasized *us* sounded and corrected myself: "For both of us, I mean."

"You'd do that? For me?" His voice sounded weird, and I decided not to analyze it. Nothing good lay in analyzing Chris's voice.

"Yeah," I said, and then because he looked surprisingly floored by this, I added, "I like it when you're happy. And we could both use a destressor. So . . ."

"So you're going to bone that guy. While I watch." He tilted his head. "Do I get to jerk it?"

"Jesus, Chris, I'm not a *monster*." I offered him a cheeky half smile. "Of course you can. I probably won't be paying that much attention to you anyway."

"Cool," he said. "Well then, you'd better get back out there."

CHAPTER TWENTY-FOUR

I walked back out to the bar and sat on my stool, then smiled at Brandon. "So where were we?"

Brandon finished off his beer and a slow smile spread across his face. "I was about to ask you if you wanted to find somewhere less public to talk."

Which was exactly what I'd been planning on, but I still blushed a little. Mostly because I'd never had sex while someone watched from the sidelines, but also because I hadn't expected this to move *that* fast. I'd thought it would take a couple more beers at least. But this was better. Less time to get weirded out by the nerves.

"That sounds good." I smiled extra big to make up for my hesitation.

Brandon gave me a full-body once-over that was even less subtle than mine had been earlier. "Then do you want to get out of here?"

"Oh, fuck yeah." Chris actually bounced on the balls of his feet. "This is gonna be hot as hell."

And between the beer, Brandon's muscles, Chris's encouragement, and the fact that it had been months since I'd gotten laid, it didn't take long at all for me to nod in agreement.

"My place or yours?" he asked, sliding off the barstool and turning to face me.

I stood up too and gave his lips a good long gaze. They were full and looked very soft, and I had a flash of what it might feel like to have them on my cock.

"You're shivering," Chris said. "You're already hot for him, aren't you?"

I took a deep breath and shrugged. "I'm staying in a hotel not far from here. Let's go there."

"All right," Brandon said, and then he slid an arm around my waist and kissed me.

I sighed, let myself relax into it, and raised a hand to his neck. He teased at my lips with his tongue, and I opened them to let him in. He tasted like cinnamon, and I wondered for a second when he'd had time to pop a mint before I realized that it probably had been when I was watching Chris like an obsessed fangirl. Or when I'd been in the bathroom asking Chris if it was okay if I exercised my own sexual freedom like he had any right to have an opinion about that. Probably the latter.

I pulled back and smiled warmly. "Let's get to my room, yeah?"

He nodded, and we left the bar. I led the way to the hotel as quickly as I could manage without actually breaking into a run. My brain whispered that maybe this wasn't an ideal way to lose my gay virginity, but my dick didn't seem to have any such moral qualms, and anybody on the streets who looked too closely would be able to tell what I was thinking about, so speed was of the essence.

There was a little drugstore across the street from the hotel, and I paused briefly before we went into the hotel lobby. "Do I need to run over there?" I asked Brandon, giving the store a pointed glance.

He glanced at the store. "If you don't have stuff in your room, then yeah."

Chris gave Brandon a withering death glare. "Seriously? He goes to a bar to pick up dudes and doesn't make sure he's packing?"

"Okay," I said to Brandon, then motioned at a liquor store just down the street. "Why don't you go grab us a six-pack and I'll meet you back here in ten?"

"Yeah, sounds good." Brandon picked up my hand and kissed it with an eyebrow waggle, then headed off toward the liquor store.

"I don't think people call it 'packing' when they're talking about sex supplies," I told Chris, turning around and walking quickly across the street and into the drugstore.

"Whatever," he said. "He should have planned ahead."

I made my way to the back of the store where they kept the lube and started considering my options. "I didn't have anything either," I said. "I should have planned ahead too, I guess."

Chris shrugged. "You didn't go out expecting to pick up a piece of ass. He did."

"Good point." I motioned at the wide array of lubrication products on the shelf. "You've done this before. What do you recommend?"

I felt his eyes on me for an uncomfortably long time. Finally, he looked away and waved his hand at a plain variety. "It's your first time," he said, in a husky voice. "Probably best to go with regular."

"I trust you." I grabbed the box from the shelf.

"Condoms too," he reminded me. "Don't forget them."

I gave Chris a Look.

"What?" Chris said. "No glove, no love."

I flipped him off. "Who are you, my high school health teacher?"

"I'm serious, Tyler," Chris warned, less lighthearted this time. "Tell him to use a rubber or I will haunt the shit out of you forever. And not in a fun way. I mean it."

"Fuck, dude, calm down." I reached for a box of regular, no-frills condoms. "Of course I'm going to make him use one. Do I look like a fucking moron?"

"No," Chris said after a second. "Sorry. I'm kind of an activist."

I raised an eyebrow at him. "You. Are a safe-sex activist."

He rolled his eyes. "I'm an intravenous drug user who likes to have indiscriminate sex with strangers. I would have been the poster child for bad things happening when you don't use condoms," he said. "So I always, *always* made sure I was safe. Rewatch all my videos if you don't believe me. That shit's important."

"I believe you," I said, because it actually did seem very *him* to be careful about some things while being shockingly lax with others. Like drug dosages, for example. I carried the boxes up to the counter and gave the cashier an I-dare-you-to-comment glance while she rang me up.

Chris was standing close behind me again. I could just *tell*.

"I finally get to see you naked," he purred into my ear.

A weird squeaking noise escaped my throat. I hurriedly finished paying and stuffed the boxes into my jacket pockets, then headed for the exit. When I was far enough away that the cashier couldn't hear me, I muttered, "Dude, not cool."

"What do you mean?" Chris asked. He was smirking like a fucker, so I scowled at him.

"You know what you were doing," I said. "Now shut up. Brandon's back."

I walked over to Brandon and grinned at him. "All covered." I patted my pockets. "Now, where were we?"

"I was about to give you the ride of your life," Brandon said, his eyes dark and heavy-lidded.

"Cool," I said, then grabbed his hand and pulled him into the hotel.

The door to the room had barely shut behind us before we were kissing again, and I couldn't remember if I'd made the move or if he had. The kiss was faster, harder this time than in the bar, and my heart rate sped up as he started push-walking me over to the bed.

We fell onto it together, which was far less comfortable than it looks in the movies—his elbow hit what must have been my pancreas and I'm about eighty percent sure I kneed him in the crotch. Must not have been very hard, though, because after a couple of seconds of rearranging our limbs, he settled between my legs and pressed up against me, and the hot length of his cock tenting the front of his pants didn't seem like something that had sustained a recent injury, so I grabbed his hair and pulled his face back down to mine.

If getting on the bed had been awkward, the kissing was definitely not. He kissed like he had a fucking doctorate in the subject, teasing my lips and the inside of my mouth with his tongue and making low noises in his throat when I kissed back. I curled my fingers in his hair and tugged at it while he ground down against me.

Brandon leaned up and pulled off his jacket and T-shirt, tossing them off to the side. I took the opportunity to yank mine off too. He had a light dusting of hair on his chest that tapered into a line that ran over his toned abs and disappeared into the waist of his jeans, and I let my eyes follow it as far down as I could see. He grinned and reached down to press his palm against my cock through my jeans.

The pressure made me close my eyes and arch off the bed, moaning loudly. I wasn't a virgin schoolboy or anything, but damn, it had been a long time since anybody touched me, and the sensation was intense.

Brandon lay down on top of me again and then started rocking against me so that our dicks pressed into each other through two layers of clothes. I moved my hands to his back and dug my fingers into his shoulder blades while he kissed my neck with just as much skill as he'd been kissing my mouth earlier.

He used his teeth to nip at my earlobe, and my eyes flew open in a delighted kind of surprise, and that's when I noticed Chris standing there beside the bed staring at us.

I'd actually forgotten for a few minutes that he was there, but now that I'd seen him, I couldn't go back to ignoring him. And besides, he wasn't looking quite as . . . *pleased* as I'd imagined he would.

I mouthed "What's wrong?" at Chris, but he just shrugged. He put a hand on his stomach and slowly dragged it down toward his waistline. I put forth a huge effort to pull my eyes away from where his hand was heading, but that turned out to be a bad idea because the only place my eyes were willing to go from there was straight up to *his* eyes.

"Tell me what you want," I whispered, my eyes still locked on Chris's. I hadn't intended to say it out loud, but Brandon clearly took it as a request meant for him, while Chris licked his lips (the bastard) and smiled at me.

Brandon put a hand between us and started unbuttoning his pants. "Just keep doing what you're doing, baby," he said, his voice low and thick with lust. "I'll take it from here."

Chris kept his eyes on mine and said, "Lick his neck. Just the tip of your tongue."

I shivered and ran my tongue over Brandon's neck, pausing to suck lightly at the place where his pulse beat against his skin.

"Eyes on me," Chris said. "Don't stop watching me."

I moaned, and my eyes crossed as Brandon started undoing *my* pants. Chris took a step closer, and I used my teeth to nip at Brandon's neck while still keeping eye contact with Chris.

"I want to see your face," Chris said. "I want to know what you look like when you have a dick in you for the first time." He took another step closer. "You're going to love it. I can already tell. You're going to be such a bottom, Tyler."

Brandon's hand slipped into my open pants and past my underwear, and I hissed in pleasure when his fingers wrapped around me. I dug my nails in to his shoulders harder and sucked on his neck.

Chris broke eye contact then and slid his gaze down to where Brandon's hand was. I wasn't sure how much he could see from his angle, but it must have been enough to keep his attention.

"Does that feel good?" Brandon asked, and it took me a few seconds to realize that I could answer him out loud without seeming like a psycho.

"Yeah," I choked out. "Yeah, that's good."

"You act like you want to bottom." He leaned back enough to see my face. "Is that cool with you?"

I pulled my eyes away from Chris to look at Brandon. "Yes." I bit my lip for a moment. "Just . . . it's my first time bottoming so . . . you know. Go slow."

"And use a fucking condom," Chris snapped. "Don't let the bastard act like he forgot."

Brandon was reaching for my jacket and wasn't watching my face anymore, so I shot Chris the dirtiest look I could muster given that my cock was hanging out of my pants. Chris opened his mouth like he was going to keep hassling me, but luckily at that moment Brandon pulled the condoms and lube out of my jacket pocket and tossed them on the bed beside us, in full view of Chris. I raised my eyebrow at Chris and tried to tailor my expression to mean "There, now shut the hell up." He just nodded and crossed his arms.

Brandon pressed a kiss against my jaw and kissed his way down my chest and stomach. I momentarily forgot that Chris was watching and squirmed on the bed, letting out a choked half moan when Brandon's chin bumped into my cock. He smiled and licked a stripe up the back side of it, and I hissed through my teeth and closed my eyes.

Brandon pushed my pants down farther to give himself more room, and he raked his fingernails over the tops of my thighs while he leaned down to nuzzle my balls. They tightened, and I moaned again, not particularly caring that I was turning into much more of a moaner than I usually was with women.

Did Chris ever do this when he was alive? Did he like giving head? Did he use his tongue like Brandon was doing? I imagined how it would have felt in the morning, before he'd shaved, the rough stubble rubbing my inner thighs while he pressed his nose lightly against the sensitive skin there. I could picture him with his mouth on my cock. He'd probably do that thing where he looked up at me through his eyelashes while he slid his lips down over me . . .

I opened my eyes and looked at Chris, my vision swimming a little with lust. "Chris," I whispered, embarrassingly desperate, and my hand lifted off the bed of its own accord like I was reaching for him. Chris jerked forward before he took a step backward and swallowed hard.

Brandon either hadn't heard me say some other dude's name or was ignoring it. He gave my cock another lick, earning himself a low moan that I didn't actually intend to give, then rolled over to the side of me. "Take your pants off and flip over," he said. "It's easier that way the first time. Don't worry, I'll go slow." He gave me a big smile and a wink before starting to remove the last of his clothes.

Chris cleared his throat. "I don't think I'm gonna watch after all," he said. "I'll give you privacy. I'll, um, wait in the hall."

I pushed myself up on my elbows and tried to search his face to see why he was backing out, but he was already walking toward the wall of the room. A pretty alarming surge of disappointment flooded through me as I watched him go, and it occurred to me that I wasn't going to enjoy this if he wasn't there.

The non-lust-crazed parts of my brain had an explanation for that, and I didn't have my wits about me enough to push it away. I had it bad. For a ghost. And not in a sexual way, either—that at least would have been more or less easy to ignore. But no, I had it *emotionally* bad. For a ghost.

Fuck my life.

"Wait," I said, out loud. Chris stopped and turned around slowly. I could feel his eyes on me, and I knew he was metaphorically holding his breath. As if there was really any choice other than Chris at this point.

I looked at Brandon. "I'm sorry, man, I need a minute first. I'll be right back, okay?"

Brandon's eyes narrowed a little. "Are you bailing on me?"

"No." I fought the urge to look over and lock eyes with Chris. "Maybe? I told you back at the bar that I had a boyfriend. I need to know that he's okay with this first."

"You've got to be kidding me," Brandon said. He motioned down at himself. "*Now* you need to call him?"

"I'm sorry," I said. "I'll just go call him, and I'll be back."

Brandon narrowed his eyes even more but nodded, and I scrambled off the bed and made a beeline for the bathroom.

CHAPTER
TWENTY-FIVE

In the bathroom, I closed the door behind me. Chris had followed me in and stood there with his hands shoved in his pockets and the tips of his ears tinged red as he stared down at the floor. "You don't have to stop," he said. "You want him. And you deserve some stress relief after everything I'm putting you through."

It felt weird to be having this discussion with my straining dick pointing at Chris through my open pants, so I tucked it back inside and refastened the button of my jeans. Not the zipper, though—it was way too dangerous to zip my pants when I was in this condition, so he'd just have to deal with an unzipped tent for a few minutes.

"Just, um, make sure he actually puts the condom *on*, you know? It's important. Don't be silly, wrap the willy." He continued staring at the floor.

"Okay, I'm going to need you to stop with the condom rhymes," I murmured. Then, more seriously: "Don't go."

He still didn't look up, and I wanted very, very badly to grab his chin and force his eyes up to mine. After a moment, he shrugged at the ugly green tile on the bathroom floor. "I just wasn't having fun anymore."

"I want you to be there, okay?" I said. "I . . ." Fuck, how could I explain this without saying something stupid? Ugh. "It won't feel right if you're not there."

"I'm just watching him touch you and hearing the sounds you're making and I keep thinking . . ." He sighed. "That, you know, it should have been me."

"Because you're horny?" I asked, ignoring how much I hoped he would disagree.

"Because—" He broke off. "I don't know. I just wish it was me, that's all."

"Chris," I started, but I wasn't sure exactly what to say after that. *I was closing my eyes and imagining it was you* seemed awfully melodramatic. So did *If you weren't noncorporeal I'd let you have me against the sink right now.* And I especially couldn't say *Why the fuck did you have to kill yourself an hour before we would have met anyway?* So instead I just shrugged and said, "I wish it was you, too."

The outer door of the hotel room shut heavily, and Chris and I both jumped at the sudden sound. Chris turned and stuck his head through the bathroom wall to check the room. "He's gone," he said when he pulled his head back. His eyes shot to the floor again.

"I don't blame him," I said. There was a long silence, then Chris finally looked up at me. "What the fuck are we going to do?"

"God only knows," I said, laughing a little under my breath. "This situation is about sixty kinds of fucked up."

He smiled a tiny, tiny smile. "Yeah. It really is."

And then, because thoughts of the night Chris died had snagged in my mind and this whole thing was feeling shimmery and unreal anyway: "Could I have saved you?"

His forehead wrinkled. "What do you mean?"

"Nothing," I said, shaking my head hard. "Never mind."

"Well," he said after it became clear I wasn't going to relent and tell him. "This whole idea backfired dramatically, didn't it?"

I snorted. "Yeah. I guess it did."

"Do you want to go find a theater and see a movie or something?"

"Sure." I left the bathroom and found my discarded shirt, Chris trailing behind me as always. "I'm gonna go, um, freshen up. Don't follow me."

Chris raised an eyebrow. "I just watched a guy suck your cock. How is watching you in the bathroom any different from that?"

"You're a dick," I said, a little more centered now that I could go back to insulting him. It just felt more natural. "I need like five minutes."

"Are you going to, you know . . .?" Chris waggled his eyebrows at me and made a lewd motion with his hand.

"No, you asshole," I snapped. "I'm going to go wash some dude's spit off of myself and brush my teeth so my mouth doesn't taste like a bar. Now leave me alone."

"Okay," he said, sitting down on the rumpled bed. "Hurry up, though. I'm already bored."

I rolled my eyes and turned on the TV for him, then took my shirt in the bathroom. I'd already showered once that day—like I could forget after what I'd learned about myself as a result of *that* shower—but I felt gross and I probably reeked of cigarette smoke from the bar, so another one wouldn't hurt. I stripped out of my clothes and jumped in the shower, letting the water run over my skin and wash Brandon's fingerprints off of me.

I did seriously consider jerking it in the shower again, but it didn't seem quite right since . . . since whatever had just happened. Which was also fucking ridiculous. I'm not some kind of raging horndog or anything, but it wasn't like I could be celibate for the rest of my life, especially if I was going to be faced with a famous sex icon in my room every morning.

I finished rinsing myself off and climbed out of the shower, then tied a towel around my waist and reached for my phone. Between the noise from the bathroom fan and the chatter of the TV, I hoped I could risk a quick call.

I tapped my fingers on the cheap laminate countertop beside the sink while I waited for Gemma to answer.

"Hi, Tyler," she said. "Aren't you in California?"

"Yeah," I said, keeping my voice low just in case. "Hey . . . I have a favor to ask you."

"Okay, go ahead."

I took a deep breath and stared into my own eyes in the mirror. "I need you to do some research. Find some, you know, credible-sounding sources. As much as any source about ghosts can be credible, I guess."

"I've been doing some research already. It seems like the whole clichéd unfinished business thing is the consensus, as far as I can tell. So you're doing the right thing."

"Yeah, well . . ." I sighed. "I need you to find out if, um, anyone's ever touched one. And how they did it, you know?"

There was a beat too long of silence. "Oh," she said. "I see."

I wrinkled my nose. "I'm also going to need you not to *see*."

"All right, all right," she said, laughing a little. "I'll see what I can find out."

"Thanks," I said. "I wish I knew what the hell I was doing."

"Do you want me to do a reading for you? I just got a new tarot deck and I've been wanting to try it out."

I thought about that for a second. On the one hand, yes, I absolutely wanted to know what the hell I was doing and what was going to happen. But on the other hand, I was sort of afraid of what cards would come up. I didn't know much about tarot beyond what she'd told me before. Maybe there was a card called "Just a Heads-up that the Bellboy is Making Googly Eyes at You Behind Your Back" and if so, Chris really didn't need to know that. His ego was too big to fit through standard doorways as it was. But still, if we were doing readings about Chris's business, then he deserved to be in the room to hear it, so I'd just have to hope she wouldn't pull any especially embarrassing cards to describe my feelings.

"Tyler?" Gemma prompted.

"Oh," I said, blinking myself back into reality. "Um, sure. Can I hang up and call you again in a couple of minutes?"

"Okay. I'll get my deck out and get ready."

"Thanks."

After I hung up with her, I finished drying off and making myself presentable, then started toward the door before I stopped and opened my toiletry bag. Chris's ring was tucked inside and there was some other assorted jewelry in the bag too. I didn't wear jewelry that often, but every once in a while I put some on, and there was a punk-looking chain necklace in there that I wore when I was trying to come across as badass. I pulled out the ring, threaded it onto the chain necklace, and then put it over my head and tucked it into my shirt.

Before I could change my mind about how ridiculously sappy that was, I made myself go out into the hotel room. Chris was sprawled on the dingy couch watching some action movie with a lot of motorcycles and explosions, and it really wasn't fair how sexy he looked when I couldn't do anything about it.

"Up for a long-distance tarot reading before we head out?" I tried to keep my voice normal.

"That could be useful, I guess," he said, standing and giving me a lopsided smile. "By the way, that douche stole your lube."

"Shit." I glanced over toward the bed. "Well, I guess he can have it." It wasn't like I was going to be using it. Unfortunately.

Chris watched me for a few seconds. "Thanks," he said, putting his hands in his jeans pockets. "For, you know, stopping."

I shrugged. "No problem, man. I'll call Gemma back, and she'll help us figure out what we're supposed to be doing."

He sat back down on the couch, and I sat on the other end, keeping as much distance between us as I could manage. Touching or no touching, it would have felt kind of weird to sit close to him after whatever had just happened. Whatever that had been.

Now that he'd seen me naked, I wondered what he thought about me, how I stacked up to the others, but I couldn't think of a way to ask that didn't sound *way* more than five percent homo, which seemed to be the rule in this relationship. Or at least it was the rule in the spoken-out-loud part of the relationship, "I wish it was you" notwithstanding.

Shit. Maybe that rule was shot to hell now. Maybe we should up the percentage limit to twenty percent—even though to be honest, we were probably way past that too.

"What did you mean earlier?" Chris said. "When you asked if you could have saved me?"

I pulled out my phone and focused on the screen instead of on him. "Nothing."

He angled his body toward me. "It's going to bug me. Did you mean could you have done CPR or something?"

I sighed. "I meant . . . if I'd gotten to your room faster. Before you shot up. If I'd said fuck the seedless grapes and taken you the steak. I just wanted to know if I could have saved you."

"Probably not," he said after a moment. "I would have just shot up later."

That was a bit of a punch to the gut even though I logically knew that's probably what would have happened. "I guess dying is one way to kick the habit."

"Yeah," he said, then leaned back against the couch and looked up at the ceiling. "Probably not the *best* way, though. But I never really did what was best for me."

I pulled up Gemma's number and tried not to think about Chris's body lying on the floor with blood on his arms. "I'm calling her now."

She answered quickly. "Hi again."

"I'm putting you on speaker," I told her. "So Chris can hear you too."

I pressed the speakerphone button and set the phone between us on the couch. The sound of shuffling cards came through the receiver and Gemma said, "Hi, Chris."

"He says hi," I said, even though he hadn't. "So what's the plan?"

"I figured I'd just do a basic reading," she answered. "You know. Past, present, near future, ultimate outcome. And then something about what you want and what you'll need going forward."

"Can we leave out the 'what you want' part?" I asked, and Chris snapped his head up to look at me, but I refused to meet his eyes.

"Um, sure," she said. "All right, so let's do this."

"What is it that you want, Tyler?" Chris said. He was still staring at me. I could feel it.

"Nothing she needs to know about," I mumbled.

He seemed to accept that as a legitimate answer, which was good because like hell was I going to really get into it.

"Okay," Gemma said. "So first. Your past." There was a pause and the rustle of a flipping card. "Eight of Swords. That's a card that means stagnation, being trapped."

"Makes sense," I said, "especially for Chris. Being as he was dead." I looked up at him and corrected myself. "Still is dead. But I mean when he was dead and not a ghost yet."

He smirked at me, and I made a face at him. Gemma continued, "Okay, the present. Page of Cups."

"Wasn't that what I drew for Chris before?" I asked her.

"No, that was the Knight of Cups. This is the Page. This one means the beginning of a journey."

Chris said, "That's a little on the nose, don't you think?" at the same time I said it. I groaned, and Gemma asked what was going on.

"Nothing," I told her. "We just said the 'on the nose' thing at the same time. It was gross. Okay, cool, next?"

"Well, let's do what you need going forward first." A flip of a card. "Tyler, you got Strength. So that's what you'll need going forward." She paused. "It means more or less what you think it means. Be strong. Be brave. All that. But it also means that you need to have faith in yourself. To believe that you're important, even if you don't feel that way."

Chris winked at me. "You're important, dude. Don't worry."

I rolled my eyes at him. "Chris says he's a prick," I told Gemma. "Next?"

"And for what you need, Chris," she said. "The Eight of Cups. It's a card about letting go of past relationships and finding happiness somewhere else."

"Noted." I looked at Chris and shrugged. He shrugged back. "Do you think that means you need to talk to Tori after all?"

He snorted. "No, I'm pretty sure Tori and I are not unfinished business. We were about as finished as you can get."

There was no rush of dread when he said that like there had been the one time we'd talked about procrastinating on important things, so I decided he was telling the truth. "He says no, Gems. I'm guessing all of that will make sense when it's important?"

"Hopefully," she answered. "I mean, sometimes it doesn't make sense until it's all over. Hindsight and everything."

"I guess that's better than nothing," I said.

"Okay, so near future."

While we waited for her to flip the cards, I smiled at Chris, getting a smile back that made my blood race more than I wanted to admit.

"The Lovers," she said, then kept talking really quickly. "That doesn't necessarily mean romantic love. Kind of like how Death almost never means death? I read the Lovers as a choice card. You're going to have to make a choice."

Chris frowned at the phone. "What choice?"

I repeated the question to Gemma, and she responded, "I don't know. But it will be a big one. And a hard one to make. But after that . . ." The sound of a card flipping again, then nothing.

"Okay, I'm really not liking the ominous silence when you flip a 'future' card," I told her, trying to infuse my voice with a stern edge.

"Well," she said, "I don't know what to tell you. See, I do this thing where I use a blank card. Remember when Chris said that one of the cards I held up was just a list of contact information?"

"Yeah, I remember. So what does that mean? Basically 'Hell if I know'?"

"Pretty much," she admitted. "It's a blind spot. Something that we can't see for some reason. It could be because the Lovers' choice will make a difference on what happens."

Or it could be that Chris would be gone, and the cards couldn't see into the afterlife. Somehow that made more sense to me than the easier explanation that we just didn't know yet. And the possibility that the cards knew he was going to be leaving turned the acid in my stomach to ice.

"Well, those are the cards," Gemma said. "I'll do some more readings and I'll keep up my research and keep you posted, okay?"

I thanked her and hung up, then smiled at Chris with a little more cheer than I actually felt. "Well, that wasn't terribly helpful. Ready to go to the movie?"

"Yeah," he said. "Lead on."

We headed back into the dark that had fallen over the city. And if, while we walked, our fingers stretched out toward each other like they didn't understand that they couldn't touch, neither of us mentioned it.

CHAPTER TWENTY-SIX

T he next morning, we got up early and went downstairs for the hotel's crappy free breakfast. The east-facing windows of the hotel lobby were too bright to look at, so I found a table in the corner of the lobby that faced away from them and sat down to eat rubbery eggs and weirdly dry sausage. None of the other guests had come down for breakfast—which probably should have tipped me off about the quality—and the desk clerk was nowhere to be seen, so I didn't worry too much about being overheard while Chris and I talked.

We knew Eric was in town. He had a house in Los Angeles where he stayed while he wasn't touring, and he was there now. I'd made sure of that before I booked the trip—entertainment news was good for something after all. But I had no idea how I was going to get in to see him. Chris, of course, was no help.

"Just text him," he said as he watched me eat. "Tell him you want to talk to him."

"He doesn't know my number, dude. He'll just think I'm some creepy stalker fan who hacked a database to get his cell number."

Chris pursed his lips. "True."

"I could try to talk to the band manager," I suggested. "I might be able to get through to him, and then I could convince him to get Eric to call me back?"

"No good," Chris said. "Woman's a hard-ass. She'd never let you through. She'd brush off God himself instead of getting him an interview. And she'd be *really* pissed that you called her a 'him.'"

"Well, I guess I could try to stalk what club he goes to and happen to show up there," I said. The coffee was terrible, but it was coffee, and it was free, so I forced it down. I had the feeling I would need it.

"He hardly ever goes out except to private parties," Chris said. "And only to ones with very strict guest lists."

"Well, I don't know, then. We probably should have worked out a game plan before we came here."

"Probably," he said, then sighed. "Well, there's nothing for it. You'll have to break in to his house."

I almost spit out the coffee I was drinking. "You want me to *break in* to his *house*?"

He shrugged like it wasn't a big deal. "I know his security password," he said. "It wouldn't be breaking in so much as just going in uninvited. Which I did all the time."

"You *knew* him, though," I pointed out. "That's different from some random stranger barging into his kitchen while he's trying to fry up some bacon."

"You're not a random stranger," Chris said. "You're me."

"Gee, thanks for making me nothing more than a vessel for your divine possession," I deadpanned.

"Dude, if I could use you as a vessel, I totally would. That would make all of this way easier."

I rolled my eyes. "You'd just spend all day boning random people and watching *The Meadow Larks*. Probably at the same time."

He laughed. "Yeah, probably. At least until I got it out of my system."

I started to say that he'd also probably shoot my body up with illegal substances, but that seemed mean after everything that had happened, so instead I went back to the problem at hand. "So you want me to just walk up into his house and tell him you're haunting me."

"Yeah, something like that," Chris said, sticking his hands in his pockets and gazing out the window.

"And then relay you telling him how much you appreciate him."

"And that I'm sorry I broke out of rehab when he put me in there."

I blinked. "You broke out of rehab?"

Chris nodded, then paused and shook his head. "Yes and no. I checked myself in voluntarily because he interventioned me."

"I'm not sure 'interventioned' is a word," I said, "but okay."

He rolled his eyes at me. "And then because I'd checked myself in, I could check myself out. So I did. After two days."

"Why?"

He shrugged. "Because I didn't like it there."

"You didn't like it because you were a junkie and you were jonesing." I waggled a finger at him for emphasis.

"Well, yeah," he said. "But it really sucked."

"I'm sure it did. I'm also willing to bet that Eric was pretty pissed when he found out you'd bailed on it."

He frowned. "Eric is a self-centered asshole. He didn't care about me, he just wanted to make sure the band survived and he knew I wasn't giving the music my full attention anymore. He should have booted me out and hired fucking Nathan Vale back then and saved us all a lot of grief."

"Not that much grief," I said. "Since you probably would have just ended up dying even sooner and then I wouldn't have found you."

Chris hesitated for a moment, eyeing me. "Would that be a bad thing?"

I shrugged. "My life is definitely more interesting with you in it. I mean, without you I wouldn't be able to say I'd been held at gunpoint by a drug dealer in an LA florist shop. That would make the autobiography I might write someday a lot more boring."

"Yeah," he said. "You would have just married Gemma and had a couple of little Bostonian kids and never come to Los Angeles at all."

"Dude, I wouldn't have married Gemma. I wouldn't have even *met* Gemma if it wasn't for you."

He flexed his fingers and followed the movements of his tendons with his eyes.

The silence got awkward, so I continued. "So . . . I'm breaking into a celebrity's house, huh?"

He looked back up at me and offered a small smile. "Yeah, I guess that's best."

"You know his codes? You're *sure* you know his codes?"

"I remember everything, dude. Of course I know his codes."

"You knew what they were a month ago," I pointed out. "Do you know for sure he hasn't changed them?"

"If he's changed them, I might move on out of pure shock," he said. "Eric never changes his codes. Never. He still has the same PIN for his bank account that he did when he opened up his junior saver savings account in fourth grade." He smiled at me. "And his PIN is the same as his security passcode for his house. And the safe in his bedroom. And his safety deposit box at the bank. And his locker code for the gym. Basically if you know Eric's first dog's birthdate, you can clean the man out."

I laughed. "He uses his dog's birthdate as his personal code?"

"He loved that dog," Chris said, still smiling. "Said when it died, that was the worst day of his life." He paused for a moment, his smile slipping a little. "It probably still is."

Awkward. I reached out to pat his hand before I remembered I couldn't. "I'm sure he misses you. I mean, you guys were best friends."

"He hated me," Chris said, kind of scary-softly. "He wouldn't answer my phone calls and he wouldn't even look at me unless he absolutely had to. He'd bail on interviews if I was going to be there. He . . ." His voice broke, then he cleared his throat and repeated himself. "He hated me."

I considered arguing with him, but that seemed to be pretty good evidence of the whole hatred thing. So instead I went into damage-control mode. "There at the end, maybe. But you know . . . people who are as close as you and Eric used to be . . . they can fix things. If you had that much, you know, love-or-whatever there between you before things went downhill, there's hope to fix it."

He was silent for a minute. "Maybe it's too late. Maybe it's stupid to want to talk to him."

I shook my head. "No, it's not stupid. I mean, maybe it's really not going to change or fix anything. Maybe he's just an ass and won't accept your apology. But you have to try it, for you. You can't move on without at least attempting to make things right."

"Will you eat some ice cream for me and let me complain about it if he doesn't want to listen?" he asked, smiling once more, just a little.

I rolled my eyes but smiled back. "Sure. We'll go on a double date with Ben and Jerry."

"So . . ." He stood, taking his time getting out of his chair and straightening up. "I guess we should go now?"

I sighed and stood too. "Maybe I'll change all my PIN codes to today's date. To commemorate the first time I was ever arrested."

Chris scoffed. "You're not going to get arrested."

"I just always thought that the first time I had gay sex would be because of something like last night, not because *prison*." I grinned at him.

"You're so dramatic," Chris said, rolling his eyes. "The worst that will happen is he'll throw you out of his house."

"And call the FBI."

"Not unless you really piss him off," Chris said.

"Well." I took a deep breath. "I guess now is as good a time as any."

"We're going now?" he asked, his voice a little weaker than before.

I nodded. "That's what you just said. We should go now."

"I know," he said. "I just . . . This is kind of a huge deal for me."

I dumped my plate into the trash receptacle and stretched, then started walking toward the hotel entrance. "You'll feel better once you've talked to him, though."

"Or worse," Chris muttered, then spoke louder. "You should know that a lot of my conversations with Eric tend to end in tears or yelling. Or both."

"Was it always like that?"

"No." He stopped walking, and I faced him.

"So . . . are you sure you're ready for this?" I asked after a moment.

He fixed his eyes on the dingy orange carpet of the deserted hotel foyer. "No. Maybe I shouldn't."

"If it's this terrifying to you, then that probably means you need to do it," I pointed out. "If you want to move on and all, I mean."

"Do I?" he asked, then lifted his gaze to mine.

I looked away immediately. "I'm pretty sure that's what ghosts are supposed to do, dude."

"But I thought maybe . . ."

I knew what he meant, obviously, but I wasn't sure I could handle a conversation about it yet. But he hadn't finished his sentence, and so

I offered a compromise. "Well, you'll still have to talk to your sister. So this isn't all, you know?"

"Do you think—?"

"What's his address?" I interrupted, a little desperately. We'd said plenty of things last night, and I really didn't want to add more to the processing pile just yet.

Chris sighed, letting his shoulders sag. "You wrote it down."

I nodded and pulled the scrap of paper out of my pocket, then turned around and started walking briskly again. "Do you think we could go to Death Valley after we talk to him? I have a couple of days left to kill and I've always wanted to go."

Chris didn't say anything for several seconds, then sighed. "It's a four-and-a-half-hour drive to Death Valley."

"I know." My voice was a little too bright and filled with the pathetic stench of overcompensation, but I couldn't seem to tone it down. "But who knows if I'll ever be this close to it again? I should go while I can, right?"

"You don't have a car," he pointed out.

I stepped out of the hotel and headed for the nearest intersection, where I figured I should be able to find a cab. "Maybe I could rent one. Or get a bus."

"You don't have enough money for that," Chris said. "You know . . . Eric probably still has my car. I left it at his house when we went on tour, and I can't imagine he would have ditched it after I died."

I glanced over at him and raised an eyebrow as I put in my phone earpiece for the cab driver's benefit. "You want me to drive your car to Death Valley."

Chris shrugged. "If he believes us, he'll loan it to you."

"What kind of car is it?" I asked. "Oh God, is it a Maserati? I've always wanted to drive a Maserati."

"You just want to drive one because of the song," he accused, but he was smiling a little bit again.

"Yeah, mostly," I said. "But I swear I won't do 185 in it. I need my license."

Chris laughed. "You don't need your license. I don't even know for sure that you *have* a license. You take the subway everywhere."

"I have a license," I assured him. "It's been like a year and a half since I've driven, but it's still valid and everything."

He shook his head. "I'm not letting you drive my Mas if you haven't even driven a golf cart in over a year."

"I can still drive," I began, then paused. "Wait. You actually have a Maserati?"

He dimple-smiled at me and shrugged. "I had money. I spent a lot of it."

"Does it really do 185? I mean, really?"

He laughed again. "It does a hell of a lot more than that, actually. Not that I would know from experience driving out in the desert in the middle of the night or anything." He gave me an exaggerated shifty-eyed innocent look and grinned.

"Dude," I said. "*Dude.*"

"Now you have even more incentive to convince him we're for real," he said, still grinning.

We took a taxi to Eric's neighborhood, then just walked up to the gate and casually punched in the key code like this was just an everyday thing and not a B&E on a celebrity home. I caught myself wishing it hadn't been so easy, wishing that we'd had to give up so we could just go back to the hotel and . . . do whatever it was we did now. Painting our toenails and talking about feelings, probably. Or, more accurately, awkwardly watching bad reality TV and pointedly *not* talking about feelings.

Not that there were feelings. No sirree Bob. No feelings.

And then it was just a short walk across a paved courtyard and the same key code on the front door, and we were in.

Chris stopped just inside and looked around.

"Has it changed?" I asked, keeping my voice low.

"No," Chris murmured. "Not really."

I gave him a second to get his game face back on, then I cleared my throat. "So . . . where should I go?"

"He's upstairs," Chris said, staring up at the ceiling.

"How do you know?" It wasn't like there was music or loud talking or anything, so I wasn't sure if he really *knew* or if he was just making shit up.

Chris took a really long time to drag his gaze away from the ceiling. "What time is it?"

I pulled out my phone. "Nine fifteen," I said, holding it out to show him. He didn't look, and after a couple of seconds I put the phone back in my pocket.

He didn't speak, so I continued. "Why does it matter what time it is?"

"He sleeps until nine thirty every morning unless there's a reason to get up earlier," Chris said quietly. "His keys are on the table over there," he pointed to a small marble-top table by the door, "so he's not gone. So he's upstairs. Asleep. For fifteen more minutes."

"Jesus, dude, you know his patterns super well," I said, lowering my voice to a whisper even though there was no way Eric could hear me from all the way upstairs anyway.

Chris shrugged. "He's been pretty much the only person who gave a shit about me since mom got sick," he said, finally forcing his eyes down from the ceiling. "I just filed the information away."

"Well, cool, I guess." I shuffled my feet. "So . . . where should I go?"

"He'll go down to the kitchen first. Best to meet him there," he said, then started walking through the house toward what I assumed was the kitchen.

I trailed along behind him, looking around and trying not to think about the fact that I'd just broken into a celebrity's home and I'd be lucky if I wasn't body-slammed into the floor by an overzealous burly bodyguard. My skin was tingling like I'd just slathered myself in aloe vera cooling gel, but I put that down to nerves and followed Chris into the kitchen.

It was a large room with big east-facing windows behind the counters and an island with expensive appliances—the kind of kitchen you'd see in a display house but wouldn't necessarily expect to see in a hard rocker's home.

"Does he cook a lot?" I asked, running a hand over the cold granite countertop of the island.

"What?" Chris looked up sharply.

"Sorry, dude, didn't mean to scare you." I motioned vaguely at the stove. "Does he cook a lot? Eric?"

He shrugged. "He cooks enough."

Well, thank goodness we only had to make small talk for another fourteen minutes, because damn if Chris wasn't making this whole thing difficult. I went over to a pub table in the corner of the room and sat down on one of the chairs. The minutes crawled by so slowly that I was sure I'd aged at least a decade in the fifteen minutes before a loud buzzing came from upstairs.

"He's up," Chris said, every muscle in his body tensing.

Not that I was noticing every muscle in his body.

I had a few more seconds to change my mind about the whole thing and bolt out through the front door, but I wasted them worrying about how Chris was going to handle all this. So by the time my feet got the message from my brain to *move right now*, Eric had walked into the room.

CHAPTER
TWENTY-SEVEN

He was wearing gray sweatpants and a fitted navy-blue T-shirt, and my first thought was, *Wow, Carmen would lose her shit if she knew I'd gotten to see Eric Painter in his pajamas.*

My second thought was, *Fuck my life, I'm going to prison for sure.*

I didn't have time to formulate a third thought before he saw me. He yelled, "Fuck!" and scrambled away, slamming his back into the refrigerator with enough force to knock the magnets off of it. They skittered across the floor like frightened mice.

I held my hands in the air. "It's okay, it's okay, I'm not going to hurt you."

He shook his index finger at me hard, still leaning backward against the fridge door. "Who the hell are you? What are you doing in my house?"

"Okay, I can explain."

"You sure as hell better start," he said, straightening up.

"It's a great explanation, but you have to hear me out all the way, okay?" I spread my hands again so he could see I wasn't armed, with a weapon or a camera. "What I'm going to say is going to sound batshit crazy, but I swear I can prove it to you, you just have to give me a chance."

"Talk faster," he snapped. "Is it an exclusive? That's what you want? Who's paying you?"

"Nobody," I said, then I took a deep breath and spoke really fast. "My name's Tyler Lindsey, I'm from Boston, and I came here because I'm, um, being haunted by the ghost of Chris Raiden and he wants me to tell you some things so that he can go on to whatever afterlife awaits him. And I know there's no way in hell you're going to take my word for that, but I can prove it."

There was a long silence. Chris didn't even appear to be breathing, but I guessed that wasn't a huge problem seeing as he didn't even have physical lungs.

Finally, Eric gave me a death glare and growled, "Get the fuck out of my house before I call the police."

"I'm serious," I begged. I took a step forward. "It's super hella cliché, I know, but you can ask me anything. Something only he would know. And I'll be able to answer because he's standing right here and he'll tell me what the answer is."

Eric stared at me. "You're insane."

"I wondered that myself at first," I admitted. "But I'm pretty sure I'm sane. Otherwise how else would I have gotten in here? He told me your passcode."

Chris was being very, very silent. I wasn't even sure he'd moved a single muscle since Eric walked into the room. I wanted to ask if he was okay, but getting Eric to believe me was step one, and so I didn't ask.

"You're insane," Eric said again. "I'm calling the cops."

"Chris," I said, looking deliberately over at him. "I need something, man."

He forced his eyes over to me, and I flinched at the raw emotion in them. "I—I don't know what to say. Maybe we should just go."

"Dude, he's going to call the cops," I said, raising my voice a little. "If you wanted to bail, you should have done it ten minutes ago."

Eric started inching in the direction of the door he'd come in.

"Wait." I took another step toward him. "Just give him a second. He'll tell me something."

"Fuck you," Eric said. "Fuck you for breaking into my house and for trying to cash in on my best friend's death." He whirled around and started stalking out of the kitchen.

Chris blinked several times and shook his head hard. "Eric," he said, loudly, and then he took three running steps and grabbed Eric's arm.

Sometimes in movies they do this thing where all the noise fades out, everything stops moving, and the whole scene grinds to a deathly silent halt, and I swear to God that's what it felt like here. Eric froze in his tracks, Chris's mouth fell open as he stared at his own hand gripping Eric's arm, and my whole thought process shut completely down for a few heartbeats.

And then: "Oh, you *asshole.*"

For a moment there I wasn't even sure who had said it. It was certainly something that could have come from any of us. But after further mental inventory, I decided that yep, it was me. Because Chris was a huge fucking asshole.

Standing there with his fingers curled into Eric's biceps and his eyes sparkling like the whole goddamn world was a great place to be again. While here I stood, over in Eric fucking Painter's kitchen risking jail time for him, and he didn't even *tell* me. Not once, in all of our conversations about coming out here and talking to Eric, had he seen fit to mention . . . *this.*

I couldn't even put a name to it in my own brain because I was so pissed off, but the look on Chris's face was really all the name I needed.

"I should have fucking known," I muttered. "I should have seen it. God*damn* it, Chris."

Chris slowly released Eric's arm and turned to look back at me. "What?"

"*That,*" I almost yelled, gesturing at Eric's arm. "I'm guessing that probably means something. And I'm pretty sure I know what the something is, Chris."

"You're being hysterical," he said. "I don't know why that happened. I don't know why it worked."

Eric cleared his throat and faced me, moving very slowly. "I'm assuming that wasn't you."

"No," I ground out. "No, it wasn't."

"Why didn't you lead with that?" he asked.

I shot Chris the dirtiest look I could muster. "I didn't know he could touch people. He's never done it before."

There was a long silence, then Eric spoke. "Tell him to do it again. While I'm watching you."

"He can hear you," I spat out. "Tell him yourself."

Eric looked at the air near his arm and swallowed visibly. "Um . . . Chris?"

Chris lifted his hand and let it hang in the air for a moment like he was deciding where to touch, then let his hand fall onto Eric's shoulder. Eric jumped and put a hand on Chris's torso for a second before he pushed too hard and it went through Chris's back.

"He can touch me too," Chris murmured. "Did you see that?"

I ground my teeth. "I saw."

"I wonder why that is?" Chris said, sounding like he was talking to himself.

"I don't know," I snapped. "Just tell me what you want me to tell him so I can go home."

Eric looked over at me. His blue eyes met mine and I swear I felt legitimately sick to my stomach. "He's really here?" he asked in a somewhat shaky voice.

I nodded, setting my jaw and crossing my arms. "Right in front of you."

Eric reached his hand out again and laid it against Chris's chest. Chris sucked in a breath I could hear from across the room, and I hated both of them.

"I'm going to need you to prove it's him," Eric said, leaving his hand on Chris.

And I'm going to need you *to stop fucking caressing him*, but I didn't say that out loud. "Fine." I worked my jaw back and forth a little and then looked at Chris. "Anytime you're ready, Christopher."

Chris hung his head for a moment and then picked it up and met Eric's eyes as best he could. "Tell him I remember the night when we were in Berlin and . . . and we were drinking together in the hotel and . . ."

He trailed off, and I contemplated what act of violence I would commit if the next words out of his whore mouth were *and then we made love in the moonlight* or some shit. Some light vandalism, maybe. Or maybe I would just scream until Eric called the psych ward instead of the police.

Luckily, though, the actual end to his sentence was less horrible than that: "And he told me that he'd written a song about my dad. About . . . how it was for me. The feeling like a monster for not missing him. And he sang part of it for me and I had to make him stop."

"That's disgusting," I said. I repeated it to Eric anyway, who turned pale but nodded.

Chris kept his hand on Eric's shoulder, digging his fingers in a little like Eric's body was his only anchor to the world. He turned, though, and gave me a glance. "Tyler. What's wrong?"

"Don't fucking talk to me," I snapped. I knew I was being incredibly bitchy, but I couldn't bring myself to give a damn. "Talk to him and I'll translate and then I'm going back to Boston and you can go to hell."

Chris narrowed his eyes and tilted his head, and I *hated* that I found the head-tilting adorable, even under the circumstances. In a better situation I might have relented and forgiven him, but right now he had his damn hand on Eric like he was Prince fucking Charming and I wondered if I should go back to the same bar tonight to find Brandon and tell him I'd made a mistake and would he please fuck me up against a wall or something.

"Okay," Chris said at last. "Well. Tell him . . . I'm sorry."

"He says he's sorry," I repeated in the flattest voice I could manage. Eric swallowed again. "Ask him for what."

"Just talk to him, Jesus." I narrowed my eyes at Eric. "He can hear you and this translating is exhausting enough when it's just one-way."

Eric frowned. "What are you sorry for?"

Chris turned back to look him in the eyes, for whatever good it did. "I should have listened to you. I should have stayed in rehab when you sent me. I should have been the friend you deserved."

I repeated it after him, even using the *I*'s instead of switching them to *he*'s.

"Damn right you should have." Eric's voice was low-pitched and gravelly and he sounded like fucking *sex* and I wanted to throw something at him.

"I didn't think it would kill me," Chris said, his words breaking slightly. He lifted his other hand and put it on Eric's other shoulder. "I meant to stop. I always meant to stop one day."

While I repeated him, I even dropped the pissy monotone to try to match his tone as much as I could. Just because I was pissed at Chris didn't mean that Eric didn't deserve his closure. It wasn't like any of this was Eric's fault, even if my stomach insisted on giving a sick twist every time I remembered that Chris's hands were on him. Which I seemed to remember at least twice a second.

Eric was answering. "I can't believe that. If you hadn't died you would have kept going at it forever. I was tired of giving you chances to change."

Chris kept his hands on Eric's shoulders and tightened his fingers, digging them in harder. "I'm sorry. I don't know what else I can say."

Eric didn't say anything when I repeated that, and after a second Chris spoke again. "Did you go to the funeral?"

"Of course I did," Eric replied, furrowing his brow and scowling. "I loved you. You were my brother. You used to be my best friend before the drugs fucked that up. Of course I went."

The way that Chris flinched when Eric said the word "love" gave my stomach another twist, and I wasn't sure if this twist was sympathy or jealousy or anger or some screwed-up combination of all three. And the only thing that saved Eric from getting my fist in his testicles was that he'd definitely used the word in a platonic, brotherly sense.

Chris went for humor quickly enough that it was clear he'd had to recover from this sort of thing a lot in the past. "And then you hired Nathan Vale."

Eric groaned when I repeated that. "Oh, for God's sake. It's not like bassists grow on trees, you know. And he was available and he already knew most of our songs."

"Don't you dare hire him permanently," Chris growled.

"I will if I want to," Eric grumbled back. "You're dead." He laughed a little hysterically. "Oh my God, I'm standing in my kitchen talking to a *ghost*."

I wrinkled my nose. "I've been putting up with the bastard for months. You get used to it."

"So what now?" Eric asked. He stepped back, and Chris let him go, dropping his hands to his sides.

I sighed. "We're here so you guys can say what you need to say to each other. And then we're going to see his sister. And then . . ." I shrugged.

"And then he . . . disappears?"

"We have no idea, actually," I admitted. "That's the current theory. Finish up his business and then he leaves for whatever comes afterwards."

Chris turned again and looked at me. "Is that what you're hoping?"

"Shut up," I said in a flat voice. "I'm too pissed to talk about that right now."

Eric knitted his forehead. "Too pissed about what?"

"Nothing," I muttered. "Can we just continue with your good-byes and then we can get the hell out of here?"

"Ask him if he has my car," Chris said.

I clamped my jaw shut and ground my teeth for a second, then said, "He wants to know if you have his car."

"Yeah, it's in the garage," Eric said. "I got our manager to contact Allison and see if she wanted any of his other stuff, but . . . Well, she wanted the ring. But I didn't have that. Nobody really knows where it went when he . . ." He scowled. "When he died."

"Oh." I pulled the chain out from inside my shirt, only realizing how incredibly obvious that was when it was too late to change my mind. "This ring?"

Chris's eyes snapped to my hand. "You still have it?"

"Of course I still have it, you dick," I said. "You've been with me 24/7 since I picked it up. When would I have had time to get rid of it?"

"You . . . you *wear* it, though?" He looked floored by this, and I hated it.

"Shut up," I said. I pulled the necklace over my head and put it in my pocket. "I'll pass it off to Allison when we go to see her."

Chris opened his mouth, presumably to be a dick and keep talking about it, so I threw him a Death Glare and he sighed. "Well, ask him what he has that's mine."

I asked Eric the question. "Lots of things," he said. "I mean, his money went to Allison as his next of kin. She almost didn't take it, but his mom's care is expensive so I think she used it for that. But she didn't want any of his actual stuff, so I ended up with most of it, and I kept the important things. Some of his clothes. His car. His guitars."

Chris sucked in a breath. "Which guitar?"

"He wants to know which guitar you have," I told Eric.

Eric shrugged. "All of them."

Chris stepped forward and reached for Eric's arm again. Eric jumped when Chris's fingers wrapped around his biceps, then relaxed. "Do you want to see them?" he asked, so softly I almost didn't hear the question.

"He does," I said loudly, causing both of them to raise their stupid perfect rock star eyebrows at me. "Just show us."

CHAPTER
TWENTY-EIGHT

We followed Eric up to the second story, where he opened the door to what looked like a music room. On one wall was a sizable collection of guitars. Most of them were basses, but there were a couple of six-strings in the mix, including one that was significantly cheaper and more beat-up than the others.

"Holy shit," Chris said. "He has my first one."

Eric was talking too. "These are all the guitars he had in his house when they cleaned it out. They didn't know who else to give them to. Allison didn't want them, and I guess I was next in line for everything." He sighed. "I'd been thinking about auctioning them off for charity, but I just hadn't worked myself up to that yet."

Chris walked slowly over to the wall and reached for the old guitar. It didn't even surprise me when he wrapped his fingers around the neck and pulled it down off the wall—I'd known the second the bastard reached for it that he was going to be able to touch it. Since the second he'd laid eyes on it, he'd been looking at it like he'd looked at Eric a few minutes ago, so of course he could touch it. Of *course* he could.

My guts started to feel like they were going to fall out, so I wrapped my arms around my stomach. I stared down at the floor and focused on the grain of the wood, the way the varnish played with the light pouring in through the window and gave the boards the illusion of being lit from the inside. It was a little steadying, which was good, because I wasn't the one who had the right to break down over all of this. After all, it wasn't like Chris would have ever even talked to me if it wasn't for this cage I had him in. And it wasn't like this was a cage he would be in for much longer, so . . . the hollow wrenching feeling in my insides was going to happen sometime. I shouldn't have been surprised.

That didn't make me feel any better, though.

I had no real concept of how long I spent wrapped up in my wood-gazing reverie, but it couldn't have been very long because Eric clearly hadn't seen Chris pick up the guitar. I know this because it was him yelling "Fuck!" really loudly and stumbling backward that broke into my thoughts.

I laughed at him. It felt good.

"You can see Chris?" Eric asked me.

I thought about being sarcastic, but instead I just nodded.

"Then as far as you can see, there's not a levitating guitar in the middle of the room?" He gestured toward Chris and the guitar.

"No, just some guy fondling his guitar like it's made of tits," I answered. I could hear the bitterness in my voice and knew how obvious it must be to everybody else, but I wasn't sure I could do anything about it. So I didn't bother trying.

Chris flashed Eric a grin like he'd forgotten that Eric couldn't see him and strummed a chord on the guitar. It sounded horrible, and we all cringed.

"Oh my God, it's so out of tune." Chris started tuning the guitar, and I let my gaze fall back down to the floor.

"Um," Eric said. I glanced at him, but it seemed like "um" was all he had to say, and I wasn't in the mood to take the conversational bait.

So I didn't say anything, and after a moment Eric cleared his throat, and even *that* sounded like it was coated in caramel-flavored lube, which wasn't fucking fair. "I can get you a tuner if you need one."

Chris shook his head without looking up. "I don't need one. Almost done."

"He says no," I relayed to Eric as I pulled my arms tighter against my stomach.

And then when Chris strummed a chord that finally sounded right, we all sighed in unison, and I suddenly understood the insanity defense a lot more, because sighing in unison with Chris and Eric fucking Painter made me want to grab a guitar off the wall and smash it into the floor until it was nothing more than splinters and curled strings.

"It's been a long time," Chris murmured, caressing the neck of the guitar and probably getting a ghost boner from it if the look on his face was any indication. He found a stool in the corner of the room and sat on it, then started playing a simple melody.

Eric watched Chris and the guitar move across the room, and then he took a few steps toward the stool. "Do you want me to go get mine?"

"Oh, for fuck's sake," I said, but neither of them seemed to have heard me. Chris was just staring at him with a thunderstruck expression and so I spoke louder, "He says yes."

"Okay," Eric said. "I'll be right back." He left the room.

Chris stopped playing and raised an eyebrow at me. "What's wrong?"

"Nothing," I snapped, and he looked so confused that I took pity on him for being as dumb as a jar of paste, and went for a toned-down version of the explanation. "I just didn't expect . . ." I waved vaguely at the guitar. "This."

"I didn't either," he said, going back to plucking out a tune I'd heard before but couldn't place.

"Chris," I started, but then Eric walked back in the room carrying a black acoustic guitar—of *course* it was black—and another wooden stool. He'd also changed from his sweatpants into blue jeans and a Def Leppard T-shirt, and I specifically didn't look at Chris because I didn't want to see his eyes light up. Eric put the stool down near Chris and perched on it, swinging his guitar strap up over his neck.

He fidgeted a little as he got ready and took far too long positioning his guitar, then glanced at Chris's guitar and then up to where Chris's face would be. His eyes didn't point exactly at Chris's, which was good because I was pretty sure I would have a rage-induced aneurysm if Eric could *see* him too.

"Do you remember 'Houses on Fire'?" Eric asked.

Chris smiled softly and bent his head back to his guitar, then started playing the first part of the song—the rhythm guitar part instead of the bass line. I did recognize this one from the many times Carmen had played their first album, which had a hokey fire theme but was decent anyway, I guess.

Eric nodded and joined in. The song had an instrumental beginning and so it took them a while to get to the lyrics, but when Eric started to sing and Chris harmonized with him, my stomach dropped again and the shitty hotel breakfast suddenly seemed like an even worse idea than it had before.

"This is bullshit," I muttered. I needed some physical distance— even fifteen feet still felt way too close to me—so I backed away from them, walking backward until I saw Chris move forward a little as I got him to the end of his invisible chain, then I sat down on the floor and pulled out my phone so that I could have something to stare at besides the jam session in front of me.

The acoustic version of the song without the driving bass line and without the drums sounded a lot more wistful than the album version. It was a song about losing everything, falling into a void, and on the album and on stage it was one of those angry dark metal thrashing songs that made even the daintiest church mouse start headbanging and yelling about fucking The Man. But here in Eric's guitar room with the two of them perched on wooden stools and Chris staring into Eric's stupid blue eyes, it was almost like a ballad. I mean, a *power* ballad, but still. It was nauseating.

And it was fucking *gorgeous*, which made the whole thing even worse. But when would I ever hear this version of the song again? I found the voice recorder on my phone and pushed Record, hating myself a little as I did it.

They sang well together—Eric's deep powerful voice layered with Chris's lighter baritone—and they played and sang with the ease of years of practice. Chris closed his eyes and an effortless smile started to hover around the corners of his mouth, and Eric's angry-badass stage presence disappeared under the peace of the room and left the two of them looking like just guys with their music.

And *this* was where Chris belonged. Sitting beside Eric Painter and singing a triple-platinum song while the troubles visibly faded off his face. In a multiroomed house in Los Angeles where the temperature was kept at a comfortable level regardless of the power bill. With someone who was in his league instead of six floors below it.

I'd never really kidded myself into thinking Chris would ever belong in my shitty apartment and my shitty life. He'd always seemed like a visitor there, just passing through. But I guess I'd started to hope for . . . something. Some kind of . . . holding pattern, at least. A way to keep him around a little longer while I sorted out what I wanted from all of this and what I was likely to end up getting after this unfinished business was wrapped up.

But fuck that. I would never be enough to make him as happy as he looked right now at Eric's side. And now that I'd seen him really *happy*, I felt like an asshole for being the reason he would have to leave this behind at the end of the day, even though it wasn't like it was my choice to pull him around with me like one of those leash-kids.

They got to another instrumental part of the song, and without stopping, Eric lifted his head and caught my gaze. "Is he enjoying this?"

I swallowed around the softball lodged in my esophagus. "Yeah," I said. "He's singing with you. And he's smiling like an idiot."

Chris shot me a dirty look that he'd given me a thousand times since we met, but this was the first time that it really cut down into me. I pressed the button to stop recording and slipped my phone back in my pocket, pulling in a deep breath that wasn't at *all* shaky, no way.

"Tell him I've missed this," Chris said. "Being with him when he didn't hate me."

The softball swelled to more of a grapefruit, and I couldn't imagine how I was even breathing around it. "He says—" I started, but my voice cracked and it was just too much. I scrambled to my feet. "Fuck this," I said. The door wasn't that far from Chris and the hallway shouldn't be past his range of movement, so I mumbled something about needing to make a call and practically ran into the hall, slamming the door behind me.

Once I was outside, I leaned against the wall of the hallway and let my head fall back with a thump that was pretty satisfying. I did it again. *Thump.* Nice. Let those assholes have their mating session with some damn privacy instead of doing it in front of me. Leaving me out of it was just common decency.

What was so fucking *fascinating* about Eric? I mean, sure, he was pretty hot. But not, like, the hottest guy I'd ever seen. More like upper-middle hotness. And sure, I couldn't sing or play any instruments or whatever, but Jesus, what the fuck was wrong with *me*?

The guitar music had stopped. I wrinkled my nose and wondered if they had their tongues down each other's throats already or if they were going to gaze into each other's eyes for a while first. Chris had told me several times that Eric was totally straight, but then Chris had *also* told me that there was nothing between them. Well, all evidence to the fucking contrary, now.

Chris had never promised me anything. And the whole point of this thing was to finish up his business so he could go back to being dead. So why did I feel like such a dick for wanting it over with all of a sudden? I thumped my head against the wall again.

"What's your problem?"

I jumped about a foot in the air. You'd think that after being around Chris for so long I would have stopped freaking out like an excitable squirrel whenever he snuck up on me, but so far no luck. So I just glared at him. "Nothing," I snapped. Then, because that was obviously not true: "You could have told me. You *should* have told me."

"Told you what?"

"That Eric isn't just your best friend." The last two words came out a little hard, like they tasted bad. Which I guess they did.

"He *is* my best friend. My brother, sort of."

I shot him a look that was probably deadly enough to be illegal in at least eleven states. "I'm not fucking stupid, Chris."

He was silent for several seconds, shifting on his feet, but I wouldn't give him the satisfaction of saving him from the awkward pause. Finally, he just sighed. "It's not like that."

"Well, what the hell *is* it like?" I asked, then felt my throat closing up again, so I waved my hand in the air and continued, "You know what? I don't want to have this discussion. Fuck you, okay? Fuck you."

"This isn't what it looks like," he said in a quiet, low voice.

"Oh, I'm pretty sure it's exactly what it looks like," I snapped. "But whatever. You just go in there and finish talking to him and then I'll take you to see your sister and then we can be *done* with this whole fucked-up mess and I can go home and try to go back to a normal life."

Chris stared at me for a second, still frowning. "I can't talk to him."

"I'm pretty sure you can figure something out. Try writing letters on his stomach with your dick. I bet *that* would work." I gazed determinedly away from him and scowled at nothing in particular.

"You're being ridiculous."

"Yeah, well, fuck you." It wasn't my finest comeback moment, but it was the best I could do under the circumstances.

"Tyler," he started, then reached out.

I flinched away from him before his hand made contact, then I took a step backward. "Don't fucking touch me. Don't even *try*. Keep your hands to yourself."

"I don't know why you're so angry," he said, but he sounded defeated now instead of defensive.

"Because . . ." *Because it's not* fair *that you can touch him and you can touch your guitar and you can't touch me. Because if you try to touch me now and you can't, that's even worse. Because I really should have fucked Brandon last night so I wouldn't be standing here feeling like such a loser today.* Ugh. "It doesn't matter. It's just I thought that, you know, you and me . . ." I waved between us but I couldn't quite dredge up the courage to finish that sentence the way it should be finished. So I just cleared my throat and said, "I thought that we were close enough that you could have told me." Which was true. Just not the whole truth so-help-me-God. But it wasn't like Chris was giving *me* the whole truth, so fuck him.

"We should probably talk about this," Chris said after a moment. "But not . . . right now."

"Yeah," I said with a scoff. "Yeah, now's not the time."

"Will you help me finish saying good-bye?"

I ground my teeth for a second and then nodded. "I'll help you say good bye." I mean, that *was* the point of this.

"And I'll try to . . ." He shrugged. "I'll try to tone down the poetics."

"*Thank* you," I said. "Because, Jesus, with the Shakespearian sonnets, man." I gave him a half smile as a peace offering, even though I didn't feel like smiling *at all*. The things we do for the people we care about.

I saw his return smile happening a second before it broke across his face like heat lightning on a summer night and my brain sent off an "Incoming Dimples" warning just in time for me to look away so I wouldn't forget how pissed I was at him. "Okay," I said quickly to head off something *really* dangerous from him like a joke or worse, the low chuckle that had made me feel off-center late at night when we'd talked over *Star Trek* reruns until it had been time for me to sleep. "Let's go back in. And I'll be nice."

"Thanks," he said. His hand twitched like he was going to try to touch me again, and I flinched like before. He frowned and then walked through the wall.

I sighed and went back in the room.

Chris did manage to keep things relatively platonic after that, although there were still some glances that lasted just a little too long for my stomach to support. The jam session didn't start up again, but the conversation flowed as easily as it could given that I was having to parrot everything Chris said to Eric.

"So . . ." Eric said eventually. "Are you staying in LA for long? Or are you going to just, you know, go?"

"My flight back's in two days," I said.

"Cool," he said. "Where are you staying?"

I wrinkled my nose. "Just some hotel. Nowhere special."

Eric raised an eyebrow at me. "Does that mean it's a shithole in a bad neighborhood?"

I hesitated. Chris was nodding his head so hard I was worried it might fall off.

Eric crossed his arms loosely across his chest. His toned chest. Bastard. "That sounds like a yes."

"It's not a *bad* neighborhood," I insisted. "I walked home from a bar last night and it was fine."

"But not a great place, either," Eric finished for me. "Let me get you a better hotel."

I flicked my eyes at Chris. "No, that's okay. I'm fine where I am."

"It's the least I can do," Eric said. "Let me help you out. And you should take his car too. That stupid fucking Mas. I mean, as long as you bring it back."

"Told you he'd have my car." Chris folded his arms over his chest and smirked at me. "Let's go down to the garage. I'll show you."

I huffed out a breath and eyed Eric. "He wants to see his car."

"I'm sure he does," Eric said, rolling his eyes. "Fine, let's go let him see it."

Eric led the way—or technically, *Chris* led the way, although I let Eric walk in front of me too—and when we got to the garage, Eric walked over to the far corner of the huge room and pulled the heavy white cover off of a sleek, beautiful silver car.

Chris made a beeline for it and barely even hesitated before throwing himself over the hood, arms spread like he was giving the car a hug. He didn't even blink in surprise at being able to touch the damn thing, and his nonreaction to it like there was never a question that he'd be able to touch it made me grind my teeth again.

Eric grinned at me. "So what do you say? Want to give her a spin?"

I let out a sarcastic half chuckle. "No way in hell am I driving a Maserati through LA."

Chris slapped his hand down on the hood of the car, then stood up. "I'll drive," he practically chirped.

"No," I said. "Don't be stupid."

Eric looked in Chris's general direction. Chris took a large step to the side to place himself in line with Eric's eyes.

Eric's eyes were pointed at exactly the right height this time too, which made it a little easier to remember that this was all bullshit and I didn't want to be here any longer than I had to. Fuck them for being so goddamn perfect for each other, Eric's straightness aside.

"Did you just offer to drive, Chris?" Eric asked.

"He did." My voice was flat again, and I didn't give a rat's ass about it.

"Do you think he can?" Eric raised an eyebrow at me.

"Yes," I answered, because of course he could drive it. The way he'd leaned over the hood of the car like he wanted to fuck it . . . yeah. He totally could. Then, just in case anyone had any doubts, I continued: "But this is bullshit. For the record."

"What's bullshit?" Chris said, tearing his gaze away from Eric.

"All of this." I crossed my arms again. Then to Eric, "But yeah, he probably can drive. As long as I go with him, because he can't get more than twenty feet from me." I glared at Chris. "Or can you suddenly do *that* too? I don't fucking know anymore."

"You're being bitchy," Chris said, crossing his arms as well and frowning at me.

I let my arms drop so that we wouldn't be mirroring each other. "Sorry. Whatever. Do you want to drive? Let's just go."

"Now?" Eric asked.

"Yes, now," I said at exactly the same time that Chris did. Ugh.

CHAPTER TWENTY-NINE

I refused to touch the steering wheel of the car on principle, and
we decided that it wasn't the greatest idea to have the cops see a
driverless car speeding down the road, so Eric drove us back to the
shitty hotel and let me run up to get my stuff while he sat in the car
and made some calls to find us—me—a better place to stay.

Chris stood in the doorway of the bathroom and watched me
shoving my toiletries and underwear into my bag. "Are you going to
explain what's with all the attitude?"

"I always have attitude," I grumbled, shaking my toothbrush
viciously to get the moisture off of it. "It's just part of my charm."

"Yeah, well, this is different," Chris said. "Is it because I can
touch him?"

I slammed my toiletry case down on the fake marble counter with
far more force than necessary and glared at him. "Do you really not
fucking *get* it?"

"No," he said, wrinkling his brow. "I mean, it's not like I *knew* I'd
be able to touch him. So I couldn't have warned you beforehand."

"You knew you were in love with him, you son of a bitch."

Chris blinked and drew his head back a bit, and it was just too
fucking much, so I grabbed the complimentary conditioner and
hurled it at his face. It sailed right through, but he flinched anyway,
which gave me a little satisfaction. After it hit the wall and bounced
off, I continued staring at him until it became clear that he wasn't
going to say anything.

So I decided to expand on what I'd said. "You knew. And that's why you wanted to come say good-bye to him this much, and that's why you've had your G-string in a twist this whole time about seeing him. And that's why you get that faraway look in your eyes when you talk about him and that's why Jerri told you not to go see him and you should have *told* me. I mean, I'm a fucking idiot myself because I should have known. I should have seen right through all your *bullshit* and known what it all meant." I glared even harder. "And stop looking so damn shocked, because we just had this same conversation in the hall outside his stupid Christopher Raiden shrine and so you knew I knew."

"I didn't know you knew . . . the extent of it."

"Yeah, well, like I said, I'm not fucking stupid." I picked my bag back up and stalked out of the bathroom to finish shoving my clothes into the backpack. "And it's not just him, Chris. It's not. I mean, you're a human being and you had a life before I met you and so of course you have people who you care about more than you care about me. That's fine. I don't care. That's just part of life. But, Jesus, you can touch your *car*."

He stared at me blankly, and I hated him for how dense he was being.

"You can touch your car," I repeated. "And you can touch that beat-up old guitar. And you can touch Eric. And those things . . ." I decided to man up a little. "I don't really know that much about the laws of physics and how they relate to ghosts, but the thing that those three have in common is that you care about them. So I'm guessing that's it. You can touch the things you care about." I took a deep breath and looked him in the eyes. "And you can't touch me."

He just stood there staring at me, but he did drop his arms to his sides, so at least that was some kind of reaction. I'd take it.

"So yeah," I said after a second of hella awkward silence. "That's why I'm pissed. I thought that you gave a shit about me and this has all proved that you don't."

"I want to touch you," he said, his voice low in both volume and pitch. "I do."

I held out my hand, extending my fingers toward him, and raised a challenging eyebrow.

He lifted his own hand and reached for mine, but stopped before our fingers touched. "I don't want to try it."

"Why not?" I snapped and wiggled my fingers at him. "Prove you care. Do it."

"This is bullshit," Chris said. He lowered his hand. "I don't know if I can do it and if I try and it doesn't work, I'm going to lose my chance with you."

"You lost your chance with me when you made me give you your teary fucking reunion with your ex-boyfriend without warning me first." I dropped my own hand and then wrapped my arms around my stomach again. "That was just cruel, Chris. Especially after last night. You can't be so thick that you didn't realize what last night meant."

He was silent for a second, then nodded slowly. "I knew what it meant."

"Then fuck you," I said. "For leading me on when you knew what was going to happen today."

His eyes flashed. "You know what? This isn't all about you. I've been in love with that bastard since I was fourteen years old and I've had to watch him fucking girls right in front of me and I've had to sit with him while he was drunk and weepy after breakups and I've had to make myself get over him time after fucking time and it's *exhausting*. And let me tell you, Tyler, he's not blameless in all this. He knew what he was doing and what I wanted and how much it fucked with me and he didn't care. But I was so head over heels for him that I let him do it because the alternative was losing him altogether, and I'd already lost my family and I couldn't lose him too."

He glared at me, both eyebrows raised and his jaw set. I decided to let the challenge slide and just nodded curtly.

"I'm not blaming him for everything," Chris continued. "My choices were my own and I think I've fucking paid for them. And I don't think he was doing it to be a jerk. But I do know that it hurt, all the time, and I couldn't even look at him for a long time without wanting to throw myself off a bridge. And then I met Jerri and I popped my first pill and suddenly I just didn't give a shit anymore. I could get on stage with him and let girls blow us in the tour bus and watch him flirt with all the groupies and not feel like he had a switchblade in my gut, and after years of feeling like every single day was a huge miserable struggle with wanting to burst into tears like a fucking pussy every time he looked at me, it just felt good not to care. Okay?"

He ran a hand through his hair, grabbing on to the ends of the strands and tugging at it hard enough to make himself grimace. "And I didn't care about how my sister hated me or how my mom didn't know me or how disappointed my dad would have been in me. And I didn't care that my girlfriend didn't love me or that she was using me for fame and money and I didn't care that everyone stopped returning my phone calls. Everything just felt fine and I felt okay with everything and I could function. The heroin made me feel *human* again."

He paused for a moment, sucking in a deep breath and letting it out slowly through his nose. "And maybe I shouldn't have done it. Maybe I should have gotten clean. But every single morning I decided to give it up and then every afternoon I decided that instead of quitting cold turkey I deserved just one more night of oblivion before I went back to the knife in my gut. And you don't understand that. Nobody understands that. And so you can take your judgment and shove it." He clamped his mouth closed and shot me the darkest glare I'd ever seen, on him or on anyone else.

After a few seconds it became obvious that he expected me to respond. I had no idea what to say, though. I finally settled on, "I'm sorry." It seemed like a safe choice.

"I know you're pissed at me and I guess you have a right to be," he said, speaking a little less like a pit viper now. "But for fuck's sake, Tyler, it's not like I *want* to feel this way about him. I've spent my entire adult life trying to get over him. But he's my best friend too, and this is probably the last time I'll ever see him, and so let me have this, okay? Let me say good-bye the way I want to so I can at least get one thing in my entire relationship with Eric right."

And that was true, and I'd already decided to keep going with the stupid good-byes even though I hated seeing the two of them in the same room together. But he didn't deserve a free pass on this one, lengthy ranting explanations aside. "You still should have told me."

"I know," he said, deflating. "I know. I shouldn't have kept it from you. That was a dick move."

"You think?" I raised a sarcastic eyebrow at him. "I just—" I thought for a second. "Just tell me *why*. Why didn't you warn me?

You had a shitload of opportunities to give me a heads-up about this and I want to know why you didn't."

He ran a hand through his hair again, more gently this time, and looked at the floor. "I just . . . at first I didn't want to out myself. You thought I was totally straight and I thought *you* were totally straight and I didn't want to make things weird. And then when you found out I was bi and you were okay with it, I wanted you to think I was cool and so I didn't want to come across like a sappy pining teenager. Then things started to get . . . you know. More intense. Between you and me. And it just got harder to tell you because I hadn't *already* told you, and . . ."

He shrugged. "And also, like I said, I've been dealing with it for twelve years and I thought I could hide it when I saw him. I'd gotten good at hiding it. And since after today I'll probably never see him again, I didn't think it would matter anymore. So, yeah. I'm sorry."

"Thanks. For the apology." It wasn't *okay*, but he seemed sincere. It would have to do for now.

"You can tell him to leave if you want," he said. "I figure I'll have to finish talking to him before we leave so that the whole trip wasn't a waste of time, but you can tell him to fuck off for tonight. And we can see another movie, or just hang out, or something. Just us."

I seriously considered that for a few seconds, then shook my head. "Might as well get it over with," I said. "You have unfinished business with him, and I'm cool with helping you wrap things up." I paused. "Well, mostly cool. Kissing him will piss me off. And no more singing love ballads while you stare into each other's eyes."

He raised an eyebrow. "Um, 'Houses on Fire' is not a love ballad."

"It is the way the two of you were singing it," I said, frowning at him and trying not to relive the scene in too much detail.

He had the decency to look sheepish. "It wasn't meant to be. I'm sorry about that too."

"Well, okay, but it was sort of bullshit."

"I know," he said, sighing. "I've never known how to act around him. We were best friends, we really were, but things were always . . . weird. Like we were dating but we weren't romantic. Or sometimes it felt like we *were* romantic but we weren't physical. Or . . . Jesus, I can't even describe it. I fucked up that relationship right from the beginning and never figured out how to fix it."

I wasn't really sure how to respond to that. "From what you said a few minutes ago, it seems like it's his fault too," I mumbled finally.

He heard me, though, and the corner of his mouth quirked upward. "Thanks."

My eyes had snapped to his cheek when I'd seen his mouth move and then snagged there, waiting for a dimple that never showed up. "Thanks for what?"

"For taking my side," he answered. "Nobody does that anymore. I'm an easy scapegoat."

"Well, to be fair, I didn't say that *none* of it was your fault," I clarified, and I was pleasantly surprised to hear some of the bantering quality sneak back into my voice. That was one thing I liked about Chris, the easy conversations we'd fallen into like flannel footie pajamas. It was nice to know we hadn't lost that.

Which reminded me. "By the way," I said, turning away from him and shoving the last of my clothes in my backpack so I could be sure to look nonchalant as fuck, "you haven't lost your chance. With me. If you still want, you know, a chance. Whatever that means here."

A beat of silence, then he let out a breath. "I have no idea what it means. But I'll take what I can get."

I nodded slowly. "Okay. Well . . . we should go back downstairs. He probably thinks we're fucking. We've been up here long enough."

"I don't give a shit what he thinks about you and me." Chris smiled. "We are what we are and this is one part of my life that he has no control over, and I like it that way."

"Did you know that you have dimples?" The words were out before I'd had a chance to vet them, and the cheek-burning started up.

"Did you know that you blush?"

"Fuck you."

He grinned at me and my pants suddenly felt a lot tighter than they had been a few moments before. "Stop that."

"Stop what?" Chris asked, his eyes wide and ridiculously innocent.

"You know what, you crotch-nugget. The smiling. The grinning. The general aura of sexy rock star. It's unfair and I have to go out in public now." I crossed my arms.

Chris raised an eyebrow. "Did you just call me a crotch-nugget?"

"Fuck you," I said again.

He laughed. "You keep me on my toes. That counts for something."

I stuck my tongue out at him and zipped up my backpack. "I guess we should go down, huh?"

"Yeah, I guess," he said. "Tell me, what exactly *is* a crotch-nugget?"

"Shut up," I said, even though he'd never obeyed that command before. And I didn't even *want* him to. "Let's go."

Chris was determined to have one last drive in his car, so Eric drove us out of LA and past the thickest of the suburbs and then pulled over at a gas station. He climbed out of the car and we all congregated in front of it. Chris leaned against the hood and stared off into the distance.

"Are you sure you can drive?" Eric asked Chris.

"Yeah, I'm pretty sure," he said, looking back at Eric but not quite looking *at* him like he'd done before. His eyes seemed to be pointed at Eric's forehead. It was a small gesture, but it grounded me a little.

"Okay," I said after I repeated Chris's answer. "Well, I guess we'll just see how it goes?"

"Less talk, more engine revving." Chris walked around and got in the driver's seat. He cranked the car and Eric and I walked back over to the passenger side. Without asking, Eric opened the front passenger door and held the seat forward for me to slide into the backseat with a pout on my face.

Chris caught my eyes in the rearview mirror as Eric pushed the seat back and climbed into the front. "You can tell him to move."

"It's fine," I said. It wasn't, not really, but I didn't really feel like getting into a cock-swinging contest with Eric Painter. And besides, just the fact that Chris was giving me the go-ahead to kick Eric out of the front seat made not sitting beside Chris better. I could deal with it.

Eric rummaged around in the glove compartment and produced an Incite the Masses CD—which seemed a little egotistical to me, but whatever—and popped it in the car's stereo system. The music came on, and Chris grinned and stomped on the gas, sending us flying out of the gas station parking lot and tearing down the road at a speed that would have ripped my Grandma's Taurus to shreds.

The music was too loud to talk over and no one made a move to turn down the volume, so I just leaned against the window and stared out at the desert speeding by outside. After a few minutes, "Houses on Fire" came on and I couldn't listen to it without hearing the slowed-down acoustic version in the back of my head. The album version was almost completely different from what I'd listened to earlier during the impromptu jam session, which was nice because I'd always liked this song and that would keep the acoustic version from ruining the album for me forever.

I caught Chris's eyes in the rearview mirror again. He smiled at me, and I was caught between wanting to scream in sexual frustration and wanting to dissolve into his eyes. The only safe course of action was to look back out the window and keep my eyes there, imagining the scorching heat we'd be feeling if it were summer.

I wondered if by the time it actually *was* summer, I'd be single again.

My backpack was in the seat beside me, and I reached over to fish out my headphones, then plugged them into my phone and pulled up the recorded version of "Houses on Fire" that I'd made earlier. I didn't realize I was holding my breath until the song reached the part where Chris had started harmonizing with Eric and I didn't hear his voice. Both guitars were audible, but only one voice. I couldn't decide if that was better or worse.

But there was no need to torture myself like that, so I switched to my phone's music storage and pulled up a random track, which turned out to be a drum-heavy hipster song. Fine by me. Really anything that didn't feature Eric on vocals was a pretty good choice. I cranked up the volume so I could hear it over the Incite the Masses CD and put my cheek against the cool glass of the window.

CHAPTER THIRTY

E ric had a radio spot that night. He offered to cancel it, but even without knowing the guy very well I could tell he didn't want to, so I unselfishly offered to just call it an early night and say our last good-byes in the morning. He dropped us off at the new hotel, a much nicer place in a *much* nicer part of town, and Chris gave me a lecture about being careful with his guitar before he would finally let me carry it up to the room. We watched Eric drive off into the afternoon sun and then headed upstairs.

The room at the new hotel was fancy, with a kitchen and sitting area in addition to a king-size bed with more pillows than I'd personally ever seen on one bed in my life. I dropped my backpack on the couch and put Chris's guitar case on the coffee table, then threw myself face-first onto the bed.

"I'm guessing you're comfortable," Chris said.

I didn't lift my head when I answered, so my voice came out as an indistinguishable mumble. Chris didn't ask what I'd said, which was probably good since I wasn't one hundred percent sure it had even been English. Or any other language, for that matter. But the bed was so much more comfortable than my lumpy one back home that lying there motionless seemed like a wasted opportunity, so I scooted into a more comfortable position and snuggled into the fluffy comforter and just let myself enjoy it.

"So what are we going to do now?" Chris said after letting me writhe around on the bed moaning ecstatically about thread counts and memory foam for a while. "The night is young."

I stopped wriggling and shrugged. "We could watch a movie or something. Or find something dumb on TV."

"Or I could play for you," he offered, glancing away like he was embarrassed at the suggestion.

"That would be really cool," I said. "But nothing that *he* sings on. I can't handle that yet."

Chris's eyes met mine, and I felt raw, like my skin had been removed and the air was hitting my exposed nerve endings all at once. After a second, he nodded. "No ITM. Got it. I'm sorry about the 'Houses on Fire' thing. Again."

"It's cool," I said, because it was actually starting to feel like it *was* cool. "I forgive you."

"I have a few covers I remember," he said. "And I do still know some classical guitar solos from when I was first learning. Sonata in A and all that."

"That sounds nice. But first let me make a phone call." I sat up on the bed and motioned at the door to the balcony. "I'm going to go out there."

He watched me for a moment before nodding again. "I'll make sure it's tuned while you talk."

"Cool." I stood up and went out onto the balcony, closing the door behind me. I waited until I heard the faint thrumming of guitar strings before pulling out my phone and looking up Aunt Greta's number, then took a deep breath and dialed it.

"Marshall residence." Aunt Greta's voice was tinny and strained over the phone.

"Hey, Aunt Greta, it's Tyler," I said, making an effort to sound chipper.

There was a pause. "Tyler whom?" she said, emphasizing the *m* in "whom."

I rolled my eyes hard. "Tyler Lindsey. Your nephew."

"Oh, *Tyler*," she exclaimed. "I don't believe you've ever called me before."

I forced out a laugh. "I don't think I have. Listen, can I talk to Chad for a second?"

Another long pause.

"Aunt Greta?" A car sped by on the road below me and distant sirens and car horns flowed into the slanting light of the early evening. The auditory cues were the same as the ones in Boston, but the cities had different personalities. Boston and I were friends, maybe even more than that. LA and I ... well, we could become close acquaintances if we spent enough time together, but I could already tell I'd never *love* it like I loved Boston.

I wondered how I would feel if I ever went to Denver.

"Yes, I'm still here," Aunt Greta said after another second. "I don't know if that's a good idea, Tyler. You know how upset he gets in new situations."

"He'll be okay, I promise," I told her, trying to infuse my voice with trustworthiness. I put one hand on the balcony railing and leaned against it, closing my eyes, while I waited for her response.

Aunt Greta made a frustrated but oddly ladylike grunt. When she spoke again, her voice was lower in pitch and more gravelly. "I suppose a few minutes won't hurt. Don't upset him."

"I won't," I assured her, even though it wasn't like I knew I could actually keep that promise. Who knew what would upset Chad? Was having someone to talk to about the ghost issue better for him, or would it just make everything worse?

There was a fumbling noise on the other end of the line, then Chad spoke in his slow, slurred voice. "Hi, Tyler. Why are you calling me?"

"She made you take your meds again, didn't she?" It wasn't how I'd planned to start the conversation, but the poor guy sounded like he was about to start snoring.

"Yes."

I waited for a second to see if he was going to elaborate, then continued, "I had some questions about your nana."

The silence stretched on for long enough that I was afraid he'd hung up. I wondered if his awkwardness was a product of the medicine or if he just took after his mother. Finally, he whispered, "I'm going to my room so I can talk," and then the phone went muffled as if he'd put his hand over the receiver.

I waited patiently while he made his way to his bedroom. There was a loud noise, then the muffling was gone and he spoke a little louder. "Okay. Nana. She's dead."

"I know," I said. "But I had a question about when she was with you."

"Before? Or ... after?"

"After." I suddenly realized that my eyes were still closed, and I opened them again and looked back out over the city. "Just humor me and pretend she was real, okay?"

He sighed. "You know, I've been thinking about it since Christmas, and I can't come up with a good explanation for why we would both be able to see the same guy saying the same things if he wasn't real. So ... yeah." He took an audible breath. "She was real."

Awesome. That would make this whole conversation a lot easier. "Okay, cool. So I was wondering ... did she ever touch you?"

Another long, long pause. "Nana wasn't like that," Chad said after a second. "And believe me, all the psychiatrists have asked that question to death, and I've never been abused so there's nothing—"

Shit. "No, no, no, I didn't mean *touch* you. Sorry. Not like that. I just mean . . . she was a ghost. Could you touch her? Or was she just . . . feel-through? Jesus, man, of course I didn't mean did she abuse you. Fuck."

"Oh," Chad said, and I could practically feel the heat from his cheeks through the phone. It probably matched the heat-production of my own cheeks. "Um, yes."

I guess that shouldn't have surprised me since I now had pretty good proof that ghosts could touch some people, but knowing that the Eric thing wasn't a fluke was kind of encouraging. "She touched you? Or you touched her?"

"Both," he said. "We hugged. Before she left. And one time I was crying and she wiped my tears." A slight pause, then in a defensive tone: "I was a little kid. That's why I cried."

"It's cool," I said. "I don't think any less of you. Could you *always* touch her? Like, when she first appeared?"

"I don't remember," he said, then continued in a small voice. "I don't remember much about my life."

"You've got to get out of there, man," I told him. "This is no way to live."

"I can't leave." His voice was still small and a little afraid.

"You're a grown man." He acted even younger than the twenty-three or so that he was, but still. "You can leave if you want to. They shouldn't drug you when you're not crazy."

"My parents want what's best for me," he replied. "And it's not like I can support myself since I've got the psych records I have. Nobody will ever hire me."

"Well, that's all bullshit," I said, "but I'll let it go for now. Anyway. You don't remember at all?"

"I don't remember ever *not* being able to touch her," he said after a few seconds. "But maybe I couldn't sometimes and I just don't remember."

"Okay." I shifted my weight to one foot and pulled my jacket tighter around me. It was so much warmer here than back home, but it was still a little chilly when the wind blew. I missed having someone to curl up with. Chris looked like the sort of person who would radiate heat if he had a real body. Had Eric felt that warmth when Chris touched him today?

"But I couldn't touch Lucas," Chad said, breaking into my thoughts. "If that helps."

I'd forgotten about Lucas. Now that Chad had said the name I had a vague recollection he'd mentioned him before, but I hadn't known who he was so I guess I hadn't committed it to memory. "Who was Lucas?"

"Nobody I know," he said, then corrected himself. "Well, nobody I *knew*. Before he appeared."

"How did you end up with him?"

"Nana had been gone for a while and I was starting to feel normal again," he said, and I noticed that his voice had gotten stronger. By now he almost sounded awake. "I could still see ghosts, I think, but I didn't have one of my own and they were easy to ignore. So I thought it was over and then Mom took me to a garage sale. I guess I was about fifteen or sixteen then. I picked up a cool necktie—I was in a 'maybe if

I dress nice the girls will forget how weird I am' phase—and there was a tie tack on it, and then there he was."

"So he was just some random guy?"

"Yeah, he was the son of the man running the garage sale. He'd died about six months before that and his dad was finally cleaning out his stuff." A sigh filtered through the phone. "Lucas was a suicide. It really upset him to find out that he still had to deal with all the things he thought he was leaving behind."

"Did you guys become friends?"

Chad sighed. "We tolerated each other. He was depressed and only spoke when he had to. It took me a while to convince him that we should find some way to help him go on to the afterlife."

"Wait. Didn't he *want* to go on to the afterlife?"

"He wanted to be dead. He wanted there to be nothing. And since there was clearly *something* . . ." He trailed off meaningfully like the sentence didn't need an ending, but I still wasn't quite sure where that was going.

"Then isn't that all the more reason to want to go to heaven?" I asked.

"Not when you don't think it's heaven you're going to."

He had a valid point, so I grunted in agreement. After a second, Chad continued. "So even after we got his unfinished business done, he didn't leave for a while. He was very resistant. He stayed and he cried and he fretted until I just couldn't take it anymore and I yelled at him to stop being afraid and move on. And he did. I hope he went to heaven because that's on my conscience if he didn't."

I thought about what Chris had said before about the afterlife question. "It seems like a cruel trick for the universe to play, though, if he didn't. You'd think if he was going to hell anyway, he wouldn't have gotten the chance to make things right."

"That's what I told him, but he didn't believe me. Not that I blame him. I was a sixteen-year-old boy on trippy medication trying to lecture him about religion and philosophy like I had a clue what I was talking about."

"Yeah, I get that." I took a deep breath. "So you never touched him."

"No," he said. "I didn't really want to. And I don't think he liked me much either, so it wasn't a big deal."

"Okay." I let out my breath slowly. "Well, thanks for the info."

He didn't say anything for a few seconds, then: "So you're gay?"

Jesus. "No," I said, a little too fast and too loud. Then the guilt kicked in because here I was on the verge of an emotional meltdown because Chris was going to leave soon and I wanted to fucking kiss him just once, so denying it felt a little shady. So I decided to man up. "I mean, not totally. I'm bi." And then, when he didn't say anything: "Surprise?"

"I saw the way you stared at him," Chad said quietly. "At Christmas."

"There wasn't anything there at Christmas," I said, but we both knew that was sort of untrue. There hadn't been anything I was ready to acknowledge, though.

"Okay."

"Is that . . . okay? That I'm bi?" I asked him. "You're not going to rat me out to Grandma, are you?"

"No, I won't. And it's fine." Aunt Greta yelled in the background. "I have to go," he said. "Mom's getting nervous."

"Thanks, Chad," I said.

"Yeah, no problem," he responded, then hung up.

CHAPTER
THIRTY·ONE

I let my hand drop to my side, holding the phone loosely. The city was alive in the sunset, and the air was full of tension and the ocean, and Chris was inside the hotel room playing something soft and intricate on his guitar. I took another deep breath, letting the salt in the air mingle with the space in my life that I was starting to realize was the same size and shape as the man waiting in the room for me, and I wanted him so much it just *had* to make a difference.

I turned around and went back inside. He glanced up like I'd just woken him up from an awesome dream, then smiled at me. I dropped my phone on the bed and then walked toward him with purpose in my steps.

He put the guitar down and was on his feet by the time I reached him, and I put my hands on the sides of his face and kissed him.

It wasn't . . . perfect. There was enough resistance now that my fingers and lips didn't automatically go through him unless I pushed hard, but he wasn't exactly solid and touching him didn't feel like touching skin. The warmth wasn't there, and I couldn't feel smoothness or roughness or any real sensation other than pressure and movement, but fuck, it was better than nothing, and it was more than we'd had before, and surely that meant it could get even better than this.

I threw myself into the kiss, closing my eyes and trying to pretend like my tongue wouldn't go straight through his head if I pushed too hard. And it did at first, a few times, until we found a rhythm and it was almost—*almost*—like kissing someone who was made of flesh and blood, and it turns out that "almost" counts in both horseshoes and making out with ghosts.

I'd never been the kind of guy who talked while kissing before, but this time I pulled away just long enough to whisper "Can you feel me?" before diving back into the sensation of almost-teeth and almost-lips and almost-tongue.

He moaned softly, and his hands slid from my waist around to the small of my back. I opened my eyes for a second to find out that *his* eyes were closed. Chris put a hand in my hair and it actually moved under his touch. I broke the kiss to push my head backward into his hand like a cat being stroked.

Chris pressed his lips to the spot on my neck where my pulse was pounding against the skin. "How can we be doing this?" he asked, breathless and with his eyes still closed.

"I don't know," I murmured back. I put my own hand in his hair like he'd done to me and if I concentrated hard, I could not-quite-but-almost feel the texture of it on my fingers. "Don't stop."

He kissed the spot on my neck again and dragged his lips up to my ear. "Don't stop what?"

I shivered. Maybe some things weren't quite so tangible yet, but his voice wasn't just *almost* and the low, husky tone was right there in my ear as if the rest of him was as solid. "Anything," I said, closing my eyes and leaning into him as much as I could without pressing through. "Whatever you're thinking of doing, don't stop."

His fingers tightened on my back, and he pulled away from my ear so he could look me in the eyes. "Are you sure?"

I swallowed hard. My whole body was vibrating with the urge to pull him down on the bed and see how solid I could make him. But that would mean officially crossing the line of what I'd done with another guy before, and that was scary enough without adding in the fact that if I went ahead with this and then Chris disappeared, it might literally kill me.

But then again, it wasn't like living the rest of my life without him and never knowing what it would have been like would actually be *better*, so I nodded and leaned my forehead against his. "I want you," I said as if that explained everything, and maybe it did.

"You have me," he said in a low voice. "I'm yours."

I wanted to ask if he meant that as a for-tonight-only thing or if I was getting more than just sex from him, but it didn't seem like the greatest time to check. My fingers itched to curl into the fabric of his shirt and walk backward to the bed while I pulled him along behind me, and I put my hand on his chest and tried it, but I couldn't get a grip on the fabric or feel the difference between shirt and skin. So instead I kissed him again and then left my lips against his while I whispered, "Bed?"

"Yes," he said, but he didn't let go immediately. I let him hold on to me and concentrated on the way my heart was beating fast and staccato like an action-movie machine gun. He leaned his forehead against mine, and I closed my eyes and tried to imagine how he would have smelled, how hot his mouth would have been, how fast his own heart would have been beating if it still could.

And then he was kissing me again, and it was hard and hungry and desperate, and I threw my arms around his neck and stepped closer to him as I kissed back with matching enthusiasm.

He felt more solid now, and it seemed to take more effort to push through the resistance and dip my fingers into the back of his head, or maybe that was an illusion. But illusion or not, it made it easier to hold on to him and to pour everything I had into the kiss.

I felt his fingers on my waist again, not stroking or digging in or any movement I recognized, but I was having trouble caring as long as he was doing things to my knees by way of my mouth. I stepped backward toward the bed, and he followed me.

His fingers moved again, and he whispered, "Fuck" against my lips in a frustrated tone.

"What?" I asked, then experimentally pulled at his bottom lip with my teeth.

He groaned and stepped back to put a little distance between us. I held on to his lip for as long as I could. "I can't get a grip on your fucking shirt," he said. He yanked his own shirt off over his head. "Take it off. I want to see you."

I'd never seen his chest and abs bare before—not in person, at least—and he wasn't gym-rat-ripped or anything, but he was toned and sexy and there was enough definition in his abs to give me the ridiculous urge to play them like a xylophone and use my cock as the mallet. And he had muscular arms that wouldn't have any trouble pinning my hands above my head while he fucked me into the mattress, and even though the thought of bottoming had always seemed a little scary before, the idea of Chris topping me somehow didn't worry me at all.

I pulled off my shirt and tossed it on the floor, then decided to hell with modesty and dropped my pants and boxers too. My dick sprang free and bobbed around for a second before settling down to point hopefully in Chris's direction. I fought off a blush and kicked my pants to the side while Chris looked me over.

"Nice," he said after his eyes finished making me feel even more naked than I already was. "My turn." He undid his pants and slid them down his legs, not exactly doing a striptease but definitely going a lot slower than I had the patience for. Then he looked up at me with a wicked grin, and I took two steps toward him, pulled him upright, and kissed him again with all the impatience I felt.

He put his shaking hands back on my waist, the motion like the thrum in my throat from a particularly awesome bass line in a song. "You're shaking," I whispered while I kissed the corner of his mouth.

"I'm nervous." His eyes were closed, and when he swallowed, my eyes followed the bob of his Adam's apple.

But this was Chris Raiden, international rock star with videos of himself boning super-hot celebrities, and I couldn't imagine him being *nervous*. Not about sex. "Why?"

He looked at me with a weirdly vulnerable glint in his eyes. "Because I want to do this right."

"You'll do fine," I said, and I put my hands on his cheeks again and pulled him in for another breathless kiss.

During a natural pause in the kiss, he said, "But I want to do better than fine." Kiss.

I love you, I thought, and the words seared through my body like someone had injected refrigerated fire directly into my bloodstream. Maybe it was just the sex talking—but I'd never even considered the words with anyone before, even during the best sex I'd ever had. He was gorgeous and he was funny and he was *mine*, at least for tonight, and I loved him so much that each individual cell in my body ached with it, but I couldn't tell him. Not yet. Not when everything was so fragile and uncertain.

So instead of saying it out loud, I grabbed his hand and pulled it between us. It felt almost as warm as a living hand now, complete with a phantom pulse in his wrist.

Or maybe his increased realness was just wishful thinking. But either way, it was definitely doing it for me, because Chris wrapped his fingers around me and gave me a long, firm stroke, and I threw my head back and hissed through my teeth at the jolt of *yes* that crackled through. While my neck was exposed, Chris took the opportunity to lean forward and nip at my throat with teeth that were almost solid enough to be sharp, and his mouth was *definitely* warmer than it had been before.

He urged me back toward the bed while he stroked slowly, twisting his wrist as he moved his hand to give me the maximum amount of sensation. I followed him willingly, even gratefully, because I was pretty sure that my legs were going to mutiny any second and send me to the floor in an ungraceful heap.

I lay down on the bed, reaching for Chris even before I got settled. He followed and climbed on top of me, straddling my hips and then taking both of our cocks in his hand. He held them together and moved his hips so that his dick slid against mine and we both moaned in unison.

"We're the same size," he said, looking down between us.

I put my hands on his ass and tried to concentrate on not embarrassing myself like a nervous virgin. "That's good," I managed to choke out. "Wouldn't want you to feel inadequate."

He grinned at me, and looked so damn *happy* that I almost didn't recognize him.

Who knew that giving a shit about the person you're with could be hot? That sounded pretty good in my head, so I said it out loud, grinning back up at him.

Chris smiled and leaned down quickly to kiss me. "I give a shit about you too," he said after one brief peck, then slanted his lips against mine and started kissing me like there'd be a winner at the end of it. There was no way I was going to lose that fight, though, so I left one hand on his ass and buried the other one in his hair, giving back as good as I got.

He started stroking again, keeping his hand around both of us and thrusting into his fist so that the undersides of our cocks rubbed together. He broke the kiss and sucked at the pulse point on my neck, then licked his way up to my ear. "I would let you fuck me right now if I could," he growled, then ran his tongue over the curve of my ear.

I shivered and dug my fingers into his ass cheek, forgetting for a second that he wasn't entirely solid. My fingers pushed through the resistance and I mumbled an apology.

He chuckled into my ear. "That's what I'm afraid would happen if we tried it." He took my earlobe in his teeth and pulled at it.

I arched against him and moaned, then spent a couple of seconds reciting the preamble to the Constitution in my head to get myself under control. "We'll figure it out," I said once I fought my orgasm back to a manageable distance.

"Lucky for you," he said, his husky voice sending daggers of lust through me, "I give head like a fucking pro and I'm going to suck you until your eyes cross."

"*Fuck*." My hips bucked up against him and there was nothing I could do about it.

He let go of us and kissed his way down my body, and when he got to my cock he didn't waste time teasing me—which was good, because if he'd done any of that bullshit right now I would have had to use my newfound Chris-touching ability to strangle him until he stopped. He licked me from the base to the tip and then took me in his mouth and slid his lips down, running his fingers over my balls. Whimpering, I tried unsuccessfully to keep myself from writhing under him.

I looked at him and put one hand in his hair, twisting it in my fingers and pulling just a little, mostly to prove I could. He glanced up and smiled at me with his eyes. And it turned out that the fucker had dimples while he was smiling *and* while he was sucking cock, and that was just unfair.

Chris bobbed his head, swirling his tongue on the head of my cock at the end of each movement, and my body felt like pieces of it were splintering off and floating in the air around us. I wasn't sure how long I could hold myself together before the rest of me exploded, and

God only knew what words would come pouring out of my mouth when that happened.

But then there was no time to worry about that, because Chris came to the upward swing of his latest head bob and moved his lips back down and then . . . kept going, taking even more of me in than before. His mouth was warmer than it had been when we'd started kissing. Then his lips got all the way down to the base of me and he pressed his fingers against the sensitive skin below my balls; my whole body shuddered, and I tightened my fist in his hair and slammed my other hand down on the bed as an orgasm dragged me under like a red-flag undercurrent, and fuck, it was such a relief that I almost started sobbing.

When it was over, I took a second to evaluate what I'd yelled when I came down his throat, and I decided that the only words had been a combination of "fuck" and "shit" and "hell yes" and Chris's name. All of which were totally legit. Good job, Tyler. Gold star.

Chris crawled up my body and kissed me, and I moaned into his mouth and held him as tightly as I could. *I love you, I love you, I love you*, I thought, and with that came a bone-deep certainty that Chris was The One. And he just *had* to feel the same way. Surely this couldn't all be me.

After letting me have a couple of seconds to come down, he thrust his hips so his cock slid over my stomach. The kiss deepened, and he started shuddering at the end of each thrust, so I pulled back enough to ask if he wanted me to suck him, and he moaned loudly and came as soon as the words were past my lips. His mouth was open against my neck, and he was doing that desperate gasping breath that only happens when you're totally letting yourself go, and he kept thrusting even after he was done.

A while passed—only thirty seconds or so, but it seemed longer—and then he slowly lifted himself up and met my eyes, sort of shell-shocked. I wondered if I had the same look in my own eyes. Probably, to be honest.

It would have been so easy to say it, to pull him down for a softer kiss and whisper it into his mouth, but I'd read enough of the magazine articles that Carmen had just *happened* to leave around the apartment to know that you were never supposed to say it right after sex, especially not for the first time. So instead we just fucking gazed into each other's eyes while we got our breathing under control.

"Fucking hell," I whispered after he blinked and lost the Staring Game. And then, because I didn't have any other appropriate response, "Fucking hell, Chris."

He let out a breathless chuckle. "Wow. That was . . ."

"Ridiculously overdue," I finished. "Jesus, you don't know how long I've wanted that."

"I can guess," he said, and he dipped his head and kissed me before rolling off and lying on his side facing me. He traced his fingers over my stomach. "See? Blue."

I looked down at myself and grinned. He was right—there was a glowing blue puddle smeared all over my stomach. I dipped my fingers in it and brought them to my mouth. A barely there salty taste spread over my tongue—more the *suggestion* of salt than the actual taste, but it was definitely there.

"Can you taste it?" he asked, kissing my chest.

"Surprisingly, yeah," I said. "I mean, a little bit."

"Do you like it? Your first time tasting spunk?"

I rolled my eyes. "Dude, that's not my first time tasting spunk." He gave me a Look, and I shrugged. "Well, fine, it's the first time I've tasted someone *else's* spunk. But yeah, I like it."

"Good," he said. He smiled at me with that same *happy* smile as before, and I swear I felt butterflies. "Yours shot through the back of my neck, you know. Which was an odd sensation."

I laughed out loud. "Seriously?"

"Yep," he said. "Apparently this whole 'touching' thing doesn't apply to your bodily secretions."

I looked down at my stomach again, and it was clean now. "Sad," I said. "Yours disappear pretty fast."

He shrugged and grinned at me. "Less cleanup this way."

"So I'm guessing this means we're dating now?" I asked him, running a hand over my stomach just in case there was still something there to feel.

He laughed and kissed the side of my head. "Yeah, I'd say that's a valid assumption."

I rolled over onto my side and propped my head on my hand. "Maybe . . . we should wait a while before we go see your sister."

And then it hit me—a shattering feeling of *wrong*, of *no*, that curled around my lungs and squeezed until I could barely breathe, and then raced up my skin, leaving goose bumps behind it. It was the same soul-crushing dread that we'd both felt when I suggested putting off the LA trip, only worse this time. I shivered and scooted closer to him like his almost-warmth would help take the cold away.

He let out a long, shaky breath. "As much as I want to say yes . . . I don't think it works that way."

"How do you know?" I asked, even though it was pretty obvious.

He hooked his leg around my waist so we were pressed together again. "I don't, really. I've just been giving that some thought and I keep getting this feeling that if I'm not actively trying to finish my business, then . . ."

I didn't need him to continue. So I just ran a hand down his arm and kissed him, slow and deep, and we gave in to each other's hands and mouths and heat and didn't talk about it again.

CHAPTER THIRTY-TWO

Since we'd gone to bed before the sun had even gone down all the way, I woke up ridiculously early the next morning, when the city itself was just starting to go to sleep. Chris was curled up behind me with his arm draped over my waist and his chin tucked into my shoulder. His chest was warm on my back and his breath fanned against my neck and holy shit, I was getting spooned by a dude.

It wasn't as awkward and weird as I'd always thought it would be back before I had ever acted on the gay side of my bisexuality. It was actually nice, to be held instead of being the one doing the holding, and I was enjoying feeling a soft cock pressed along the curve of my ass, so I snuggled back against him and smiled to myself.

"Good morning," he said, and kissed my shoulder.

"Morning," I said back. My voice was sleep-slurred and a little rough, so I cleared my throat. "Have you been there all night?"

"Yeah," he said. "No big deal. I was comfortable."

"I should have turned on the TV for you so you wouldn't get bored."

He laid his hand flat on my stomach, playing with the light line of hair that led downward from my belly button. "I wasn't bored. Not this time."

"You're warm," I said. "I can feel you."

"All the way?"

I gave that some thought, experimentally evaluating all of the parts of my body that were in contact with parts of *his* body, and I sighed. "Not yet. You're still . . . fuzzy. Not totally solid. But you're getting there. Maybe—" I stopped myself. There wasn't much more time now. It felt like time was speeding up, rushing us toward the inevitable end of all this.

His hand slipped lower, following the trail down but not quite reaching its destination. My body started taking notice of where Chris was touching it and extrapolating from that where he would be touching next, and I let out a tiny moan and was rewarded by Chris's cock stirring against my ass.

"I want to fuck you," he whispered in my ear. "We could try it."

And *that* jump-started what had been a slow rise to power on my dick's part, because I wanted that too. I rolled over to face him, and we both hissed through our teeth in unison as our cocks made contact.

"Brandon stole my lube, remember?" I said. My cheeks started to burn with the words, but it wasn't like there was any other way to say it.

"Fuck," he said, stroking us both again like he'd done last night. "You'll have to go buy some more today."

I put a hand on his hip and dug my fingers in. "Yes," I said, drawing out the *s* and answering both the lube question and the unspoken question in Chris's eyes. I wasn't even sure what that question was— *Can I touch you? Are you horny? Do you love me?*—but regardless of the question, my answer would be yes.

Later, I batted Chris's hands away when they started in on a round three for the morning. Which would have been round six overall, and Jesus, I hadn't even come six times in one night back during my freshman year of college when I'd been furiously sowing my wild oats.

He pouted at me. "You're done?"

"Fuck, dude, I'm gross and my balls are tired and empty. I need to take a shower and find some food to refuel."

"I don't want to let you out of bed," he said. He moved his hand away from the danger zone but curled his arm around me to pull me closer. "You might not come back."

I kissed him and smiled. "I'll come back. With lube."

He laughed. "I guess maybe it's worth the risk, then."

A dimple appeared, and I flicked my tongue at it. Chris's breath caught in his throat, and I decided what the hell, there's not *that* much difference between five rounds and six in the grand scheme of things, and it wasn't like the shower was going anywhere.

When Chris finally let me out of bed, it was still well before sunrise. We'd had a brief bargaining session that had ended with me promising to blow him later if he left me alone while I showered, and then I grabbed my toiletry bag and scampered to the bathroom before he could change his mind about the deal.

The cold tile floor of the hotel bathroom was more of a shock than usual after the nice warm bed, and as I carried my soap over to the shower, the easy contentment seeped out through the soles of my feet to be replaced with something a lot less like magic and a lot more like fear. I turned on the shower and stepped in.

We had to go see Allison, and soon. I wasn't sure what would happen if we didn't, but there was no doubt in my mind that if we tried to cheat the system, bad things would happen. And I got the uneasy feeling that whatever those bad things were, they'd be a lot worse for Chris than for me, which was unacceptable.

I wondered if it would have been better to have held all these feelings inside me and kept up the boundaries that we'd had before last night. If that would make it easier for both of us after Allison. I didn't regret what had happened, but that didn't stop me from feeling like it had been a bad idea, at least on some level. Specifically, the level where I had to learn to live after he was gone. The thought of letting anyone else in like this made me nauseous, and it occurred to me that maybe this was how widowers felt.

The shower relaxed me a little, and I definitely felt less disgusting after I'd scrubbed all the sweat and jizz (mine, obviously, since his was self-cleaning) off, so that was something. We'd made plans to see Eric again today, and I had to be on my game. Last night, the thought of talking to Eric again had pissed me the fuck off, but after spending the night hearing only *my* name come gasping out of Chris's mouth, I felt much better about the whole thing.

It didn't matter that he'd loved Eric before. It didn't even matter if he *still* loved him. All that mattered was that he wanted to be with me for as long as we had left. And I believed he did.

I dried off and tied a towel around my waist to go out into the main room. Chris was back in the sitting area with his guitar, dressed again and playing—I kid you not—"Free Bird." Which was a perfect opening to get back to the ragging and bickering.

I rolled my eyes at him and pulled a pair of jeans and some underwear out of my backpack. "Of *course* you'd be playing that."

He raised an eyebrow. "What's wrong with it?"

"You just must have known that I was going to come out here and yell 'Play some Skynyrd!' at you, and you decided to beat me to the punch," I explained. "Because you're a dick."

He smirked at me. "You seem like the type to do something cliché like that."

"Well, carry on," I said. "Don't let me rain on your little Skynyrd parade." I let the towel drop to the ground and smirked when Chris fumbled and missed a note.

"If you're not back on the bed in thirty seconds, you're going to be getting rug burns on your ass," he warned me.

I smirked even harder and was about to say something snotty when there was a knock on the door. "Fuck," I said, grabbing my boxers and jeans, and struggling into them. "It's like 5 a.m. Who the fuck knocks on a door at five in the morning?"

"Didn't you put the sign on the door?" Chris asked, putting his guitar down.

"I did," I said. "I don't think it's housekeeping." I went to the door and looked through the peephole, then frowned. "It's Eric."

Chris must have sat back down, because after a second I heard the guitar start again. Still with the "Free Bird." I groaned and opened the door.

Eric glanced at my bare chest and raised his eyebrows just a bit. "Good, you're up. I would have called but I didn't get your number yesterday."

"That's cool." I held the door open. He walked inside, and Chris didn't react as Eric walked over to what must have seemed like a floating guitar to him. I cleared my throat. "It's really fucking early, dude. What do you need?"

He looked a little sheepish. "I had trouble sleeping. So I decided I might as well see if you were awake."

"Well, you're in luck," I told him. "I'm almost never up this early."

Eric sat down beside Chris and put his hand on Chris's arm, which didn't piss me off as much as it had the day before, especially since Chris didn't react to his touch with that broken sort of hope he'd had on his face yesterday morning. I tried to be subtle as I sauntered over to the bed and nonchalantly rearranged the sheets so that the spots all over them weren't so obvious, but Chris and Eric both turned to stare at me. Chris chuckled, and Eric's eyes flicked back and forth between the sheets and my bare chest and then back to the guitar.

"He knows our secret," Chris said.

"Fuck off," I told him, helpfully holding up a middle finger in case he wasn't sure what I'd said.

Chris gave me a shit-eating grin, and I rolled my eyes and got a T-shirt out of my backpack and tugged it on over my head.

"So," Eric said after a second, "I thought you couldn't, um . . . I mean, I thought he wasn't a physical presence for you."

"He means he thought I couldn't shag you until you screamed," Chris translated.

I started to point out that he hadn't *technically* shagged me, but instead I just flipped Chris off again. It was good for him to be reminded that sappy feelings aside, he was still a douche. "I'm not talking about my sex life with you," I told Eric. That was vague enough that I wasn't giving away too much detail, but it also made it clear that yes, Chris and I had fucked, and so I had a claim on him now, and Eric could back off on that level.

Eric's brow wrinkled for a moment, then he loosened his shoulders and took a breath. "I was thinking. You said yesterday that you would have to save up some money to get to Allison's house."

Shit. I looked at Chris with wide eyes. He put the guitar down and stood up again.

"If he offers," Chris said softly, "we have to take it, don't we?"

I nodded, both at Chris and at Eric's question. The feeling was back, the one that said it was time for Chris to go. It wasn't quite as intense as the sense of dread from actively trying to delay things, but my pulse still sped up and my nerves still sang with adrenaline like I was late for a job interview, like I was wasting too much time. I wondered where that feeling had been before today and why it had to show up *now*. Why I couldn't have a few weeks to enjoy this before letting him go. It seemed ridiculously unfair.

Eric didn't seem to be fazed by the look on my face, and he hadn't heard Chris's question, so he took a breath to continue.

Please don't say it, please don't say it, please . . .

"I can get you a flight if you want," he said. "You can fly out there today and I'll give you some cash to rent a car and drive back to Boston. That way you could finish what he needs to do without it being a big burden on you."

"You rat bastard," Chris said to Eric.

"Thank you," I heard myself saying. "That would be nice of you."

"Awesome," Eric said. "I'll make a phone call and get you a flight. Then I can drive you to the airport." He stepped onto the balcony, pulling out his phone.

I sat on the end of the bed and closed my eyes.

"Tyler," Chris said, loudly. "Don't do this. I'm not ready, okay?"

I looked at him but not at his eyes. "I know you feel it too. Bad things will happen if we don't go."

"Fuck the bad things," he said. "I'm not fucking ready. I won't go."

"I'm not going to risk it," I said, putting my elbows on my knees.

"I don't care," Chris said. He knelt in front of the bed so he was at my level. "I'm not ready. I don't care what happens. I'm not ready to go yet."

"What if you go anyway?" I whispered, voicing the fear that had dug its way into the base of my spine. "What if we decide not to go see her and you lose your chance and just fade away?"

"Then we won't be any worse off," he said. "And there's always the possibility—"

I cut him off there. "There's obviously an afterlife. And if the religious crowd is right, you get into one by being a good person and you get into the other by doing the wrong thing. I'm not sending you to hell because I was selfish, Chris."

"I don't care," he said again. He put his hands on the sides of my face. "Tyler. I don't care."

I moved back, sitting upright to pull my head out of his hands. "That's really sweet and everything, but if I turned out to be right, then you'd care after a few millennia. And I can't have that on my conscience."

"This is bullshit," Chris said, rocking back on his heels and glaring—in my direction, but not at *me*. "Why the *fuck* would they," he motioned at the ceiling, "let me stay just to fuck with me like this? To fuck with *us* like this?"

"I don't think it was supposed to happen this way," I pointed out. "It didn't happen like this for Chad. He just helped them finish their business and then they left and he was fine."

"Will *you* be fine?"

"Fuck you." I twisted away from him. "I'm not having this conversation right now."

"Tyler—"

"No," I said, loudly. "I can't talk about it. Not when he's right out there." I waved my hand at the balcony.

He was quiet for a few seconds. "This is bullshit," he said again.

"Oh, man," I said, turning my gaze back to his. "I know."

He leaned up to kiss me, and I had never in my life been so conflicted in what I wanted. Half of me wanted to push him away because kissing him now would feel like saying good-bye and I wasn't ready for that yet, but the other half of me wanted to pour every ounce of my soul into the kiss and let him help me bear it.

And after all, he was only a couple of days from being gone forever, and every kiss was numbered now. So I let him kiss me and I tried to concentrate on his lips and how they felt on mine, and I tried to burn it into my memory without acknowledging to myself that that's what I was doing. My eyes started stinging like venom was pooling behind them, and I fought hard against the tears. I mostly won the battle, although when the balcony door slid open and Chris pulled away, I knew that my eyes were just a little too bright.

Eric smiled at me. "I got you an early flight to Albany," he said. "We can go out for breakfast and then I'll take you to the airport."

"Thanks," I said. My throat felt raw, and I couldn't look at Chris. If Eric noticed, he didn't say anything.

In the end, saying good-bye to Eric was far less climactic than I'd expected. The check came, and Eric paid it, then leaned back in his seat and cleared his throat.

"This is it, huh?" he asked.

"Yeah," I said. Chris was clutching my hand under the table like he'd forgotten how to let go, and I gave his hand a squeeze. "I guess so."

"I brought a case for the guitar," Eric said. "I thought maybe he would want to keep it. So he could play it sometimes."

"I doubt he'll be around that long," I said, and my voice cracked in the middle but none of us acknowledged it.

"Then you should keep it," Eric said. "I think he'd like that."

"I would," Chris said. "Keep it."

I just nodded. Words were tough, and I didn't feel like fucking with them at the moment.

"Do you want the rest of his stuff?" Eric asked. "There are a couple of things I'd like to keep, but I can send you—"

I spoke over him, a little too loudly. "Can we talk about this some other time?" *Like maybe never.* But that might not be strictly true. I could envision a night, years from now, when I would be on the brink of convincing myself that I'd bought the guitar on eBay and I would need something else to hold on to so that I could remind myself that it had been real, and Eric might be my only link to that.

"Sure," Eric said. "Give me your phone, and I'll put my number in it."

I handed it to him, and he fumbled with it while he tried to figure out how to enter contacts. Chris squeezed my hand, and I looked over at him.

"You should get a selfie with him and send it to Carmen," he said. He was grinning and the mischievous twinkle I loved was back in his eyes, but his hand still had a death grip on mine.

I smiled. "You're right. That would be hilarious."

"What would be hilarious?" Eric asked, handing the phone back to me.

"My ex-girlfriend is a huge fan, and she's a bitch, so Chris suggested that I take a selfie with you and send it to her." It would be even funnier if Chris were alive and I could also mention that I'd had breakfast with Eric Painter *and* gotten head from Chris Raiden, but I didn't think I could bring that up. Not now. And anyway, even under better circumstances, pics or it didn't happen, and taking a picture of Chris sucking me off would pretty much amount to a dick pic, and nothing good ever came of sending dick pics to disgruntled ex-girlfriends.

"A big fan, huh?" Eric asked. "The kind who just happen to get lost at the concert and find themselves naked in our dressing rooms, but while they're there would we bone them please?"

"Pretty much," I said. "You were number one on her free-pass list."

Eric laughed. "I'm number one on a lot of girlfriends' free-pass lists."

"You're also so fucking humble, dude. Just like I assumed you would be."

He laughed again. "Show me this chick."

I pulled my hand out of Chris's with some difficulty and found the picture I'd shown Chris before. I held it out to Eric.

He leaned forward and inspected the picture, then lounged back in his chair and smirked. "I'd fuck her."

I raised an eyebrow. "Did you miss the part where I said she was a bitch? Trust me, you don't want anything to do with her brand of crazy."

He shrugged. "Great tits make up for a world of bitchiness."

"So do you want me to give her your number?" I asked, my voice dripping with sarcasm. "I mean, she *did* leave me like seven hundred voice mails about how I'd killed Chris by not magically making a steak cook faster. I'm not sure you really want that type of girl knowing your phone number."

Chris purred in my ear, "You're so hot when you're being snarky."

"Jesus, dude, we're in public," I hissed back at him. He kissed me full on the mouth and it was the hardest thing ever to not let my lips react to it while people could see.

From the corner of my eye, I could tell that Eric was watching us—or me, rather, but still—with what appeared to be great interest. "I guess you're not hoping to get back together with her?"

Chris had moved his lips from my mouth to my neck, and I tried to swat at him surreptitiously. "Not at all," I said. "I'm kind of involved elsewhere. And besides, seriously, I'm lucky I didn't need therapy with all the guilt-tripping she gave me." Chris started sliding his hand across my thigh, and I groaned. "Christopher David Raiden, *behave yourself.*"

He put his lips next to my ear and sex-growled, "You know my middle name, baby?"

"I read the band bio, remember?" I pushed him back to a safe distance on the bench. "Fuck. I have to walk out of here, you know."

Eric chuckled. "I see he hasn't changed."

Chris stuck his tongue out in a fake-sexy way and rubbed at his own nipples. I rolled my eyes at him. It felt good to be normal again, even if I wasn't sure how long it would last.

Eric held out his hand. "Phone, please."

I tore my eyes away from Chris, who had licked his own finger and was trailing it down his chest with an exaggerated porny expression on his face. "You're such a dweeb," I told him, then realized I hadn't followed what Eric had said. "Wait. What?"

"I'm going to call her," he said. "Give me your phone."

Chris stopped with his ridiculous display of sleaze and grinned. "Oh, shit, she's going to flip."

"She's not going to believe him," I said, but I handed Eric the phone. "Carmen Anders. Might still be listed as 'Psycho Bitch.'"

He pressed some buttons and then held it up to his ear. "Hey, is this Carmen? Cool. Listen, this is Eric Painter." He paused for a few seconds, listening. "Do I sound like Tyler?" Another pause. "Well, I was going to offer to fly you out to California and fuck you senseless, but not if you're going to be like *that.*" Another pause, and then he took the phone away from his ear. "She said to tell you that you're a jackass. And then she hung up."

"I told you she was a bitch," I pointed out. "To be fair, though, I *am* a jackass. So she's right about that. You shouldn't fly her out here, though. I guarantee you'll regret getting involved with her."

"Oh, believe me, I wasn't really going to." Eric stood up and walked around to my side of the table, then crouched beside me outside the booth so our heads were at the same level. "How do you work the camera on this thing?"

I snorted a laugh and took the phone from him. "I give it three seconds after she gets this before she's calling back. Do I answer?" I snapped a picture of us and then started putting it in a text.

"Hell yeah," Eric said. Chris slithered closer to me in the booth and slipped his arm across my shoulders as I hit Send on the text. I leaned in to Chris and waited for Carmen's inevitable reaction. Eric slid back into his seat on the other side of the booth and tapped his fingers in a drum beat on the table.

The phone rang, and I answered it. "Hey, babe, how's it going?"

"TYLER LINDSEY, YOU GIVE HIM THE PHONE RIGHT NOW," she screeched.

I held out the phone to Eric. "It's for you."

He took the phone and put it up to his ear. "Believe me now, princess?" A pause. I couldn't hear what Carmen was saying, but he rolled his eyes super hard so it was probably saccharine-sweet and over-the-top. "Well," Eric said, "I mean, yeah, I *would* have offered to fly you out here and give you a full backstage pass, if you know what I mean. But Tyler here says you were a Grade A bitch to him after my buddy Chris died."

Chris nibbled at my ear, and I lost any hope that I was going to be able to walk out of this restaurant without a full-on boner.

"Well, listen here, sweetheart. You can't treat people that way," Eric was saying. "Chris's death was an accident, and I'm offended on Tyler's behalf that you'd try to blame him for it." Another pause. "Yeah, I absolutely would have flown you out here. If you'd been nicer to my boy. But I guess that ship has sailed, huh? Peace." He hung up and slid the phone across the table to me.

I laughed, and it was only a little throaty. "Way to tell her what's what."

Eric shrugged. "Least I could do." His phone started to buzz then, and he checked it. "It's our publicist. I have to take this." He pressed the screen to accept the call. "Eric here."

Chris leaned over again and whispered, "He'll be a few minutes. Bathroom?"

I scoffed, but the shiver that his voice gave me kind of ruined the sarcasm. "You're such a horndog."

"For you, yeah," he said, then ducked his head to nip at my neck.

I slid out of the booth. "Bathroom break," I mumbled to Eric, then scurried toward the restroom as quickly as I could so as not to traumatize any children.

As soon as I got inside and locked the door, Chris threw me against the wall and started kissing me, wasting no time in shoving his tongue in my mouth and fumbling at the fastenings of his jeans with one hand. "Open your pants," he growled, biting at my lower lip.

"Jesus, you're pushy all the sudden," I managed to say between assaults on my mouth, but I reached down and pulled my cock out of my pants.

"You're mine," he said, his voice low and rough. "I want to make damn sure you know it. I want to show you."

I knew he wouldn't hurt me, that he would stop if I told him to, but this lack of control wasn't what I wanted to remember from our last day. Today wasn't supposed to be desperate and fatalistic, even if that was how we felt. So I pulled away as much as I could with the wall at my back and concentrated on bringing him back to me.

"Chris," I said, and I put my hands on his cheeks and held him far enough from me that he could see my face. His dark-brown eyes were dilated, and he seemed almost like he couldn't focus on me for a second before I whispered his name again. Then his eyes locked on mine and he looked utterly lost.

"I'm here," I said softly. "Okay? I'm here and I'm yours. You have nothing to prove to me. I know I'm yours, okay?"

"You'll forget eventually," he said, but he relaxed and sagged against me.

"Never." I tucked my head into his neck. "Never. I promise." I slid my hands around his back and held on to him tightly. "I promise, Chris."

He let out a ragged breath. "I'm sorry."

"It's fine," I said, then I glanced behind him into the mirror, and couldn't see him. I looked like a hunched-over crazy person petting the air with my cock hanging out, and I couldn't help but laugh at the visual.

"What?" he asked, a little humor evident in his voice.

"I look like a psycho in the mirror," I told him, and he pulled away and turned around to see. I smiled at him and took his hand, lacing our fingers together.

"I have a lot of things I want to say—" Chris started, and I cut him off quickly.

"I know. Me too. But not here. Not in a restaurant bathroom, okay? We'll talk. I promise. We'll say everything we need to say. Just not here."

He nodded, and we tucked ourselves inside our pants and went back to the table. I picked up my phone and put it in my pocket but didn't sit down. "I guess we're ready to go," I told Eric. "Want to go outside to say good-byes?"

Eric nodded, and we went to the parking lot and stood by the car. "So," he said.

Chris took a deep breath. "Tell him I'm happy," he said. "Tell him I'm sorry I didn't listen to him, but I'm happy now and I'm going to be okay."

I repeated his words to Eric, forcing myself to think of it as reciting lines in a play instead of something that was really happening to me.

Eric nodded. "I shouldn't have given up on you," he said. "I'm sorry. I should have tried harder to get through to you."

Chris answered, and I repeated after him as unobtrusively as I could. "I was stubborn and there was nothing else you could have done. It wasn't your fault."

"I'm sorry I couldn't ever be what you wanted me to be." Eric gazed down at the concrete, and Chris took a step forward and put a hand on his shoulder. It didn't cause my gut to clench like it had the day before.

"You were my friend," he said. "You still are my friend. You always will be."

Eric nodded. "I miss you," he said after a beat of silence.

"I miss you too," Chris said. He took another step forward and put his arms around Eric. Eric slid his arms around Chris too, and it wasn't romantic but it *was* intimate enough that I averted my eyes.

"Okay," Eric said after a moment. "I'll take you to the airport."

CHAPTER THIRTY-THREE

They hugged again when Eric dropped us off, and then Eric surprised me by giving *me* a quick bro-hug too. He pressed an envelope containing a couple hundred dollars and a check with a rather unsettling number of zeroes on it into my hand right before he jumped in the car and then drove off before I got my eyes back in my skull. I thought about tearing the check up and throwing it away on principle, but the poor side of me balked at that and after a few seconds of indecision, I slipped the envelope in my backpack.

Chris got flustered and unhappy at the mere suggestion that I might hand his guitar over at the check-in desk as a checked bag, so I carried it with me into the line at security. This time he didn't talk about double-ended dildos or harass me about how much better rock stars had it when they flew. As a matter of fact, he didn't say much of anything as we waited in line, which was nice because I wouldn't have been able to answer him without getting weird looks from the people around me, and if there's any place you don't want to come across as crazy, the airport security line is it.

He stayed close by my side, though, and at one point he stood behind me and slid his arms around my waist, holding me to his chest and putting his cheek against the side of my head. We stood like that for a long time, breaking apart for a few seconds now and then to move forward in the line, but eventually the lump in my throat reached critical mass and I had to step away from him so I wouldn't start bawling like a newborn in the middle of the airport.

We got up to the metal detectors, and I heaved his guitar up onto the conveyor belt and took off my shoes to put in another bin. Then I reached for one of the little bowls for jewelry and pocket change and slowly pulled the necklace with his ring threaded on it over my head and dropped it in the bowl.

Chris stared at it, and the look in his eyes made me wonder if ghosts could cry. "Tyler . . ." he started, like he had in the restaurant, but the TSA line at the airport wasn't really the time to start the discussion either, so I turned quickly and went through the metal detector. He followed me and didn't try to finish the sentence.

They started boarding almost immediately after we got to the gate, so there wasn't much of an opportunity to talk until we got on the plane. They insisted that I gate-check the guitar, which made Chris frown, but he let it go.

For then, at least. Once I found my row, he plopped down in the aisle seat beside me and started grumbling. "If anything happens to that guitar, I'll bust some heads."

Eric had gotten us a first-class ticket and the seat next to us seemed to be empty, so I didn't worry too much about being overheard, but I put my earpiece in anyway. "I'm sure it will be fine," I told him. "People gate-check things all the time."

"Yeah," he said, "but it's not like I can just go out and buy another guitar if they lose this one or break it or whatever."

"True," I admitted. "But still. Don't worry about it." He put his arm around my shoulders, and I relaxed into him. "It was your first one?"

He nodded. "I got it right after my dad died. We weren't rich or anything, but Dad had some life insurance and Mom was pretty focused on using the money to make me and Allison happy, so she didn't put up a fight when I asked for a guitar. She even paid for lessons for a while, until I decided I didn't need them anymore."

"Wait," I said, "I thought your mom got Alzheimer's when you were twelve?"

A flash of something unpleasant crossed his face. "No, that didn't happen until later. After we signed with the record label and started actually making money off our music," he explained. "It was just that when it happened, she regressed back to the year before Dad died. I guess that was her safe place. That's what the doctors told us, anyway." He tightened his arm around my shoulders, and I leaned in a little. "I want to tell you so much, you know. Everything. But I feel like that's weird, to unload everything on you at once. And I want to know everything about you too, but there's just not . . . time."

"We'll go back and forth, then," I said. "You ask a question and I'll answer, and then I'll ask you one. No secrets and no lies, though. Everything has to be true."

He hesitated for a second. "Even the Eric stuff?"

I thought about that, weighing my personal distaste at talking about how awesome Eric was against my desperate need to know all Chris's stories before it was too late, and eventually I nodded. "Yeah, even the Eric stuff. But let's keep it at a storytelling level and not a waxing-poetic level, yeah?"

"That seems fair." He reached up and ruffled my hair, laughing when I wrinkled my nose. "Well, let's start with a small one. Are you a cat person or a dog person?"

I shrugged. "I've never really had either one. I had a ferret once. His name was Lorenzo."

"A ferret, huh?" He paused, tilting his head. "I guess I can see that."

"He was a handful, but I liked him." I leaned against Chris a little more. "I had to get rid of him when I went to college. He wasn't allowed in the dorms, and I didn't want Grandma to have to take care of a ferret while I was gone. They're a lot of work, you know? So I gave him to this dude I went to high school with. He was a good guy who would give Renny a good life."

Chris started to say something, but the plane doors closed and the safety video came on, and he seemed to want to watch it. So I took off my earpiece and put my hand on his thigh, then experimented with pressure. He was a lot more solid now than he'd even been earlier in the day—solid enough that I had to put forth a little effort to put my hand through him. Not *much* effort, but enough to show that we might actually be able to have full-on sex if we were careful about it, which was such a nice thought that I had to stop thinking it. I had no idea if we were ever going to have the chance, and *that* made my gut clench and my mouth go dry.

Funny how on the plane out to Los Angeles we were just a couple of guys and I was sure I could let him go when he finished up his business, and now, on the plane back from LA, I was legitimately worried about how I would manage to get out of bed tomorrow if he wasn't there harassing me to tell my streaming service that yes, he was still watching.

Jesus, I was going to need therapy after this. And to make the whole shitty situation worse, I wasn't going to be able to talk to anyone about it. *Yeah, Richard, I'm upset because my dead boyfriend got a lot deader over the weekend.* Gemma and Chad would talk to me, but they'd probably get sick of listening to me moan about said dead boyfriend really fast, and that just left Eric, and fuck Eric. I didn't know if I could stand talking to *Eric* about Chris. It would just feel . . . awkward. At best.

"Tyler," Chris said, using the arm around my shoulders to jostle me a little bit. I gazed up at him with a question in my eyes, and he kissed my forehead. "You seemed like you were somewhere else for a minute there."

I considered lying, but I'd been the one who said that everything had to be true. "I was just trying to figure out what I'm going to do without you." And then quickly, because I didn't want to sound *too* pitiful: "I'll definitely have to redecorate."

He laughed. "Yeah, we're going to have to redecorate either way. It's super weird to have to look up and see myself on the wall all the time."

"Carmen hung that shit up," I pointed out. "I keep telling you that."

"Yeah, but Carmen doesn't live there anymore and you left it up," he argued. "So that says something about it."

"I told you, I was just too lazy to redecorate."

He made a *tsk-tsk* noise at me. "No lies, you said."

I laughed a little, snuggling in even more and not caring how odd my posture must look to the flight attendant. "Okay, well, part of it was laziness."

"And the other part?" he prodded.

I rolled my eyes. "I *might* have been a slightly bigger fan than I said I was. *Slightly.*"

He smirked at me like he'd fucking known it all along, and my stomach did a flip at the way his mouth curved. "Did you think I was sexy?"

"Hell yes," I told him. "I mean, I didn't give it *too* much thought because it wasn't like I was ever going to meet you. But yeah, I thought you were hot."

"If I'd been alive when you got there with room service and I'd invited you in, would you have taken me up on it?"

I considered that for a few seconds. "Yeah," I said. "Yeah, I totally would have. Richard would have fired me, but it actually would have been worth it."

"That's pretty serious," he said, smiling at me. "You admitting I would have been worth losing your job over. You, who never ever bones guests, ever."

"Yeah, yeah, don't let it go to your head." I looked past him at the woman in the window seat across from us, who had headphones on and was staring out the window and, most importantly, not watching us. I put my hand on Chris's cheek and pulled him around for a kiss that was supposed to be brief and hard but quickly turned velvet, soft and warm and so slow that it made my toes curl and my throat ache. It took all my willpower to break the kiss after a few seconds so that the flight attendant wouldn't notice.

I imagined that kiss in my bed on a Sunday afternoon, both of us warm from the blankets and with ruffled hair from the more energetic kisses that we'd been drowning in earlier, Chris pulling back and staring at me with the same happiness from this morning and none of the fear that had crept into the rest of the day. I would throw my leg over his hip and press myself against him, our bodies lining up and fitting together like they'd been designed to align perfectly, and we could just lie there, kissing slowly and learning and relearning each other's skin. And maybe we would have sex and maybe we wouldn't need to, but either way, the world could end in a fiery apocalypse right outside our apartment and we probably wouldn't even notice, and it had never been like that for me with anyone before.

"Nobody has ever kissed me like you do," I told him, whispering, and normally I would have never admitted something like that, but the thought of losing him made my entire esophagus hurt, from my mouth all the way down to my stomach, and so fuck appearances.

He searched my eyes for a few seconds, and I took that time to memorize the patterns in his irises. Finally he leaned forward again and brushed his lips across mine. "Same here," he said, quietly.

I remembered the way Gabriel had kissed him in the video and how the intimacy of it had made me click away when not even their ejaculations had seemed that private. "Did you love Gabriel?"

"No," he said. He laced our fingers back together and held my hand pretty tightly. "I mean, I cared about him a little. Maybe I even had something like a crush on him. But I didn't love him, no."

"You seemed . . . close," I said. "In the video. When you were kissing."

He shrugged. "Gabe's a good kisser, and I was projecting."

I paused, then cautiously asked, "Eric?"

"It was always Eric," he said. "All my life, it was him. And it shouldn't have been."

"Because he didn't love you back?" I wondered if it was okay to talk about this, but we'd said no secrets and no lies. And even though talking about Eric still sort of made me want to punch something, I wanted to know.

"Because love should make you happy," he answered. "And loving Eric never made me happy. It was always this desperate, awful thing, this void in my life that he just kept hacking at with a chainsaw, and once I realized that he *knew* I was in love with him and he was hurting me anyway, it was even worse. I would see love stories in the movies and on TV and in song lyrics, and I wouldn't be able to connect with them because I didn't know what love was like when it didn't have a serrated edge."

"And now?" It was a selfish question and I knew it, but I had to hear the answer.

He smiled a very small smile and tightened his arm around my shoulders. "I'm letting go of him and all the bullshit baggage that came with him. He never made me happy, and you do. So this is what I want. For however long I have left."

"And it's not just because I'm your only option?" I picked at a string on the hem of my shirt.

"Tyler . . ." He touched my chin. "I would have gone to rehab for you. And I wouldn't have checked myself out."

"Fuck, man," I said, smiling a little. "That's serious."

He leaned over and kissed my nose. "Yeah, well, I mean it. You make me want to be better, you know? For you." He reached up and brushed some of my hair back from my forehead. "I guess I'm just lucky that I don't have to go through withdrawal as a ghost."

"Yeah, no kidding." I fought back a good shiver at his touch and almost suggested taking this to the airplane bathroom, but there was something sort of heartwarming about cuddling for a while without sex being a factor, so I snuggled into his side and tried to ignore the way the salt kept creeping closer to the corners of my eyes with each passing mile.

CHAPTER
THIRTY-FOUR

When the plane landed late in the afternoon, I carefully untangled myself from Chris's arms and was surprised at how cool the air was when I wasn't pressed up against him. LA had been warm, but now we were back in the Northeast, and it was going to be cold, and I wasn't sure I'd ever be able to warm up again. Chris kept his hand on my lower back as we filed out of the plane and down the jet bridge. Once we got into the airport itself, I put my earpiece back in and reached for Chris's hand.

He let me lace our fingers together, but he raised an eyebrow at me. "In public?"

"Hi, Mom," I said, loudly, for the benefit of the people around me. Then, to Chris: "Yeah, I want to."

Chris smiled. "I guess it's not that obvious. Maybe you just have a weird claw hand or something."

"Shut up." I hefted the guitar case up and started heading for the exit. "I want to hold hands with my boyfriend, okay?" I didn't say *while I still can*, but both of us knew it was implied.

"I'm cool with that." He tightened his grip on my hand and damn, that was weird. Girls always expected me to be the strong one with the iron grip and the ability to, I don't know, club a saber-toothed tiger, and the last time someone had gripped my hand this tightly was back in fourth grade when Rob Lewis nearly broke my wrist because he was *really* into not losing at Red Rover. This was significantly more pleasant than that had been.

We went to the taxi platform and got in line for a ride. Chris put a hand on my arm. "Are you sure we have to go now?"

I shrugged, not meeting his eyes. "There's no use in waiting, is there? Not if we're going to be forced into it anyway. At least now it will sort of be our choice."

"Are you hungry?" he asked. "Surely a pit stop for food would be okay with whoever's in charge of this thing."

I paused and took an inventory of my body, searching for hunger and the icy dread that I'd gotten when we considered putting Allison off indefinitely. Neither feeling was there, although I was fairly sure I'd be hungry if this whole situation wasn't keeping my stomach filled with acid. So I nodded. "Yeah, I guess I could eat."

He slid an arm around my waist, which felt pretty weird since his arm had gone through my backpack. "I don't want to go," he said, softly.

"Yeah, no," I said, frowning deeply. "We're not talking about that in public. Not in the taxi line, Chris. I can't do it."

He nodded and let his arm drop away from me. "All right."

"Actually," I said after a moment, "I don't think I can eat right now."

Chris laced his fingers back into mine. "I understand. I just want more time."

"Me too," I said, eyeing the taxi that was approaching the line. "But we should probably . . . you know. Go see her."

"I know," he said, so softly that I almost didn't hear him. We climbed into the taxi after a struggle with the guitar case, and I relayed the address Chris gave me to the taxi driver.

It was still winter, so the sun had set when we pulled up to Allison's house, but there was some residual light on the horizon, an orange line that quickly faded up into the deeper blue above. Allison's house was a respectable two-story on a respectable street, and the windows glowed and made the whole house seem warm and inviting.

We stood on the sidewalk and looked at the house and not at each other for a long time. I put my backpack and the guitar case on the grass in front of us.

"Is this when we're going to talk?" Chris asked quietly.

My natural instinct was to be bitchy and tell him that we'd talked on the plane, but we were past that now. "Yeah," I said, and held up a pinky finger. "Solemn vow that we're suspending the Cool Points Tally for the time being and we will not rag each other about being sappy right now."

Chris smiled softly and hooked his pinky around my own. "It's a little late to be worried about being sappy. But agreed."

When we'd finished shaking, I lowered my hand slowly to my side. "Chad said that Lucas stayed for a bit after he finished his business. So once we're done talking to her . . . try and stay. Just for a while. So I can be the last one."

Chris moved backward so that a large shrub blocked us from the view of the house, and when I didn't immediately follow him, he put his hands on my arms and gently tugged me with him. I didn't resist it. I wasn't even sure that I *could* resist it. "Tyler," he said, and then didn't say anything else for a few seconds.

I sighed. "I don't want you to go."

"I know," he said. "I don't want to leave you."

"You're going somewhere better, though," I pointed out. My voice sounded strange, like cracks on the sidewalk where weeds could grow. "I don't know where that is, but it's got to be good."

He put his hand on my cheek. "Here is good," he said. "Boston is good."

I smiled a wavery smile and raised an eyebrow at him. It probably wasn't convincing in the least, but it was enough to help me survive a little longer. "You're saying that you'd rather be in my shitty apartment with the beat-up TV and the saggy couch than in *heaven*," I said, then I paused and grimaced. "Don't answer that. You'd just say something gross."

Chris laughed, a low rumbly baritone laugh, and then he raised his other hand so that he was holding my face and gazing into my eyes. "If I go, I'll wait for you. They won't be able to drag me through the gates without you."

"That's disgusting," I told him, but my lips were shaking.

He smiled. "Maybe, but it's true." His eyes got oddly intense, and I couldn't have looked away if a nuclear bomb had gone off down the street. "Can I say it now?"

I nodded, mostly because I was pretty sure my voice would have cracked if I'd tried to say an actual word.

His hands were still on my cheeks, and I leaned my face into one of them without breaking eye contact with him. He rubbed his thumb against my cheekbone. "I love you, Tyler Lindsey."

The words ripped my heart out of my chest and made me want to curl up in the fetal position and never stop sobbing. I tried to focus on how fucking amazing it would have felt to hear him say that to me if it wasn't so close to the end of all of this. I put my hands on his upper arms, then moved forward so that our foreheads touched, squeezing my eyes shut. "I love you too."

He let out a tiny sigh and slid his hands up into my hair. "I want you to be happy," he said. "Promise me you'll be happy."

I snorted and pulled back. "I can't believe you're asking me to promise that right now."

"I don't want to move on and not know that you'll be okay," he said. "Don't make me do that. Please."

I sucked in a deep, shaking breath. I couldn't imagine ever being happy again, not without him there giving me shit about my toothpaste choices or the way I cut my sandwiches or whatever. But he needed to hear it, and I would figure it out somehow. Once he was gone. "Yeah," I said after a moment. "It'll take a long time. But I'll make it."

"Good," he breathed, smiling at me with quivering lips. "I don't want you to forget me, but I don't want you to be alone for the rest of your life pining for me, either."

"Chris," I started, but I couldn't come up with the words for what I wanted to say, so I just closed my eyes again and shook my head.

"Find someone." He touched my lips with two of his fingers, and I pulled away from his touch. "Find someone and be happy."

"You can't fucking tell me what to do," I said, giving him what I hoped was a snarky bitch-face but was probably a watery-eyed tragic stare. "If I want to pine for you forever, I'll do it, and you can't do shit about it."

He smiled, even though I was only sort of joking. "You should go back to school too."

"I don't want to go back," I said, but it was the automatic answer that I always had ready to go in case Grandma brought it up sometime.

"Yes, you do," Chris said. "You can't lie to me. I can tell when you're lying. You do a thing with your nose." He flicked it with the tip of his finger and smiled softly. "And you do want to go back to school."

I sighed. "I do. I don't know how I'd afford it now, though."

"Maybe they'd give you your scholarship back, since you left instead of flunking out."

"I don't know," I said. "I doubt it. Those things are pretty prestigious and pretty picky."

"You could ask," he pressed.

I nodded, resting my forehead against him again. "I could ask."

We stood there like that for a long time, leaning against each other. I had to remind myself every few seconds that I needed to breathe. Chris didn't seem to be bothering, because his body was firm and unmoving against mine. I didn't ever want to let go of him.

It was getting cold out, though, and even the warmth of Chris's skin couldn't keep the tips of my ears from turning into ice, so we reluctantly stepped back and stared at each other with desperate, shining eyes.

After a beat of silence, he asked, "Listen . . . you have my ring, right?"

"Yeah." I slowly pulled the necklace out of my shirt and unhooked it, dropping the ring into my hand. "I was going to give it to her. Eric said this was the only thing she wanted of yours."

He kissed me, his lips trembling in a way I would have made fun of in any other circumstance. "Don't give it to her."

I swallowed hard around the softball in my throat. "What?"

"My mom gave that to me after Dad died," he said. "I always wore it on my right hand, and I figured I'd switch it to my left one day. It's mine. It's not Allison's." He touched the side of my neck. "Wear it. Please. For me."

I shook my head hard. "No, I can't, I . . ."

"Please. I want you to have it. It's yours now, okay?"

I took a deep breath and looked down at the ring in my hand, the Celtic symbols and the woman's name engraved on the inside. "My name isn't Emma," I said, looking up at him with a weak smile.

He laughed at that, one of those sounds that's half laugh and half something that resists labeling. "God, Tyler, I love you so fucking much," he said, smiling and leaning in to kiss me again.

I let him kiss me, and I tried my hardest not to wonder if this was going to be the very last one. "This is so goddamn unfair," I muttered once he'd pulled back.

"I know," he said. "But it is what it is."

I stepped back and held up the ring. "Are you sure?"

"I'm sure," he said, nodding for emphasis.

My hands were shaking. I slid the ring onto my finger. It lay there, warm against my skin, and I grabbed his shirt and pulled him to me. "Stay as long as you can after," I whispered fiercely into his ear. "Swear you'll try and let me have a few more minutes with you. Okay?"

"I swear," he said. "You can be the last one."

We clung to each other for what felt like hours before I finally pushed myself away from him. "Okay," I said, forcing a snarky smile onto my face. "That's enough sappiness for one evening. Pinky Vow expired. Let's go talk to your sister."

"Does that mean I can give you shit again now? About how you said you're going to pine for me forever?" His eyes were twinkling and only part of the twinkle was salt water.

"Um, no. The Pinky Vow covered the whole conversation and now we can never give each other shit about it." I raised an eyebrow at him. "And I wouldn't push it, Mr. I Won't Go Through the Pearly Gates Without You."

He showed me his stupid dimples again, and I kissed him one more time. "Let's go," I said, walking over to pick the guitar case up and then looking toward the house.

CHAPTER
THIRTY-FIVE

We walked up to the porch, and I rang the doorbell. I would have known that the woman who answered was Chris's sister even if he hadn't told me. They had the same dark-brown eyes and the same nose, and I was pretty sure that their hair would be identical too if his were longer and hers didn't have highlights in it. I smiled at her.

"Can I help you?" she said, holding the door mostly closed.

"Her husband, Joe, is deployed overseas," Chris murmured. "She's nervous when he's gone."

"My name is Tyler. I'm here to talk to you," I said. "And I know this is going to sound crazy, but hear me out." Not that it had worked so far, but there was a first time for everything.

Unfortunately, that was not true of *this* time. She started to close the door.

"Wait!" I said. "Give me two minutes, and then if you still don't want to talk to me, I'll leave. I promise. No questions asked."

She didn't open the door back up, but she also didn't finish closing it. "What do you want?"

"I'm here with a message from your brother."

"Chris is dead," she shot back. "Are you another reporter?"

"No," I told her. "This is where it's going to sound crazy. I have his ghost here with me and—" The door slammed in my face.

"Shit," I said under my breath. I pressed myself against the door and tried to speak through it. "He loves you," I called. "He loves you and he's sorry."

There was no answer, so I looked at Chris and raised my eyebrows in a "What now?" gesture.

He stepped through the wall and then came back outside. "She's still by the door. She's listening." He knitted his brow. "She's crying."

"Can you touch her?" I asked him. "That worked with Eric."

Chris paused for a second, tilting his head. "I'm sure I can." He took a deep breath and went in the house again.

I pressed myself back against the door, putting my lips close to the seam, and called out, "He really is here. He's going to touch your arm, okay? So you know he's real."

There was a moment of silence, then a soft squeak. The door opened again, and I stumbled backward so I wouldn't fall through. "How did you do that?" she demanded, the tears already drying on her cheeks.

"Chris did that," I said. "He wanted you to know he was really here."

She glared at me. "Even if that was true, I have nothing to say to him."

"Fuck," Chris said. "I told you she hated me."

She did look pretty pissed, but she wasn't closing the door, so I decided to continue. "Okay, he made some mistakes, but he always loved you. He missed you. And he wants to tell you that he's sorry and that . . . well, that he loves you."

"And Abigail," Chris said. "Her daughter. My niece."

"And he loves Abigail," I repeated.

"If he'd loved us, he wouldn't have done the things he did," she said. She glanced back inside the house, then stepped all the way out on the porch and closed the door. "Abby doesn't even know he's dead. I didn't tell her. Because I don't want to lie to her and I don't want to tell her that her Uncle Chris was a narcissist and an addict who didn't care about anyone but himself."

Which—okay, granted, the narcissist/addict part was true, but geez, surely his *sister* should know he was more than that. "Lady, he's dead," I snapped. "Can't you cut him a little slack given that he's paid his dues now?"

"He's not sorry," she countered. "If he'd been sorry, then he would have stopped a long time ago. If he's sorry now it's only because he's dead. Not because he really saw the error of his ways."

"Welcome to my life," Chris said. "This is how she always is with me." He put a hand on her shoulder, and she jumped again.

"Well, he's dead now," I said. "And you're his unfinished business. So at least hear him out."

"Who *are* you?" she said, narrowing her eyes.

"Nobody," I said, then rolled *my* eyes when Chris glared at me. "Okay, I'm not *nobody*. My name's Tyler Lindsey. Chris's ghost is attached to me, and I have no idea why. But I've been helping him say his good-byes so he can . . ." I waved my hand at the sky since I wasn't sure I could say it without my voice breaking.

"And he wanted to see *me*." She seemed skeptical about that, which was kind of weird. "The last time I saw him, he told me he was never coming back here again and that I was a terrible sister."

Chris looked down at the wooden slats on the floor of the porch. "Yeah, well, she told me I wasn't welcome anymore anyway, so there's that."

I sighed. "He says you said he wasn't welcome anymore."

"Yeah," she said, "*after* he told our mother in great detail about how he was a degenerate, then tried to shoot up in our bathroom, and *then* had sex with one of my PTA friends in our guest bedroom. At a *children's birthday party*."

"*Chris*," I gasped, raising my eyebrows at him. "You didn't."

He shrugged. "I didn't try to shoot up in the bathroom. I didn't have anything with me even if I'd wanted to. But the rest of it . . . yeah."

I looked back at Allison. "He says he didn't try to shoot up in the bathroom. And he's sorry for the rest of it." Which he hadn't said in so many words, but I figured he must be, and he didn't contradict me.

"It's too late for that now," she said, her shoulders slumping.

I sighed again. "Look, you guys had problems. I get that. But it sounds like you were on really bad terms when he died and surely you want to resolve some of that, right? Not everybody gets a chance like this, you know."

The corners of her mouth tightened, but she gave a tiny nod. "I don't know what you want me to say. I begged him to get help. I tried so hard to convince him. He wouldn't listen."

"Yeah, he's a stubborn jerk sometimes," I agreed. "But he really does love you."

"Why didn't he stop, then?" Her eyes were a little shiny, and that made me pretty nervous because I am *not* good at dealing with crying.

Chris sighed. "I don't know what to tell her that would make it better."

I looked back at Allison. "There was a lot going on with him that he thought the drugs were helping him cope with. He was wrong about that, and he knows he was wrong. But that's not what's important right now anyway. He just wants you to know that he's sorry for everything."

"That doesn't help," she said. "I'm really sorry, Chris, but that doesn't help. I've got nobody now. Do you realize that? No grandparents, no father, no brother, and a mother who only knows me on good days—and I can't even remember the last good day." Her voice broke a little on the last word, and she took a second to regroup. "You left me alone in the world and thank God for Joe because if I hadn't met him . . ." She didn't attempt to finish the sentence.

Chris ran his hands through his own hair. "I was alone too. We sort of left each other."

I met Allison's eyes. "He missed you too. And he really is sorry about everything. He felt alone just like you did."

"I can't forgive him," she said. "I'm sorry, but I can't. There's too much to forgive and not enough reason to do it."

Chris winced, squeezing his eyes shut, and it made me want to gather him up in my arms and tell him that everything was going to be okay. But this wasn't really the time for that, so I replied: "If he was alive, he could prove it to you. But I don't know how he can do it when you can't see him and talk to him and tell how sincere he's being."

"And you can tell he's being sincere," she said, not sounding particularly convinced about that. "How?"

I shrugged. "I've gotten to know him really well. He's been with me for a while now."

"*With* you?" She raised an eyebrow.

Jesus, she was going to make me come out to her. I glanced at Chris for help.

He made a face. "She knows. About Eric. I didn't ever tell her, but she figured it out."

That was all very interesting, but it didn't exactly help me decide how to answer her. Finally I sighed. "Yeah, with me."

"Meaning...?"

"Meaning what you think it means," I said, then tried to make my peace with my maker quickly just in case she killed me right there on her front porch. "But that's a pretty recent development."

She wrinkled her nose but didn't make a move to murder me, which I took as a good sign. "I was hoping he was past that sort of thing."

Chris took a step closer to me and slipped his arm around my waist. "If she starts insulting you, I want you to walk away. Being bitchy about Eric and my one-nighters was one thing, but I refuse to let her talk smack about you."

I turned to him, mostly so Allison would know he was talking. His fingers pressed firmly into my side, and fuck, I wanted him to stay around long enough for me to let him be the first one inside me. Probably the only one. I couldn't imagine letting another guy sneak his way into my circulatory system like this, so yeah. The only.

But it wasn't the time to be thinking about that, so I just nodded and gave him an almost-bashful half smile. "Thank you," I said to him, then turned back to Allison. "Well, he seems happy. With me. And that's what's important, right?"

She shrugged. "That's between him and God, I guess. But I was hopeful about that girl he was dating."

Then it was my turn to wrinkle my nose. "He didn't love her. And they really weren't a good match for each other."

"And the two of you are?" she asked, and it sounded a lot more like a challenge than an honest question, so I bristled and narrowed my eyes.

"Yeah, we are," I answered, trying to keep the bitchiness out of my voice.

She didn't say anything for a second, then shrugged again. "Fine, I suppose. The homosexuality was never the big problem, anyway."

"What was?" I asked. "The drugs, you mean?"

Allison shook her head. "The drugs were a symptom of a bigger problem."

I gave her a moment to elaborate, but she didn't, which kind of pissed me off because I hate taking the bait like that, but somebody had to keep the conversation going. "Which was?"

"I don't think he had a heart," she said flatly.

"Oh, fuck her," Chris bit out.

I shot him a warning look and then turned back to Allison. "That's an awful thing to say about your brother."

"You don't know how he was," she snapped. "You didn't see him after Dad died. You didn't see him the day we took Mom to the nursing home. You don't know how it felt to hear he'd given up on rehab and then how it felt to buy a cemetery plot for him and pick out a headstone for a man in his twenties. He never cared about any of us, just himself, and I hated him for it. I know that's wrong, but it's true. I hated him."

Chris flinched and then closed his eyes. I moved my hand up to my waist and laid it over his. "It wasn't that he didn't have a heart," I told her. "Not about your parents, anyway."

"He didn't care," she insisted. "He just stood there with that blank, kind-of-annoyed look on his face and shut everybody down if they tried to talk about anything meaningful."

"I'm sorry, did you *know* him?" I asked her. "Because I've only really known him since around Thanksgiving and I can already tell that that's his coping mechanism."

"Being a jerk to everyone who loves him?" she challenged.

I paused for a second. "I'm sure that's how it comes off, yeah. But it's more complicated than that, you know?"

"I just never saw it," she said, raising one shoulder in a helpless shrug. "I'm sorry. I could forgive him if I believed that he cared about us at all. But he never showed it. Not once."

Chris stared down at his feet and didn't say anything for a long time. "I cared," he said finally, so softly I almost didn't hear it.

"He cared about you," I said to Allison. "He just wasn't good at showing it."

There was an awkward silence.

I frowned, took a minute to be thankful I didn't have any siblings, then tried again. "How can he show you?"

Allison raised an eyebrow at me. "He's dead. He can't show me anything."

"He's right here," I said, pointing at him. "And he wants to make it right. So tell him how he can show you he cares. That's why we're here, you know. He needs to resolve things with you. So if there's anything he can do that will show you he cares about you, anything he can say or explain or whatever, he'll do it."

She pursed her lips. "Can he hear me?"

"Yeah," I said. "And I can hear him, so I can relay what he says back to you."

"Who else have you talked to, Chris?" she asked him.

He glanced at me. "For the love of God, don't tell her about Jerri."

"We went out to LA and saw Eric," I said to Allison. I felt a little bad about the half truth, but then again, if she *already* didn't want to forgive him, throwing in a reference to his dealer might have sealed the deal. And the point of this was to settle things between them, not to stir up even more shit.

She curled her lip at that, but nodded. "I expected as much."

"And now we're here talking to you," I continued, "and we're thinking that you're the last one. He can move on after this." My voice didn't crack or anything, and I was super proud of myself.

"She's not going to be the last one," Chris said. "You said you wanted to be. And I'm going to make sure you are."

Tyler-to-ghost telepathy would really have come in handy during this whole ordeal, but sadly that didn't seem to be one of my new ghost-related abilities. So instead I let my weight rest against him and tried to communicate through just touch and warmth that I appreciated him.

Allison, however, didn't look pleased. "So he's not going to go see Mom."

Chris's fingers tightened in my skin. "We talked about this. You and me. Should I go?"

"I don't know," I said. "He seemed to think that it wouldn't make any difference." I figured that was an answer to both questions.

"Well, that's how he can prove it, then," Allison said. "We'll go see Mom and depending on how that goes, maybe I'll believe him. *Maybe*."

Chris sucked in a deep breath, then nodded.

"Okay," I said. "Now?"

She paused, glancing back into the house. "Yes. I'll meet you there. Chris knows where it is. Give me half an hour." She stepped inside quickly and closed the door.

I looked at Chris. "You fucked a PTA mom at your niece's birthday party?"

He grimaced. "Yeah. Not my proudest moment, definitely."

I rolled my eyes and turned around to head back down the sidewalk. "How far away is this place?"

"A few miles," he said. "You should go ask if she'll drive us."

"I'll just call a cab," I said. "I mean, I'm a strange man with a crazy story, so I wouldn't be alone in a car with me either. And besides, I'm guessing this is a secondary test. See if I know where to show up without her telling me."

"Good point," Chris said. "Do you have the money for a cab?"

I patted my backpack. "Got it covered. Eric was pretty generous." I pulled out my phone, looked up the number for a cab company, and called a ride. The guy who'd dropped us off earlier wasn't too far away, so they just sent him back to get us. I struggled to get the guitar inside the cab and repeated the address of the nursing home to the driver.

"I haven't seen her in a long time," Chris said softly while we were driving through town.

The cab driver was engrossed in his talk radio and not paying attention to me, so I answered, keeping my voice low. "I don't know what she wants us to do. I mean, she can't see you and so she won't understand what I'm talking about."

"And even if she did, she wouldn't remember me," he agreed. "Or at least not me now. She remembers she has a son. When I was alive, she'd always tell me I looked like him."

"Do you care about her?" I asked. "I mean, for real. You can be honest."

He watched the city speed by outside for a long time without speaking. I stayed quiet, but I put my hand on his leg.

Finally, he spoke, drawing the words out like he was still coming up with them while he was talking. "She's my mom. I love her. But . . ." He sighed and ran a hand through his hair. "I don't know what to say to her. Not since she got like this. And I feel like coming to see her doesn't help her out at all because she doesn't remember, and it hurts me to see her like that, so why bother going?"

"Are you really asking, or was it a rhetorical question?" I traced circles on his leg and kept my eyes on his profile.

He shrugged, still staring out the window. "If you have an answer, I'd be happy to hear it."

"For Allison," I said. "You should bother going for Allison. Because she needs you to be there. To show her she's not alone, you know?"

He frowned, but after a few seconds he nodded. "Yeah. I get that. But she should have done something to show me *she* cared. Come to a show, or called me on my birthday, or even just sent me a Christmas card."

I leaned against him and shifted so that our legs pressed together. "Hey, I'm not saying it was all your fault. She did shitty things to you, and she should apologize. I'm just saying that going to see your mom today is for you to say good-bye and for Allison to see you caring. It's really not about your mom at all. So don't worry so much about what to say, you know? Just be there."

He put his hand on top of mine. "I guess I can do that. Even though they won't be able to tell if I'm there or not."

"I'll tell them you are," I reminded him. "Your sister seemed to believe me well enough on the porch."

"Yeah," he said. "Let's hope for that."

CHAPTER
THIRTY-SIX

I t was a really nice nursing home, one of those where the rooms looked more like apartments than hospital rooms, and there were lots of common areas where people were sitting around watching TV and playing board games with each other. There was even a piano in one corner where an elderly man was playing some sort of jazz tune. If you had to live in a nursing home, this wasn't a bad one to live in.

I wondered how much of this Chris had paid for before he died. I decided to ask him.

He shrugged at the question. "All of it."

"And Allison let you?" I asked. "Didn't call it hell-money and set it on fire?"

He shrugged again. "I sent the checks directly here. They cashed them. There wasn't anything she could do about it."

"That was good of you, though, to take care of your mom like that." I propped the guitar and my backpack up behind a potted plant so I wouldn't have to lug them around, then sat on a bench just inside the main doors and waited for Allison.

"Allison didn't think so." He paced back and forth, and I took a moment to appreciate how he moved, how inhumanly gorgeous he was. It was hard to believe I'd ever thought I'd be happy with anyone else when there was someone like him in the world.

"Really?" I asked him after I got my thoughts back under control. Because honestly, that had been gross. True, but gross. "Why not?"

"She thought I was paying Mom off. You know, putting her somewhere so I didn't have to feel guilty about not taking care of her." He paused in his pacing and bit his bottom lip. "It wasn't like that. I just . . . had money. And Allison didn't—not a lot of it, anyway. And so I paid for the best place I could. So Allison wouldn't have to have all the pressure on her to take care of Mom and so Mom could be somewhere nice."

I smiled. "That's good of you, though. Whether she believes you or not."

"Thanks," he said. "Jesus, I don't deserve you, Tyler."

"You really don't," I agreed, but I gave him a little grin.

The door opened, and Allison walked inside. She saw me sitting on the bench, and her mouth fell open. "You're here."

"We're here," I corrected. "Chris and me."

Chris stepped forward and raised a hand to touch her, but paused before his hand landed and glanced over at me. "Give her a warning."

Good thinking. "He's going to touch you. To show you he's here. On your arm."

She nodded, wide-eyed even though this wasn't the first time he'd touched her, and only jumped a bit when his hand landed lightly on her shoulder. "Hi, Chris," she said softly.

He sucked in a surprised breath. "Hi, Allison." I repeated after him, which felt sort of weird in this case since I'd been the one doing most of the talking back at her house.

"I called ahead," she said. "They're prepping her to see us."

Chris sighed. "She gets flustered and confused if they don't warn her first. We think that something in her recognizes us just enough to set her on edge, but not enough to actually register."

I nodded and stood up from the bench. "I'm ready whenever she is."

"Chris," Allison said, pursing her lips, "please don't say anything awful this time."

"He won't," I assured her. And besides, I had to parrot everything he said anyway, so even if he decided to be a jerk, I'd cover for him. But I didn't want to tell her so because that would make it seem like I thought him being a jerk was a distinct possibility.

Chris nodded. "I won't. I'll be good."

"What did you say last time?" I asked him.

"That I was in love with Eric and that our music was satanic," he answered. "Only half of that was true, though."

I rolled my eyes. "Okay, then. Don't say any of that this time."

He smiled at me, with tiny dimples. "I won't."

"And don't tell her about . . . the two of you," Allison said. "Either."

"Um . . ." I looked at Chris. "I won't? I guess?"

He shrugged. "She won't know who we are, so it won't come up. Just tell her you're a friend of her son's."

A nurse walked up at that point and told us that Mrs. Raiden was ready to see us. We followed her to Chris's mom's apartment and went inside. The nurse headed back for the lobby but left the door open. The woman sitting in the room was a lot younger than the residents I'd seen out in the lobby, who'd been mostly elderly people with canes and walkers. She had dark-brown hair with no gray in it at all—although it may have been dyed, I don't know—and a pleasant smile, and when Chris saw her he deflated like all the air had been sucked out of the room.

"It's been a while," he murmured. "She looks so much older."

Allison went over to her mother and gave her a kiss on the cheek.

"Hello there," Mrs. Raiden said. "They said that you were friends of my kids? Aren't you a little old to be friends with my kids?" She narrowed her eyes a bit and watched us.

"My name is Allison." She stepped forward. "We've met before."

"I love the name Allison. It's my daughter's name, you know. I'm Emma," she said, smiling. "I don't really remember meeting you. I'm sorry." She peered at me expectantly, folding her hands in her lap.

"Oh. Hi. I'm Tyler. I'm Chris's friend," I told her. It gave me a twinge of regret that I couldn't tell her that I was head over heels in love with her son, but she thought her Chris was just a child and I didn't want to have to lunge for the phone so she wouldn't call the police.

"It's very nice to meet you," she said. "What can I do for you today, Allison and Tyler?"

Allison smiled. "We just wanted to spend some time with you."

Mrs. Raiden smiled back. "Well, that's kind of you. I don't have a lot of visitors."

"I have a message for you from your son," I said to Mrs. Raiden.

Allison raised her eyebrows at me and started to speak, but I continued over her. "He said to tell you that he loves you, and that he's sorry for all the things he did that made you think he didn't," I told her. "And he wishes he could be here right now to tell you this stuff himself, but he sent me to tell you so he could be sure you knew."

Mrs. Raiden blinked rapidly. "Chris is just a kid," she said after a moment. "He hasn't done anything wrong, not really. And even if he had, I would still love him. He's my little boy."

Chris squatted down in front of her chair and looked up into her eyes with the most open expression I'd ever seen him give anyone other than me. "Tell her she's beautiful."

I swallowed. "He thinks you're a wonderful mom and that you're beautiful."

She blushed. "That's so sweet of him."

I shrugged and gave her a half smile. "That's what he said to tell you. And also that he might not see you for a while, but he will always love you."

She raised her eyebrow at that. "He'd better see me soon. He knows he's supposed to be home by the time it gets dark out." She looked over at the window and frowned. "He should be back any minute."

Allison did jump in then. "He called to say he was staying at Darren's house tonight, remember?"

Mrs. Raiden's gaze clouded for a moment, then her face smoothed out. "Oh, that's right." She peered at me again. "Darren is Christopher's friend from school," she explained. "Do you know Darren too?"

I glanced over at Chris, and he shrugged. "No, I don't think I do."

"So tell me, Tyler, have you met my husband?" she continued. "He's at the church right now, but he should be home soon."

Chris sighed heavily and looked at Allison, who was picking at a loose thread on the hem of her shirt. I wondered how often she came here, how often she had to deal with talking about her father as though he were still alive. That had to suck. And judging by her total nonreaction to the question, it happened a lot.

"I haven't met him, no," I said.

"That's his picture, over there." She pointed to a framed family portrait on the wall. "Chris looks so much like his father, you know. I've always said so."

I glanced at Chris for permission and he nodded, and I had no doubt in my mind that he knew what I was asking with my eyes. Funny how we'd gotten close enough since we met to communicate through glances, and I hadn't realized it was even happening before we were all the way there. I stood and walked over to the picture.

It was a staged professional portrait. Allison looked like she was about fifteen or so, and she had her hair braided in an elaborate French braid and was wearing a blue dress that matched her mother's dress. Mrs. Raiden was much younger, much happier, and it was hard to reconcile the portrait with the woman in the room with us now. She'd aged a lot more than the fifteen or so years that had passed since the portrait.

Chris and his father didn't resemble each other at all at first glance, and I couldn't imagine why in the world Mrs. Raiden—or anybody else, for that matter—could possibly think they were identical. But then I noticed the slight shading on Mr. Raiden's cheeks that indicated dimples, and I smiled. And as I kept surveying the picture, I saw more similarities: the same nose, the same cheekbones, the same eyebrows. Nothing that contributed to an overall twinliness, but there was enough there that yes, I could totally tell that Chris was this man's son.

And young Chris was just adorable. Standing there with his junior-high haircut and his generic blue tie, his hands in fists at his sides, frowning but with just the slightest upward curve at the corners of his mouth. How much of his life was summed up by that: wanting things as much as he didn't want them and not being able to reconcile that with everything else?

"Don't they look alike?" Mrs. Raiden asked, and it wasn't until she said something that I realized I'd been staring at the portrait for longer than was really socially acceptable.

"Yeah," I said. "Yeah, they do. I can see the resemblance."

"I loved my father," Chris murmured from behind me. "I did. And I wish he was here."

We were far enough away from the women that I could whisper back. "Really?"

"Yes." He slipped his arms around my waist. "I miss him."

"It took dying to make you miss him?" I asked softly, carefully modulating my voice so it wouldn't sound bitchy.

There was a long pause. "It took dying to make me realize I did."

He was holding on to me really tightly. I brushed my fingers against his and asked, "Do you want to go outside for a minute?"

"Yeah," he said, his mouth close to my ear, but not in a sexy way for once. "Yeah, I think I need a minute."

I turned around and headed for the door, speaking to Allison before Chris and I left the room. "I'll be back in just a minute. Promise."

She tightened her mouth but nodded. Mrs. Raiden kept her eyes on me until I got outside and closed the door behind me.

Chris was already pacing, clenching his left hand into a fist over and over while he walked. I waited a few seconds before I spoke, letting him get settled. "Are you okay?"

"No," he snapped. "No, I am not okay." He ran a hand through his hair, tugging on it and working his jaw back and forth.

"What can I do?" I asked him. "I want to help."

He kept pacing, spinning around so quickly at the end of each circuit that I was worried he was going to fall over. "There's nothing you can do. There's nothing anyone can do."

"What's wrong? Is it just the situation or is it something else?" I crossed my arms loosely and watched him pace.

"How do you *stand* it, Tyler?" he demanded, stopping in front of me with his brow knitted and his teeth clenched around the words. "How can anybody deal with all this without breaking the fuck down all the time?"

My first instinct was to snap back at him, but down underneath the anger I could see a much younger Chris, one that was scared and broken and mad at the universe in general instead of me specifically. So instead of letting myself get defensive, I shrugged and said, "We don't, not really."

He blinked and then wrinkled his brow. "What do you mean, you don't?"

"We break the fuck down all the time," I said, keeping my eyes on his. "It's okay to not be okay, you know?"

Chris raised an eyebrow. "I've never seen *you* break down."

I rolled my eyes, then regretted it because this was serious, then decided it was okay because this was us. "That's totally untrue," I said. "You saw me curled up in the fetal position screaming my head off the night we met."

He gave me a dirty glare but didn't actually seem offended. "Not the same thing."

"I know." I reached out and touched his cheek. "Look, you didn't know me when Grandma was sick. I was a sobbing mess for weeks—I just didn't do it in public. And that's what most people do, you know? We hold it together until we're at home, and then we let it go."

"It's too much," he said. "It's always been too much. Especially with Dad. God, he would hate me so much if he was alive."

"He wouldn't," I told him. "You're his son, and he would love you."

Chris scoffed. "I'm a screwup."

"You're a work in progress," I corrected. "And nobody expects you to get there all at once. They just want to see that you're making an effort, you know?"

He didn't say anything to that, but he let his eyes drift downward to the floor.

"Chris," I said, quietly, "you don't have to do this alone anymore."

Chris's throat twitched, and he drew a long, ragged breath. I managed to grab him and pull him close before he fell apart, burying his face in my neck and clutching at my back like he physically needed me to be there. I rubbed his back and held him tight against me while he let the tension flow out of his eyes, and I wondered if he'd ever really cried like this before. From what he'd told me, it didn't seem like he had.

The heavy part of the crying session didn't last long, but I'd be damned if I was going to let go of him before he was ready, so I held on, running my hands over his back and murmuring some disgustingly sappy things into his ear until the sobs faded into sniffles and finally stopped. He left his head on my shoulder for a few seconds after he was done crying and then slowly pulled away.

"My eyeliner probably looks like shit," he said, shooting me a weak smile.

I smirked at him. "It's cool. I'm sure it will reset soon. And it's not like anybody but me will know how crappy it looks, so you're good."

"You're going to rag me so hard about this, aren't you?" he asked, rubbing at his eyes and smearing the eyeliner even more.

I dropped the smirk and looked him in the eye. "Fuck no," I said. "I only give you shit when you're being a bitch. This was you letting me in and I'm good with that. No judgment."

"And no Cool Points deduction?"

"Nope," I said. "I promise."

He didn't say anything for several seconds, but it didn't seem like a silence that needed to be filled, so I let him process things a bit more. Finally, he whispered, "I love them."

"I know." I pressed a quick kiss to his lips. "So go in there and show them that."

"How?" he asked. "I don't know what to say to them."

"Let me do the talking, then," I offered. "You just show them."

He nodded slowly. "Okay."

Allison frowned at us when we came back in the room. I ignored the expression and walked over to sit beside Mrs. Raiden. "Sorry about that," I said.

"Did Chris want to say anything else?" Allison said, a bitter edge to her voice.

Chris walked over to the love seat where Allison was sitting and sat beside her, then pulled her into his arms and kissed her cheek. She jumped about ten feet in the air and then carefully reached out and smoothed his hair.

"He loves you," I told her.

Mrs. Raiden gave me a strange look. "What's going on?"

I considered telling her the truth, and if she'd known that Chris was dead I probably would have. But I didn't want to slam her with that much information at once, and I didn't want her to freak out and disrupt the brother-sister bonding time, so I just smiled. "Tell me about your kids," I said, mostly to distract her but also because it was a sacred tradition to find out embarrassing stories about one's boyfriend. "Tell me a story about them. Chris and Allison, when they were kids."

"They're still kids," she said wistfully. "They're growing up so fast but they're still kids to me."

Allison and Chris had broken their hug and were just sitting beside each other, but Allison had a shell-shocked look on her face indicating that she probably wasn't ready to talk about anything heavy just yet, so I smiled at Mrs. Raiden again. "When they were younger, then."

Mrs. Raiden appeared lost in thought for a few seconds, then she nodded. "When Allison was in second grade, I sent her out to get on the school bus. I walked outside on the porch to watch her and make sure she got on board safely. And then just as the doors went to close, little Chris ran out from behind an azalea bush and tried to sneak on to the bus after her," she said, smiling really big. "He was in so much trouble, but it was hard because I was trying to discipline him at the same time that I was laughing like crazy."

Chris flushed and scratched his head. "She talked like school was so awesome. I was jealous. I wanted to go too."

Allison laughed. "I remember that," she said. "He was so mad when Momma dragged him down off the bus steps. He was wearing a Ninja Turtles T-shirt, and she had it all twisted up in her fist." She moved her hand in the air beside her for a moment, clearly feeling around for Chris, and then once she'd located Chris's arm, she patted it.

Mrs. Raiden frowned at her. "How do you remember that? You weren't there. I don't know you."

Allison bit her lip, then said slowly, "I'm your daughter, Momma. Allison. That's me."

Mrs. Raiden stared for a few seconds. "That's not funny."

"Oh, I know it's not," Allison said. "But it's true."

"You're not Allison," Mrs. Raiden insisted. "Allison is fifteen and she's at school right now."

"What happened yesterday, Momma?" Allison asked. "Tell me what happened yesterday."

Mrs. Raiden opened her mouth to speak but couldn't seem to find the words. "I don't remember."

"Because you never remember," Allison said softly. "Never." She looked at me. "She used to remember sometimes. Every once in a while, she'd have a few minutes of memory. I could tell her who I was and she'd know I was telling the truth because she'd remember things."

I just sort of stared at her. I mean, what the fuck was I supposed to say to that? Family drama, man. I can barely handle my own family, much less one I don't know. So I said nothing.

"Chris never saw it," she continued. "He was only here a few times after she got sick and she never remembered while he was here."

Chris bristled at that and inched away from her on the love seat, so subtly that I wasn't even sure he realized he was doing it. "I didn't know she *ever* remembered," he said, a note of bitterness in his voice. "You didn't tell me."

"He didn't know," I relayed to her. "You should have told him. He would have tried harder if he'd known."

"He should have come anyway," she said, raising her voice slightly. "He should have come for me, even if Momma didn't remember him."

"Look, I don't know what happened in the past other than what little bit you and Chris have told me, but maybe you should have been nicer to him. Treated him like you wanted him around," I said, then kept talking when it looked like she was going to interrupt. "I know he was a jerk to you, and there's no excuse for how he acted and that's part of why he wanted me to come tell you that he loves you and that he's sorry. But he wasn't the only one at fault in this thing."

"Excuse me," Mrs. Raiden said, loudly. "What is going on here?"

Allison turned to her with a softer expression. "You don't remember things, Momma. It's okay. I'm your daughter."

Mrs. Raiden squinted at her. "I guess you do look like Allie," she said. "But you're crazy. My daughter is a teenager and my son is just a boy."

"Your daughter is a wife and a mom," Allison said, "and your son is dead."

Chris jumped up off of the love seat and glared daggers down at Allison. I hissed and then muttered, "Damn" under my breath. Mrs. Raiden just stared at her.

"I don't believe you," she said after a moment, "and you need to leave."

Chris grabbed Allison's arm and hauled her to a standing position. "Tell her to stop upsetting Mom," he growled in my direction.

"Let's calm down," I said to the room at large—how the hell had I become a mediator in this business?

Probably because Chris needed me to be one, which shouldn't have been as much of an incentive as it was. Fucker turning my life upside down and then making me realize I liked it that way.

Allison frowned and yanked her arm away from Chris. "I'm sorry," she said, more to Mrs. Raiden than to me and Chris, "I shouldn't have said anything."

"What happened to my son?" Mrs. Raiden said. "Not that I believe you. But what happened to Chris if what you're saying is true?"

Allison opened her mouth but I spoke over her, "It was an accident."

"He killed himself," Allison said. "It wasn't an accident."

"Chris . . . killed himself?" Mrs. Raiden said, her eyes huge and distant, and it was exactly the same expression Chris had worn on his face in the bathroom when he thought I would forget about him, and that was a punch to the gut.

"He didn't," I said, glaring at Allison. "It was an accident."

Allison frowned at me even more deeply than before. "He knew what would happen."

"Um, just a second, Mrs. Raiden." I gave Allison my most lethal bitch-face. "Come outside."

"I don't want to."

"Stop being a child," I snapped at her. "Stop it. Come outside for a minute."

She stuck her nose in the air as if to say "I'm doing this because I want to and not because you're making me" and stalked over to the door. I followed her outside into the hall.

"What the fuck was that?" I demanded.

"Don't use that language around me," she practically hissed.

I crossed my arms. "You just tried to tell your mother that Chris was a suicidal junkie. So I can say whatever the *fuck* I want." I emphasized the word "fuck" even though it was a little childish. Still.

"Chris *was* a suicidal junkie," she said, crossing her arms too. "It's true, and you can't tell me it isn't."

"He was a junkie," I admitted, because there was no sense in denying that. "And he did the wrong thing a lot of the time. But he wasn't suicidal, and he wasn't a bad man."

"You don't know him." She let her arms drop to her sides, and then seemed to reconsider and crossed them again. "You don't know what he was like."

I glared at her. "I know him pretty well by now," I said, "and I'd be willing to bet that you don't know him nearly as well as you think you do."

"He's my brother," she argued. "I think I know him better than someone who only met him a few months ago. If you're even for real with this ghost business."

"He just hugged you on the couch," I pointed out. My voice kept wanting to rise, and I kept telling it to stay cool. "I don't know how I can prove it any better than that."

"I don't know how you did that." She stared at the door to the room like she could see through it.

I sighed. "Look, I didn't come here to stir shit up. He just wanted to show you that he cares. And you said this was the way he could show you. So here we are."

"He needs to say good-bye to Momma too," she said. "He needs to show her he cares. Not just me."

I shrugged. "Not really."

She stared at me with wide, suspicious eyes. "What do you mean? Of course he does."

"Well, look at it from his point of view," I said, prying my arms from their crossed position and trying to relax my tightened muscles. "Your mom doesn't know he's dead. She doesn't know he was a junkie. She thinks he's a twelve-year-old boy who hasn't done anything really bad in his life. And I'm willing to bet that when he was the age she thinks he is, he was more open with showing her he cared."

Allison kept frowning, but after a moment she gave a curt nod.

"So as far as she's concerned, he's good. Their relationship is good. He has nothing he needs to say to her." I spread my hands in front of me. "And besides, she won't remember. Why upset her when she won't remember?"

"He needs to say good-bye."

"That's what he's doing," I said. "That's what he's trying to do, anyway. But the important thing is that he wants to show you that he loves *you*. Because it won't matter tomorrow what she thinks about what he says and does today, but it will matter what you think."

"And he thinks that one hug will change the years he was awful to me?" she demanded, and I was briefly concerned that the poison in her words would burn my face.

"No, he doesn't think that," I snapped back at her. "But he's got to start somewhere. And besides, we don't know how long he has. He could disappear any second and do you want *that*," I motioned back at the room, "to be the last thing you said to him?"

She grimaced, her nose wrinkling like she'd smelled something bad, but after a moment she sighed. "No. I don't want that."

"He can't make up for everything in one afternoon," I told her, "but you have to cut him some slack and believe that he's trying. You know?"

Allison dropped her gaze to the white tile on the floor of the hallway. "And *you* believe he's trying."

"Yeah, completely," I said, nodding for emphasis. "Trust me, if you could see his face and the way it crumpled when you said you didn't forgive him, you would believe him too."

"And you're . . . *with* him," she said, curling her lip when the words were out.

I shrugged. "He said you wouldn't be okay with it. But yes."

"I don't understand why he couldn't find a nice girl," she said, shaking her head.

I sighed again. "I'm not going to have this argument with you. Just know that we're happy together. For however long this lasts."

She didn't respond to that, just kept staring at the floor with her jaw set. After a moment, I sighed deeply. "Look, it doesn't matter right now, okay? Give him a break and assume he's sincere. And stop talking about the drugs and claiming he killed himself, because that upsets everyone and it doesn't help the situation at all."

She nodded slowly. "Yeah." She was still frowning, but at least she wasn't arguing with me. I would take it.

"Hey, again, I'm not saying Chris is a pure innocent snowflake who hasn't done anything wrong," I said. "I'm just saying that you should forgive him. Just like you'd want him to forgive you."

Another long pause. "I'll *think* about it."

"Well, that's all I can ask," I said. "Now give him a hug and don't tell your mom anything that isn't helpful to the situation."

She grimaced again, but lifted her nose in the air and walked back in the room.

It wasn't until I'd followed her inside that I realized Chris hadn't been in the hall with us, and I had a flash of sheer blind panic before I saw him sitting beside his mother. He looked up at me and smiled and that was just fucking unfair, to make my heart skip a beat after it had stopped for a moment only a few seconds before. And it was even *more* fucking unfair to make me start thinking things like that when six months ago I would have laughed at myself so hard my spleen would have ruptured for that sort of shit.

"I was telling Mom about *The Meadow Larks*," he said. "I think she would have liked it."

I raised both eyebrows, and he continued: "She can't hear me, no. But it feels nice to just . . . sit here and tell her about my day. You know?"

I nodded at him and then jerked my head toward Allison. Chris must have figured out what I meant, because he got to his feet and walked over to her. He placed his hand on her shoulder for a second and then pulled her in for a tight hug. She put her arms around him and this embrace seemed way less tense and awkward than the one they'd had on the couch a few minutes before.

I looked at Mrs. Raiden, who was watching Allison move all weird with the air and knitting her brow. "Mrs. Raiden, you're not going to remember any of this," I told her. "But Chris really does love you."

"You mean my dead son?" She folded her hands primly in her lap.

I sighed. "She wasn't supposed to say that. Just take comfort in knowing that you won't remember any of this tomorrow."

"So he's really . . ." She tried again. "He's really dead. Christopher is dead."

"Yeah," I admitted. "But he's a ghost. So he's not gone."

"He's here?" she asked, looking around.

"He's hugging Allison," I said, turning to address Chris. "Do you want to hug your mom too?"

"Yeah," he answered, "I do." He walked over to Mrs. Raiden's chair and took her hands in his, then gently pulled her to her feet. She didn't resist it, which was sort of weird, but then again she was clearly overwhelmed so maybe she was just on autopilot. He put his arms around her like he had with Allison, and she stood there stiffly for a few seconds before she gave in and sagged against his chest.

"I love you," he whispered to her.

"He loves you," I told Mrs. Raiden.

"I love him too," she said. "He's my little boy. No matter what, he's my little boy."

Allison sniffled behind me and Mrs. Raiden sniffled in front of me and while I was totally cool with being strong for Chris while he cried, that coolness did not extend to women I didn't know. "Oh, come on, guys, don't cry."

As it turned out, that was the wrong thing to say, because it made Allison burst into tears and push her way into the hug so that the three of them were all clinging to each other in a circle.

Chris buried his face in his mother's hair and I could hear him taking deep breaths through it, and when he looked up at me, his eyes were red and bright. His posture was sagging and his fingers were clenched in the fabric of the women's shirts, and it tore at my heart. I remembered that I'd just promised him he wouldn't ever have to do this alone again, so I took a step forward and slipped my arms around his waist, splaying my fingers out over his stomach and pressing my lips against the back of his neck.

"I love you," I whispered, hoping it was soft enough that the women wouldn't hear. "I love you and I'm here."

When we all finally broke apart, Chris turned around and pulled me all the way into his arms, holding me tightly for a few seconds before releasing me. He still looked shattered, but now the pain seemed like something that would heal, like when doctors rebreak bones so that they can knit back up the right way. It probably still hurt like fuck, but he had peace in the depths of his eyes, and I wondered how long it had been since he'd felt at peace about anything.

When visiting hours were over, Allison drove us back to her house. I let Chris sit up front with her even though he was invisible to her, and I sat diagonally from him, but it totally wasn't because I couldn't deal with not being able to see his face. Not at all. And I was definitely not mapping the way his profile stood out against the city passing by outside the windows, and I was absolutely not desperately hoping that he would turn and look back at me. And when he *did* turn around in his seat and look back at me, I most certainly did not smile like an idiot and go starry-eyed at him. Because that would be dumb.

He told me a few more things to tell Allison, but nothing too life-altering. Mostly just repetitions of "I love you" and "I'm sorry" and "tell Abigail I loved her" and things like that. Allison burst into tears one more time before we got back to her house, but this one was short-lived.

She parked the car in her driveway and got out. "So . . . you'll be going now, I guess?"

"Yeah," I said. "Heading back to Boston."

"Is Chris still here?"

I laughed, and it was much closer to hysterical than it had been at the nursing home. "Oh, you'd be able to tell if he wasn't. I would have flipped out by now."

"Okay," she said. "Well, I should get your contact information. In case he stays around."

We exchanged phones and typed in our respective numbers, then stood there awkwardly.

Chris cleared his throat. "Ask her if I can see Abby."

I relayed the question, and Allison hesitated. "I don't know if that's a good idea."

"I just want to see her," he said. "I won't touch her or try and talk to her or anything. She doesn't even have to know I'm there."

After I passed that along, Allison's shoulders sagged. "I guess that would be okay."

"I love her," he said, and I repeated it.

"I know. She loves her Uncle Chris too."

She led us up to the porch and unlocked the door. "She's probably in the living room with the babysitter."

Chris walked inside, and I followed him at as much of a distance as I could, because I really didn't need Abby telling her dad that Mom brought a strange man in the house one night. Chris stood in the doorway of the living room for a long time while Allison stayed beside me.

"God, she's so pretty," he said after a while. "She's going to be a heartbreaker one day. Tell Allison she's got a wonderful daughter."

I spoke softly so Abby wouldn't hear. "He says she's beautiful and she's going to break a lot of hearts one day. And that she's wonderful."

"Thank you, Chris," she whispered.

"Do you think she forgives me? Allison?" Chris asked me.

I did think so, but I decided to ask anyway. "He wants to know if you forgive him."

She paused, then nodded slowly. "If he's sincerely sorry, then I can sincerely forgive him."

Chris broke into a brilliant, high-octane smile that stole my breath, and by the time I caught it again, Allison was continuing.

"And I'm sorry for . . . abandoning him. For throwing him out." She sighed. "We both should have been better to each other. I'm sorry I didn't do my part."

"Forgiven," Chris said immediately. "She's forgiven."

"He forgives you," I told her.

"One more hug?" she asked, her eyes getting bright.

Chris hugged her. They clung to each other for a long time before Chris finally let go and stepped back, and I let out a breath that I didn't know I'd been holding.

"Let's go home," he said to me.

"Yeah," I said, letting my nerves settle back down a bit when he didn't vanish, "let's go."

We said last good-byes and called a cab, then I picked up my backpack and guitar case yet again and headed for the road. Chris put his arm around me while we waited for the taxi to show up.

"So what's next?" I said.

He shrugged helplessly. "Fuck if I know. I'm not an expert on ghosts."

"You're still here," I pointed out. "Not that I'm complaining. But it's a little surprising after all the time I've spent imagining you just vanishing as soon as you finished talking to her."

"Well, you asked me to stay," he said. "And didn't you say that one of Chad's ghosts stuck around for a while?"

"That's what he said. Maybe we get more time, then." I viciously tamped down on the hope I was feeling. After all, just because he hadn't disappeared instantly after saying good-bye to Allison didn't mean that he was here to stay.

"Let's not waste it, then," he said. "Let's go home."

We had the taxi drop us off at a rental car station, then rented a car with some of the money Eric had forced on me and drove back to Boston. I held Chris's hand tightly the entire drive. We talked again, like we had on the plane, but this time it was a little more lighthearted, a little more hopeful. There was still a desperate edge to it, but the knots in my stomach were looser. I could smell him, feel his heat radiating from the seat beside me, and it felt . . . real.

"Why do you breathe?" I asked him at one point.

"I don't think I need to. But it makes me feel normal." He sucked in a bunch of air and let his cheeks puff out like a chipmunk, and I laughed and squeezed his hand.

As we crossed the state line into Massachusetts, I said, "I think I'm going to find a two-bedroom apartment and ask Chad to move in."

"Can you afford that?" he asked, and he sounded genuinely concerned instead of bitchy for once.

"Eric gave me a *lot* of money," I told him, then corrected myself. "Well, not a *lot*. But enough to make up the difference for a while. And Chad needs out of his mom's house, and I'm sure that eventually he'd find a job and could pitch in."

"Well, he'll have to deal with occasional screaming from our room." Chris waggled his eyebrows at me.

The use of "our" gave me a warm glowing feeling in my torso region, but the Pinky Vow time was over and I was honor-bound to give him shit again. "Only in frustration because you're a douche," I said, then shot him a sideways grin.

The road stretched on in front of us, and I let myself imagine that this was going to last forever.

CHAPTER
THIRTY-EIGHT

We got back to Boston and dropped off the rental car, then caught the subway to my apartment. I lugged the guitar case and my backpack up the stairs and put them in the corner, then turned to Chris. We hadn't spoken much since dropping off the car, but he'd stayed close by me, touching me on the arm and the back and the shoulder as much as possible.

"Do you think it's over?" Chris asked. His voice was quiet, unsteady.

I reached deep down into my mind and my gut, trying to decide whether the Powers That Be were okay with this. I didn't feel like I had when we were thinking of skipping out on talking to Allison, but things didn't feel . . . resolved either. Adrenaline still thrummed under my skin, like there was still something left to do. And I had a pretty good idea of what that was.

"We're assuming for now that you're staying. But just in case we're wrong . . ." I reached into my nightstand and produced a bottle of lube, then tossed it onto the bed and stepped up next to him with what I hoped was a sexy smile. "Fuck me."

"Hell yes," he said and pulled me toward the bed.

He lay down and yanked me on top of him. He still couldn't get a grip on my clothes, but I could take his off, and when we were naked and I put my hands on his chest it felt deliciously real—no invisible gloves this time, just heat and sweat and skin. I moaned and kissed him deeply, tasting his mouth and drinking in his heat and the scent of his cologne.

He pulled away and looked at me strangely. "Your mouth is minty."

"Yeah, I popped a mint in the car," I answered, not paying too much attention to the statement since I was preoccupied with making out with my rock star boyfriend. I kissed him again, straddling him and rubbing against him as seductively as I could given that I was still a rookie at seducing a man.

"No, you don't understand," he said, pushing me back to lock eyes with me. "I can *taste* your *mouth*."

I blinked to clear the lust haze from my eyes, then groaned as I figured out what he meant. "Shit, that means you're going to make me eat scones and then you're going to kiss me to taste them, aren't you?"

"Fuck yes. But first . . ." He touched my jawline with just the tips of his fingers. "Are you sure? That you want to do this?"

"Of course I'm sure, you idiot," I said. "Can't you tell?" I ground down against him so he could *feel* how sure I was.

"I can tell." His hand fell away from my face, and his fingers trailed over my chest and stomach as he brought it down. "I just mean . . . if I'm not going to be here anymore. If you're going to go out and find someone else—"

I tapped his cheek lightly. "Stop that. Number one, if you leave, I don't think I'll ever want to find anyone else. And number two, even if I did . . ." I kissed him. "I still want you to be the one, okay? If you're going to go, that's even more reason for me to want it to be you."

He considered that for a moment, then flipped us over so that my back was against the bed and he was on top of me. "You'll have to get yourself ready since I can't touch the bottle." I must have looked nervous, because he shot a skin-searing grin at me and nibbled at my earlobe. "Don't worry, I'll be distracting you," he rasped into my ear.

I groaned and pushed him off of me so that I could roll onto my side, then grabbed the lube from where I'd tossed it earlier and worked on opening myself for him. Chris pressed himself against me and licked at my neck while his hands roamed over the rest of me, pausing whenever he touched a place that made me gasp, as if he was making a mental map of my hot spots.

Not that finding my hot spots was hard—it seemed like anywhere his fingers brushed made my skin catch fire. I'd always enjoyed sex, but this was different. Nobody else had ever cared about making me squirm, about watching the looks on my face as they touched me. Everyone had always treated my pleasure like a price of admission—something to give me so that I would give it to them too—but Chris seemed to get off on making *me* get off, which was hot as hell.

By the time I was ready for him, my fingers were shaking and my breath had started coming out in gasps, and he hadn't even gotten to my dick yet. I rocked my hips so that my cock slid against his warm abs and hissed in pleasure.

Chris grabbed my chin. "Focus. Come back down."

"*Fuck*," I gasped, giving him the most pleading eyes I could muster. "I'm too close." My hips moved again without my permission and it was almost over right then, but Chris dug his fingernails into my side, just hard enough to hurt a little and to bring me back down.

"Not yet," he said, his already-dark eyes dilated to the point that they were nearly black. "I want to be in you when you let go."

I gritted my teeth and tried to remember Grandma's raspberry muffin recipe. "Then for fuck's sake, do it *now*."

Chris rolled me over onto my back again, and I opened my legs to let him settle between them. He lifted my hips up and positioned himself, and I felt the head of his cock pressing against me. "Are you ready?" he asked.

"Yes," I gasped. "Yes yes yes yes." I put my hands on his sides and tried to pull him forward into me. "Do it now, before I fucking *die*."

I couldn't remember if you were supposed to preheat the oven to 350° or 400° and I tried to picture the recipe card in my head, and then he was pushing in and the sensation was strange enough to distract me from the orgasm I'd been barely holding off. I looked up into Chris's eyes and our gazes locked, and I wouldn't have been able to look away if there'd been a gun to my head.

He smiled and stopped moving with just the head inside me. "You okay?" he asked, his voice rough but carefully controlled.

He was a decent-sized guy and I'd never had anything inside me except my own fingers, and even *that* had been a long time ago.

There was no way in hell this was going to work. It stung a little, and I was having trouble relaxing to allow him in, and the fear that Chris was going to be disappointed rushed over me and trailed icicles down my skin.

But then he kissed me gently, using his tongue to tease my lips open and moving inside my mouth slowly and with a lot of emotion. The fear melted as my skin heated up again. This was *Chris*, and he loved me, and I wanted this, so I put my arms around his neck and kissed back and moaned softly into his mouth as he slid farther inside me.

And then he was all the way in, and I wondered if my eyes were as huge as his and if my skin was flushed like his. Probably so. The discomfort was fading as I adjusted around him, and soon it was minor enough to be easily overtaken by the rising tide of delirious *want* that seeing him above me and feeling him inside me was triggering again.

I gave Chris a nervous smile and wiggled my hips, and his eyes crossed slightly and lost focus on the world. I decided to make it my personal mission to cause him to make that face as often as possible for however long he stayed around.

So I did it again. He groaned. "You need time," he said through his clenched jaw.

"Fuck that," I said, experimentally squeezing around him, which tore a guttural whimper out of his throat. "I'm fine. Go."

He started moving then, slowly at first. The last of the stinging and discomfort faded as I got used to having him in me, and my cock didn't waste any time getting rock-hard again when Chris's stomach rubbed against it with each thrust. I tilted my hips to give myself a better chance of hitting his abs, and the new angle had the added bonus of making his dick press into just the right spot inside me, and I thought for a second that I was going to pass out.

"Oh," he breathed, grinning down at me. "You like that, don't you?" He sped up a little, moving faster and harder. After a few thrusts, he hit that spot again, and I arched up off the bed and clutched at his biceps to steady myself.

He took my cock in his hand. I was so incredibly hard that it almost hurt to be touched, and I hissed and writhed underneath him, which just made him hit my prostate again. He moaned loudly and let go of my cock to grab my hips.

"Sorry," I gasped out, barely keeping myself together again.

"Don't apologize," he breathed, and then started really going for it, slamming into me like he couldn't hold back anymore. "Fuck, you feel good."

Every thrust seemed to hit the fuck-yes button inside me, which made sparkles appear at the edge of my vision. I tried to reach between us and give myself the last couple of rubs I needed, but he shifted his weight and knocked my hand away before I got hold of myself. "No," he gasped. "*I'm* going to make you come. Me."

Do it, then, I thought, but I couldn't force the words past my lips, so I just locked eyes with him and tried to communicate through moans instead.

He seemed to get the drift, though, because he wrapped his hand around me and started pumping his fist in time with his thrusts. The blood behind my ears roared, and I grabbed the bedsheets, twisting my fingers into them and holding off for as long as I could until he hit my prostate one more time and holy shit, I hadn't known it was *possible* to come that hard without literally flying apart. My body left the bed and every muscle in it clenched impossibly tight before exploding into boneless relaxation, and I barely had time to refocus before Chris was coming too, yelling my name and pulsing inside me with a glazed look in his eyes.

I attempted to say something coherent like "Why yes, good sir, that was an excellent orgasm you provided me with" but instead I just started babbling about love and want and need and saying Chris's name far too many times while he collapsed on top of me, breathing hard and burying his lips into the spot where my neck met my shoulder. I put my hands in his hair, stroking it and murmuring nonsense until our hearts began to slow down and our breathing returned to normal.

After what seemed like a long time, Chris slowly pulled the rest of the way out. He lay down beside me, and I rolled over to face him.

He smiled and kissed my forehead, then gave me a wicked grin. "I told you that you'd love being a bottom."

I smacked him, but I was too exhausted to make it a very painful smack, and my hands were shaking just a bit so that made it less convincing too. "Shut up. You'll get it hard when it's your turn."

"Oh, baby, I'm looking forward to it," he breathed. He brushed my hair away from my face. "You're fucking gorgeous, did you know that?"

I rolled my eyes and experimentally worked my muscles. Ow. But the good kind of ow. "I don't know about gorgeous. I'm okay, though, I guess."

"I've always thought you were gorgeous," he said. "Even before I realized it was more than just an aesthetic observation."

"Well, thank you." I started to smile at him before I noticed that I was already smiling like an idiot. Gross.

"I want this to be my forever," he said, and I should have groaned in disgust but didn't because fuck if I didn't want that too.

But it wouldn't be, and we both knew it. The achy panic had already made my hands begin shaking, and I could feel my pulse speeding up again as the now-familiar dread started to creep in, but I could ignore it for a while. Surely we'd earned a few minutes of happiness and postsex cuddling before we had to talk about it. So I didn't say anything, just put my head against his chest and draped my arm over his side.

He kissed the top of my head. "It's weird, you know. To have everything resolved. It feels weird."

"I can imagine," I murmured into his chest. "You've had so much you've wanted to say for so long, it must be strange not to have that stuff inside you anymore."

"Yeah. And now I have you."

"Gross," I said. "You know . . . I'm not even jealous of Eric now."

"Really? I mean, you never actually needed to feel that way. But really?"

"Yeah. I feel pretty secure in how deep my talons are lodged in you now," I said, lifting my head up to grin at him.

"Eric is my past, and you are my present and my future." He leaned in and kissed me softly.

"Ugh," I said once the kiss was over. "The poetics are a bit much, don't you think?"

"Not at all," he said, smirking. "I'm a songwriter. Poetics are what I do."

Now that we weren't boning, the cold February air seeping in through the edges of the window was starting to get to me. I wriggled out of Chris's arms and got up to find some clothes that didn't smell like airplane. Chris sat up too and put his ghosty clothes back on while I tugged on some warm pajamas and a pair of wool socks. The tightness in my chest and the gradual quickening of my pulse was getting harder to ignore, but I did it anyway. Based on the tightness in Chris's eyes, I was pretty sure he was feeling the same thing.

"Want to watch a movie?" I asked, smiling a little shakily.

Chris smiled back. "Sure." He sat down on the couch, and I picked something random out of my stack of DVDs and popped it in. I walked back over to the couch and cuddled up beside him. We watched the movie for a long time without talking, communicating through occasional light kisses and fingers running over each others' skin, while I tried to work up the strength to do the right thing.

Suddenly a shiver ran through me, and my throat felt like it was going to close up. It was time. I pressed pause on the movie and took a deep breath. "Chris," I started.

"No." He pulled me close to him and held on, his arms shaking. "No, don't."

I swallowed a couple of times to loosen up my esophagus. "You have to go."

"I don't want to," he whispered.

"I know," I whispered back, then cleared my throat and spoke at a normal volume. "And fuck knows *I* don't want you to, but you're done here. I . . ." I regrouped and tried again. "I have to let you go, you know? So you can go wherever you're going. Into the light or whatever. I don't want to keep you from that."

"This is where I want to be, though." He dug his fingers into my skin.

I sighed. I didn't have it in me to keep arguing with him much longer, not when we were on the same side. But somebody had to say it. "Chris, it's going to be bad for you if we don't say good-bye. You can feel that just like I can."

He took in a long breath even though he didn't need to. "I don't care."

"Well, *I* do," I told him. And *that* part was true. "I don't want to trade in your soul for my happiness. I can't do that. Don't ask me to do that."

His fingers loosened in my flesh, then started to run lightly over my back. "I'm glad we had this," he said after a moment. "I'm glad I got to be part of you before I left."

I rolled my eyes and kissed his shoulder. "Fuck, you've been part of me since Christmas, at *least*. The sex was just a nice bonus."

He laughed, and I took that time to pry myself away from him and sit back a bit. He watched my movements and then slowly sat up too and faced me. "So this is it, huh?" he said.

Our eyes snagged together, and I didn't try to look away. "Yeah. Just . . . know that the reason I'm telling you to go isn't because I don't want you here."

"I'll wait for you," he told me again. He touched my chin, and I dipped my head to kiss the palm of his hand.

"You don't have to," I said, leaving my lips against his skin. "Just promise you'll be somewhere I can find you."

"I promise." He tangled his hand in my hair and leaned forward to kiss my forehead. "I would have loved you for the rest of my life."

I squeezed my eyes shut. "I know. Me too." When my eyes opened, a couple of tears sneaked out the corners of them, but I wiped them away quickly and Chris didn't mention it. "And I still will, no matter what."

He kissed me again, and I let myself melt into the feeling for a few seconds, reaching up and gripping the sides of his face with shaking hands. When the kiss ended, we stayed there with our foreheads together for a long time before I finally convinced myself to say the words. "Good-bye, Chris."

He sucked in another shuddering breath and rubbed his thumb over my neck. "Good-bye, Tyler."

There wasn't a dramatic exit or anything. He didn't look up at the ceiling and start glowing with light from another world. There were no angels or trumpets or harp solos. He was just there, and then he was gone, and he took all the air in my lungs with him.

I reached forward and touched the empty space where he had been to make sure he wasn't still there but invisible. Then I took a deep breath and let it out in a long stream while I tried to center myself. Vaguely, in the back of my mind, I knew I should be breaking down. I should be lying on my bed with my face in the pillow sobbing my eyes out. But instead I just felt . . . drained. Numb. I could hear a bunch of drunks stumbling by outside my window, talking way too loudly like drunks do, but they sounded even farther away than normal. When they were gone, the silence in the apartment seemed almost alive, like it was an intruder waiting in the shadows to strangle me.

I got up and went to my bed and crawled under the covers. I lay there for a while with my eyes open and tried to ignore the fact that the ring on my hand felt like it weighed at least a ton and seemed to be made of ice. Finally, I squeezed my eyes shut and took it off, slipping it into the drawer of the nightstand. After that, sleep took over quickly, and I had a flash of gratefulness for human exhaustion before it pulled me under.

CHAPTER
THIRTY-NINE

In the morning, I forgot he wasn't there.

I woke up buried in my mountain of blankets. It was warm, and it smelled like home instead of like hotels, and I let the corners of my mouth slide upwards while I stretched like a cat. After a moment, I mumbled, "Good morning," and sat up in bed. My eyes automatically jumped to the empty couch. And that was when the sledgehammer hit my gut.

I wish I could say I was strong or that I accepted the whole thing with grace and style. But instead I immediately started fucking sobbing, making these awful gasping sounds even before my eyes got with the program and pumped out tears to go along with the noise. I lay back down and curled into a fetal position. The sobs just kept coming, and I didn't want to stop them even if I'd had the ability to. He was gone and surely after all that had happened, I'd earned the right to lie in my bed and cry over him for a while.

So I did, for what I swear to God felt like decades. Every time I was sure that I had nothing left in me, that I'd cried out every tear my body could produce, another memory would surface and I'd find a few more.

And then, finally, they slowed down and stopped. I realized dimly that I hadn't sobbed in a few minutes and that the tears were mostly drying on my face. Oh, I wasn't *okay*, not really. The loss of him made all my internal organs feel like they had jagged edges that were all bumping into each other, and I was sure I'd been reduced to half a lung because it was tough to take in a decent breath. And I knew all of that would come back later—tonight, tomorrow morning, next week, a year from now in the dairy aisle at some grocery store out of the fucking blue. But for the moment, I was more or less done. I slowly sat up in bed again and braced myself to look around.

He was still gone. But at least this time I expected it.

My phone buzzed on the nightstand. I picked it up, fully prepared not to answer. After all, there was only one person I wanted to talk to, and he wasn't what you would call "alive" or even necessarily "in existence" anymore. But the name on the phone was Vic Mitchell. Another bellboy at the hotel. Who only ever called me to get me to cover for him.

Suddenly, the thought of getting back to work felt really good. I still had a couple of days off since Eric had sent us—*me*—back early, and moping around my apartment with all the ITM paraphernalia was probably the worst thing I could do. It wasn't like the hotel was a place I could forget Chris, but it was at least a place where I could maybe think about something *other* than him from time to time.

I answered the phone and was pretty pleased with how strong my voice came out. "Hey, Vic. What's up?"

"Hey, Tyler. I'm sick as a dog and I can't go in today. Can you cover?"

Fucker didn't *sound* sick as a dog. More like he'd rolled over away from his girlfriend's tits and muffled his voice with a pillow. But hey, I would take it. "Fuck you, man," I said, because that was what I always said when Vic asked me to cover. Reputation was important.

"Oh, come on," he said. "I'll give you Friday if you take today."

I let out a super heavy sigh for appearances' sake, even though I was already climbing out of bed to find my work suit. "Okay."

He thanked me and hung up, and I grabbed a quick shower and put on my uniform. I went to the nightstand and took out Chris's ring, then stood there and stared at it for a long time before I decided I just couldn't fucking do it. Having it on my hand all day would just make it impossible to keep it together. But I also didn't want to *not* wear it, because that felt like betraying him, so I finally settled on threading it back onto the chain I'd had it on in Los Angeles and tucking it under my shirt.

I'd done the right thing by letting him go. That didn't change the fact that thinking about his stupid fucking eyeliner made me want to curl up in the fetal position again, but the desperate, panicky feeling was gone. When I thought about Chris, the ache that shot through me was just because we weren't together, not because I felt like he was unhappy wherever he was. Most people don't get the luxury of knowing with total certainty that there's an afterlife and their loved one is in the good part of it. At least I had that. It didn't really help, not right now, but it seemed like the sort of thing that would help in the future when I had a little more distance, so I was grateful for it.

I went to work, taking a different route than usual to avoid the places where I could see Chris in my mind's eye. I had to stop more than once to stand in the chilly breeze and regroup so I didn't burst into tears again, and all over stupid things, too. A pigeon that looked like the pigeon he'd been petting the day he appeared. A pair of jeans in a store window that were the same style as the ones he was always wearing. Some guy on a cell phone at the end of the street who had the same hair color as him. A couple of times, I almost decided to go back home and tell Vic to go fuck himself, but the thought of being in my room, on my bed, on my couch, fuck, even in my shower—it all made me want to never stop screaming. So I kept walking.

I eventually made it to the hotel. It was ridiculously busy for some reason, which was awesome because it gave me less time to stand in the hotel entryway with Mark the doorman staring at the street and thinking about what I'd lost. Break time came and went, and I kept working, smiling way too brightly at all the guests and racking up a fuck-load of tips even though I didn't really care anymore. I didn't bother to count them, because Chris used to count them and I couldn't do something that he'd done. Not yet.

After a while, Richard came up to me and put a hand on my shoulder. "Take a break, Tyler."

I swallowed and shook my head. Downtime was bad. I couldn't do downtime. "I'm fine. I'm working. It's cool."

"It's not cool," Richard said. "You look like you're about to pass out, and I know you skipped your break earlier. I'm not having you faint and then claim I was working you to death."

"I'm fine, really," I said, but my voice was a little weaker than usual, and Richard must have picked up on that.

"Go take fifteen minutes in the break room. Drink some coffee. Get yourself a candy bar. I don't care what you do, just don't come back out until you've had a rest." I opened my mouth to protest, but he narrowed his eyes and spoke over me. "It's the law, Tyler. I have to give you a lunch break. So take fifteen minutes *at least.*"

I sighed and nodded, and he let go of my shoulder and watched me wander off to the tiny staff break room. I got myself a paper cup of water from the water cooler and sat at the little metal table, pointedly not looking at the counter where Chris had liked to sit, swinging his legs and playing air guitar. I stayed for exactly fifteen minutes and then hurried back out to the lobby.

When I got to my apartment building that night, I stood outside, staring up at the windows from the outside for a long time. The walk had been exhausting. Without Chris to distract me, I'd felt every single step of it. And I was going to have to go upstairs and see his face on that stupid poster and his guitar propped against the wall, and every morning from now on I was going to have to remember that he wouldn't be sitting on the couch waiting for me to get up.

I didn't want to go inside. There was too much of him there. And even without all that had happened . . . I hated that stupid apartment. Always had. There was too much Carmen and too much Chris and too much impoverished bellboy without a future there. And I probably would have been content to stay there forever, going to work and coming home and eating Ramen and going to bed just to do it all again the next day, if Chris hadn't shaken up my routine.

Maybe it would be good to just . . . get out of here. Not out of Boston, of course. I fucking love this city and I wasn't going to let a broken heart drive me out of it. But even before Chris had gone, we'd talked about me finding a better place to live. That made it seem a little less like I was running from memories and more like I was just . . . doing what we'd planned on doing. And maybe while I was at it, I could shake up someone else's routine too.

I pulled my phone out of my pocket and dialed Chad's number. When Aunt Greta put him on the phone, I looked back up at the apartment windows and took a deep breath. "Hey, Chad. How'd you like to come live with me?"

I spent a while trying to persuade Chad to move out of his parents' house, and in the end I didn't actually manage it. But I did convince him to come stay with me for a few days while I looked at apartments. I figured I'd be able to win him over once he was here and not having to put up with his mom screening his phone calls anymore.

When I hung up with Chad, I stared at my apartment building for a few more minutes before I finally decided that I couldn't do it. Not tonight. So I started walking again. At first I wasn't sure where I was going, but eventually it dawned on me that I was heading for the subway line that would take me to Gemma's apartment. Which didn't seem like a terrible idea. Chris and I had been there, but only a couple of times and never for very long, so it wasn't filled with him like my apartment was. I could deal with it.

I knocked on Gemma's door, and when she opened it I started talking before she could say anything because I didn't want to waste time with formalities. "He's gone," I said, a little desperately but oh well. "Can I crash here tonight? I can't . . . go back to our place. Not yet."

"Yeah, of course." She stepped forward and crushed me in a hug, and I clung to her for a while, letting her anchor me, until I had the thought that Chris would have given me shit for it. And when that occurred to me, I had to pull back.

"What happened?" she asked, quietly.

I took a second to make sure I was going to hold it together. "I told him to go. We did what he needed to do and I told him to go. I did the right thing. But still . . ." I couldn't finish that sentence, so I just hoped she'd be able to fill in the blanks.

She put a hand on my cheek. "You loved him, didn't you?"

A little bubble of hysterical, humorless laughter escaped from my chest. "Jesus, yes. More than . . ." I stopped myself before I said something really gross that he would have rolled his eyes at.

"Of course," she said. "I get it." She led me to the couch and we sat down.

A long time passed in silence before I finally said, "Hey. Can we, you know, check on him?"

"The cards, you mean?"

"Yeah," I said. "I mean, I feel it. That he's okay. I know he is. But it would be nice if the cards confirmed it a little."

She nodded and went to get her deck of tarot cards, then came back. We both shifted so that we were sitting cross-legged on the couch facing each other. She shuffled, then spread the cards out in a wide fan between us. "Pick five cards."

I didn't even hesitate, just picked five in a rapid series of pointing fingers. She flipped the first one over. "The Knight of Cups," she announced.

"Fuck," I whispered, staring down at the same card I'd picked for Chris back at the beginning. The emo-narcissist, charging forward into battle on a stupid white horse. God, Chris was such a douche. It was the perfect card for him. But also I couldn't look at it anymore because it made my breathing feel too ragged, so I flipped it back over. "Next," I said, a little hoarsely.

Gemma flipped the next card. It was the Hierophant. "That's what he picked for you, wasn't it?"

"Yeah," I said. "The Knight of Cups and the Hierophant. The dick and the prude." I looked up at the ceiling. "I'm not a prude, you jackass," I said to the sky, then felt stupid for doing it. He was probably up there exploring whatever came next and teaching the angels to play "God of Thunder" on the harp, not watching me sit here with Gemma and talk to the ceiling.

Gemma sighed and flipped the next three quickly, one after the other. "The Sun, the Lovers, and the World."

I swallowed hard. "Yeah?"

"The Sun is very positive," she said. "It's happiness, contentment. Joy. Really it's the most positive card in the whole deck."

"So he's happy," I said. "And then the Lovers is the choice card, you said before. So he's happy with the choice we made."

She shrugged. "I guess so."

"Well, good for him." I stretched. "I think . . . I think I'm just going to go to bed." She looked surprised at the sudden end to the conversation, but I just couldn't think about Chris anymore. I'd hit my limit for the day. She got up and found me a pillow and some blankets, and I kicked off my shoes and took off my suit jacket but otherwise just lay down to sleep in my clothes. Chris's ring felt cool against my chest and I fell asleep with it clutched in my hand.

CHAPTER FORTY

Two weeks passed, and although Chris's absence didn't start hurting any less, it at least got easier to fake it when I was in public. Richard stopped giving me those "you're a huge insurance risk" looks, and people stopped asking why I was so pale. Malika called me out on looking miserable on my mandatory breaks, and started taking hers at the same time so she could sit with me in the break room and play cards for a few minutes, and I was grateful for that. I got some moderately threatening texts from Carmen demanding that I give her Eric's number—like *that* was going to happen—but I ignored them. Gemma met up with me for lunch a few times, and she didn't make me talk about Chris.

Not that it mattered, because he kept showing up anyway. Gemma did a few more tarot readings for me, and the same cards kept cropping up every time. Mostly the Knight of Cups and usually at least some combination of the Lovers and the Sun and the World. The Knight, though, came up in every reading unless we specifically removed it from the deck.

After it became obvious that the Knight was going to keep showing up, Gemma took me back to the new age store where I'd first told her about Chris. She bought a new deck ("Just in case the one I'm using is corrupted," she said, like I knew what that meant), and while she was paying for it, a different deck in the glass case caught my eye.

"Hey." I motioned one of the employees over. "Can I look at that deck?" I pointed to it.

"The dragon one?" the guy asked. "Sure." He took it out of the case and handed it to me. "We have a sample deck you can look through if you want to see some of the cards before you buy it."

"Thanks," I said. He pulled out a much more beat-up box of the same cards and handed that over, too. I opened it and picked a card at random, which surprisingly was not the Knight of Cups.

It was, however, the *Ace* of Cups. Which was new. I held up the card to the guy behind the counter. "What does this one mean?"

"Well, you should probably ask your girlfriend if she's pregnant," he said, smirking.

I frowned and glanced over at Gemma. "She's not my girlfriend."

"Well, traditionally that's the pregnancy card. Or, on a broader level, the 'beginning of an emotional journey' card. It also means marriage or engagement." He smiled. "So . . . congratulations?"

I thought about snapping at him that my boyfriend was dead, thanks, so I really didn't see any marriage in my future, but it wasn't like *he* knew that. So I just let it go and pulled out another one. This time it *was* the Knight of Cups.

I pinched the bridge of my nose. "Fine, I'll buy the deck."

He rang me up, and Gemma and I sat down at the table where we'd sat with Chris before. She shuffled her deck, and I pulled my new one out of the wrapping and started mixing my cards up too.

A card fell out of my deck. It was the Ace of Cups. I glared at it, then put it back in the deck and kept shuffling.

After we were sure that the cards were all nicely randomized, Gemma spread her whole deck out facedown on the table in a big arc. I did the same.

"Pick one," she said.

I picked a card from her deck and flipped it over. The Hierophant. I stared at the card for a few seconds and then looked up at Gemma. "Why the fuck is this happening?"

She bit her bottom lip before responding. "It's probably just because you're thinking about him so much, you know? You're calling his cards to you subconsciously. Maybe you should try to pick a card while you're specifically thinking of some other question."

I paused with my hand hovering over her deck. Then I took a deep breath and then clenched my fingers into a fist. "I don't know how to think of anything else."

"Yes, you do," she said. "Listen, you and Chris talked about this, right? You said that he told you to have a happy life after he was gone. So what are you going to do to try and have a happy life? Think about that."

I swallowed hard. "That's still Chris, though. Everything is about him. The whole rest of my life is going to be about him."

"No, it's not," she said. She reached across the table, and I put my hand down so she could pat it. "The rest of your life is about *you*, Tyler. And besides, you being happy is what he would have wanted anyway."

My throat was starting to feel tight again, but I managed a snarky eye-roll. "He's an asshole, and he doesn't always get what he wants," I said, then sighed. "But you're right."

"So what are you going to do?"

I flipped another card. It was the Page of Pentacles. I picked up the tiny booklet that had come with my deck and flipped to the section that described it—it was the education card, plain and simple. A student, a scholar, someone on an educational venture. Which, if I was being honest about it, was what I'd always wanted to go back to. Maybe this was the time to revisit that. The cards certainly seemed to think so.

I turned my head and looked out the window at the people going by outside. If I found him again when I died one day and I was still a broke-ass bellboy without any friends, Chris would rag me about it for fucking *eternity*. And I really wanted our eternity to be about other things. Happier things. Gross things. So maybe this card was right. "I think I'm going to go back to school," I said after a moment. "He told me that I should. And . . . I want to."

Gemma beamed at me. "Good. See? You thought about something else and you got a different card. So think about that. Think about school. And pick a card."

I focused on college in my mind and tried to remember the way it felt to be in a classroom, to be making something of my life. Good, was how it felt. I just wished Chris could be here to see it. He would have been proud of me.

I picked a card. It was the Ace of Cups.

"Oh, for God's sake." I thumped my head down on the table, which caused a few of my cards to skitter off the table. I didn't look up. "Those cards that just fell on the floor . . ."

"The Sun, the Lovers, the World. And the Knight of Cups."

"What the fuck does he want from me?" I picked my head up off the table and stared at the cards. "I mean . . . is this him? Is he fucking with me?" I glared up at the ceiling. "I get it. You're up there and you're happy, I know. You don't have to keep . . ." I blinked back a few tears that were only half-angry.

Gemma sat there in silence. I didn't blame her for not saying anything. I wouldn't have said anything to me right then either.

I swiped my eyes to get rid of whatever moisture was still there, then sighed. "I'm sorry. I shouldn't get so upset."

"It will get easier," she said softly. "Maybe we should lay off on the readings for a few days. Just while you get more settled."

"Yeah, maybe." I slowly raked my cards together into a pile and put them back in the box along with the booklet of explanations. "I should go. I'll call you, yeah?"

"Anytime," she told me, and I put the deck in my jacket pocket and headed home.

I got to my apartment and stood there just inside the door for a while, looking around at all my stuff. I made a mental note to start bringing home some of the cardboard boxes they delivered those little bottles of hotel shampoo in. It probably wouldn't take very many boxes to pack everything, especially if I finally threw out all of Carmen's crap. Not the Incite the Masses stuff, because let's be real—that was mine now. But the rest of her stuff could go. I could be packed and ready to move in just a few days if I really put my back into it.

I looked up at the big concert poster on the wall—really *looked* at it, for the first time since Chris had disappeared. Even before Chris had gone, I'd gotten in the habit of just letting my eyes skip over it, and it was a little jarring to give it such a long stare at this point. Chris was still sexy, still larger-than-life, but now that I knew him I could see the deep unhappiness in the tilt of his head and the angle of his shoulders. It was nice to know that he hadn't been like that when he was with me. Maybe I really had made him happy while he was here. Maybe that was part of why the cards were telling me he was happy now.

I walked over to the poster and reached up to touch his face. "I miss you," I said to it. Then I gripped the sides of the poster and took it down off the wall. There was enough space behind my TV to fit the frame, so I turned it around and slid it behind the TV stand. It just wasn't healthy to have a giant picture of your dead boyfriend staring down at you all the time.

Dead fiancé, I corrected myself, then felt silly for that too. Just because the fucker had given me the ring that he'd always meant to use as his wedding ring and told me to wear it didn't mean he would have married me. But then that made me think about the Ace of Cups, the marriage and engagement card that had started to come up in readings, so maybe he would have. Maybe that *was* what giving me the ring meant. And if he'd been alive, I would have said yes and then married the shit out of him. Which was ridiculously sappy, and I would have lost a ton of Cool Points for saying it if he'd been here, but it was true.

That line of thought would only lead to a pint of ice cream and crying into my pillow, so I abandoned it for the moment. There was other shit I needed to do. I sat down on my couch and opened my laptop, then typed *readmission to Emerson College* in the search bar.

"So they won't just readmit me because it's been too long," I told Gemma a few days later when we met for lunch again, "but I talked to an advisor and she said that I can reapply and I should be able to get back in without too much trouble since I was in good standing when I left."

"What about your scholarship?" she asked, picking up a piece of sushi in her chopsticks and popping it into her mouth.

I shrugged. "It's gone for now, but there are a few others I can apply for. And besides, Grandma was so excited when I told her

I was reapplying that she's going to help pay. I think between that and financial aid and my job, I can swing it without too much trouble."

"You're going to stay at your job? I thought you hated it."

I shook my head. "I don't hate my job. I just hated what it stood for, you know? I didn't want to be sixty and still working as a bellboy. But now that it's not seeming like such a life sentence, I'm cool with working there for a couple more years while I finish school." I pulled open an edamame shell and popped the beans into my mouth. "And besides, Richard is being pretty cool about working around my schedule once classes start. So it's going to be fine."

Gemma smiled at me. "I'm so happy for you, Tyler."

"Well, thanks," I said. "I just wish . . ." I didn't even need to finish the sentence. We both knew what I wished.

"I know," she said after a second. "He'd be happy for you too, you know."

"Yeah." I pushed my empty plate away. "And you were right, too. He made me promise to try and be happy. And I can't be *totally* happy, not without him here, but I can do this much. I can try."

"That's a good attitude to have."

I picked up my napkin and wiped the table with it, then pulled my tarot deck out of my jacket pocket. "I think I'm ready to try again."

She smiled and pulled her own deck out of her purse. "All right," she said. "Let's see what the cards have to say today."

The first card was the Page of Pentacles again. The school card. I held it up and showed it to Gemma, and she smiled.

And then the next four were the Knight of Cups, the Sun, the Lovers, and the World. A lump formed in my throat. "Maybe I should have waited a little longer after all."

Gemma stared at the cards. "I have never seen anything like this. It feels like the cards are rigged."

"Or they're coming up this way for a reason," I said, frowning at them. "I mean . . . do you think the cards are really trying to tell me something? Do you think *he's* trying to tell me something?"

"I don't know," she said. "But something's going on. There's no way that keeps happening just randomly."

I pulled two more cards out of the middle of my deck. "The Hierophant and the Ace of Cups," I said before even looking at them.

I laid them down on the table and wasn't even surprised that I was right. I mean, by this point it would have been weirder if I *hadn't* been right.

She didn't say anything, and I spread my cards out in an arc and stared at the table. "I mean—" I tried again. "If it's him, why is he showing me the same thing over and over? It can't just be him telling me that we made the right choice. I fucking get it. Why would he just keep telling me that?"

"I don't know," Gemma said.

I flipped another card, then burst into almost-hysterical laughter.

"What is it?" Gemma asked. When I just kept laughing, she reached over and gently took the card from me. "The Fool. Well, that's new."

I buried my face in my hands and tried to get a grip on myself. After all, this wasn't funny. But then again, it sort of was.

"The Fool means—" she started.

"No, I don't need to know what the books say it means," I interrupted her, sitting back up and wiping my eyes. "He's calling me an idiot."

Gemma stared at me. "What?"

"It's not just him telling me that he's okay." I tapped the Lovers card with one finger as my pulse started to race.

"Then what's he telling you?"

I laughed, and it was only a little crazy sounding. "The fucking Knight of Cups with the Lovers. Chris and a choice. Between the Sun and the World. Holy shit." I had to stop and take a few deep breaths so I didn't hyperventilate. "And then the Hierophant and the Ace of Cups. Me and the marriage card. Me and his ring."

"Are you sure—"

"I have to go." I stood quickly and scooped all my cards up into a messy pile, then crammed them in my jacket pocket. "I'll call you later."

I let myself in the outer door of my apartment building and headed down the hallway toward my place. This was a long shot,

I kept trying to tell myself. It was more likely that I was just seeing what I wanted to see in the cards. But still. It was worth a try. I pushed the door to my apartment open and rushed inside, nearly tripping over the stack of moving boxes I'd left in the middle of the floor.

"Okay, motherfucker," I said to the ceiling. "If you're just fucking with me, then I will burn your guitar. I swear I'll do it."

I pulled the chain with the ring on it out of my shirt and unhooked it, dropping the ring into my hand. "Come back to me if you can," I whispered to it. "I love you."

I slipped the ring onto my finger.

"Jesus," Chris said from the couch. "It took you long enough."

I stood there staring at him for anywhere between two and five thousand seconds. He smirked at me, complete with a single dimple, and I clenched my fists and opened my mouth a couple of times before words started to come out. But when they did, I didn't· even make it through the first syllable before my voice broke and my knees hit the floor. I knelt there, wrapping my arms around my stomach, and started to wheeze.

"Tyler," Chris said. He walked over to slide down onto his knees a couple of inches away from me. "It's okay."

"It's *not* okay, you dick," I choked out, surprisingly loudly. I hadn't intended to yell, but I'd sort of lost the ability to modulate my voice. And there he was kneeling in front of me looking fucking beautiful and I wanted to reach up and touch him except that I was afraid that if I let go of my stomach, my guts would fall out. "I thought you were *gone.*"

"I was," he said. "I'm back now." He put his hand on my shoulder, and I shrugged it off.

"What does this mean?" I demanded. "Are you . . . Did you give it up?"

"Give what up?" He pulled me into his arms, and this time I didn't resist.

"Fucking *heaven*, you asshole. If you gave it up for me after everything . . ." I couldn't come up with a threat to end that sentence, so I just smacked him in the chest and then tucked my face into his neck and tried to get a grip on myself.

"I didn't," he said, reaching up to stroke my hair. "At least . . . not permanently." He kissed the top of my head. "I wouldn't do that to you. You told me not to make you do that and I didn't."

"So what the fuck is happening?" I twisted his shirt in my fingers. "You better be back for a while because I will *kill* you if you came back just to make me let you go again after a few days."

"I think I'm back for as long as I want to be." He shifted so that he was sitting on the floor, and pulled me into his lap. "I got to choose."

I kept my head on his shoulder and tightened my grip on his shirt. "Why?"

He ran his hand up and down my back lightly. "I think because we did the right thing, I got to decide. And of course I chose you. After that, it was just a matter of convincing you to put the ring back on."

"You *think* it was because we did the right thing," I said, and a hiccup slipped out as my breathing started calming down. "This is too important not to be *sure*."

He was quiet for long enough that I leaned back and looked up at him. His eyes were distant. "I'm sure about it being my choice," he said finally. "I know that I can leave again whenever I want. And go back there, and not somewhere else. That's what matters, right?"

"You're *sure*?" I pressed. "You're absolutely one hundred percent positive?"

He thought for another few seconds, then nodded slowly. "Yeah. Yeah, I am."

I watched his face to make sure he wasn't lying, then leaned forward and kissed him hard. He chuckled against my mouth and kissed me back, and when he stood and pulled me up with him, I shucked off my outer coat and started kissing him again, pushing him backward toward the bed.

"Have I ever told you how hot you look in that shirt?" he asked me, then reached over his own head and pulled his T-shirt off.

"It's just a shirt," I said, going for his belt and kissing his throat while I worked on it.

"A sexy one, though," he said in a voice that was already sex-rough. "Take it off."

I shoved him playfully, and he fell back onto the bed and grinned up at me while I gave him my best seductive smile. "I have to do all the work?"

"I can touch the things I care about," he said, his eyes sliding up and down my body hungrily, "and let me tell you that I do not give the slightest shit about your clothes right now."

I laughed, and for some reason laughing nearly made me lose it. "Chris," I said, staring down at him. My voice wavered a little on his name and the corners of my eyes started stinging.

He dropped his sexy rock star grin and looked me in the eyes. "I'm here. This is real."

"It better be." I took a deep breath and started pulling off my clothes again. "Pants off, *now*."

"Bossy," he said, the grin reappearing along with the heat in his eyes. "I like it." He unbuttoned his pants and shimmied them off without getting up from the bed.

I finished dropping the rest of my own clothes and crawled on top of him, straddling his waist and moving my hips so that our cocks slid together. We both made strangled moans at the contact, and Chris's hands flew up to my hips and dug into the skin there.

"Do you want to fuck me?" he asked, a little breathlessly.

"Next time, I promise," I said. "This time I want it like this." I leaned off to the side and grabbed the bottle of lube out of the nightstand, then got to work getting ready for him.

Chris trailed his fingers around to my abdomen and then down to my cock, and he started stroking it with both hands while I worked on myself, and it was almost too much. My dick twitched in his hands and his responded with a jerk of its own under me.

"Take as long as you need," he rasped, "but fucking hurry up too."

I rolled my eyes and smacked his chest with my free hand, then shifted around and positioned myself over him. "Fast or slow?"

"Oh fuck," he said, his eyes glazing over a little bit. "Whatever you want, just do it now."

I leaned down and kissed him, then sat back up and we locked eyes as I slid down on him, taking him in with a gasp and a moan. Chris lifted his hips off the bed to meet me, never taking his eyes off mine, and then he was all the way in and I suddenly felt *whole* again.

I started riding him, slowly at first but then faster, working myself on his dick until I figured out just the right angle. When I found it, my back arched and I threw my head back and gasped.

"That is so fucking sexy," Chris growled. "Ride me, baby."

I kept my head tilted up toward the ceiling and rolled my hips faster, grinding myself down onto him, and when he hit my prostate again my eyes flew open and a loud breathy moan escaped my lips. I dropped my eyes back to his and grabbed his biceps, digging my nails in and riding harder, faster, getting him as deep inside me as I could. He stroked my cock, matching my rhythm and wringing more moans out of me.

"Come for me, baby," he whispered. He cupped my balls with one hand, and I let out a noise that was almost a scream.

It got harder to keep the rhythm as my body started tensing up. His cock brushed my prostate on an upswing, and I froze there, the orgasm rushing toward me. My mouth opened and my back arched and I hovered on the edge for several seconds, my knuckles turning white with the force of their grip on Chris's arm.

"*Now*." Chris grabbed my hips and slammed himself up into me, and I exploded into so many pieces that I might never come back together again.

Chris slipped an arm around my back and executed a maneuver that would have impressed me if my thoughts had been anything close to coherent. Suddenly, he was on top of me, thrusting into me like he couldn't stop. He kissed me hard on the mouth, using his tongue to mimic the movements of his cock, and then I got with the program enough to tighten around him. He moaned loudly into my mouth and unloaded into me, his whole body jerking with it. He broke the kiss and moved his mouth to my ear, alternately gasping and whispering my name.

I wrapped my legs around his waist and my arms around his neck. "Don't leave me again."

"Never," he said into my ear.

"I mean it, Chris." I tangled my hand in his hair. "I can't lose you again."

"I know." He rested his forehead against mine and closed his eyes. "I can't lose you either."

We stayed like that for several seconds, then I relaxed my grip and let him slide out of my body and lie down beside me. I kissed him and he kissed back, but this time it was a slow, lazy kiss, the type that meant we had all the time in the world and didn't need to rush anymore. I hooked my leg over his waist and pressed our bodies together and let the kiss go on. When we finally pulled away, we just sort of gazed into each other's eyes for a long time, brushing hair back from each other's faces and smiling like we'd never smiled before.

"Thank you," I whispered once my pulse had returned to normal.

"For what?" he asked, even though I was sure he knew.

"For coming back to me. For choosing this." I made a vague motion at the two of us.

"Don't thank me for that." He brushed his fingers through my hair. "It was at least fifty percent selfish. I mean, come on, you're a pretty good fuck and you have a cute butt. Why wouldn't I want to keep you a little longer?" He grinned at me and kissed the tip of my nose.

I rolled my eyes at him. "Jesus, the Cool Points Tally rises again."

"Damn straight."

I put my head back down on his chest and snaked my arm around his side. I considered making an innuendo about all the things that were going to rise again, but I just couldn't muster the shit-eating grin that would need to accompany that. "Fuck, I'm tired. I need to rest."

"You sleep as long as you need to," he said. "I'll watch over you."

I shook my head against his chest. "No way can I sleep right now. I'm way too wired for that. I just need to *not move* for about eight hours."

He nodded and sat up in bed. I pushed myself to a sitting position too and watched him stand and put his clothes back on, then I leaned over the side of the bed and picked up my boxers and shimmied them back on as quickly as I could.

"Grab your blanket," Chris said. "I'll carry you to the couch, and I'll let you force me to watch *Star Trek* all night long."

"*Next Generation*?" I asked, wrapping the blanket and my sheets around myself and preparing to be scooped up.

He wrinkled his nose. "If we *must*."

"I keep telling you I don't know if I can associate with someone whose favorite *Trek* is *Voyager*," I said, giving him a mock-stern look.

"Well, you're stuck with me." He picked me up and carried me over to the couch, and I took a moment to imagine how this would look to an outside source—me levitating across the living room. We would have to figure out a way to get some fun out of that someday.

"At the risk of losing Cool Points," I told him, running my fingers over his jaw with a silly smile on my face, "I'm totally okay with that."

Dear Reader,

Thank you for reading Lauren Sattersby's *Rock N Soul*!

We know your time is precious and you have many, many entertainment options, so it means a lot that you've chosen to spend your time reading. We really hope you enjoyed it.

We'd be honored if you'd consider posting a review—good or bad—on sites like **Amazon, Barnes & Noble, Kobo, Goodreads, Twitter, Facebook, Tumblr,** and your blog or website. We'd also be honored if you told your friends and family about this book. Word of mouth is a book's lifeblood!

For more information on upcoming releases, author interviews, blog tours, contests, giveaways, and more, please sign up for our weekly, spam-free newsletter and visit us around the web:

    Newsletter: tinyurl.com/RiptideSignup
    Twitter: twitter.com/RiptideBooks
    Facebook: facebook.com/RiptidePublishing
    Goodreads: tinyurl.com/RiptideOnGoodreads
    Tumblr: riptidepublishing.tumblr.com

Thank you so much for Reading the Rainbow!

RiptidePublishing.com

ACKNOWLEDGMENTS

This book would not have been possible without the unwavering support of my family and friends. In particular, I am thankful to Sarah for listening to hours upon hours of me alternately ranting, gushing, crying, and cheering about the story, and for allowing me to talk about my characters like they were real people without having me committed. Other people who also deserve my deepest gratitude on this front are: Kasey, Wendy (aka Mom), Alicia, Bill, Brandy, Kai, and Kim, all of whom served as test readers, cheerleaders, and amateur therapists at some point during the journey. I'm not kidding when I say I couldn't have done it without you.

I am also grateful to the FBI for turning a blind eye to my incessant internet searches about dead bodies, heroin abuse, and how one would go about finding a drug dealer if one needed to do so. I sincerely doubt I could have written this from prison, so here's to you guys for not putting me there.

Finally, I am extremely grateful to the wonderful team at Riptide Publishing who took a chance on a first-time writer and helped make this novel what it is today. Every single person at Riptide is a joy to work with and I look forward to many more collaborations in the future.

ABOUT THE
AUTHOR

Lauren Sattersby has always been a writer, but it took her a while to discover that M/M romance was her passion. For a while, she thought she was a poet. That didn't end well. She then attempted to write traditional heterosexual romances, but it became painfully clear very quickly that her main characters were never quite as traditional as she'd intended. Then when she realized that the hero of one of the novels was *obviously* making out with his male best friend in-between scenes, she decided to just let her characters be who they wanted to be. After that, there was no going back.

Lauren lives in Eau Claire, Wisconsin, with her partner and their three terrible cats. She grew up in the US Deep South and still has a Southern accent that immediately exposes her as an outsider in the Midwest, but that's okay because she likes her drawl. She likes birdwatching, Indian food, and (of course) happily ever afters.

Website: www.laurensattersby.com
Twitter: @LaurenSattersby
Facebook: facebook.com/laurensattersby

Enjoy more stories like
Rock N Soul
at RiptidePublishing.com!